Bleeding Hearts

Bleeding Hearts

3429

by Teri White

THE MYSTERIOUS PRESS · NEW YORK

Design by Holly Johnson at the Angelica Design Group, Ltd.

Cover illustration © 1983 by Gerry Daly

Library of Congress Catalogue Number: 83-63040
ISBN: 0-89296-077-9

FIRST EDITION

To my family

.

It's like a lion at the door;
And when the door begins to crack,
It's like a stick across your back;
And when your back begins to smart,
It's like a penknife in your heart;
And when your heart begins to bleed,
You're dead, and dead, and dead, indeed.

— Nursery Rhyme

Bleeding Hearts

Chapter 1

HE was getting out.

Tom Hitchcock had been planning this night for a very long time, waiting for it, hanging onto it as a fragile thread of hope. Now the moment was here and nothing could spoil it for him. He felt as if he could afford to savor each minute of anticipation.

Tom knew that the secret of his master plan was in its simplicity. Complicated plots, he'd decided a long time ago, just led to complications. His was the kind of mind able to grasp that basic truth, which was why he deserved to get out, while all the other idiots would stay locked up.

Survival of the fittest.

No one on the inside knew what was going to happen this night. Some of the assholes in here were so damned stupid that they blabbed their clever escape plans to all, even their stupider friends. Sooner or later word would get back to the cut-rate Nazis in charge, and bingo, another big break-out attempt would fall flat on its face.

That wasn't going to happen to him. Tom never let slip even the slightest hint of what he was going to do. It was pretty simple for him to keep the secret, of course, because he didn't have any friends to spill the beans to. After almost ten years spent within the walls of this place, the last three in the minimum security ward, he was as alone as he'd been on the day they locked him up.

There was only one person in the whole universe that Tom Hitchcock trusted, and that person was waiting for him on the outside.

3

Tom went into supper just as he did every other evening, although his stomach was feeling sort of queasy. There couldn't be any change at all in his routine or attitude; anything like that might alert the shrinks that something was up. They had their sneaky ways of reading people, even him sometimes. So he sat for what would be the last time in the steamy cafeteria, with its dirty green walls and damp smells, and shoveled the meal into his mouth.

He ate meat loaf, canned peas, and tapioca pudding with the same lack of interest as always.

When the meal was finally over, he even forced himself to parade into the dayroom with several others to watch the television. They took a vote and everybody wanted to see the same thing for a change, the Clint Eastwood movie. But the bitch of a nurse checked the Forbidden Viewing list and found *Dirty Harry* there, so that was out. They ended up with *Love Boat*.

Tom thought it was a dumb show, made even worse because much of the hour was peppered with comments from members of the group, mostly dealing with how much they'd like to get into the pants of the blonde broad. It was always the same with those jerks. Tom sat silently through the whole program, not wanting the others to see how disgusted he was by their words. They had no respect for themselves or others.

But then he decided: To hell with all these creeps and crazies anyway. Before long, Tom Hitchcock would be just a memory around here. Or maybe more than that; maybe he'd be a legend.

When the show finally ended, it was almost time for lights out. Tom headed for his room quickly, needing to use the john. It was about the tenth time of the day. Nerves, he knew. Yet he also knew that there wasn't a damned thing to be nervous about. The careful planning he'd done insured that nothing could go wrong.

4

It was thirty minutes before the night nurse showed up with his bedtime medication. He pretended to swallow the brightly colored capsules, just as he'd been doing for months. When the nurse was gone, he added the pills to his secret stash, which also included a couple of filled hypodermic syringes he'd managed to lift from the medications cart once.

Another hour passed before things were quiet on the floor. Tom, still wearing his khaki pants, was in bed, covered by a thin sheet, when the aide, Lang, made his final room check. Tom kept his eyes closed and his breathing even. As soon as the door closed again, he slid from the bed. The adrenaline was flowing through his body much too fast, and he took a couple of deep breaths to stop the slight shaking in his hands.

A faint light leaked in from beneath the door, and in the pale glow it created Tom crouched to pull the knife from its hiding place behind the dresser. He tested the blade lovingly and smiled.

He was ready to leave the room. This part had all been rehearsed so many times that the late-night hallway was a familiar place to him. He knew just who on the staff would be where at any given moment. Timing was the most crucial thing in an operation like this one. Being in just the right spot at the right second.

As he had expected, the door to the employee lounge was locked. The lock was such a shoddy piece of equipment, though, that it took him only an instant to snap it open. He stepped into the empty room, closing the door again, hearing the lock click into place once more.

There was a large metal wardrobe in one corner of the room, where the aides and nurses hung their jackets and things. Between the wardrobe and the wall was a niche just large enough for Tom's purposes.

The wait seemed much longer that the twenty minutes he knew it was. Lang left at the same time every night.

5

Routine. It would be the downfall of mankind. At last Tom heard the door open again, and then footsteps approaching the wardrobe. He tensed, holding the knife more firmly in his left hand.

Hangers clattered as Lang reached into the closet to hang up the white lab coat and pull out something else. The wardrobe door clanged closed. Lang had just donned a light windbreaker when Tom made his move. The knife was at Lang's throat before he could react.

"Shh," Tom cautioned. Then he smiled. "I wouldn't like to cut you by accident," he said politely.

Lang's eyes darted from side to side, dark pools in his suddenly pale face.

Tom edged out of his hiding place, wrapping an arm tightly around Lang; the point of the knife just pricked lightly at the skin of his neck. "You won't go all stupid on me, will you, buddy?"

Lang opened his mouth as if to say something, but the extra pressure Tom exerted on the knife made him close it again. He just shook his head very slightly.

"Good boy. Now listen up. You and me, we're gonna take a little walk right down the hall to my room. No noise. Nothing, you understand? Because if anything goes wrong, you'll get hurt. Hurt bad. What've I got to lose by cutting you, right?"

Lang jerked his head once in mute understanding.,

They moved out of the lounge, still locked together in the macabre embrace. They were almost of a size, of course; that was an important part of the plan. Also, Lang's hair, like Tom's, was black and curly. He had waited a long time for someone like Lang to come along.

The hallway was empty, although they could hear soft night voices coming from the nurses' station. As they walked in a sidewise crab style, the point of the knife never wavered.

The journey seemed to take a century at least, but finally

they reached his room. Feeling safe again, Tom allowed himself a small sigh of relief. He switched the lamp on. "Lay down on the floor," he ordered. "Spread-eagled."

Lang obeyed. It helped the plan that he was a coward, Tom thought. But then most people were.

Tom knelt next to him. "Listen up again. I want you to undress. You might be thinking about trying something. And you might even be able to fuck up my plans. That would make you a hero, probably." He poked the knife into Lang's ribcage. "But you'd be a dead hero, I promise. William Lang would be one dead motherfucker, because I'd kill you before anybody else could get in here. Do you believe what I'm saying?"

Lang nodded.

"Good. Now you just stay right where you are and get those clothes off."

Lang began to wriggle out of shoes, pants, jacket, and shirt. His desperate gaze never left Tom's face. He didn't look at the knife even once. In moments, he was still again, clad now only in pale blue briefs and white athletic socks. His Giants baseball cap, which he seemed always to be wearing, on or off duty, had fallen to the floor. Tom reached over with one hand and removed the man's glasses. Then he pushed everything safely out of the way.

The knife blade grazed the front of the briefs lightly. "You can keep those on. See what a nice guy I am?"

"Yeah," Lang said in a hoarse whisper.

"Yeah what?"

"Yeah, you're a nice guy."

Tom smiled at Lang and then with one swift gesture, cut the man's throat. Blood spurted and he pulled away quickly. He'd forgotten how much blood a human being had inside. Lang was still looking at him, bewildered. Finally, his body gave one terrible shudder, and Lang died with a soft gurgling noise.

Tom didn't have a chance to congratulate himself on

how well things were going so far. Timing, timing. He hoisted Lang's body and dumped it into the bed, facing the wall. Blood made a dark trail across the floor, but that couldn't be helped. When the sheet was pulled high enough, all that could be seen of the dead man was a thatch of tangled dark hair.

Still moving quickly but calmly, Tom pulled off his pants and used them to wipe up some of the blood. It was a lousy cleaning job, but he reassured himself by remembering that it wouldn't have to stand a close inspection until morning. By that time, he'd be long gone.

If his luck held.

He went into the bathroom and washed carefully, leaving the bloody towel and pants in a pile on the floor. Returning to the other room, he donned Lang's slacks, red knit shirt with the little fox on the front, and sneakers. The clothes fit well enough, although Lang had about ten pounds on him. Tom added the navy windbreaker, the baseball cap, and finally the tinted aviator glasses. That idiot Lang had made it all so simple. It was almost as if he were asking for something like this to happen.

But the easy part was over now.

Tom retrieved his hidden drug stash, shoving the plastic bag into the windbreaker pocket. The supply might come in very handy later. If nothing else, he could always sell the shit.

The knife went into the other pocket.

He glanced at the cheap alarm clock sitting on the dresser. Right on schedule. After one more glance around, he turned off the light and left the crummy little room forever.

The shoes, he discovered immediately, were a little too small, but he forced himself to walk naturally, ignoring the twinges of pain in his toes. There was, as always, a paperback book shoved into the left rear pocket of Lang's jeans. Tom tugged at the book until it slid out. He opened it at random and started to read, paying no attention to the words, not even knowing what they were.

He could feel his gut tighten as he got closer to the circle of light that marked the nurses' station. A few feet to the left of that was the guard's desk. It had always seemed to Tom that this place couldn't make up its mind whether to be a jail or a hospital. Now he didn't care.

The guard, Morgan, had his face buried in a copy of *Playboy*. There was only one nurse at the station. The second, he knew, would be checking rooms in the east wing, and the third was on her break now, in the lounge. None of this knowledge was a result of luck or divine blessing. Tom knew that things were going so well only because he was so smart and had planned so carefully.

This part, however, had not been rehearsed; he was going in cold.

Keeping his head bent low over the book, Tom walked precisely in the narrow band of shadow that fell between the nurse and where Morgan sat. No man's land.

The nurse glanced his way, barely looking up from some papers she was working on. " 'Night, Billy," she said.

He raised a hand in absent-minded farewell.

Morgan was still huddled over his magazine.

Tom hardly allowed himself to breathe as he moved down the hall. He stopped at the electronically controlled door. "Hey," he said in a muffled voice, not turning.

"Sorry, Lang," Morgan said, belatedly pressing the release button. "See you."

"Yeah." He stepped through the doorway.

When he heard the lock click shut behind him, Tom had to bite his tongue to keep from shouting. But he held the emotional urge in. There were still plenty of ways for things to go wrong.

He didn't lift his head as he stepped into the elevator and turned toward the front, away from the gaze of the operator. The ride down was silent, with Tom reading and

9

the other man yawning. When the doors slid open again, Tom got out quickly.

It was all so unbelievably goddamned simple.

He paused long enough in the lobby to sign out, scribbling Lang's name in the thick book shoved at him. He could sense the guard look quickly at the picture on the badge that was pinned to the front of the windbreaker, then at him.

One part of his mind expected an outcry, and he was ready for it. They wouldn't stop him now, no matter what. Not when freedom was so close that he could almost taste it. His fingers curled around the knife inside the pocket as he crossed the lobby.

But nothing happened.

Tom smiled a little. There would probably be some changes made around this place when it was discovered that he'd gotten out. Heads would roll. Still smiling, he nodded to the guard by the door and walked out.

Freedom.

There was still one more hurdle in his path, but Tom was absolutely calm as he turned away from the employee parking lot and headed, instead, for the front gate.

Still another damned uniformed man stepped out of the cubicle as he saw Tom approach. "What's up?" he asked, checking the badge in the dim light.

"Fucking car died. I think it's the battery."

"Want me to call the auto club?"

Tom shook his head. "Thanks, but I already called a friend to pick me up. I'll worry about the car in the morning. Right now, I just wanna get home."

"I can dig that."

Tom peered down the road and saw two faint pinpoints of light. They blinked once, then again. "There's my ride."

The guard opened the gate and waved Tom through.

He walked rapidly away, feeling the darkness close

10

around him protectively. As he got closer to the lights, he could see a solitary figure inside the old brown pick-up.

Jody. His brother hadn't let him down.

Tom felt a smile beginning on his face, although he knew that Jody couldn't see him yet. It didn't matter. He was free. They were together again.

It was great to be alive.

Chapter 2

"So? What about it?"

"So what about what?"

"You want to screw or not?"

Her name was Pamela, and no one would ever have the guts to call her Pam. She had very long, absolutely straight silver-blonde hair, tortoise shell glasses, and at the moment, an expression of exquisite disgust on her face. "You really enjoy playing the role, don't you?" she asked, instead of answering his question.

Blue Maguire paused in the middle of what he was doing, which happened to be mixing another pitcher of margaritas. "What role is that?" He supposed that dialogue like this was what he deserved for getting involved with a professor of sociology. Knowing that, unfortunately, didn't make it any easier to live with.

Pamela sighed. "The role of macho cop," she said wearily.

"Oh, that role. Sure, I enjoy it." He gestured toward the just-silenced television with one salt-rimmed glass. "Me and Dirty Harry Callahan. Just a couple of tough guys walking the mean streets."

"Maybe the part suits him. It doesn't suit you."

"No?" He crossed the room and gave her one of the drinks, then sat facing her, his own glass in hand. "Why doesn't it 'suit' me, as you say?" Stretching his legs out onto the glass-topped table, he stared at her.

"You're far too intelligent to be very believable as a dumb cop."

"Cops are dumb?"

12

She shrugged. "You must admit that there aren't very many brilliant minds in the field."

He nodded slowly and sipped the drink. "Anything besides my extraordinary mind makes you think I don't belong?"

A faint smile tugged at her lips, but she suppressed it; this was, apparently, to be a Serious Discussion. "You don't dress for the part," she said.

"Which would be how?"

"In a baggy suit that hasn't been pressed since Ike left office. Jesus, you don't even have a beer gut."

He was wearing a pale green Lacoste shirt, with tailored jeans, and soft leather Italian-made loafers. Still, his wardrobe seemed fairly irrelevant to the issue at hand. "But I am a cop," he said. "And cops are supposed to be team players. So shouldn't I try to fit the mold? Shouldn't I try to belong as much as I can?"

She didn't say anything to that. They drank in silence for a moment.

"Besides," Blue said eventually, "if I'm not a cop like all the others, what am I?" He said the words with a smile, but there was a real question in the tone.

Pamela licked salt from the edge of her glass. "That's the crucial question we have to deal with."

Ah, this went even beyond Serious. It was Crucial. "Why do we have to deal with it?" he asked.

"Because if you don't know yourself, what becomes of us? How can there even be an us?"

He was beginning to see where all this talk was heading; it didn't take a baseball bat across the skull for him to get the point. He swallowed another gulp of tequila. "I don't think that follows. Necessarily."

But she said that it did, of necessity, follow. Her line of reasoning had something to do with the parts being greater than the whole. Or maybe it was the other way around.

13

Blue wasn't sure, because he wasn't really listening. There were grains of salt stuck along her upper lip, and she swiped at them absently with the tip of her tongue. Instead of paying attention to her words, Blue was thinking about how much he'd like to fuck her. He toyed with the idea of just throwing her down on the rug, ripping off the black denim skirt she was wearing, and going at it hot and heavy. Probably, if he were any other man within the ranks of L.A.P.D.'s macho finest, he would have done just that. She might even have liked it.

But no matter how strong the urge, he just couldn't picture Detective Second Blue Maguire, with his fancy master's degree in criminology and his three-hundred dollar shoes, doing something like that. And maybe when all was said and done, or undone, that was the real problem.

She was still talking, using her lecture room voice. "Maybe we just shouldn't see one another for a while."

"How long a while?" he asked, mostly so that his end of the conversation would be held up.

"I don't know. A while. Time enough for both of us to try and understand who we are. What we want out of life. I think that would be a very good idea, don't you?" Her mouth pursed thoughtfully. "A period of personal evaluation."

Blue pushed himself up from the chair and walked around the room for a moment. Then he turned to face her. "Pamela, if you want to split, just say so. Why do you always have to cloak everything in some kind of damned sociological garbage-speak?"

"I'm sorry you think that's what I'm doing," she said stiffly. It was bad manners to dispute the professor.

"It's what you always do."

"Always is a very loaded word. An angry word. I wish you wouldn't react this way."

14

"I always react with hostility when I'm in the process of getting dumped. Rejection is a real downer, you know?"

"Let's not take off on a self-pity kick. Those kinds of feelings are very counter-productive."

"Go to hell," he muttered, stopping by the vast picture window that filled one entire wall of the room. He had a great view of the city from up here. It sometimes seemed as if all of L.A. belonged to him. No other cop he knew could afford to live this way. No honest cop, anyway.

Of course, no other cop he knew had a daddy who made a fortune in the early days of computers and was then kind enough to drop dead, leaving only one son and heir.

Pamela stood. "I think I'll just get my things and leave. Obviously you're not prepared to discuss this on any kind of rational level."

"Great. Fine. Leave. If I want to be irrational in my own damned house, I will be, thank you."

He followed her up the winding staircase to the bedroom and stood watching as she collected the residue of her time in his life. There wasn't much to collect. A short white nightgown styled like a man's shirt, a toothbrush, some make-up. A couple of impossibly thick textbooks and the new *Cosmopolitan*. Pamela was a modern woman who believed in traveling light. She didn't seem to want much baggage, either real or emotional.

She wasn't alone, of course; it seemed as if he kept meeting women who liked to move on sooner than he'd been ready for them to. He probably should have been used to this scene by now.

Just once he'd like to do the leaving.

Pamela had all of her things together very quickly, shoving them into a large canvas tote bag from the UCLA bookstore. "We'll talk," she said. It wasn't said with much conviction.

"Sure."

15

"You sound so bitter."

He gave a soft laugh. "No, babe, not bitter. Just sort of resigned."

She sighed, hoisted the bag, and started out of the room.

He let her get past him — she did it carefully, so they didn't touch — and down the stairs before he spoke again. "Pamela?"

"What?"

He went down into the living room. Her hand was on the doorknob. "Does this have anything to do with — " He broke off, then said savagely, "Maybe I'm just not very good in bed. Is that what this is all about?"

She looked at him for a long moment, then sighed and shook her head. "Oh, Blue. This is about a lot of things. Maybe mostly it's about the fact that you feel as if you have to ask that question." She looked as if there might be more to say, but then she only waved and left.

It was too quiet after she had gone. Blue turned on the television, flipped around the dial a couple of times, and finally settled on the cable news station, just for the background noise it provided.

Blue wasn't sure why he felt so bad. Pamela's walking out didn't come as any real surprise; he'd known for several days that it was coming. The signs had all been there. He walked over to the window again and leaned against the glass.

Shit.

What was it with him and broads? He couldn't seem to keep one around long enough to get tired of. They all got tired first. Some of them couldn't seem to handle the fact that he was a cop. The weird hours and broken dates made them crazy. At least, that was the excuse they offered. But maybe it was something else.

Far below he could see the fast moving, flashing light of a squad car. Something was happening. Whatever it was had

16

to be more interesting than a continued reflection on the sad saga of his love life.

Blue straightened and crossed the room again. He lowered the volume on the television, leaving the picture flickering, and switched on the police radio, hoping to find out what was coming down.

After turning off the lamp, he took the pitcher of margaritas and sat cross-legged on the floor. What was needed, he decided, was an attitude change. A shifting of his priorities. Nobody ever said he had to be his father's son. The old bastard had been an electronics genius who made a bundle. True enough. He'd also had a cock that was famous in most of the civilized world. Horny Hank Maguire, the gossip columnists used to call him.

Fine and good. When he died, there were a lot of unhappy women in the world. But that was Hank. Did that mean that Blue had to keep trying for stud of the year honors?

No, damnit, it didn't.

Blue liked being a cop, and he was good at it. What else did he need? Not to keep on competing with his father, that was for sure. And not to have his gut kicked by another broad walking out. To hell with it. From now on, all his energies would be devoted to being a better cop. Hell, he'd be the best damned cop in the history of the department.

And for the rest of it, he'd just buddy up to somebody in vice and find out where a man could get some of what he needed for cash on the line and no emotional investment.

Blue sat for a long time in the dark apartment, watching the city below and listening to the police calls, as he finished off the warm tequila.

17

Chapter 3

PROBABLY he should have been a whole lot smarter about it.

After all, he was no dummy, no virgin, for Chrissake, to the realities of life on the street. He'd been on the hustle for almost two years now, ever since splitting from Wichita, and he knew the ropes as well as anyone, better than some.

The gimmick was in learning how to read people, to spot the possible nutcases. More than once he'd thumbed a car to stop, then after getting a good look at the driver, moved on without getting in.

Pete had a lot of smarts. He knew the rules, and he lived by them, knowing how bad it could be if he didn't.

But what the hell. Nobody made exactly the right moves all the time. It was a hot night. The city was smack in the middle of the hottest damned summer on record, and the weight of that heat hung over everything oppressively, like a too-heavy wool blanket. People were getting itchy. He had been standing on the same corner of Santa Monica Boulevard for almost an hour, his thumb stuck uselessly in the air. He took off his Who concert tee shirt and shoved it into the waistband of his cutoffs, but it didn't seem to make him any cooler or to increase his desirability to the passing drivers.

It pissed him off that nobody would stop. Pete wasn't very good about keeping his temper. He tried to be mellow, but it just didn't work sometimes.

When the truck pulled to a grinding halt just a few feet past the corner, Pete didn't use all the brains and street smarts that he had.

The truck itself should have given him his first warning.

18

It was an old Ford, dirty grey-brown in color, with too many dents to count and what sounded like the beginnings of a bad muffler.

But he ran up to the truck anyway, because he was so tired of standing on that corner, feeling like the fucking invisible man. He stepped onto the running board and peered into the cab. There were two men inside. That fact set off a small buzz way in the back of his mind. Usually he tried to avoid cars with more than one person inside. Not because he had anything against an orgy now and then, if he knew the others involved. What he didn't like was being outnumbered by strangers.

"Where you heading?" the passenger asked.

"Downtown. The bus depot."

" 'Kay. Get in."

The other guy, the driver, didn't say anything. Pete balanced where he was, listening to the warning buzz that was telling him to skip this and wait for something better.

But it was so damned hot. And more important, if he didn't get downtown pretty damned soon, Doc would be gone, taking his supply of rainbow-colored goodies with him. Pete was feeling wired; he needed some of what Doc had to offer. And broke as he was, Doc was his only hope for feeling better. It had been two weeks since the last time, and the fat pharmacist was undoubtedly horny again.

"Make up your mind," the man said impatiently.

"Okay, sure," Pete said, opening the door. The man shifted over a little to make room. "Thanks for stopping."

"No problem."

Although he was grateful for the ride, Pete still couldn't relax. He sat as close to the door as he could get, ready to make a fast exit if it became necessary.

After a few minutes, the silence in the truck became uncomfortable, so he cleared his throat. "I'm Pete."

"Nice to meet you, Pete," the man next to him said. "I'm Tom, and this here is Jody."

19

"Terrific. Sure is hot, huh?"

"Yeah, sure is." Tom moved in the seat slightly so that he was a little closer. He stank of beer and sweat. "Kinda late to be out, ain't it?"

"I gotta meet a guy."

"Right away?"

"Yeah, sort of." Pete leaned forward so that he could see better through the grimy windshield. "I don't think we're going the right way."

"Don't worry about it."

"But I'm in this hurry, see. If I don't connect—" He shut up.

"What're you hoping to connect for, Pete?"

He frowned. "Nothing, I guess." He tried to judge the speed of the truck. Too fast; he'd break a fucking leg if he tried to jump out now. Maybe if he just waited until a red light. Could these pricks be narcs? Or maybe vice?

Tom reached into the glove compartment and pulled something out.

Pete waited for him to flash a badge, but when he looked all he saw was a plastic baggie filled with pills. "What's that?" he asked, trying to sound as if it didn't matter much.

"A little bit of everything. You want some?"

"Well, to be honest, Tom," he hedged, "I'm a little short right now, cashwise."

Tom laughed and poked an elbow into the driver's ribs. "Hell, Pete here thinks we wanna sell him some of this shit. He thinks we're dealing. That's a laugh, huh?"

Jody glanced at Pete and smiled a little. He was a slightly younger edition of Tom, with the same lean, dark face and curly hair.

"You think we're dealing? No way, Petey." Tom grinned and patted Pete's bare knee. "We were thinking more of having a party. Just you and me and Jody here. You like the sound of that?"

Pete swallowed, considering. Okay, so he'd miss Doc

20

this time around. But maybe with these guys he could cop some joy medicine and pick up some bread at the same time. "Ten bucks extra for both of you," he said, wanting to get things clear right up front.

"Ten? That's a little steep, don't you think? Especially since we're willing to share the goodies."

"Five extra, then. I got overhead to meet."

"That's more like it. Sounds good to me. How's that seem to you, Jody?"

"Fine," he said, speaking for the first time.

"Great. So let's get a move on. Time to party."

"Where are we going for this party?" Pete asked.

"The park. Old Griffith Park. I haven't been there in a long time. Years. That sounds like a good place to have a party, don't you think?"

"I guess so," Pete said.

He still wasn't sure about this, but it was too late now. Besides, he thought, at least these guys weren't fat and gross, like Doc. He looked at Tom and forced a smile to his lips. "We'll have fun."

Tom stared at him for a moment. His eyes, startlingly pale blue in the dark face, held a hungry, fevered look. "Count on it, Pete," he said. He reached out a hand and ruffled Pete's sweaty hair.

Pete was used to hungry eyes and eager hands. He leaned against the door and closed his eyes. He hoped to hell the creeps had the bread to pay him. He hoped the little baggie had some really high-powered shit in it. And mostly he hoped that the two of them weren't kinky. It was too damned hot for any of the funny stuff.

21

Chapter 4

THE PHONE RANG.

"Shut the hell up."

It rang again.

"Gonna pull your fucking cord out."

Again.

One hand reached out, groping, searching for the offending instrument. The damned thing wasn't there. It kept ringing, but it wasn't there.

Spaceman Kowalski yanked the pillow from over his head, grunting as an explosion of daylight crashed against him. He blinked and then stared. The ceiling above was pale blue. With little silver stars painted all over it. Most definitely not his ceiling.

The other occupant of the bed finally answered the phone, which happened to be on her side of the room. The same goddamned thing happened everytime he spent the night here. He never got used to either the ceiling or to having the phone in the wrong place.

"Hello," she said. Perkily. She sounded perky at the frigging crack of dawn. Like Sandra Dee in some old movie. There really was no justice in the world.

And what the hell had ever happened to Sandra Dee?

Spaceman shrugged away that momentous question and managed to focus on his Timex. Seven-thirty. Almost time for work, anyway.

Mandy held the receiver out toward him. "It's for you," she said. The voice now held only disappointment, and he knew it was because the call wasn't from her agent.

He took the phone and sat up. "Yeah?" The taste in his mouth reminded him vaguely of the smell hovering over a garbage dump where he'd once spent three days looking for a body. He belched into the receiver.

"Detective Kowalski?"

"No, it's fucking Princess Di. Whattaya want?"

"The lieutenant wants you should go over to Griffith Park."

"Why?"

"Maybe he wants to have a picnic." The voice was end-of-the-shift snippy.

Spaceman watched as Mandy got out of bed and walked, naked, across the room. She had great tits. They bounced just enough. "Why does McGannon want me to go to the park at seven-thirty in the morning?" he asked pleasantly, proud of his restraint. He was determined that the word "surly" wouldn't appear anywhere in his next fitness report.

"Somebody found a stiff. You're still working homicide, right? Maybe, just maybe, that's why McGannon wants you there."

He wished he could put a name to the voice, but Los Angeles could freeze over before he'd ask. "Wonderful," he said instead. "That's just what I need this morning." He was hung-over and had gas, but did the killers of this city care? Fat chance. He belched again and asked just where in the park the picnic was happening.

The voice told him.

He hung up without saying good-bye.

Mandy came out of the bathroom and, still naked, started her exercises. "What's up?"

He thought about saying something real clever, like "I am, and what're you gonna do about it?" But a quick check under the sheet revealed the dismal truth. It was hell to be thirty-eight. What would life be like after forty? It didn't even bear thinking of. So he told her about the stiff in the park that he had to go see.

23

In the middle of a leg lift, she made a face. "Gross," she said. "Before breakfast, even?"

He watched the exercise routine for a moment, then realized that unless he got out of the bed immediately, even his aging flesh would start to react.

And he had a picnic to go to.

He got out of bed and headed for the bathroom. "Make some coffee," he ordered.

Even the lukewarm water the old pipes churned up felt good as it washed away the sweat and sticky wine from his chest. As he scrubbed with a bar of lime green glycerine soap, Spaceman wasn't thinking about what might have happened in the park. He was wondering, not for the first time, why the devil anybody would put the Big Dipper on her bedroom ceiling.

She had instant coffee made and some frozen orange juice about half-thawed by the time he came out, trying to smooth the wrinkles from his old brown suit. It was a fairly hopeless task.

He swallowed the lumpy juice in one gulp and started on the coffee. As he drank, he worked on his tie with a damp paper towel. Mandy had donned an old sweatshirt and a pair of white panties. She sat in a chair, watching him and eating a bagel that dripped strawberry jam. "You want something to eat?"

His stomach did a flip-flop. "No time," was all he said to her. Couldn't let the twenty-year-old know that middle age took some things harder than did youth.

One of these days, he thought, giving up on the tie, I'll find a woman my own age.

The young stuff was going to kill him off before his time. How many late night parties with cheap wine, pepperoni pizza, and pot could a man of his age take before the damage got serious?

24

The thick black coffee burned his gullet. "Gotta go," he said, taking one last gulp.

She untwined herself from the chair to give him a hug. "What about tonight?"

"I'll have to see. No promises. The thing in the park might screw up my whole day." His hands slid down her back until the fingers were gently massaging the firm flesh inside the silky panties.

"Well, lemme know," she said, going back to her bagel.

Wondering what she did on the nights he worked, Spaceman moved carefully down the narrow outside staircase that led to her third floor apartment. One good tremor and the whole damned thing would collapse. Probably with him on it.

Maybe it was time to think about losing those fifteen extra pounds.

Except that it would probably be easier to find a girl who lived on the ground floor.

Once inside his car, he radioed headquarters that he was rolling on the dead body in Griffith Park. As he spoke, he stared into the rearview mirror.

The pink Lady Schick had done a perfectly miserable job of shaving his face.

25

Chapter 5

SPACEMAN KOWALSKI liked being a cop.

He didn't like morning traffic. Hunched over the steering wheel of his '76 Chevy, he swore and sweated his way from Mandy's place on Beverly toward the park. Finally, he pulled the bubblegum light from under the seat and shoved it onto the roof. With that flashing and the siren cranked up, his progress was made a little easier, though not much. Nostalgically, he thought about the good old days when he was a kid. Back then, the other traffic would pull over to make room for a cop on a run. There was respect.

But then came the Sixties and the old world fell apart. Now a few drivers got out of his way, most didn't, and a goodly number swore at him or made some obscene gesture. All of which he returned in kind.

Something else he didn't like, besides traffic, was looking at dead bodies.

If the departed citizen was reasonably tidy, he could usually handle it with no problem. The old farts who just expired in bed, for example. That wasn't fun, but if the carcass didn't lie around too long before being found, it was at least tolerable. Maybe this case was just some old fart who stretched out in the grass and passed away.

He could hope, anyway.

Two zone cars and a black van from the medical examiner's office were parked near the bird sanctuary when he arrived. Nobody was doing much, however; nobody would until he had a chance to view the scene intact. The routine was part of the mystique surrounding police work. Spaceman was supposed to see something, the clue, that would set the wheels of justice turning, no matter how slowly.

The first thing he saw was that this body wasn't neat and tidy.

The stiff was just a kid. About the age of his own son, he realized, remembering suddenly, parenthetically, that Robbie had a birthday coming up soon. He'd have to buy something for the occasion.

This boy wouldn't be having any more birthdays. He'd been a good-looking boy, maybe sixteen, with longish blond hair and the pouty kind of face that was popular in some circles. A bloody tee shirt and some shorts were next to the body. There was a lot of blood.

"Shit," Spaceman said.

Gardner, from the pathologist's office, nodded. "That just about says it all."

"Pictures?"

"All done."

When he had given the whole area a fast once-over, Spaceman gave a short nod. Gardner promptly knelt beside the body.

Spaceman bent over and picked up the shorts. He pulled a worn black wallet out of the rear pocket, then handed the shorts themselves to a cop holding a plastic evidence bag.

The only money in the wallet was a single dollar bill, well-creased, that had been tucked into a hidden compartment. Obviously, the buck was intended to be used only in case of the direst emergency. There wasn't much else to see. Two pictures. The first was of a family group standing at stiff attention in front of a house. A middle-aged man in a checkered sport coat, a thin, tense looking woman, and three children. A girl, middle teens, wearing a short pleated skirt and a letter sweater. A much younger boy in a Cub Scout uniform. The third child was obviously the dead boy, looking a couple years younger,

27

but otherwise much the same. He was wearing jeans, a black tee shirt, and a petulant, dissatisfied expression.

Except for that one false note, the photo might have served as the basis for a Norman Rockwell *Saturday Evening Post* cover. There was even a dog that might have been Lassie. Americana preserved by Kodak.

And if not for that expression of dissatisfaction and the feelings behind it, the dead boy might still be a part of the picture. Spaceman knew, without knowing anything else about the people in the photo, that it was the boy's search for something different from what he had in that house that had brought him to this bloody and terrible end in Griffith Park.

The other picture was from one of the quickie booths downtown. The dead boy, looking drunk and silly, grinned up at Spaceman.

There were only a few other things in the wallet, none of them very significant, except for the ID card tucked behind the pictures. It was the kind of card that came with cheap wallets like this one. The name on the card was Peter Lowe, and the address was on Honeydew Lane in Wichita, Kansas.

There wasn't much else in the wallet: A shiny gold token from some game arcade, maybe used as a good luck piece, and a stub from a downtown movie house.

That was all.

Spaceman walked back to Gardner just as the other man stood. "Anything?"

"Not much beyond the obvious so far. Somebody used a knife on him. I stopped counting the stab wounds at fifteen. About one for every year of his life. Some indication of sexual activity just before death."

"He was raped?"

Gardner looked slightly annoyed. "Sexual activity and rape are not synonymous." He shrugged. "Anyway, the poor bastard didn't die easy."

28

"Let me know when the post is scheduled."

"Sure thing."

Spaceman watched as the body was tagged, bagged, and loaded into the black van. A minicam crew from one of the stations had appeared on the scene, drawn by the smell of blood, and the reporter stuck the mike into Spaceman's face. "No comment," he said. That was all he ever said to them, and he sometimes wondered why they kept asking.

"Can't you tell us anything about this brutal crime?"

"No comment," he repeated. Too many cops got themselves into trouble by opening their traps on camera or for the newspaper.

They filmed him anyway, walking to his car and getting in. He sat behind the wheel for a moment, then belched again.

"Shit," he said once more, this time to himself.

And to anyone who might catch the tape on the noon news and who could read lips.

Chapter 6

SPACEMAN decided that he needed some breakfast

He parked his car in the police lot and walked around the corner. There wasn't any name on the front of the tiny building he entered, just the stark word DINER over the door. The place was owned and operated by an ex-homicide dick named Joe Spinoza. Not surprisingly, considering the location, cops made up almost his entire clientele. Whatever Joe's talents had been as a detective, they did not, unfortunately, extend to his culinary efforts. The food he served up reminded a lot of the men of home cooking, and that wasn't a compliment. But he dearly loved to have the guys from the precinct come in, the prices were more than reasonable, and it was convenient. Also, Joe was always willing to let you run a tab.

Spaceman perched at the otherwise empty counter and without even glancing at the mimeographed menu, ordered his usual: three eggs over easy, sausage links, hash browns, toast, and coffee.

Joe cracked the eggs and poured them onto the sizzling grill. "So what's doing?" he asked. He spoke in a raised voice, in order to be heard over the steady drone of the police radio and the small black and white television, both of which sat behind the counter, always on.

Spaceman wondered if Joe ever left this place, ever slept beyond the catnaps that he was sometimes seen taking behind the counter. It seemed that whenever a customer came in, day or night, the plump, balding man was on the job. His wife of forty years was dead, and Spaceman always figured that Joe was happier here than in an empty house.

"I caught the stiff in Griffith," Spaceman said in glum response to Joe's question. The coffee wasn't much better than Mandy's. He added another little packet of sugar.

"I heard about that on the box. Sounded messy."

"Yeah."

Joe flipped the eggs with concentration a brain surgeon might have envied, then slid them onto a plate. He added three sausages, a mound of potatoes that were only slightly burned, and two pieces of toasted Wonder Bread. "Any leads?"

"*Nada.*"

Joe moved a sticky pot of orange marmalade down the counter to within Spaceman's reach. "Well, I'll keep my eyes and ears open. You never know." He always said that, no matter what the case. In all his years of running the diner and offering to "keep my eyes and ears open" Joe had never turned up one piece of solid dope, as far as Spaceman knew. But that didn't stop him from trying.

"Yeah, do that," Spaceman said. "Any help gratefully received." He lowered his head over the plate and began to shovel the food in.

The lieutenant was waiting when Spaceman strolled into the squadroom. "Took your sweet time getting here," he complained.

Spaceman removed the toothpick from his mouth, contemplated the well-chewed sliver, then shoved it back. "I had to catch some breakfast. Can't think on an empty stomach."

McGannon only snorted. His own body was whippet-thin compared to Spaceman's bulkier form. He waved Spaceman into his office. Inside, McGannon sat behind the vast desk that took up most of the space in the small room. The desk gave his men a lot of laughs.

McGannon's father and grandfather had both been lawyers, real movers and shakers in the legal

31

establishment, and the big hunk of oak had been part of their prestigious offices. McGannon himself flunked out of law school and became a cop. His most driving ambition over the years had been to work his way far enough up the ladder of command to rate his own office. The very day he landed this job, the desk was moved in.

Now he leaned back in the chair and clasped both hands behind his head. "So?" he said. "Any first impressions?"

Spaceman broke the toothpick in half and tossed the pieces into the heavy cut-glass ashtray on the corner of the desk. "Some sex freako," he said flatly.

McGannon frowned. He didn't like cases that had anything at all to do with sex. He was what used to be known as a "good Catholic." In his view, sex was for married couples only, to be committed once a week in the dark, with its only object being the propagation of the faithful. Any pleasure that might happen along the way was permitted, but never acknowledged. Kathleen and he had six kids, with a seventh on the way, and even they never talked about sex.

Money was a motive that he could understand. Or even drugs. But anything to do with sex made him very nervous. "But this was just a kid," he objected.

"Want a theory?" Spaceman asked.

McGannon looked tired suddenly, a man who knew he wasn't going to like what he was about to hear. He nodded anyway.

"I think the kid was hustling and picked up the wrong customer."

McGannon sighed.

"Whoever he picked up wasted him. Did a very messy job of it, too."

"That's really sick," McGannon said, his voice ringing with a moral ferocity that Spaceman used to think was phony, but which he finally decided was real. It sometimes made him feel kind of sorry for the other man.

32

Spaceman smiled faintly. "Sick? Yeah, that's probably just what the defense attorney will claim when we bust him."

"If we bust him."

Spaceman spread his hands to indicate helplessness. "If we lose hope, there's nothing left."

"And even if we do bust him, chances are it'll never come to trial."

The damned gloomy Irishman. "That's not my look-out."

McGannon was quiet, swiveling from side to side in his fancy chair. "Kids. What the hell is going on? When I was his age, there wasn't any of the shit that goes on today."

"Sex, you mean?"

"I mean, all this weird stuff. Who the hell started it all anyway?"

"Beats me, boss. Maybe it was the hippies. Or the Beatles."

"The damned Commies, probably," McGannon said darkly.

Spaceman shook his head. "All the Reds I ever knew were puritans. Worse than Republicans, even." He lit a Camel and waited for McGannon to get back on the track.

Finally he did so, crisply. "You want to call the parents?"

No, he didn't want to.

He was tired of making that same dismal call. Kids, the damned little shitheads, seemed to come from all over the country just to get killed or kill themselves in his city.

See Los Angeles and die.

That would make a great bumper sticker.

So he made the call, time after time, and broke the news. The reactions he got never seemed to vary much in type, only in degree. Disbelief, followed by anger, then painful and weary acknowledgement. At bottom, it never seemed to come as much of a surprise. Parents today apparently expect something like this to happen, sooner or later.

33

He thought again about his own son. What the devil did a boy just turning seventeen want for his birthday?

"I'll make the call," he said.

It was a crummy job, yeah, but he always did it himself. Maybe he hoped that by talking to a mother or father in that first unguarded moment, he might uncover something that would lead him to the why.

McGannon was still frowning. "Well, keep me on top of it," he said, closing the discussion.

"Sure thing." Spaceman started for the door.

"Oh, by the way, Kowalski — "

"Yeah?"

McGannon studied him, smiling faintly now. Then he shook his head. "Later."

"There a problem?"

"No. No problem. Just something we need to talk about. Drop in after lunch."

Spaceman shrugged. "Sure."

He went out to his own desk. Several other detectives were in the room as well, talking, writing reports, or just drinking coffee from styrofoam cups. Spaceman picked up his phone and dialed information.

He scribbled down the number a bored operator gave him a moment later. Frowning, he traced the numbers over more firmly as he mentally figured time differences. Getting on toward eleven here, which meant almost one there. One o'clock on a summer Saturday. What were the chances of finding anyone home?

But he dialed anyway, because he had no choice. The ringing of the other phone sounded very far away. Once, twice, three times, then the ringing stopped. "Hello?"

It was a male voice, for which he was glad. Easier to break news like this to a man than a woman. The voice sounded a little winded, as if its owner had to run to catch the call. Probably he'd been outside, cutting the grass or feeding the cows or whatever else one does in Kansas on Saturday.

"Mr. Lowe?"

"Speaking."

"My name is Kowalski. Detective Kowalski, Los Angeles Police Department."

"What's that? California?"

"Yes, sir."

"Whatever trouble he's got himself into, I'm not bailing him out." The words were immediate and harsh.

"You're talking about your son, Peter Lowe?"

"He's no son of mine, not any more."

Spaceman picked up his pen again. He wrote the dead boy's name on the notepad, then drew hard black lines through it. "The trouble he has now, you can't bail him out of."

"What?"

"I'm afraid it's very bad news, Mr. Lowe. A boy we've identified as Peter was found deceased this morning."

"He's dead?"

"Yes. Apparently Peter was the victim of a homicide."

Lowe seemed to mull that over for a time. "Somebody killed him is what you're saying?" The flat midwestern voice never wavered.

"Yes."

There was still another pause. "You sure it's him?"

"Yes. As sure as we can be without an official ID." He thought maybe that sounded a little hopeful, and hope was a commodity that nobody could afford anymore. "It's Peter," he said.

"I told him that sooner or later he'd get just what he deserved."

"Sir?" Spaceman stopped scribbling and set the pen down carefully.

"Peter was no good. He's been nothing but trouble to us

35

since he was ten. I knew he'd end up bad. And you want to know something? I'm glad it's over. Yeah, I really am."

Spaceman didn't know what to say. It wasn't the first time he'd had this kind of reaction; usually he put it down to shock. Lowe didn't sound shocked, though. He didn't sound anyway in particular. Spaceman took a deep breath. "This is difficult," he began awkwardly. "But — "

"He left us two years ago. This was a good home, officer. We gave him everything a boy needs."

Spaceman thought about the dissatisfied expression on the young face in the family photograph. Not everything, he wanted to tell Lowe. At least, not all the things Peter thought he needed. Or wanted.

"We're good Christians, church-going people. I'm an alderman. But Peter threw all that back in our faces. Made out like it was us in the wrong instead of him. You want to know how many times we heard from him in the past two years?"

Spaceman made a noncommittal sound.

"I'll tell you. Once. Just about a year ago. And that once was too much for me."

"What did he want?"

"What else? Money, of course."

"Did you send him some?"

"Certainly not. That would have condoned his lifestyle. I did the only thing a righteous man could."

"Which was?"

"I told him that if he was willing to renounce the way he was living, and come home, we would forgive him."

"You would forgive him."

"Yes." Lowe was obviously very pleased with himself. "Even after all he'd done, I was willing to accept him back. To give him one more chance at a decent life."

"But he refused your generous offer?"

Lowe missed the sarcasm. "He did. And worse. Told me in plain words just how ugly and degraded his life had

36

become. About the drugs. About. . .unspeakable things. I just thank the good Lord that my wife never had to hear the things Peter told me that night."

"Okay," Spaceman said briskly. "I can understand how you felt. But that's all in the past now. Your son is dead. What arrangements do you want to make for the body?"

"I'm not interested in making any arrangements at all."

"Lowe, despite the problems he caused you, Peter was your son. Your responsibility."

"You must have some kind of potter's field out there, don't you?"

Spaceman nodded wearily, then remembered that the man couldn't see him. "Yes, I guess we do."

"Put him there. Put him anywhere you want. He's not a part of us anymore."

"Don't you want —"

"That's all I have to say." He hung up.

Spaceman slowly followed suit. He was thinking about the bloody, ravaged body he'd seen in the park, and about the cold, hard voice of Lowe. "The world sucks," he announced.

Jefferies, a skinny black man, looked his way and laughed softly. "That supposed to be some kind of news?"

"No, but I keep forgetting how damned much it sucks, until somebody reminds me."

Nobody said anything to that.

Spaceman had a report to type from another case, the killing of one wino by another over the disputed ownership of a bottle of Thunderbird. Said bottle, in fact, being the death weapon. It wasn't a very long report, but he was a slow typist, so it took a while.

Just as he was finishing, the phone rang.

"Kowalski," he answered, yanking the completed report from the grip of the ancient Smith-Corona, and tossing it toward his out basket.

"Hi." It was a woman's voice, not Mandy's.

"Yes?"

There was a sigh from the other end. "I thought you might recognize my voice. But I guess ex-wives are very forgettable."

"Hi, Karen." Just what he needed to put the finishing touch on a morning that was already the pits. "The check's in the mail," he said automatically.

"The check came last week," she replied. "That's not why I'm calling."

"Oh?" He shifted the phone to his other ear and initialed an earlier report that he'd forgotten to initial the first time around, causing McGannon to send it back. "What's up?"

"We have to talk. Can I see you? Maybe for lunch?"

"It's not a good day, Karen. Things are closing in."

"It's never a good day for you. But this is important. It's about Robbie."

"I haven't forgotten his birthday."

"This isn't about his birthday, either." Her voice sounded strained.

"Then what?"

"Damnit, I can't talk now; I'm at work. Can we just meet for lunch?"

"All right, all right. Is Denny's okay?"

"Fine. How about——" She paused, probably checking her watch. "Forty minutes?"

"Be on time. I'm really pressed."

She hung up without saying any more.

Spaceman sat still for a moment, frowning. Karen never called him, except to bitch about the child support check being late. He hoped to hell this wasn't anything important; there was no room in his day for a major hassle.

Chapter 7

HE woke without knowing where he was.

Panic filled him in the first terrifying moment; as he stared at the ceiling of the unfamiliar room, his breathing quickened. He began to hyperventilate.

Remembering what the shrinks had told him, Tom closed his eyes again, squeezing them tight, and tried to relax. Consciously, he slowed the workings of his lungs. The fear that was gripping him began to fade.

And then he remembered: I'm free.

A smile began as he rolled over and opened his eyes once again. "Hey," he said.

Jody sat up in the other bed, looking like he'd been awake for a while. "Hey, yourself," he responded listlessly.

Tom felt a rush of feeling for his little brother. Jody was the only person in the world who really understood him. Who really loved him.

With the happiness in his chest pounding hard enough to hurt, Tom got out of bed. "I'm hungry," he said. "Let's have a really big breakfast." He grinned. "No oatmeal, though. They serve that every damned morning back at the hospital."

"We can go a couple blocks over," Jody said. "There's a good place on Figueroa." His voice was flat.

Tom called first dibs on the bathroom, then stopped in the doorway. "You okay?"

"Sure. Why?"

"You just seem kind of down."

Jody looked at him for a long moment, then shrugged. "I'm fine."

Tom nodded and went into the bathroom.

While the water in the shower slowly warmed up, he brushed his teeth and urinated. He noticed that there was still some blood caked beneath his fingernails.

When the water was finally hot, he stepped in under the spray and began to scrub. He used lots of soap, almost the whole of the little bar the motel provided, rubbing with the worn cloth until his skin was red and stinging.

Last night already seemed very far away. All that remained with him clearly was the memory of the excitement he'd felt, the almost unbearably beautiful agony of the moment. He'd never known such feelings, such complete release when it was over.

Just thinking about it made his groin ache.

He stroked himself slowly with soapy fingers. Then, abruptly, he pulled his hand back. Hell, no time for that now. He turned off the hot water and let the sudden icy blast hit him full force. It helped.

Jody got out of the bed and walked over to the mirror.

He looked the same. Maybe his eyes were a little bloodshot and his face pale, but beyond that Jody Hitchcock seemed to be the same man as he'd always been. Which was ridiculous, of course.

A shiny nail clipper was lying on the top of the dresser and Jody picked it up. He carefully removed a hangnail that had been bothering him for a couple of days.

His reflection in the mirror stared out at him. Jody could almost see the blood that should have covered his hands. "Shit," he whispered to the glass image. "What the hell is going on?"

The figure in the mirror had no answer.

Since the restaurant was so close, they left the truck parked at the motel and walked over. On the way, Tom breathed deeply of the hot, fume-filled air. To him, it was freedom he was inhaling and that made it sweet, no matter what.

40

Then he frowned a little. The morning newscaster on the television had talked about fires burning around Los Angeles, out-of-control flames, fanned by the Santa Ana winds blowing hot and fierce. According to the news story, arson was suspected in some of the fires. That bothered Tom. This was his city, and nobody had the right to destroy it.

The Original Pantry Cafe was crowded, and so it took several minutes for them to get a table. Jody said he never ate much in the mornings, so all he wanted was some orange juice and scrambled eggs. Tom, however, gave in to his hunger, ordering a pile of buttermilk pancakes, some eggs and ham, toast, and coffee. He was stunned to see what the prices were. It had been so long since he'd been in the real world. He had a lot of catching up to do.

The coffee was strong and hot. He sipped it carefully while waiting for the food. "We've got a lot to do," he said.

Jody was folding and unfolding his napkin. "What?"

"First of all, we have to lose the truck."

"My truck? Why"

"Because we've used it enough. For my break and for all the rest. Somebody just might remember it."

"That's my truck," Jody said. "It's a good vehicle."

Tom didn't like the tone of Jody's voice. He looked at him for a moment. "We have to lose the truck," he said again, very quietly.

Jody frowned, but didn't say any more about it.

The food arrived and for several minutes they ate in silence. Tom poured more syrup over his plate. "Then we need to pick up some new wheels," he said, as if there had been no pause in the conversation.

"You mean steal a car?" Jody asked, playing with his eggs more than eating them.

"No, asshole, we'll walk into a dealer and buy a new Caddy," Tom said. "Of course steal one."

"And then?"

41

Tom just smiled. He pushed a piece of pancake around in the blueberry puddle.

After another moment, Jody leaned across the table toward him. "About what happened last night," he began softly.

"Yeah?"

"Are we going to do that anymore?"

"Do you want to?"

"Not the way it ended."

"Forget about the way it ended. What about the rest? You liked that, didn't you?"

Jody didn't say anything.

Tom concentrated on cutting a piece of ham. Then he looked up and smiled again. "Maybe," he said. "Maybe we'll do it some more."

Chapter 8

KAREN was already sitting at a table near the back when Spaceman walked into Denny's five minutes late. She glanced pointedly at her watch, but didn't say anything. She looked good. In the years since their divorce, Karen had worked hard to get her act together, and it was clear that she had succeeded. There wasn't much left of the girl he'd married: a plump eighteen-year-old, with a puppy dog's eagerness to please. Now, with the extra weight long gone, the dishwater hair lightened to a radiant gold color, and a wardrobe that was too costly for a cop's wife, Karen was a different woman.

Maybe, he mused, if she'd been more like this during their marriage, the divorce never would have happened. He didn't know whether that should make him feel bad or not. Then he decided not. Life, as his old man used to say, was life, which was philosophy enough for Spaceman.

The waitress scurried over as soon as he sat down. She knew he was a cop, and most waitresses liked cops. He rewarded her promptness with a smile. Karen, obviously aware of the byplay, sighed, then ordered a chef's salad and iced tea. Spaceman went for a cheeseburger, fries, and a Coke. It was his favorite lunch.

When they were alone, Karen opened her purse, a large duffel of soft butterscotch leather, and removed a lighter and cigarettes. Her fingers were steady as she lit a Virginia Slims menthol. "Thank you for coming," she said, exhaling a cloud of smoke across the table toward him.

He couldn't quite tell whether the tone of her words was sarcastic or sincere. He never could with her. "You made it sound important."

43

She nodded, looking distracted. "Yes. Yes, it's about Robbie."

The drinks arrived and he took a long gulp. "You said that before."

"He's gone."

"Gone? What the hell does that mean?"

Now, suddenly, he could see the tiny lines of tension etched around her mouth. "It means just what I said. He's gone. G-o-n-e. He hasn't been home for three days."

"Three days?" Spaceman realized that he was beginning to sound like an echo, and he gave himself a mental shake. "Why don't you just start at the beginning?" he suggested. "Give me all the facts."

"Just the facts, ma'am? What the hell is this, your Joe Friday imitation?"

He sighed patiently. "I just want to know what's going on."

"Okay, okay, but don't play cop with me. This is your son we're talking about, not just one of your damned cases."

Spaceman didn't say anything.

Karen smoked in silence for a moment, watching something across the room. "When was the last time you saw Robbie?" she asked finally.

He thought. "Couple months ago, I guess." Still trying to remember, he stirred the Coke with the straw. "Yeah, it was on opening day. When I took him to see the Dodgers play."

"Have you even spoken to him since then?"

Spaceman started to feel like he was being accused of something. "I don't know. Maybe I called him. Probably I did." He couldn't remember calling.

The food arrived. He poured catsup on the fries and smeared some mustard on the burger. "Robbie didn't seem to enjoy the game much," he said. "In fact, the whole

44

damned day seemed like nothing but a big pain in the butt to him."

"So your tender feelings got hurt and you didn't call him again."

"I've been busy, is all." He wondered if what she were saying might be true. If so, it didn't seem to say much for him in the fathering department.

He picked up a couple of fries and chewed them while thinking about opening day. It was an annual trek for them, going out to see the Dodgers begin the season. They'd done it since Robbie was four.

But this year had been different. Robbie and he didn't seem to have anything to say to each other anymore. The boy was obviously his son; it was there in the square jawline and the green eyes. But lately the jaw always seemed to be set stubbornly, and the eyes were full of dark secrets.

During the drive to Dodger Stadium, Robbie slouched in the passenger seat, ostentatiously lighting one cigarette after another, and staring at the traffic. Any comment offered by his father was answered with either a grunt or a sigh.

Things didn't get any better at the game itself. Robbie perched on the bleacher seat like he was sitting in the dentist's waiting room. Even when the Bums managed to pull the game out in the bottom of the ninth, he didn't seem to give a damn.

They made the ritual stop for pizza on the way home, but Spaceman was frankly glad when the day ended, and Robbie seemed just as relieved when he jumped out of the car and disappeared into the house.

The next time he was slipped a couple of tickets to see a ballgame, he had taken Mandy, who hated baseball, but loved sitting on the sunny side of the stadium in her halter top, soaking up the rays.

Spaceman took another bite of the cheeseburger and chewed slowly. "Hell," he said. "Teenagers, they all get screwy."

"Do they?"

"Sure. I see it all the time."

She shook her head. "You see the bad kids. Robbie's not like them."

"I know that." He didn't know it, not really. Any kid could make a dumb mistake and screw up his life.

Karen stared at her plate, then pushed the half-eaten salad away. "I thought at first that maybe he was just staying with a friend. I mean, it's summer, so what the hell. But when he didn't show up again last night, I called some people. Nobody's seen him."

"At least nobody would say so. They stick together. Did something happen before he left?"

"Such as?"

"Such as anything. Like maybe the two of you had a fight?"

The skin over her cheekbones turned pink. "Are you saying this is my fault?"

"I'm not saying that at all, Karen. Anyway, so far nothing's happened to be anybody's fault. I'm just asking questions."

"No, we did not fight. Not any more than usual. You've never tried living with a sixteen-year-old day in and day out. It's not easy."

"I guess not."

"And it doesn't help that you never seem to be around."

He finished the burger in one more bite, chewed, and swallowed. "That was your choice, honey, not mine." His voice held more of the old bitterness than he would have thought possible.

Shit, I'm supposed to be over that by now. I'm not supposed to care anymore.

Karen spoke coldly: "It was you who decided to sleep

46

around. Somehow, my definition of marriage didn't include sharing you with every little bitch who had the hots for a cop."

He slurped Coke through a straw.

After a moment, Karen swept a stray blonde lock out of her face. "That is not why I'm here. No matter what happened between us, you're still his father. You should care."

"I care, damnit. Maybe I don't come around too often, but you've got no right to say I don't care. I do."

"You know that. Maybe I know, too. But I'm not sure Robbie does."

"All he had to do was call, whenever he wanted anything."

"Probably he doesn't even know what he wants." The words shook a little, and her eyes were suddenly too bright. "Maybe that's why he left."

A sudden image, sharp-edged and too real, flashed through Spaceman's mind: Peter Lowe's body. Just another dumb kid, looking for something, probably not even knowing what it was.

He wiped his mouth with a paper napkin. "Shit," he said.

Karen looked up sharply. "What?"

He just shook his head.

"Can you do something?"

"I'll file a missing person sheet on him." Spaceman shrugged. "We get so damned many of those things. Especially on kids."

"So? Does that mean nobody will do anything?"

"What can be done, will be. I'll look for him myself, of course. Whenever I can."

She bristled. "Whenever you *can?*"

"I also have a job to do. Damnit, I have half a dozen open cases."

"Cases that are more important than finding your son?"

47

"Stop deliberately misinterpreting every goddamned word I say." He thought again about the dead boy, but he didn't think she needed to hear about that at the moment. "When was the last time you saw Robbie?"

That turned out to be four days ago, before she left for work. Apparently words were exchanged about taking out the garbage. Words that weren't particularly nice, on either side.

As she recounted the conversation, her smile was wryly bitter. "That's about par for our relationship lately."

"You don't have any idea where he might have gone?"

"No." She opened the purse again and took out a piece of paper. "I wrote down the names of his friends, with their addresses. The ones I know, anyway. There might be others."

"Where does he spend his time?"

"You mean besides shut up in his bedroom? At the beach, mostly, I think. Santa Monica. Venice, maybe. Wherever kids hang out these days."

"Where they hang out depends on what they're looking for."

She handed him the paper and then a picture. "I thought you might need one for the report. You probably don't have a recent one."

He shook his head. The only picture he had of his son showed a six-year-old dressed in a cowboy outfit. That smiling child in the fringed vest and matching pistols bore little likeness to the sullen teenager in this school photo. He thought that this face looked strangely angry. He put the paper and the picture into his wallet.

Karen looked at her watch again. "I have to go," she said. "I'm showing a house in twenty minutes. You'll call me tonight?"

"If I have anything."

She stood. "Even if you don't have anything, call. Just to let me know you're looking."

48

He nodded.

"Should I be scared?" The voice was a whisper, and at that moment she seemed very much like the girl he must have loved once upon a time.

Spaceman reached out to pat her hand. "Hell, no. And when I find him, I'll kick his ass all the way home for making you worry like this."

She tried a smile. It almost worked. "Talk to you later, then."

"Yeah, later."

She swung the bag over her shoulder and hurried out, looking once again like a successful woman on the move. Spaceman finished off the ice in his glass and picked up the check. This day was going from bad to shit. What the hell else could happen?

Outside, the air was hotter than ever as the temperature moved toward yet another record. He looked in the direction of the hills, wondering if the fires were still raging.

Hell of a job that, putting out fires.

Chapter 9

SPACEMAN managed to forget all about his appointment to see McGannon after lunch. He went back to the office to take care of the paperwork on Robbie, which bothered him more than he thought it should have, and then he was ready to hit the street and see what he could turn up on the Lowe boy.

But before he could get away from his desk, the phone rang. A bored voice from the medical examiner's office informed him that the autopsy on Lowe, Peter would begin in one hour. He thanked the voice and hung up.

That didn't give him enough time to do anything else first, so he was a sitting pigeon, just skimming the *Times* and working on a cigarette when McGannon opened the door of his office and waved him inside.

Spaceman swore under his breath. He didn't know what was coming, but it was damned sure not to be anything good. McGannon looked too happy; nothing made him that cheerful except finding some new way to screw up Spaceman's life. He slowly crushed the cigarette and walked with heavy steps into McGannon's cubbyhole.

McGannon, safely behind the damned desk again, had a slight and dangerous smile on his face. Spaceman's gut tightened. This was going to be nasty, no doubt about it.

It was only then that Spaceman noticed the third man in the room. The stranger smelled like Money, which made him a little nervous. He thought quickly, but couldn't come up with anything he'd done lately to get a bigshot mad at him. He tucked in his gut, smoothed his tie, and decided to tough it out.

"Kowalski, this is Maguire. I guess you heard about the

50

shift in personnel City Hall wants? 'More efficient deployment of available manpower' they call it."

"I heard."

"Well, Maguire here got caught in the winds of change. He's just been transferred into the division."

The stranger was a cop?

Spaceman took another look. Slender and tanned, Maguire looked more like a professional polo player than a homicide dick. His beige slacks and brown pinstripe didn't seem to have wilted in the heat at all. Or maybe he came wrapped in cellophane.

Maguire stood, extending a hand. One finger bore a silver ring set with a large, dull green stone. "Blue Maguire," he said, flashing a Bobby Kennedy grin.

Spaceman shook the hand quickly. "Spaceman Kowalski," he mumbled.

"Spaceman?"

"It's a long story." He dismissed Maguire and turned back to McGannon. "I gotta take off. The post on the Lowe kid."

"Good. On the way over, you can fill Maguire in on what you have so far."

Spaceman didn't say anything right away. Instead, he just looked from McGannon's shit-eating grin to the *GQ* cover boy standing next to him. "What?"

The grin widened to what seemed impossible dimensions. "As of now, the two of you are working together on this case."

Spaceman was peripherally aware that Maguire seemed to be as stunned by the news as he himself was. "Hey, lieutenant," he said in a strangled voice, "I work alone, you know? I do a solo," he explained to Maguire.

Maguire just looked at him.

McGannon snorted. "This isn't the Metropolitan Opera," he said. "We don't need any damned prima donnas."

51

"But you know I don't work so good with other people." Spaceman knew from long and painful experience that this was a losing battle, but he had to give it his best shot anyway. "My personality is like sandpaper. I antagonize people. That's what *you* told me, remember?"

The bastard didn't seem to mind having his own words thrown back in his face. He shrugged. "You'll adapt. Besides, Maguire is a college graduate. Maybe you can learn a few things from him."

Spaceman gritted his teeth together tightly so he wouldn't say something he'd be sorry for later. Then: "Oh, shit," he said anyway.

He turned on his heel and left the office.

Blue nodded a polite farewell to McGannon and followed Kowalski.

He wasn't thrilled. The unexpected transfer was bad enough, but now Spaceman Kowalski had been thrust into his life. And just when he'd decided to give his all to the damned job and make a smashing success of it. This partnership was bound to put a crimp in his grand design.

Kowalski paused next to an amazingly cluttered desk and immediately plucked a thin file from somewhere in its depths. He didn't seem to know or care whether Blue was following him. In silence, they walked out of the building and across the parking lot, coming to a stop beside a battered Chevy. "You want to be wheelman?" Kowalski asked, finally acknowledging his existence.

"I don't mind," Blue said. He looked at the car again. "We can take mine, if you want. It's air-conditioned."

Kowalski looked as if he would rather get into the hot Chevy, just to prove some point, but then he shrugged. "What the hell." His voice was slightly husky, like that of a man who smoked and drank a little too much.

They walked a short distance across the lot to where the

52

Porsche was parked. Kowalski stared at the seafoam-green car for a moment, then looked up. "One question."

"Sure," Blue said, unlocking the door.

"You on the take? I don't need a crooked partner. I've got a reputation."

That was no doubt the truth, although what kind of reputation he had was probably open to debate. Blue knew what he was getting at, though, because it wasn't the first time the question had come up. Usually, of course, it was more subtle. "No," he said. "I'm not on the take. I'm just rich. Very rich."

"Okay, then." Kowalski got inside and settled his bulk snugly into the passenger seat. "If you're so fucking rich," he said, "why are you in this racket?"

"I like it."

"You like it?" The idea seemed to amuse him.

"Sure. Don't you?"

"Well, yeah. I guess. But I'm not rich."

Blue shrugged and started the car. "What's this case?" he asked, after a moment both men spent listening to the purring engine.

Kowalski lighted a cigarette. In an obvious afterthought, he held out the pack.

"No, thanks. I quit. Found out they were screwing up my endurance."

"Yeah? Interesting." Kowalski took a long drag.

Blue jerked the blower up another notch. "The case," he said again.

"Oh, yeah. Somebody killed a kid in Griffith Park. A very bloody knife job."

Blue released his breath slowly. "Bad."

"Very." Kowalski frowned suddenly, as if a more troubling thought had crossed his mind. But he didn't say anything.

Blue concentrated on driving. "I'll try not to fuck up your life too much," he said after several minutes.

53

"What?" Kowalski seemed startled; his thoughts had obviously been someplace else.

"I know you're not crazy about working with me." Diplomatically, he refrained from saying that the feeling was definitely mutual.

"Oh, hell," Kowalski said with a shrug. "Nothing personal. This happens all the time. You'll get fed up before long, and McGannon will let you off the hook."

Blue didn't have much hope for this partnership. Starsky and Hutch they weren't. They were just a couple of departmental loose ends that somebody was hoping to tie up by tying together. The only thing he could do was make the best of it. Go along for the ride. Most importantly, he had to show them that Blue Maguire was, above all, a team player. One of the boys.

Blue inhaled some of the drifting cigarette smoke. It tasted great.

Chapter 10

SPACEMAN had stopped counting the autopsies a long time ago. He tried to be there in person as the pathologist worked, instead of just getting the facts later in a written report. Not that he got off on watching somebody cut a stiff into pieces. It was just that seeing what had been done to some poor slob inspired the cop in him, made him even more eager to hit the streets, find the bastard responsible, and in his own mind at least, exact some measure of justice.

Over the years, there had been a lot of bodies.

His feelings never changed, though. And neither did the smell of the place. It was a more subtle stink than might have been expected, but it was also unforgettable. It lingered. On the clothes, the hair, the edge of whatever soul he still had left. It made him want to turn and run away as fast as he could. The old primal instinct to survive, ignited by a dumb fear that dying, like the flu or herpes, might be contagious.

But was the fear really so dumb? He wasn't sure. A cop could see so much death that it would finally wear him down, erode his humanity until there was nothing left. Spaceman figured that would happen to him eventually.

For now, he just swallowed the fear, trying not to taste it.

Almost forgotten next to him, Maguire sighed. "I really hate this place."

Spaceman shrugged. "All part of the job," he said, not wanting to let on that it was the place of many of his worst nightmares. "Let's get to it."

He led the way through the swinging doors.

55

Three of the tables were in use. Ignoring the first two, Spaceman walked to where a slender woman in white stood checking a cart of instruments. She glanced up as they approached. "This yours, Spaceman?"

"Lucky me. I get all the good stuff." He gestured over his shoulder. "You two know each other?"

"Never had the pleasure," she said.

"Maguire. My latest partner." If there was any sarcasm in the tone of the introduction, no one seemed to notice. "And this is Sharon Engels. Doctor Engels is a very kinky broad, who gets her kicks playing around with dead bodies."

Engels and Maguire smiled at each other.

Spaceman had never been able to figure out why a woman would take a job like this. It wasn't even like Engels was some kind of dog, either. She was a damned good-looking broad.

Unfortunately, she kept sidestepping his attempts to score. Despite that, it was one of his favorite fantasies, imagining what Sharon Engels would be like in bed. Probably a real tiger. Even now, wearing the damned lab coat, and with her usually untamed auburn hair pulled into a severe bun, she had the kind of stuff that got a man thinking. In her domain, sex and death coexisted.

After a moment of mental eroticism, however, he turned his attention away from her and toward the table. A skinny Chicano seemed bored as he finished hosing the body down. Water that was still rusty pink with blood swirled through the metal grating and disappeared into the tub below.

Spaceman stood to one side, keeping both hands carefully in his pockets. A habit here. He didn't want to touch anything by accident. Engels gave a fleeting look at the tray of specimen containers, syringes, knives and then switched on the overhead tape recorder. "The body is that of a well-developed and well-nourished white male," she began in a measured tone.

Stretched out naked under the glaring lights, Peter Lowe looked even younger than he had in the park. The ugly slashes across his chest and stomach gleamed redly.

"Jesus." It was Maguire's voice.

"...approximately sixteen years old...head hair is dark blond, eyes are blue, each pupil 3.5 millimeter in diameter...all teeth present. Fingernails are chewed very short."

Spaceman moved away slightly, carefully.

Engels worked slowly, precisely, giving the boy more attention in death than he had probably ever received in life. "Evidence of sperm present in the mouth and the anus...twelve slash wounds in the chest..." It went on and on.

Spaceman listened without expression to the familiar whirring of the small electric saw used to cut through the skull. Every once in a while, a case came along that got to him more than usual. This one, he knew already, was going to be one like that. Maybe it was the fact that the victim was a kid like Robbie and Robbie was missing. Whatever. Spaceman knew that he had to get the bastard who had done this. Maybe Peter's own father didn't care, but one cop sure as hell did.

Spaceman glanced sidewise at the pale but impassive face of Maguire. Even if breaking this case meant getting along for a while with Detective Perfect here, he'd do it.

Having decided to succeed and knowing that in the end justice would be done, Spaceman could bear to tune in again to the cool discourse of Sharon Engels.

In the hallway again, Blue leaned against the wall and wished that he could ask for one of Kowalski's damned cigarettes. Instead, he said, "I want a drink."

Kowalski raised a brow. "You drink on duty?"

"Not usually. I'll make an exception."

"Really bothered you, huh?"

"And it didn't bother you, for Chrissake?"

"Hell, I'm used to it."

Blue realized that Kowalski was lying. No matter how much he might deny it, the other cop was shaken by what had been done to that kid. Maybe the surly son of a bitch was human after all.

Kowalski flipped the end of his cigarette into the overflowing sand bucket in the corner. "Let's go," he said abruptly.

"Where to?"

"First to have a drink and wash the taste of this place out of my mouth. Then we're going to find that bastard." He turned and walked out.

Blue followed. The exit line had been corny and melodramatic, like a piece of dialogue from a bad movie, but he didn't mind. Somehow he was convinced that Spaceman Kowalski meant just what he said.

Chapter 11

THERE weren't many customers in the Red Dog Lounge. Aside from one fat woman perched precariously on a stool near the door, and two old winos arguing politics with the bartender, Tom and Jody had the cool dark refuge of the rundown bar all to themselves.

Which suited Tom just fine. The backroom and the pool table there belonged to them alone. His game was very rusty, because pool had been against the hospital rules, but that didn't matter. It felt good just to have a cue in his hands again, and there was no pressure in the playing. Jody, like him, was content to take it easy, play slowly, downing lots of cold beer and rapping about things that weren't important.

Tom felt great. The whole afternoon passed in a kind of golden fog, accompanied by the soft clicking of the balls hitting against one another and the taste of the thick dark stout.

When at last Tom managed to win a game from his brother, they replaced the cues in the rack and took their drinks to the last booth. A quieter mood seemed to descend on them suddenly. Jody began to build a tower of stale pretzels. "What're we going to do, Tommy?" he asked.

Tom took a slow sip of his Guinness. This was a moment he'd known would have to come sooner or later, and maybe now was as good a time as any. Except that the day had been so nice, so perfect, that he hated to lose the good feelings by talking about the past. But it had to be done. "Time to get down to business," he said regretfully.

"You said that before, and I still don't know what the hell you're talking about. If you want my opinion, I think we should just leave town. For a while, at least."

"We will. After."

"After what?"

"After we get even, Jody." He finished off the stout in his mug, then stood. "I'll get us a couple refills, then we'll talk, okay?"

He walked to the front and waited impatiently for the husky black bartender to pull himself away from a heated discussion of Reaganomics and do his damned job. "Hope I'm not interrupting," he said sarcastically, but softly.

The bartender just filled the mugs and pushed them across the bar at him.

Jody was still playing with the pretzels when he got back to the table. Tom took one of the nonessential pieces of the emerging structure and ate it. "You remember when they sent me away?" he asked suddenly.

Jody ducked his head and nodded.

"I promised then that I was going to get even with the bastard who did it."

"Who, Tommy?"

"The cop," he said flatly. "The dumb polack pig who busted me, and then told them in court that I was crazy."

Jody's eyes were squeezed shut. "I don't remember him," he said in a strained whisper.

"What do you remember, Jody?"

They had never talked about it.

Jody stayed quiet for a long time. "Well," he said slowly, "I remember some of what happened. But I don't like to think about it. I don't remember any of the cops, especially. They put handcuffs on you, I think. And they took me over to juvie hall in the squad car."

"What about the trial?"

"Maybe. Yeah, I remember some of that." He opened his eyes and stared at Tom. "Hey, you know, I've spent

60

years trying to forget all that. Everybody said the past doesn't matter. Maybe it's better that way. Don't you think we should just let it go, Tom?"

" 'Let it go?' 'Everybody said the past doesn't matter?' Who the hell said that?"

Jody bit his lip, as if trying to recall the words. Then he shrugged. "Just friends."

"Friends?" Tom felt a surge of anger. He grabbed Jody's wrist and squeezed hard. "These friends mean more to you than I do, is that it?"

"No. No, of course not, Tommy."

"You want to forget everything that happened back then? Is that what you want?"

Jody shook his head. "No, I don't. And you know it. Would I be here if that was what I wanted?" His voice was low. "I just want to forget the bad. I want to remember all the good things, Tommy, Really. Would you let go before you break my goddamned wrist?"

Tom released his grip. "Okay. Maybe that works for you. But not me. I have to remember it all. Like the pig who dragged me away. He's the one who split us up."

"I know. But if we try to get back at him, there might be trouble." Jody's hands roamed across the tabletop, finally closing around the mug. "Shit, man, they'll send you right back."

"They have to catch me first, and that won't happen, not this time."

Jody sighed and shook his head. "So who's the cop?"

"Kowalski." He spit it out like a dirty word. "His name is Kowalski."

Just saying it aloud brought the past flooding back, washing over Tom like a tidal wave.

That summer had been hot, too, just like now. Day after steaming day of unrelenting heat. The four of them seemed trapped in the damned little house. No air conditioning.

61

Not enough money to get away even for a few days to someplace that might be cooler. Nothing. Just the four of them rubbing against the edges of one another in the simmering days and nights.

Tom was not quite twenty then. He worked part time pumping gas, but that didn't pay enough for him to be able to get out and find a place of his own. Besides, there was another reason why he couldn't go.

Their father was always out of work. He claimed that it was because of his bad back, an old war injury. But Tom knew that was just a crock of shit. The old man was nothing but a lazy son of a bitch. The only things he was good for were boozing, screwing, and beating on his sons. He was a huge bear of a man, towering over the rest of the family.

Life with him had been the same for as long as Tom could remember.

Their mother wasn't any help. She always made Tom think of a limp grey dishrag. She'd spend hours bitching about life to anyone who'd listen, but she wouldn't lift a finger to help herself or her kids. She liked the booze, too, and she liked fucking. The two of them went at it a lot, and they made a lot of noise about it.

When they were very young, Tom and Jody would crawl under the blankets and try to cover their ears against the grunts and groans coming from the other side of the thin walls. Later, as they got older, the whole thing became a dirty joke, able to disgust and excite them at the same time.

Tom hated his parents, hated the pigsty of a house where they were all trapped, hated his whole damned life.

Except for one thing. The only thing that kept him there and made it all bearable. Jody. His little brother was thirteen that summer, a boy who somehow managed to stay bright and happy even there. Jody was the one he loved, the one who loved him. That made the rest unimportant. In their bedroom was a secret and wonderful world all their own. A world that no one else knew about.

Until that terrible day in July.

It was pretty dumb, of course, to fool around like that in the middle of the afternoon. Usually they played the games only at night, when their parents were sleeping, or as was most often the case, passed out. The dark hours belonged to Tom and Jody.

But it was so hot. And the damned little fan he'd spent a whole week's pay on did nothing except move the sluggish air from one corner of their room to another. They just started goofing around a little to help them forget how hot it was and how boring.

The problem was, once they got started, it was hard to stop. A little teasing got serious too fast. Pretty soon, it was too late to stop.

Then the bitch opened the door.

Tom took a gulp of beer quickly.

Jody was watching him.

He pressed the cold wet glass to his forehead and smiled weakly. "Shit, it's just waiting to ambush me."

"What?"

"The past, little brother. The goddamned fucking past."

"That's what I mean. Maybe it's better to forget."

"No. I told that dumb porker that I'd get back at him someday. That was a solemn oath, Jody. I can't get on with my life until it's taken care of."

"I understand. I just don't want them to send you back."

"Everything will be okay. Promise." He reached across the table, this time covering his brother's hand gently. "It's just you and me. The two musketeers."

"Just like before?"

"You got it."

After another moment, Jody took a deep breath. "So," he said. "What next?"

Tom smiled and pulled his hand back. He'd known that Jody wouldn't let him down. Never. "What next. Good question. I've been thinking about it for a long time. I've had a lot of ideas. Maybe blow up his house. Maybe shoot him. I just haven't made up my mind yet what's best."

"Whatever you say."

"Right now, I say one more round. Then we'll split from here and pick up some wheels."

Jody frowned, still thinking about the damned truck. They had dumped it earlier, after taking off the plates and wiping it as free of prints as possible, just in case. Then he just nodded and got to his feet. "I'll get the beer this time," he said.

Chapter 12

IT turned into the worst kind of L.A. day. October in July. The Santa Ana blew relentlessly, spilling acrid smoke over the Pacific. The smell of the fires hung above the city, serving as one more irritant to a population already chafing. Something would have to give, sooner or later. Spaceman's mood was no better than anybody else's.

It was already fifteen minutes into the next duty shift when he slammed down the phone after one more unsuccessful attempt to find out anything at all about Peter Lowe. Vice had no file on him, nor did the local juvenile authorities. The only fact they had so far came not from anything they had done, but from the pathologist's report.

Most of what was contained in the report had been expected. One thing was not: Two men had killed Peter Lowe.

That information immediately gave the case a slightly weird aspect. Sex crimes, which this certainly seemed to be, were usually one on one. But according to Engels, the varied angles of the knife wounds indicated two distinct sets of injuries, one inflicted by a right-handed person, the other by a leftie. Further, specimens of semen found on the body confirmed the two-killer theory.

Finding that out did absolutely nothing to improve Spaceman's mood. Neither did something he found tossed on top of his in-basket. The terse memo was from up north, near Lompoc. A teenaged boy had been found dead by the highway. He'd been stabbed to death and the Lompoc cops were trying to get an ID on him. There was no picture, although one was supposed to be on its way.

65

There was only a description that might have fit any number of boys. Peter Lowe, for example. Or even Robbie Kowalski.

But Spaceman pushed that thought aside; what the hell would Robbie have been doing in Lompoc? He folded the memo and put it into his pocket. Chances were it didn't have a damned thing to do with their case, but he'd check it out. Tomorrow.

"Time to quit," he said.

Maguire settled into the desk opposite his, looked up. "What?"

"I said, shift's up. Time to go home."

The blond frowned. "I hate to leave with nothing done on this."

"Take my word for it, we can leave. Nobody's going to pick up our ball and run with it during the night."

Blue acknowledged that with a shrug and reluctantly closed the file.

Spaceman's phone rang. He looked at it balefully. "I'm off duty," he said. But the damned thing rang again.

"Might be important," Maguire said.

"Did it ever occur to you that the fucking telephone runs our lives? That it runs all of Western civilization?"

"It never even occured to me that this city was a part of Western civilization," Maguire replied. "Answer the damned phone."

"Shit." But he answered it. "Homicide."

"Officer Kowalski?" It was a woman's voice, very soft and timid.

"Detective Kowalski," he corrected. "Can I do something for you, ma'am?"

"My name is Mary Lowe."

It was hard to hear above the racket of the squad room, but the name came through loud and clear. "Yes?"

"Peter is... was my son."

66

"I see." He stuck a fingertip in his free ear so he could hear her better.

"You're the policeman who spoke to my husband earlier, aren't you?"

"Yeah. You must be calling about the body."

"Yes, about that."

"Good. I didn't think you'd just want him dumped in a hole out here and forgotten."

She made a sound that might have been a sob, but which was muffled so quickly that he couldn't be sure. "My husband is a stubborn man. He won't change his mind about that."

Spaceman swore at the ceiling. "You don't need his permission to bring your son's body home."

Maguire was watching him, listening to the one-sided conversation with interest.

"I can't go against him. Maybe that seems wrong to you, but it's the way my life is." She sounded resigned.

"Then I don't understand why the hell you're calling me."

There was a pause before she went on. "I have some money saved. Money of my own. It's not much, just fifty dollars. If I send it out there, will you see that Petey has a decent burial? Maybe some flowers?"

"You want to send me fifty dollars to bury your son?" he said, primarily for Maguire's benefit.

"It's the best I can do." Her voice seemed higher. "God knows, it's the best I can do."

"Okay," Spaceman said shortly. "I'll take care of it."

"Thank you." Another moment passed. Then: "I know what you must think of me. A woman who would treat her own child this way. But that's how life is sometimes. He's the head of the family, and I can't go against him."

"That's your business, Mrs. Lowe. My only concern is finding out who killed Peter."

"You don't know that yet?"

"Not yet."

"Can you tell me how it happened?"

"He was stabbed to death."

"My poor baby. I hope he didn't suffer much."

Although it wasn't asked as such, there was a question plainly audible in the words. Spaceman thought about the body. For one bitter moment, he wanted to tell this stupid and pathetic woman the truth. Maybe she should know about the pain and fear Peter must have gone through before dying. Maybe she should know that he must surely have greeted death with relief when it finally came. At sixteen, he was glad to die.

But he didn't say any of that. Without even knowing why he should spare the feelings of this woman, Spaceman lied. "He didn't suffer much," he said flatly. "Peter died quickly, without much pain."

She sighed. "We can thank the good Lord for that anyway."

Spaceman had a bad taste in his mouth, and he knew that unless this conversation ended quickly, he'd let her have the truth right between the eyes. "Anything else, Mrs. Lowe?"

"No. Just... I'll send the money right away."

"You do that. And I hope it helps you to sleep nights." With that, he hung up.

Maguire was still looking at him.

"That dumb bitch doesn't have the backbone of a rabbit," he said, maybe to justify his parting shot.

Maguire just shook his head, then said, "How about going across the street? I'm buying."

Spaceman knew that he had to get out there and find Robbie, but he also knew that a drink was just what he needed at the moment. "Why not?" he said. "As long as you're buying."

The Lock-up was always busiest at shift change. They picked up a couple of beers and worked their way through the crowd gathered around the television, watching a ballgame. A hand-lettered sign over the bar proclaimed the desire to outlaw liberals and not guns.

Spaceman hated that sign. He wasn't crazy about liberals or guns, but at least liberals didn't kill people. No more than the right-wingers did, anyway. Most killers seemed pretty apolitical, in his experience. He lit a cigarette. "I know a couple places downtown where boys like Peter crash," he said. "Tomorrow we'll make a run past them. Of course, it'll be a damned waste of time."

"Will it?"

"Sure. But we have to make the effort. We have to justify ourselves."

"To whom?"

"To whom?" Spaceman smiled faintly, then shrugged. "Mostly to us, I guess."

Maguire was looking at the sign. "I wonder what drives kids like that."

"What drives anybody?" He was thinking about Robbie. Where the hell could he have gotten to?

"I feel bad about the kid."

"We all feel bad. So what?"

"Maybe I could ante up for a funeral. Would that be okay?"

Spaceman studied him over the top of his beer bottle. "Why should you?"

"No reason. I'd just like to. I can afford it."

"That's right. I forgot you're loaded." He shrugged. "Fine. Bury him if you want to."

"Somebody should care." Maguire sounded defensive.

People seemed to keep telling him that he didn't care. Didn't they know how tired he was? What the hell did they

69

expect out of him? "Maybe. If anybody has room to care."
Spaceman was still looking at the other man. "How long
have you been in Homicide?" he asked.

Maguire smiled. "What time is it now?" He shrugged.
"I've been in Robbery. And the department PR office."

"Public fucking relations?"

He shrugged. "Not my choice. Can I ask a question
now?"

Spaceman knew what was coming. "What?" he said
anyway.

"Why 'Spaceman'?"

Everytime he got a new partner, it was the same thing.
Sometimes he made up elaborate stories to explain away
the nickname. One dumb shit now working for Internal
Affairs still thought that Kowalski had been one of the
original seven astronauts. But tonight he was too tired for
games. "About a million years ago," he said, "I was in
Nam. Somebody over there tagged me with it. We spent a
lot of time flying pretty high in those days. If you catch my
drift."

"I remember."

Spaceman was surprised. "What was a rich bastard like
you doing in that sewer? I thought your type knew all
about how to avoid dangerous drafts."

"I enlisted."

"Shit." He shook his head. "You really are a major fuck-
up, aren't you?"

"Some people have said so." Maguire shifted gears
again. "You have some kind of problem?"

"What?"

"All day I've had the feeling that something besides the
case is bothering you."

Spaceman was mad at himself for letting it show. "It's
personal," he said flatly. "As in, my business."

"Sure. Okay. Didn't mean to trespass."

Maybe he'd sounded like a bastard, but the last thing he needed right now was to have this guy feeling sorry for him. Anyway, Robbie was his son and his business. "Gotta go. See you in the morning," he said more quietly.

"I'll be there."

Probably right on time, too. Spaceman finished his beer in one gulp and left.

Chapter 13

Night promised to be no cooler than the day had been. Already sweating, Spaceman sat behind the wheel of his car and studied the list Karen had given him earlier. Not one of the names on the neatly typed sheet seemed even vaguely familiar, and it dawned on him that he didn't really know anything at all about his son's friends or his son's life. Pretty pathetic, that. But what the hell could he do about it? The boy wouldn't talk to him.

Things would change. When he found Robbie, they'd sit down and have a good long talk.

Finally, he just picked a name and address at random. A start had to be made someplace and it might as well be with Roger Fellows, whoever the hell he was. Or should that be whomever?

As he angled the car in the direction of the San Diego freeway, Spaceman peered toward the hills. Although the radio was saying that half a dozen fires were still burning, he couldn't see anything but the slight haze. It was early for such an outbreak, but the hot, dry spring had made the whole area prime fire territory.

Hell, it was always something around here. Fires, mudslides, earthquakes. Or else all the television actors went on strike. There was no middle ground in Los Angeles.

Long Beach was changing. Six city blocks had been torn down to make way for a shopping mall costing, rumor said, in the neighborhood of a hundred million. Spaceman would have sold the whole damned city for half that price.

The Fellowses lived just a few blocks from the house

Spaceman used to own, until the divorce took it away. Karen and Robbie still lived there. The Fellows' place, like his former residence, was a small tidy box covered with aluminum siding. The lawn was neatly trimmed, but beginning to turn brown because of the water shortage. That was one advantage of living in a fifth floor apartment in the big city. No damned lawn to worry about. Just muggers and dogshit.

Standing on the front porch, which really wasn't a porch at all, but just a four-foot square of concrete, Spaceman could hear a television blasting, as well as the steady hum of an air conditioner from inside. He pushed the bell.

Raised voices in the house seemed to be debating the issue of who should respond to this obviously unwanted intrusion. After several moments, the door was opened by a middle-aged man wearing the uniform of a city bus driver. He eyed Spaceman warily. "Yeah?" he said.

Although he hadn't really planned to go official on this, there was something in the man's tone that made Spaceman decide to play it differently. He pulled out his shield case and flashed it. "Mr. Fellows?"

"That's me. What do the cops want here?"

"I'd like to talk to your son Roger, please."

A look of weary exasperation crossed the ruddy face. "What's he done now?" There was a twang in his voice, the memory of someplace else. Maybe Missouri. Oklahoma. He was another seeker. When people in other places didn't like the lives they had, they headed west. They kept moving until there was no more land and then they stopped and waited for the good things to start happening.

Fellows looked like he was still waiting.

"He hasn't done anything, as far as I know," Spaceman said. It was a familiar lament: 'What's he done now?' Somehow tonight it seemed to ring louder than usual. "I'd just like to talk to him."

73

"Well, I guess you might as well come in." Fellows moved aside just a little.

Spaceman squeezed through the doorway and found himself in the living room. A plump woman dressed in shorts and a flowered blouse was sitting on the couch. One hand held a can of Tab and the other a paperback romance. On the table in front of the couch was a bottle of beer and a large bowl of potato chips.

"What is it?" she asked, staring at Spaceman.

"A cop," her husband said in disgust. "Wants to see Roger."

"He's been home all day," she said quickly. "So whatever happened, he couldn't of had anything to do with it."

"Nothing's happened," Spaceman said. "Can I talk to him?"

"He's in the backyard. I guess you can just go on through. Unless you need us to be there." Fellows glanced at the television as he spoke. The ballgame was all tied up.

"No, that's all right."

Relieved, Fellows returned to his beer, his television.

Spaceman walked down a short hallway and into the kitchen, a spotlessly clean room that smelled of lemon freshener, and more strongly, of an apple pie that was cooling on the table. The sight of the pie reminded Spaceman that he hadn't had any supper.

He opened the door and stepped out into the postage-stamp backyard. A boy, wearing only cut-offs, was stretched out on the ground, smoking what looked like a legal cigarette, and staring at the sky. "Roger?"

A slow hand lifted to remove the cigarette, and the boy rolled on his side to gaze up at him. "Hey," he said with a smile. "You're a cop." He spoke in the languid, spaced-out way the kids cultivated even when they weren't stoned.

"Right the first time," Spaceman said.

"Not hard." He relaxed onto his back again. "You'll

never take me alive, copper," he said in a lifeless Rich Little-doing-Cagney routine.

"William Morris is looking for you, kid."

"Who?"

"Never mind." Spaceman lowered himself into a flimsy lawn chair that teetered dangerously under his weight, but held. "Let's talk about Robbie Kowalski."

"Kowalski? Why? What'd he do?"

"Nothing. I only want to know if you've seen him lately."

Roger blinked in his direction. "If he ain't done nothing, why should I say anything to a cop? How do I know that what I'm saying won't get a buddy into trouble?"

"He a good friend of yours, is he?"

"Rob's okay. For a polack. He's a little slow sometimes, but I figure that's like genetic, right?"

"By the way, I'm Detective Kowalski."

A chuckle. "His old man?"

"Right again. You're on a roll."

"Shit. No offense meant. It was a joke."

"Have you seen Robbie lately?"

"What's going on? He split or something?"

"He hasn't been home for a couple days. His mother is concerned."

"Yeah?"

"Have you seen him?"

"Nope."

"When was the last time you did see him?" Spaceman kept his voice level, although he wanted to grab the punk and give him a good shake. He hated working with juvies.

"Couple weeks, I guess. Rob's been a little weird lately."

"What's that mean?"

"Just . . . weird."

"He doing drugs?"

"Hey, man, that's getting a little personal, you know?

75

Rob's just into his own head trip right now. I guess he'll come home when he's ready. Tell the old lady to hang loose."

Spaceman wished he could smash his fist into the smiling face. Just once would make him feel a lot better. But he didn't do it. "Rob might be in trouble," he said quietly.

"We're all in trouble, sir. The whole fucking world. Haven't you heard? I think it was in all the papers."

Spaceman was tired of him. He stood. "Do you know anyplace Rob might hang out?"

Roger ground out the cigarette in the dry grass. One blade caught and smoldered a little. He quashed it with his thumb. "Try Fat Jack's on Pacific Coast."

"Thanks."

"You didn't hear it from me."

"Right." Rather than dance another round with the senior Fellowses, Spaceman walked up the driveway and back to his car.

Chapter 14

As Blue drove home, he listened to the latest news reports about the hill fires. Over 50,000 acres gone already. Four dead. A stable of expensive horses wiped out. The account of the disaster, recited in the cool measured tones of the female reporter, worried Blue. If the winds changed by even a couple miles, the flames would get pretty close.

But then he pushed the worry aside. No sense getting himself into a panic about it; there wasn't a damned thing that Blue Maguire could do about the wraths of nature.

Once he was home, it was simple to relax a little. He poured a glass of Chateau Lafite '69, and slid into the hot tub. Immediately, life started to look better. He directed his consciousness toward only two things: the rippling of the water in the tub, and the smooth taste of the wine.

Sensual, tactile things.

Back in college, Blue had made some visits (six, actually) to a shrink. Nobody ever knew about the therapy, but Blue felt as if it had helped. It was Foreman who taught him the ability to relax. The technique of clearing all the garbage out of his mind and centering on the simple. Like the feel of the hot water swirling through his toes and the soothing effect of the wine as it glided down.

Originally, the exercise had been intended to rid him of the ubiquitous and destructive spectre of his father. And it worked to some degree. But more importantly, the ability to withdraw from the world temporarily helped save his life in the war. Blue was convinced of that.

By the time thirty minutes had passed, he felt invincible. Forgetting a towel, he got out of the tub and padded wetly into the bedroom. He sat on the edge of the bed for a moment, then picked up the phone and dialed before he had a chance to think about it.

Pamela answered on the first ring. "Oh, it's you," she said.

"It's me, yeah."

"What is it, Blue?"

"Look, babe, I've been thinking. Do we really want to leave things the way we left them? I thought maybe we could get together, have some dinner, talk about it."

"It's all been said."

"No, I don't think so, Pamela. I mean — " He broke off and took a sip of wine.

"Blue, let's not stand around watching the death throes of this relationship."

"That's not what I'm doing."

"We've had some meaningful times, but it's over. I've faced that fact; why can't you?"

Meaningful times? The broad was a walking compendium of triteness. "So that's it then?" He was almost hoping she wouldn't change her mind at the last moment.

"Yes, that's it and I've got to run."

Dispensing with good-byes, he hung up.

Fuck her.

He pulled the phone book from the shelf and thumbed the pages quickly, looking for the name he wanted. She might be married, for all he knew, or shacking up, but it was worth a try. The important thing was to move ahead, not to dwell on the end of still another relationship. Get right back on the old horse.

Engels, S. That was probably it. An initial usually meant a woman living alone. He hoped. The address was in Los Angeles proper, on Wilshire.

This time, he paused for just an instant before picking up the phone. But then he moved; what the hell. He had nothing to lose.

78

She answered on the first ring, too.

"This is Blue Maguire," he said. "We met today."

"Maguire?"

"I was with Kowalski." And I must have made a great impression, he reflected glumly.

"Oh, sure, Spaceman's partner. What can I do for you?" Her voice was brusque and businesslike, but not unfriendly. "Do you have a question about the post today?"

"No, this doesn't have anything to do with that. I was just wondering if you'd have dinner with me." He swore at himself for the bluntness of the invitation.

There was a pause on the other end of the line. "I guess I could take the frozen pizza out of the oven," she said finally, sounding amused.

"Forty-five minutes?"

"Fine."

Blue hung up. Invincible, that was the word.

Sharon Engels lived in a middle-aged apartment building that was equipped with a doorman. She was waiting in the lobby, talking to the uniformed old man when Blue arrived. He watched her walk across the room. The light summer dress did a lot more for her body than had the white lab coat, and now wild curls fell to her shoulders.

Blue was glad he'd worn the new suit.

There was an awkward silence as they walked from the building to the curb. She admired the car, then indicated the squawk box. "Always in touch?"

"Only when I want to be." Which was almost always, but he didn't say that. "I made a reservation at Jimmy's," was what he did say. "That okay?"

She nodded, looking mildly impressed.

Blue wondered about that. Sometimes maybe he tried too hard. Usually, probably. He had to work on that, maybe once in a while suggest Taco Town.

79

At the restaurant, they each had a cocktail while studying the menu. When the waiter returned, Sharon chose veal *à l'orange,* and Blue picked the poached salmon. The mechanics of decision provided a topic for some conversation, but once the order was placed and another round of drinks served, silence fell again. She seemed very interested in the decor.

"Well," he said finally and unoriginally, "do you like your job?"

"Yes. Very much. Do you find that bizarre?"

"Should I?"

"Some men do." She tasted the vodka tonic. "Of course, there are also some men who get turned on by the idea. Death as an aphrodisiac."

"I don't think I belong in either category."

"Oh?" She sounded skeptical.

"I just think a job should be enjoyable."

"Do you enjoy yours?" She smiled. "I ask, because obviously you're not in it for the money."

"I like it." Again he could have said a lot more, but didn't.

"How do you get along with Spaceman?"

"Kowalski? Well, it's only been one day. But he's definitely different."

"One of a kind." Her face grew serious, and Blue wondered just what the relationship was between Sharon and his new partner. "I've seen him work. He's very good."

Blue nodded. "Yes, I think maybe he is." Even if he didn't give a flying fuck about having a good working relationship. Maybe he just hadn't heard about that great sense of camaraderie cops were supposed to have.

Sharon played with the thin plastic stir stick. "You two have anything on the twenty-seven thirty-four?"

"What?"

"The boy who was killed."

"Peter Lowe? Nothing yet."

And with that, they reached an unspoken agreement not to talk about work anymore. They talked about themselves instead. College—her time at UCLA, his at Harvard. He told her something of his time in Nam. She gave him a fast rundown on her brief marriage to a brilliant but troubled young surgeon.

Over the baked Alaska, Blue decided that he liked Sharon Engels. A lot. The realization made him nervous. If there was some way to screw up a relationship, he'd find it.

They lingered over coffee and brandy, until she remembered an early appointment. He thought she was sincere about that, not just making an excuse to end the evening.

He hoped so anyway.

Chapter 15

THE CHINESE DINER had yellow plastic tablecloths and a jukebox with music left over from the Fifties. They had chow mein and egg rolls and listened to Gogi Grant. They both ate too much, even finishing off the fortune cookies that always tasted like cardboard to Tom. His fortune said, "Be diligent and you will prevail." He liked that.

Jody read his fortune, frowned, and threw the tiny slip of paper into the ashtray without telling Tom what it said. "Let's go," he said instead.

Before getting into the car, they walked across San Pedro to a mom-and-pop store for a six-pack. The interior of the Ford was so hot that even rolling down every damned window didn't help; all it accomplished was to blast them in a continuous stream of oven-baked air. They each popped open a beer immediately and headed out Wilshire.

With no real destination in mind, Jody simply guided the car up and down the traffic-clogged streets of Hollywood according to Tom's whim. The sticky night had brought out a lot of whores, creeps, and hustlers. Nobody seemed to have much energy, though. It was as if the continuing hot spell weighed them down, so they were just going through the motions of high-speed life.

They cruised for a long time. Tom was enjoying the hunt and didn't want to rush. As they searched, he allowed himself to wonder, fleetingly, what was going to happen this time. But then he pushed the thought aside quickly.

"How about him?" Jody asked finally, motioning with one hand.

The boy he'd indicated was standing alone in front of a

gay movie. He was slender, fair, wearing tight white pants and a red silk shirt. "Maybe," Tom said, staring at him. He chewed his lower lip. "Yeah, maybe."

But as they watched, a tall skinny black in a purple jumpsuit appeared. He greeted the boy with a hug and they both went into the movie.

"Shit," Tom said. Then he shrugged. Plenty more where that one came from.

It was almost ten minutes before Tom saw him, the one he wanted for sure, standing on the corner of Hollywood and Vine, of all places. "Stop," he ordered Jody.

Jody managed to pull to the curb, squeezing in next to an old VW bug. "Which one, Tommy?"

Tom pointed. "Him."

The chosen one had light brown hair that just covered his ears, and was wearing blue jeans with a plain white tee shirt. His face was arranged to display perfect and exquisite boredom as he leaned against a sign post and took long lazy drags on a cigarette. There was something about him that seemed to glow, that made all the others seem shabby by comparison.

"Yeah," Jody said. "I like him." His voice sounded strangely tight.

Tom looked at him sharply, then nodded. "Okay. Go get him."

"Me?"

"Yeah, you. Bring him over here."

Jody took a deep breath. He pounded both hands lightly against the steering wheel, then quickly opened the door and slid out.

Tom leaned forward a little so that he could watch as Jody walked to the corner and spoke to the boy. The boy smiled and nodded in return. It was weird, but just watching the two of them talk was giving Tom a warm itch inside. He ran one hand across the front of his jeans, then

83

pulled it away quickly. "Not yet," he muttered through gritted teeth. "Not yet, damnit."

After a time that seemed endless, Jody and the hustler came over to the car. Jody opened the door and the boy slid in. "Hi," he said. "I'm Chris."

"Nice to meet you. I'm Tom."

Close-up, Chris smelled of lime aftershave. "Jody here said you wanted to have a little party. Just us three."

"Right. Does that sound like a good idea to you?"

"Sure, why not?"

"Why not?" Tom reached over the seat and pulled out another can of beer. He offered it to Chris. "Hot tonight."

"For sure. You were lucky to catch me here, you know? I was invited out to this big bash in Malibu. A bigshot TV producer asked me to come, but I decided it was too hot for the hassle."

"We were lucky," Tom said.

Chris took a long gulp of beer, then smacked his lips together. "Good shit. Anyway, this producer, he's thinking about using me in a new series. I'm an actor," he added.

"No kidding?" Tom fished out another beer and opened it. "You done something I might've seen?"

Chris frowned. "Well, I haven't actually done anything yet. But I go to a lot of auditions. And once I even got a callback. But then that part went to some creep who was related to the producer."

"That's life, I guess."

"Yeah. But something's gonna break for me soon."

Jody was quiet, just listening to them talk as he guided the car through the clogged streets.

Chris swallowed more beer. "Where's this party gonna be, anyway?"

Tom thought about that for a moment, then shrugged. "I like Griffith Park," he said. "There might even be a breeze around."

"Okay with me. If we can dodge the bastards from vice."

"No problem. It's a big park."

Tom smiled and lifted his beer again.

Chapter 16

FAT JACK'S turned out to be just the kind of place Spaceman was expecting it to be. Greasy burgers, watered-down Cokes, and a lot of loud noise that wasn't even a reasonable facsimile of music, as far as he was concerned. In addition, a flourishing trade in controlled substances was being carried on in the parking lot.

He left his car, which was making some funny noises anytime he went over thirty, on the street and braved Jack's. He realized that every person in the crowd made him for a cop instantly, but that didn't matter. In a place like this, it didn't pay to be subtle.

He reached out at random and plucked a skinny waiter by the arm. "The manager?" he shouted.

The pimple-faced kid stared back at him stupidly. "Huh?"

"I want to see the boss."

That got him a nod in the direction of a closed door. Spaceman didn't bother to say thanks; he also didn't bother to knock on the door.

It could only have been Fat Jack himself in the office. The man couldn't have weighed less than three hundred pounds, and that was probably guessing low. He had a television turned on, the volume blaring so that it could be heard above the noise in the restaurant. Several cheeseburgers were on the desk in front of him.

When Spaceman came through the door unannounced and uninvited, the fat man was busy pouring orange soda from a quart bottle into a large glass of ice. His tiny eyes studied and dismissed Spaceman with one scathing glance. A hand reached for the remote control device and the volume on the television vanished; the picture flickered on. "I already made my cop drop for the month," he said. The voice was rusty, as if it didn't get much use.

"Did you now?" Spaceman pulled a chair closer to the desk and sat down.

"If you're trying to raise the ante, go screw yourself." He spoke and bit into the burger at the same time.

"I don't give a flying fuck about your sweetheart deals with vice or the narcs," Spaceman said almost lazily. Which wasn't exactly the truth, because he had never believed that anybody else should be making more at the job than he did. He made a mental note to snoop around a little and find out who was making his scratch from this dump. "You Jack?"

"Mr. Feldman, to you."

"Whatever. I'm looking for someone. A kid. I'm told maybe he hangs out here."

With one more bite, the first burger was gone. "Half the little pricks in Southern California hang out here, but I don't pay them any more attention than I have to."

Spaceman reached into his pocket and pulled out the picture of Robbie. "This face look familiar?"

"None of them look familiar," Feldman said, not raising his eyes.

Spaceman leaned closer, practically shoving the picture into Feldman's face. "Look again, maggot." His voice was very soft.

The eyes flickered. "Shit," he said, reaching toward the desk drawer.

Spaceman tensed a little, moving one hand in the direction of his shoulder holster.

But all Jack removed from the drawer was a pair of glasses, old-fashioned bifocals. He perched them on his moon face. "Oh, that's Rob," he said.

"You do know him then?"

"I recognize my employees when I see them."

"Robbie works here?"

"Worked. As in, I canned him about two weeks ago."

"Why?"

The fleshy shoulders moved a little. "He had a case of sticky fingers. Nothing big, but it happened."

Spaceman felt like he'd been gut-kicked. This creep was telling him that Robbie, his son, was a thief? "You sure about that?"

"I'm sure, but it was no big deal. They all do it. Kids. A certain expectation of loss is built into the prices I charge." Feldman didn't seem much bothered by the wholesale theft apparently going on around him. "Rob's problem was, he was stupid enough to get caught. That meant I had to let him go." The second burger had somehow vanished.

"What'd he do to get you guys on his case?"

"He's missing."

"Runaway?"

"Looks like."

Jack shook his head. "Makes a man glad he never had no kids."

"Can you tell me anything about Rob?"

"What's to tell? These punks are all alike." Feldman seemed to reach deep inside and pull out a thought. "Maybe Rob had something bugging him lately."

"What? Do you know?"

"What the hell do I look like? Dear fucking Abby? I don't listen to what they say. I ain't a father." The third and final burger was disappearing fast.

Spaceman tried to ignore the crack; Feldman didn't know that he was the father in question. "Is there anybody around here who might be able to help me?"

"He came to work with another kid. Lom. I think maybe they're friends."

"Lom here tonight?"

Jack redonned the glasses and consulted a hand-drawn

chart on his desk. "Should be. In the kitchen. Short, slanty-eyed kid."

"Okay, Jack." Spaceman stood.

"That's it?"

"That's it."

"You might let it be known that I cooperated, you know."

Spaceman smiled slightly. "Hoping for a discount in your monthly ante?"

"Can't hurt to try."

The smile broadened. "Sure thing, Jack. Just tell me who you're in bed with at the department, and I'll see what I can do."

Jack stared at him for a moment, then shrugged. "Fuck you."

Spaceman shrugged and left the office.

The kitchen could never have passed a health department inspection, so Feldman must have been greasing a few palms down there, too. There was certainly enough grease on the stove, the walls, and the floor of the kitchen for a liberal coat on every greedy palm in the state.

Two kids, one black and one who looked Vietnamese, were standing over the stove. "Lom?"

The boy glanced his way. "Yeah?"

"Let's talk."

"I'm busy."

Spaceman reached out and gently pulled the spatula from his hand. He gave it to the other boy, who muttered something under his breath about white men who liked to perform unnatural sex acts with their own mothers. Spaceman smiled at him. "Let's talk," he said again to Lom.

They walked over to stand in the doorway. The screen was propped open in the foolish hope of attracting a stray

89

breeze. All that had been attracted so far were a lot of flies.

"If you're from Immigration, all my papers are in order. I'm legal."

"Glad to hear that. Where's Rob Kowalski?" he asked abruptly.

The bright black eyes wavered a little and then a mask seemed to drop over Lom's face. "Rob? Beats the hell out of me. I've been wondering the same thing. We were supposed to go to a movie the other night, but he never showed."

"What kind of problems has he had lately?"

"Problems? The same ones as the rest of us, I guess." His English was very good. "Who the hell are you anyway? Why are you asking me about Rob?"

Spaceman swatted away some of the flies trying to lick the salty sweat from his face. "I'm his father."

There was a slight drawing away. "The cop?"

"Right."

"Well, man, I don't know where he is. Maybe he just dropped out and went to live on the beach. He was really tired of the scene around here."

Spaceman stared at him for another moment.

Lom returned the look. He lifted one shoulder. "Maybe he went to San Francisco."

"Why?"

The boy seemed to lose patience with him. "Maybe he wanted to see if there are any hippies left. How the hell do I know?"

"So you don't know where he is?"

"All I know, man, is flipping the fucking hamburgers."

Spaceman looked at him, then gestured. "Okay. Get back to it."

Lom went back to what he knew.

Spaceman went home. It was late and he still hadn't had any supper. He didn't really want to call Karen, but he knew that she'd call him sooner or later. So he dialed her number while peering into the fridge and trying to find something to eat.

"At last," she said when she heard his voice. "Well?"

"Well what? I haven't found him yet."

"Do you think that something's happened to him?"

"I don't think anything yet." He found some Hebrew National bologna and pulled it out, along with some bread and an almost empty jar of French's mustard. He was trying to forget what Lom had said about Robbie going to San Francisco. The memo about the dead boy in Lompoc crackled in his pocket.

"What next?"

"I keep looking. He'll turn up."

"You don't sound very concerned."

Spaceman sighed. "I'm concerned. But it's just been a real long day."

Karen asked him to keep in touch and he said he would. They hung up.

He remembered then that he'd never called Mandy. But he just couldn't take any more tonight. He made a sandwich, poured a glass of milk, and went into his bedroom. *Casablanca* was on the late show, and he watched it, stretching out on the bed to eat the sandwich.

Chapter 17

HE was a nice kid and they all had a good time.

Chris talked a lot, and he dropped the names of almost all the big stars in Hollywood, trying to make it seem like he knew them personally. Clearly it was all just a bunch of lies, but Tom didn't mind. He thought it was kind of sad, in fact, that Chris felt he had to try so hard to make people like him. Tom liked him fine, just the way he was, without the lies.

They found a quiet corner in the park, behind a large stand of trees near the picnic grounds. The moon was up by then, and bright. Chris accepted a cigarette from Tom. "We didn't talk about price," he said hesitantly.

"Price?"

He nodded.

Tom shrugged. "Whatever's fair." He felt sorry that everything in life had to have a price tag attached, even friendship.

"Twenty?"

"Sure, why not?" He made the deal easily, not even stopping to think about it.

With that out of the way, Chris seemed to relax, but Tom could tell that Jody was still uptight. He kept looking around, although they were obviously alone. The whole park belonged to them.

Tom stretched out, relaxing, feeling number-one fine. "Why don't you and Chris get to know each other better?" he suggested to Jody.

Jody licked the sweat above his upper lip. "What about you?"

"I'll just watch for a while."

92

There was an awkward moment, with Chris and Jody looking everywhere but at each other.

Tom felt a twinge of impatience. "Come on," he said sharply.

Chris made a move, reaching out to unzip Jody's jeans. He put a hand inside. Jody, his eyes locked onto Tom's face, gave a sigh. Chris smiled sheepishly and bent over him.

Tom could feel the itch beginning again inside, and this time he didn't fight it. He took a swallow of beer and thought about the first time.

He'd been sixteen and Jody just ten.

They'd had the house to themselves that day, because the old man was working for a change, and their mother was at the hospital visiting her sister, who was dying of some female thing. All the women in her family died of some female thing, and the stupid bitch was afraid that she would, too.

Jody was playing little league ball that year. He came in from a game, sweaty and dirty, and went to clean up. He'd hit the first home run of his life, winning the game for his team, and he was puffed up with pride.

A few minutes later he came into the kitchen where Tom was eating lunch. "You shoulda been there, Tommy," he said for about the tenth time. Still wet from the shower and wearing just shorts, he poured a big glass of Kool-Aid. As he drank, he got a purple moustache.

"Next time," Tom promised. He felt a sudden urge to hug his little brother, to let him know how proud he was. Jody needed to know that no matter how bad things got at home, Tom would always be there for him.

He crossed the room quickly and put both arms around him, pressing against the skinny wet body. "That was great, Jody," he said in husky voice. "I'm real proud."

Jody didn't pull out of the embrace for a long time.

93

Tom sometimes thought that their whole lives were decided in that one moment when Jody didn't pull away. The only thing he couldn't ever quite figure out was whether he should love Jody for that moment or hate him.

Jody moaned softly. The sound pulled Tom back into the present. He blinked away the memories. Chris spit into the grass a couple of times, then took a gulp of beer.

It was Tom's turn. He unsnapped and unzipped his jeans as Chris moved toward him. Jody was sitting up now, watching. Tom smiled at him, then closed his eyes and gave himself up to the wonderful feelings he was having inside.

It was real and it was a dream of the past all at the same time. He could almost believe that the practiced mouth of the hustler really belonged to somebody else. Somebody still ten years old with a grape-flavored tongue.

Tom really didn't mean to kill Chris.

The knife was in his hand.

He didn't know how it had gotten there or why he had it. Chris was flaked out on the ground, the jeans still tangled at his feet. Tom looked at him, then at the knife, surprised to find himself holding it.

"Tommy..." It was a whisper from Jody.

Tom looked up and met his brother's gaze. There was a long moment, during which neither one of them seemed even to breathe. Chris broke the mood. He sat up suddenly and reached for the beer can. Without even thinking about what he was doing or why, Tom bent forward and plunged the knife into Chris' spine. A faint scream, more a whimper than anything else, escaped the boy as he toppled over.

"*Oh God,*" Tom said to himself. Then panic seized him. If Chris told anyone what he'd done, they'd send him back to the hospital again. He yanked the knife blade free and pushed it into Chris again. Again and again. It got easier. Finally he turned and handed the knife to Jody. "Now you," he said.

Chris was still twitching, making soft mewing sounds.

Jody gripped the knife with both hands. "I can't," he whispered. "Please."

Tom leaned very close to him. "For me," he said softly. "Do it for me."

Jody shook his head. He stared into Tom's eyes, then glanced at Chris. "He hurts so bad."

"Yes," Tom said. "He hurts. I hurt."

Jody nodded once. Then he closed his eyes. "I'm sorry." He lowered the blade quickly into Chris.

Tom felt another hot wave of excitement wash over him. "Again," he said hoarsely.

Jody did it again and then so many times that Tom lost count.

Tom stayed on his knees, his body wracked by an explosive climax, better than any he'd ever had before. Jody finally stopped. Tom crawled over to him and pried the knife free from a death-like grip. Then he held Jody's hands until the sobs faded and died.

They were hungry.

"That's the trouble with chink food," Tom said. "It doesn't stick with you long."

They found a MacDonald's and drove through the pick-up window for Big Macs, fries, and shakes. It was only a short drive back to the motel.

They spread the meal out on one of the beds and ate in silence. Tom finally slurped the last of the chocolate from the bottom of the paper cup. "Tomorrow we get down to business," he said.

"The cop, you mean?"

"Kowalski the pig."

Jody crumpled his empty cup. "Does that mean no more parties?"

Tom grinned. "You like the parties?"

Jody shook his head.

"Don't lie. You like them just fine."

"I feel sorry for Chris," Jody said in a faint voice. "It's terrible what happened to him."

"Yeah." Tom didn't know why the evening had ended that way. "He might have been a famous actor someday."

That was too sad to talk about, so they cleaned up the mess and went to bed.

Jody lay awake for a long time, listening to Tommy snore. There was an ache in his gut that wouldn't quit. He felt like he had once before, way back, when his brother had taken him to a playground near their home. It was very late at night and nobody else was around. Jody got onto the small merry-go-round and held on tightly to the metal bar as Tommy began to push. The merry-go-round went faster and faster, blurring the world.

He closed his eyes and screamed for Tommy to stop, please, but the merry-go-round just spun more quickly. Above the sound of the wind crashing around his ears, he could hear Tommy laughing.

Jody pressed the heels of both hands into his eyes, wanting to scream again, wanting Tommy to stop what was happening. He kept thinking about the fortune in his cookie at the Chinese place. "Beware that your love does not lead you astray," it said.

Beware, Jody thought. Beware.

96

Chapter 18

BLUE was already out of bed when the call came.

He had finished twenty minutes of aerobics, showered and shaved, and was in the kitchen preparing a bowl of Grape-Nuts. The sudden shrill ringing startled him, causing his hand to jerk, splashing a puddle of milk across the counter. "Damn," he said mildly, then answered the phone.

"Blue?"

"Yes?" He ripped off a paper towel and tried to wipe up the milk before it ran down the side of the cupboard to the floor. "Who's this?"

"It's me. Spaceman."

He recognized the slightly raspy voice then, and wondered when they'd reached a first name basis. But what the hell. "What's up?"

"My fucking car won't start. Pick me up, okay?"

"No problem." Blue shifted the phone to his other ear and fumbled for a pencil so he could write down the address. "Be there as soon as I can."

Spaceman hung up without saying good-bye.

Blue listened to the dial tone for a moment, then shrugged and hung up, too. Maybe too much emphasis was put on the old social amenities anyway.

He carried the bowl into the bedroom, eating the hard cereal as he got dressed. His mood was good. Last night's dinner with Sharon Engels seemed like a promising beginning. It was just possible that his life was starting to turn around. There was, of course, still the problem of Kowalski to deal with, but in the morning light, even that seemed manageable.

He whistled softly as he pulled on jeans and a white Izod. Maybe casual was the way to go with his new partner. Blue was willing to make accommodations. He clipped the .357 Magnum to his belt and took a lightweight jacket from the closet. The good guys had to keep their guns covered, on the theory, he supposed, that it made the general populous nervous to see naked guns flapping around.

It was a little more than thirty minutes later when Blue pulled to a stop in front of an apartment building on Vermont and leaned on the horn. When nothing happened after a minute, he honked again. Kowalski came barreling out. He was wearing slacks and a sport jacket that had never been intended to be seen together, but at least the shirt was clean.

"Change of plans," he said, sliding into the car. "We've got another stiff in the park; headquarters just called."

Blue made a sharp righthand turn and headed toward the park. "Another kid?"

Spaceman was leaning back in the seat, his eyes closed. "What? Oh, yeah, another goddamned kid."

"Damn," Blue said.

"Yeah. And I didn't have any breakfast."

They drove through the park to the place where a couple of zone cars and a lab vehicle were already parked. The area was roped off, and a small group of sightseers stood behind the bright orange restraining lines. Joggers, maybe; what else would anybody be doing in the park so early?

It wasn't until Blue had pulled in behind the other cars and turned off the engine that Spaceman spoke again. "How much this thing set you back?"

"About thirty grand. Give or take."

"Give or take. Shit."

They got out together and headed across a patch of rugged terrain. A rookie cop standing nervous guard was still a nice shade of chartreuse. Obviously relieved to see them, he stepped aside and pointed.

It was the worst thing Blue had seen in his time as a cop. Maybe he'd seen worse in Nam, but that was a long time ago and mostly buried in memory. "My God," he whispered, looking down at the bloody fetal shape curled in the grass. It seemed an especial obscenity on this warm and sunny morning in the park.

He turned away quickly to stare at a couple of joggers who were running in place and chatting. An early morning pick-up.

"Just like the Lowe boy," Spaceman said.

Except that they both knew this was worse, for one very good reason. With the first killing, no one knew what they had. Maybe it was a one-time thing. An act of personal passion, no matter how sick and twisted that passion had been. There was always the chance that Peter had brought about his own death, that something in his actions or personality caused someone to go a whole lot crazy suddenly and kill him.

Which didn't make his death any less tragic, but which at least meant that it was a single incident, terrible but isolated.

But this body put the lie to that. This body meant that they were dealing with a genuine crazy. Or, if the two-killer theory was correct, a couple of crazies.

Blue was tired just thinking about it. For one moment, he almost missed the PR department and making speeches to the Rotary Club.

Spaceman knelt beside the body, just looking at it for a long moment. "Pictures?" he asked no one in particular.

"Done," the recovering rookie said.

He reached out and gently turned the body so they could see the face. It was a very young face, still boyishly pretty, unmarked by the brutal attack the body had endured. Spaceman said something under his breath that no one could hear.

99

Blue watched him.

Spaceman fumbled at the jeans that were tangled around the boy's feet and finally pulled out a wallet. He handed it to Blue.

Inside was an ID card, the kind that some schools issued to students. The picture on the card was of the dead boy; he was very photogenic. "Christopher Blair," Blue said. "There's an address in Pasadena, but that's been marked out. The new one is the Starlite Hotel, on Fairfax."

"I know the place."

Another van pulled up and parked.

"About time," Spaceman muttered.

Sharon Engels climbed down and walked over to where they stood. "Sorry about the delay," she said. "But they're stacked up to the ceiling already today. Old folks dropping like flies from the heat and from breathing the air. Not to mention a couple of amateur firefighters. Heart attacks."

"We have another dead boy," Spaceman said shortly, not seeming very interested in all the other people dying in L.A. that day.

Sharon pulled on thin plastic gloves and bent over the body. "Thanks again for dinner last night," she said, not looking up, both hands already busy.

"Any time," Blue said. He could feel Spaceman's curious gaze move over him, but luckily they were interrupted.

One of the uniforms came up, holding two bloody tee shirts. "Found these over there," he said. "Looks like they washed up in the drinking fountain and left them behind."

Blue opened an evidence bag and the two shirts were dropped in. "That was careless of them."

Spaceman shrugged. "They probably knew that the shirts wouldn't help us a damned bit. With the weather the way it is, two guys running around half-dressed won't attract any attention."

Sharon joined them. Her face was wearily grim, but she still looked good. Maybe it was the cheekbones. She yanked at the gloves until they peeled reluctantly away from her skin, and shoved them into her black bag. "I wonder how long this damned heat is going to last," she said.

They both shrugged.

"Everybody always talks about a full moon making people crazy," she went on, taking out a cigarette. Before anyone could move to light it, there was a Bic in her hand and it was done. "But for my money, a heat wave like this is worse. Wonder if anybody's ever done a study on that."

Blue didn't say anything. He recognized the seemingly idle chatter for what it really was, an attempt to get away from the horror of it all for a moment, to steady herself. He had done the same thing himself in the past. They all had.

She glanced back toward the body, which was being readied for transport. "This is just preliminary," she warned.

"Sure," Spaceman said.

"It looks like a match to the other killing. There's only one real difference that I could spot immediately."

"What?"

"This one was a lot worse. Escalating degree of violence, I think they call it."

"That's what they call it," Blue agreed.

"That's it, then?"

"For the moment, Spaceman. You want to be at the post?"

But he shook his head. "Not this time. I don't need a rerun. Just get the data to me as soon as possible." He turned and started for the car.

Blue hung back. "Mind if I call you again?" he asked, feeling like a junior high nerd talking to the prom queen.

"Call." She smiled fleetingly and left.

He watched until she was back in the van. When he slid

101

behind the wheel of his car again, Spaceman was smoking a cigarette and staring into the distance. "Where to?" Blue asked.

"I don't give a damn." Then he sighed. "To a telephone. But not the office. I sure as hell don't need to get trapped into listening to one of McGannon's pep talks." He glanced sidewise at Blue. "Unless you're a stickler for details like checking in."

Blue shrugged. "I'm flexible."

"Good," Spaceman said, and Blue had the feeling that he'd passed some kind of test. "We'll track down the Pasadena address, see if his family is still there." Spaceman tossed the cigarette out the window. "Put the phone someplace where I can get some breakfast."

Blue nodded and aimed the car toward San Fernando Boulevard and Biff's Coffeeshop.

Chapter 19

WHILE Spaceman downed a western sandwich, Blue checked out the address found in Blair's wallet. The family, whatever that might consist of, apparently still lived at the same place. It had been decided that they would go break the news in person.

Blue went back to the table and sat down opposite Spaceman, who was just finishing his meal. He was plainly lost in thought, and once again Blue had the feeling that something beyond the case or even the unwanted partnership was bothering him. Having learned his lesson the day before, however, he kept his mouth closed.

The coffee he'd ordered was cold now, but Blue drank it anyway. "The phone is listed to a Charles Blair," he said.

Spaceman nodded and wiped the napkin across his mouth. "That's our next stop, then," he said, reaching for his wallet.

The house was a stucco bungalow, painted a bright shade of pink. The lawn, what there was of it, needed trimming. They parked in the unpaved drive. The house and the green car clashed painfully in the vivid sunshine.

Since Spaceman seemed quite content to stand back for the moment and let him take charge, Blue led the way to the door and knocked firmly. He didn't know what game his partner was playing now, but he was willing to hang in there. If nothing else, a background in public relations taught the art of diplomacy.

The door opened slowly. A woman stood there, but it was hard to see her inside the dim hallway. "Yes, what do you want?" The voice was overly precise, as if it belonged

103

to an English teacher or a drunk. Blue tagged this one as a boozer. Not a falling down drinker, but a careful sherry sipper.

"Mrs. Blair?"

"I am Felicia Blair, yes. Who might you gentlemen be?"

"Detectives Kowalski and Maguire, ma'am, from the Los Angeles Police Department."

"Which one are you?"

"Maguire. May we step inside and speak with you?"

"Well, I suppose so. One wants to cooperate with the authorities, of course, although I cannot imagine what business the police could have with me." She unlatched the screen door and pushed it open. They entered, following her toward the living room.

Blue came to an abrupt stop on the threshold, staring. Several hundred framed pictures covered every available inch of wall space in the room. A closer look revealed that they weren't pictures at all, but the covers of movie magazines, some from as far back as the Forties and some quite recent. Each cover had been placed within a plastic frame of red or blue and hung with care.

Spaceman nudged him from behind and they walked on into the room. *The Phil Donahue Show* was on the television. Once inside, Spaceman again seemed to lose interest in the proceedings. He appeared quite content to wander around the room, studying the walls.

There was something frightening about the room. Granted, everybody in Southern California lived a media-soaked life, where nothing was real until and unless it was on the screen or in *People* magazine, but Mrs. Blair's little world went even beyond that. This room had slipped over the edge of tenuous reality into the madness that hovered all around, like the smog.

"I see you've noticed my collection," the woman said.

"Hard to miss," Spaceman replied.

She ignored him, looking at Blue instead. The

104

expression on her face could only have been described as coy. Her hair was tightly curled, her face elaborately made up. The brows had been plucked and then pencilled in again; the mouth was a vivid red slash across her face. Although she probably wasn't much over forty, she looked more like something preserved from several decades earlier.

Her gaze simmered as she took Blue in from head to toe. "Young Redford," she pronounced at last. "That's what you are. A young Redford type."

"Uh, thanks," he said. He pulled out his notebook, hoping it would make things seem more official and less like a trip into the Twilight Zone. "You have a son named Christopher Blair?"

She shook her head vigorously, but the curls didn't even flutter. "No. I was never blessed with a child of my own."

"But you do know him?"

"Of course. He's my husband's nephew. We've raised him since he was four, after the tragic accident that killed his own parents. So even though I was not blessed to give birth to him, Chris is very dear to me." It sounded like a speech she'd given before; it also sounded like a speech from an old Bette Davis movie.

"Well, I'm afraid we have some bad news for you. Chris was found this morning—"

"Found?" she broke in cheerfully. "But he hasn't been lost. Chris lives in Hollywood." She said it with the fervor a true believer might use to speak of Mecca.

"At the Starlite Hotel, right?"

"Yes. We decided that was a better place from which to launch his career. Chris is an Actor." Capital letter.

Spaceman made an impatient sound.

Blue took the hint. "I'm sorry to have to tell you, Mrs. Blair, but Chris is dead."

"What?" Lacquered fingertips sprang to the scarlet mouth, but Blue couldn't tell how much of the emotion

105

was real and how much staged. "Dead? Oh, no, you must be mistaken. It must be some other boy you're talking about. Chris is going to be a star."

"I'm afraid someone killed him," Blue said gently. "His body was found in Griffith Park."

She shook her head impatiently, angrily, rejecting this sudden thrust of reality into her dream world. "No."

"Yes," Blue said firmly.

"Chris is a wonderful actor. Who would kill him? Who would harm him at all? He's the sweetest boy."

"We don't know yet who killed him."

Spaceman, who had been studying a *Movie Screen* cover trumpeting an affair between Burt Reynolds and Loni Anderson, turned suddenly. "How old was Chris?"

"He's sixteen."

"Isn't that a little young to be on his own? Especially in a place like the Starlite?"

She drew herself up and now Blue thought of Gloria Swanson in *Sunset Boulevard*. "The Starlite Hotel is the residence of a number of promising young theatrical figures," she said with great dignity. "The giants of the business frequently lunch in the chic little cafe there."

Spaceman snorted. "Crap, lady. The giants of the business wouldn't use the toilet there because they'd probably catch something."

She fixed him with an icy glare. "Obviously one does not expect a person of your type to understand the film world. A boy like Chris needs to make contacts."

"Right," Spaceman said in obvious disgust.

Blue stepped forward. "Mrs. Blair, Chris is dead," he said softly, but firmly. "Someone killed him."

She looked at him, her mouth opening as if more protest might be forthcoming, then something within the woman seemed to crumble. She folded like a dying flower and sank to the couch. "Chris? But he was going to be a star. We had it all planned."

106

Blue touched her shoulder lightly. "Is there someone we can call for you?"

They called her husband, and since he worked only minutes away, he arrived quickly. Obviously, Charles Blair didn't share the lofty visions of his wife or his late nephew. He was a thin, nervous-looking man with a twitch. He didn't seem surprised to hear about Chris, although his twitch got a little worse. "He was my brother's boy. Nice, kid, Chris, but a dreamer. Flighty, like my wife. The two of them were always at the movies or reading through those damned magazines." He glanced across the room at his wife, who was showing Spaceman a scrapbook devoted to Chris. "I always thought the boy was a little. . . strange. Not normal, if you get my drift."

"We think he was picked up by someone for sexual purposes, then killed."

Blair nodded. "I thought it might be something like that. The poor kid."

There wasn't anything more to be learned from these people. Blair agreed to come in for an official ID, and at least they were willing to bury the boy. In fact, she was already making plans for the funeral when they left. Blair saw them to the door and stood there, twitching and looking bothered as they got into the car.

"Hooray for Hollywood," Blue said.

Spaceman slammed the car door too hard. "Goddamned fucking Tinseltown," he said.

Chapter 20

IT wasn't the first time Spaceman had been to the Starlite Hotel. Back when he was still in uniform, he'd been called out a number of times to the rundown establishment. Most of the complaints were minor — drunk and disorderly, domestic squabbles, an occasional drug OD, once a knifing. Just the ordinary kinds of things for a place like that.

Once upon a time, back in the late Forties and early Fifties, the Starlite had worn a mantle of respectability. Rumor had it that a couple of real stars actually lived there before they made it big. That rumor was enough to bring more hopefuls flocking to the tiny rooms and haphazard service. It didn't take most of them long to realize that Hollywood held nothing for them except hurt. Nevertheless, the dream persisted.

The lobby never changed, only got more like it was. The gloomy lighting did nothing except hide the worst of the stains on the rug. All the stains looked alike, so there was no way of telling which were blood, which booze, which other things that didn't bear thinking of.

On this particular day, it was occupied by several rummies and a couple of kids. The old-timers were playing a slow-motion game of poker, while the kids read the trades.

Spaceman and Blue walked through the dismal lobby to the front desk, which was under the command of a woman dressed entirely in ycllow. She could have been fifty or seventy. Blue hair was piled onto her head in a display Marie Antoinette might have envied. A small fan on the counter was blowing air right at her, but it did not seem to have much of a cooling effect on her plump redness. Obviously an old hand at her job, she watched their approach suspiciously. "Nobody called the cops," she said when they reached her.

"How do you know that, sweetheart?" Spaceman asked, leaning across the counter toward her.

"Because I work the switchboard," was the snippy reply. Not easy to scare this broad.

"And you listen in on all their calls, right?"

She ignored that.

Blue was standing to one side, hands shoved into his pockets, rocking back and forth patiently.

"Chris Blair's room," Spaceman said.

"He ain't in." She smiled prettily. "Would you like to leave a message?"

"I'd have to wait a long time for an answer. Blair is dead."

She swallowed hard. "Dead?" Her voice raised, attracting the attention of the kids in the lobby. They looked up from *Variety* and the *Hollywood Reporter*. The old men didn't bother. Death was no novelty to them.

"Blair was found murdered in Griffith Park this morning."

"How tragic. He was a very nice boy."

"Was he? Then I'm surprised he lasted very long around here. This place chews nice kids up and spits them out pretty fast. We want to see his room."

"Why?" She fumbled for an explanation. "I mean, he wasn't killed here or nothing. I don't know why you have to see his room. A thing like that gets around, it could get us a bad name."

"But not nearly as bad as the name I could give you," Spaceman said cheerfully.

She thought that over for a moment, then turned and took a key from the board behind her. "Room 203."

"Thanks so much."

As they climbed the stairs, their progress was followed all the way by several pairs of eyes. "They don't know whether to feel bad because somebody they knew is dead," Spaceman muttered, "or glad because it isn't them."

"We all do the same thing," Blue replied. "Remember Nam?"

Spaceman conceded the point silently.

Chris Blair hadn't had much to call his own. The room held an iron bedstead, made up with an oft-patched quilt, a desk and chair, and a chest of drawers. A cheap black and white portable television was sitting on the dresser, the current *TV Guide* open next to it.

Inside the drawers were only the usual underwear and socks, the expected plastic bag with a small amount of hash, toilet articles in a paper bag, ready to be hauled to the john at the end of the corridor. In the closet were several pairs of jeans, some shirts, and a grey flannel blazer complete with dress shirt, blue slacks, and regimental tie.

There was a pile of paperbacks on the desk. A French-English dictionary, some Nick Carter thrillers, and a motley collection of stage plays.

Spaceman made a face. "Depressing as hell in here."

"Maybe Chris liked it."

Before Spaceman could reply, there was a soft knock on the door. They glanced at one another, then Spaceman moved to answer it.

The girl standing there was perhaps sixteen, wearing jeans and a halter top that she didn't yet have the figure to carry off well. Her face was pretty enough, just like that of thousands of other girls. She had wide blue eyes, freckles, and not a chance in hell of making anything of herself in this town.

"Is it true?" she said in a slightly quivering voice. "About Chris being dead?"

"It's true. You knew him, did you?" Spaceman asked.

110

"He was sort of a friend of mine." She chewed on a fingernail. "Who killed him?"

"We don't know yet. Maybe you can help us."

She shook her head. "I don't know nothing. Chris was just a friend, you know? Nothing else." Surprisingly, she was still able to blush; Spaceman wondered how long she'd been here. "He didn't make it with girls, so we was just friends." She suddenly seemed to realize that she'd lost the edge of toughness necessary for life in the jungle. "Anyway, I don't screw around with guys who can't do me no good, careerwise, you know?"

They knew.

Spaceman was lighting still another cigarette. "So you can't tell me anything about who might have wanted to hurt Chris?"

"No. It was probably just one of those creeps he used to trick with. I saw him yesterday, and he was flat. He was going out to score." A sudden flash of knowledge older than her years sparkled in the blue eyes. "I guess he did. Score, I mean."

"Looks like." Spaceman could feel the taste of the cigarette searing his lungs, and he wondered how long it would be before his craving for nicotine killed him. "What's your name, sweetie?"

"Brooke Kane."

"For real?"

The smile was engaging and in a fair world she might have gone far just on the strength of that. "No. But I think it works, don't you? See, when the producers hear it, they'll think about Brooke Shields. When they can't get her, I get a break."

He could have pressed her for a real name, even hauled her in, but it would have been pointless. He couldn't run in every kid on the lam. It wasn't his job. So he just waved her out.

She turned to go, then paused. "Can I ask you something?"

111

"Ask."

The smile flashed again. "What's gonna happen to his TV?" she said brightly.

Chapter 21

ALL that got done for the rest of the day was a lot of wheel-spinning. Spaceman was used to that; it was an occupational hazard. They nosed around the area of the Starlite a while, but it wasn't the right time of day to converse with the street people, even if they wanted to pretend that the crazies and druggies would know anything. Or tell it if they did.

When the autopsy results finally showed up, they simply confirmed what was already known. What they had was two boys, two street hustlers, killed by the same hands in two days. And as far as Spaceman could see, there wasn't a damned thing he or anybody else could do to prevent a third body from popping up the next day.

Disgusted at the sense of futility that he was feeling, Spaceman gave it up for the day. The night men would pay special attention to the boys of Hollywood; beyond that, there wasn't much to be done. He called the garage, but his car wasn't ready. It made a perfect end to a perfect day.

He took out the memo from Lompoc and stared at it for a moment. Damn, there just weren't enough details. The dead boy might have been anybody; there was no reason for him to think it was Robbie. His hand rested on the telephone for a moment; simple enough to call and find out some hard info.

Then he pulled his hand back. Damnit, just because some creep said Robbie might have headed for San Francisco there was no reason to think it was the truth. There was no reason at all for Robbie to have been in Lompoc. And there was very little chance that the killing there was connected with the ones here.

He decided not to call Lompoc yet. They should have a picture down here soon, and if no photo turned up, it meant they must have identified the dead boy. No sense in borrowing trouble.

Blue came back from someplace and leaned against his desk. "I just heard that your son is missing," he said.

"Yeah?"

"Dwight told me."

"Dwight talks too damned much."

"Was it supposed to be some kind of secret?"

Spaceman shrugged. He didn't even know now why he hadn't wanted Maguire to know. It was dumb. Still, he felt obligated to try and justify himself. "I just don't like people who bring their problems to the job. It gets in the way."

"Admirable," Blue said. "Why don't you let me help? I've got a lot of time and nothing much doing."

But Spaceman shook his head. Maybe he was just being a stubborn ass — all right, no maybe about it — but that was how he felt. "Thanks, but no thanks. I can handle it."

"Your car ready?"

"No."

"I have one you can use."

Spaceman drew back and glared at him. "You have another car besides that fancy hot rod outside?"

"Just a Jeep. In my garage at home."

He hesitated, not wanting to be obligated. That was the trouble with getting close to other people; it meant losing some of your control.

"Hey, you have to look for the kid, right?"

"Yeah." He thought suddenly of the dead boys and the fact that his own son was out there somewhere. "Yeah. Okay. Thanks."

Spaceman turned down the first invitation to stay for something to eat, but when Blue asked again, he decided what the hell, and agreed.

114

The house they parked beside was all redwood and glass, making his own place seem even shabbier by comparison. Maguire didn't gloat over it, at least. In fact, he seemed almost embarrassed by the house, at the same time that his fondness for it was obvious.

Spaceman wondered how rich a person had to be before his wealth was an embarrassment.

Blue stopped long enough in the living room to pour them each a shot on the rocks and then led the way into a large kitchen. Most of Spaceman's apartment could have fit into the one room. "I better warn you, I'm not much of a cook," Blue said.

"Hell, I eat out mostly. Or make some of that frozen shit." He sat down at a round butcher block table and started to work on the drink. The whiskey was smooth all the way down.

Blue opened the refrigerator door and peered inside briefly, before starting to pull things out: lettuce, a lemon, some eggs. Cheese. "You sure I can't lend a hand looking for Robbie?" he asked, putting a pan of water on the stove and starting to wash the lettuce.

"I'm sure. But thanks." Spaceman looked for an ashtray and finally found one across the room. He brought it back to the table. "This is just something I have to do. The department has a missing person report, so I'm not exactly doing a solo." He smoked and drank in silence for a few moments. "I haven't been much of a father, maybe," he finally said in a low voice. "This seems like a way to make up for that." He cleared his throat.

Blue nodded but didn't say anything. He squeezed the lemon and tossed the lettuce with some olive oil.

"Speaking of crazy names," Spaceman said, although they hadn't been, "how'd you get stuck with something like Blue? Sounds like a name for a dog."

"It was, actually," Maguire replied. "My old man had a hunting dog that he loved more than anything else in the world. He always said that dog was the bravest, smartest, most loyal creature he'd ever known. So he over-ruled my mother's choice, David, and named me Blue." He shrugged.

Spaceman wondered if the story were true; whether it was or not, Maguire seemed determined to stick with it. He dropped the subject. "Thought you said you couldn't cook," he said.

Blue smiled sheepishly. "My old man was a real freak on food. He always had the best cooks money could buy working for him. I got used to the good stuff, so I learned a few tricks."

"Why don't you just hire somebody?"

Blue shrugged. "I like my privacy. Besides, it kind of relaxes me after a rough day. Like today."

Spaceman finished his drink and crunched thoughtfully on an ice cube. "Nothing wrong with that," he said. "They say some of the best cooks are men. Probably all of them aren't weird."

Blue just smiled a little. For the next few minutes he was very busy grating cheese, cooking the eggs fleetingly, and slicing some crusty French bread. When the Caesar salad was ready, he opened a bottle of California wine and joined Spaceman at the table. "What do you think about this case?" he asked as they started eating.

Spaceman speared a crouton with his fork and frowned at it. Or at the question. "I think it's gonna be a bad one," he said. "Real bad."

Chapter 22

THE JEEP moved easily down the steep road that led away from Maguire's castle, back to ordinary life. Spaceman had to admit to himself that he felt better after the food and wine. Maybe Maguire wasn't such a creep, after all.

Not that he was looking to get stuck with him permanently, of course. He liked working alone; but until McGannon could be persuaded to divorce them, Kowalski figured he could get along with Maguire.

He'd already picked another name from the ones Karen had given him. Becky Malloy, the only girl on the list. She lived in a fancy part of town and the sight of the house confirmed that there was money in the family.

The woman who answered the door had the class to go with the neighborhood and the house. She was outfitted for tennis, in a short white dress with some kind of ruffled thing underneath. The clothes were right for the game, but it was clear from the unruffled hair and the perfect make-up that she hadn't set foot anywhere near a tennis court. Her tan was flawless and the figure inside the dress nearly so.

Maybe, Spaceman thought, if I could find a woman my age who looked this good, I'd give up the young stuff.

Which reminded him that he hadn't called Mandy yet.

The woman eyed him speculatively. He got the impression that she looked at all men the same way, testing them to see if they met her standards.

Spaceman had the feeling that he came up a little short on her acceptability scale.

To compensate, he showed her the badge and made sure

she caught a glimpse of his gun as he replaced the wallet. Sometimes the rich bitches got turned on by an implication of brute power.

It seemed to work with her. A wet tip of tongue appeared, flicking along the frosted pink lips. "What can I do for you?" she asked.

"Is your daughter here?"

"Becky? No, not at the moment." But she stepped aside and ushered him in anyway.

He liked the living room. Done all in muted shades of blue and green, it gave off a sense of coolness.

"What did you want to see Becky about?"

"I was hoping she could help me locate my son. Robbie Kowalski."

"Robbie is missing?"

"Seems to be."

She smiled at him. "Excuse my rudeness. Please, sit down. How about a drink?"

He relaxed into the plump-cushioned sofa, but shook his head to the drink. "Do you know when Becky will be back?"

"No." She remained standing. The better to show off her health spa figure, no doubt. "I honestly don't think she'd be able to help you anyway."

"She's a friend of Robbie's, right?"

"Well, they were close at one time, but. . ." She broke off suddenly and glided across the room to a bar in one corner. "I think a little chablis would be just marvelous. Do say you'll join me?"

He gave in with a shrug. "Becky and Rob?" he said, when she came back to hand him a glass of sparkling gold liquid.

"They broke up about three weeks ago."

"Broke up? Why?"

She hesitated. "Because my husband and I insisted."

118

Spaceman took a sip of the wine; it didn't taste as good as it looked. "Why? If you don't mind telling me."

She considered her drink. "You mustn't think it had anything to do with Rob personally. He seems like a very nice boy."

"But?"

"They just weren't suited to one another. I mean, their backgrounds and..." The words dwindled off uncomfortably.

"Becky comes from here and Rob is the son of a cop, right?"

"That's a little blunt, but accurate. Becky has other interests that we feel she should be pursuing right now. Next year she's going East to school." The woman shrugged. "I think you can understand our concern."

"I understand that you thought Rob wasn't good enough for your daughter."

"Please, don't be hurt by what I said." She scooted a little closer to him on the couch. He was suddenly aware of the perfume she wore, a heavy, cloying scent. "Your job must be terrifying, what with all the animals on the streets these days."

"There are all kinds of animals," he said. "In all kinds of places." The room that had seemed so pleasantly cool before now struck him as a sterile, unfeeling place. Cold, not cool. "When will your daughter be home?"

She looked like she might want to pout, but then she shrugged instead. "Well, to be honest, I'm not sure. She went to spend a few days with a girlfriend, and I expected her home today. But she hasn't turned up yet."

"What girlfriend?"

"Why do you need to know that?"

He smiled. "I need to talk to Becky."

She leaned forward and very carefully set her glass on the polished table. He had the feeling that she wouldn't be buying any tickets for the next policeman's ball. "I will call my daughter," she said tightly. Lady of the manor addressing the stableboy. "I will ask her to come home immediately. I don't want her to be humiliated in front of others. The girl's father is in the state legislature. How would it look for a cop to come knocking on his door asking for Becky?"

Since he didn't know how it would look and he didn't much care, Spaceman didn't say anything.

She left the room.

Spaceman finished the wine. He probably wouldn't be offered any more. Or offered anything else, for that matter. Too bad. He could use a broad with some class for a change. Maybe he was hanging around Maguire too much and a taste for the expensive stuff was starting to rub off.

Spaceman made another note to himself to call Mandy.

It was several minutes before Mrs. Malloy returned. Her uppity attitude had apparently suffered a blow.

"What is it?"

"They said Becky wasn't there."

"When did she leave?"

Mrs. Malloy shook her head. "They said she never was there. I don't understand. Becky told me she was going to stay with those people. Why would she lie?"

Spaceman sighed. "So Becky is missing, too."

"No, she's. . . ." The woman shuddered and sank down onto the couch. "Do you think they're together?"

"I think it's very possible."

She made a small sound, half sigh, half sob.

Spaceman decided that she could use a dose of liquid courage, so he went to the bar and poured her some more wine. Then he poured a shot of Irish for himself. He smiled faintly. So the little bastard was shacked up someplace with a rich bitch.

Spaceman put the dead boy in Lompoc out of his mind.

Chapter 23

BLUE was restless.

He paced the living room for a while after Kowalski left, decided to hell with it finally, and left the house. Maybe he could do something about finding the kid on his own. He'd seen the picture of Robbie and it couldn't hurt to hit some of the places in Hollywood where runaways congregated. Hell, he could do some digging about the dead boys, too.

It would look very nice on his record if he somehow managed to catch the killers.

At the end of a couple hours, though, all he had managed to catch was a headache. He was allergic to marijuana, and just inhaling the smoke in some of the places he visited got his allergy raging. He found a drugstore on Sunset and went in to buy some antihistamines.

After swallowing a couple of capsules on the spot, he found a phone and called Sharon Engels.

She answered the call immediately, and said, in response to his question, that she wasn't doing much of anything.

He suggested going out for a drink.

She said it was too hot.

He suggested that maybe he could just come to her place.

She said that tomorrow was going to be a very busy day, so it would have to be an early evening.

He said okay.

She said okay.

Before leaving the drugstore, he bought a quart of Rocky Road ice cream.

She answered the door wearing shorts and a thin tee shirt. No bra. Rocky Road, as it happened, was her favorite flavor.

They sat on the living room rug, eating ice cream and watching a *Rockford Files* rerun. The first time he kissed her, she tasted like cold chocolate. It was a good taste, so he kissed her again.

Sharon Engels apparently didn't believe in playing games. She pushed herself up from the floor and carried both dishes into the kitchen, where she rinsed them carefully. Then she turned and stared at him thoughtfully.

"I don't usually go to bed with cops," she said.

"Why not?"

"They usually don't appeal. All bravado and bluster."

"Does that apply to me?"

"I don't think so." She grinned suddenly. "Besides, rules were made to be broken. Come on." She headed down the hall, pausing only long enough to put a record on the stereo.

Joan Baez began, sounding husky and filled with secrets.

The bedroom was cluttered with books, papers, mail. There was a refreshing lack of frills. Sharon smiled faintly as she slipped off the sandals and started to undress.

"Well? I said tomorrow was an early day."

"Right, you said that." He tried not to hurry as he took off his clothes and joined her in the large bed.

Joan was singing about passionate strangers.

They spent some time just getting to know one another. Her body was lean and healthy, the body of a person who enjoyed exercise. She definitely enjoyed sex.

It was a very nice couple of hours. Baez kept singing the same songs over and over until Blue felt as if the words were permanently seared into his soul. There was no big passion sweeping them away. Instead, what they had was a lot of fun. He decided that they could come to like each other very much, even if they never again went to bed. Although that would be nice, too.

Finally she sat up against the headboard. "You're a good lay," she announced.

He was a little startled, but then he smiled. "Thank you. I might say the same about you."

"We'll do it again sometime." She reached for his jeans and threw them at him. "But for right now, get the hell out of here. I have a seven o'clock date with some stiffs."

As he drove home, the sound of Joan Baez was still echoing in his head. He forgot the case and everything else, including his headache.

Chapter 24

JODY fell asleep in front of the television, but Tom was too keyed up to relax. He sat in a chair all night, staring out the window, working on two packs of cigarettes and a bottle of Old Grandad. He was thinking about Kowalski. The desire for revenge against the cop was a cold flame in his gut, but it was a fire without direction, like the ones burning in the hills. Kowalski had to pay, that much Tom knew, but the coin in which that payment should be made wasn't clear yet.

Sometime near dawn he finally dozed off.

When he woke a couple of hours later, his mind felt muddled and more weary than it had before the sleep. A shower helped some, and so did brushing his teeth to rid himself of the taste of too many cigarettes and too much booze.

They went back to the Original Pantry Cafe for breakfast, and again he ate a huge meal. Jody picked listlessly at a couple of eggs, maintaining a strained silence.

He seemed to have a problem and Tom couldn't figure out what it was. That worried him. Used to be, he could read Jody loud and clear. Now there seemed to be secret places where he wasn't welcome. It wasn't right.

When they got back to the motel, Tom fished the phone book out and looked up Kowalski's name. It was just that simple. He rubbed the listing with the tip of one finger.

The flame inside flared a little.

At last, he became aware that Jody was pacing the room like a restless cat. Tom watched him for a moment, then threw a crumpled cigarette pack at him. "What's up?"

124

"Nothing." But the single word didn't sound very convincing.

"Something's wrong. Why don't you just tell me?"

"I said, nothing's wrong," Jody snapped. He rubbed his forehead, as if it hurt. "I need a Coke. Want one?"

Tom shook his head.

"Okay." Jody picked up a handful of change from the dresser and left the room.

Tom frowned. Jody was lying to him; something was wrong. He got up and followed his brother from the room. He stood on the balcony outside and leaned far enough over the iron railing to see the soda machine below. Jody wasn't there. However, Tom could also see a phone booth and inside the booth, Jody.

Tom felt a tightening in his gut.

He walked lightly in his stockinged feet down the steps and across the small brick courtyard. Jody didn't even know he was there, until Tom reached out with one hand and depressed the lever to break the phone connection.

Jody spun around to face him. He compressed his lips tightly, then slowly replaced the receiver. "That was a stupid thing to do," he said.

"Who the hell were you talking to?"

Instead of answering, Jody pushed by him and walked to the soda machine. He dropped several coins in and took out a can of Coke. Still without speaking, he turned and went back upstairs.

Tom trailed behind.

Jody sat on his bed and opened the soda. Tom remained standing, looking down at him. "I asked you a question, Jody. Who were you talking to?"

"Don't play Big Daddy with me." Jody's voice held a coldness that Tom had never heard there before. "I'm not fucking ten years old."

"Who were you talking to? Please, Jody?" This time he spoke pleadingly.

"A friend of mine." Jody spit the words out.

"What friend?"

"Just a goddamned friend." He bent his head back and stared up at Tom. "For Chrissake, Tommy, do you think I don't know anybody? After ten years? I'm not a frigging monk. I wasn't locked up. I had a job and a home and some friends. Not many, but a few."

Tom looked at him, trying to figure out who this angry man was. What had happened to his brother? "Okay," he said finally. "I don't give a damn. But did you tell this good friend where you're at?"

"No. I didn't tell him anything, because the line was busy."

"Does he know about me?"

Jody shook his head. "I just told him I had some business." He took a quick gulp of Coke. "I had to tell him something, after four years. I couldn't just let him come home and find me gone. But he doesn't know anything about what's going on."

"Why did you call him?"

"Just to talk."

Tom wanted this conversation to end; he didn't like the ache in his chest. "Okay," he said. "Never mind. It doesn't matter."

Jody finished the soda and crushed the can.

Tom crawled under the bed and found his shoes. "We need to get busy."

"You understand about the phone call?" Jody pressed.

"Yeah, sure, why not?"

Jody didn't seem satisfied, but he didn't say anymore.

The apartment building looked like a dump to Tom. He had thought that a fascist pig like Kowalski would have a better place to live.

They sat parked on the street in front of the building for a long time, watching the comings and goings on the block.

126

"Come on," Tom said finally, opening the car door. "Let's go take a closer look."

"What if he's there?"

"Are you kidding? At this time of the day? No way. The supercop is out chasing the bad guys. He likes doing that better than anything else he does."

"Maybe it's his day off."

"Shit, he probably never takes a day off. He's only alive when he's working. Kowalski is like that. Believe me, I know."

Tom knew.

He knew because once upon a time he and Kowalski spent forty-eight hours together in an interrogation room. They got real close. Even more than those hours, though, Tom could remember the look on the cop's face at the very moment they met.

Tom was hiding under the porch, listening to the roar of a sudden thunderstorm above. He was scared and crying. A car stopped nearby and he could hear the voices of men as they searched for him. They even had a dog.

But it was Kowalski who found him, who hit him with the glare of a powerful flashlight. Tom blinked, squinted through the brightness, and saw that face. The look was clear: the hunter victorious. It was a look he never forgot.

"Somebody else might be there. His wife or something." Jody's voice brought him back to the present.

"Then we won't go in," he said, exasperated. Jody should be showing a little more enthusiasm, he thought.

They stopped in the lobby to check the row of mailboxes. Jody spotted the right one; Kowalski lived in apartment 511. The hallway was empty as they climbed the stairs and found the right door.

Tom knocked a couple of times, but as he had expected, there wasn't any answer. He smirked triumphantly at Jody.

A cop, he thought and told Jody, should have an

efficient lock on his door. The one Kowalski had was hardly better than no lock at all. Within two minutes, they were inside.

Some unopened mail had been dropped on a small table just inside the door. Tom picked it up and looked through it quickly. It was boring, just bills and ads. No wonder Kowalski hadn't bothered to open it. He dropped it back onto the table.

The living room was small, made even smaller by the clutter of old newspapers and cast-off clothes. Tom shook his head. Years of institutional living had given him an almost compulsive sense of neatness. This place was a real mess. Maybe crime didn't pay, but neither, it seemed, did being a cop.

Jody picked up the framed photo of a kid and a woman who needed to lose some weight. "His family?"

"Must be." Tom looked at the back of the picture and read the date penciled there. "Shit, this was taken the same year I got sent away."

Jody wiped the frame with the edge of his shirt and replaced it on the shelf. He sat on the couch as Tom made a tour of the rest of the place. The refrigerator was almost empty. The bathroom was reasonably neat, but the small bedroom was another clutter of clothes, papers, and several used plates and glasses.

What a slob.

If Tom had still felt any fear of Kowalski, this apartment had ended it. Somebody who lived like this couldn't be any kind of a threat to a man with a mind like his.

He went back into the living room and joined his brother on the couch. He lit a cigarette.

Jody sighed. "So?" he said. "Are we just going to sit here and kill him when he comes in?" The voice held only mild curiosity.

"You in some kind of frigging hurry?" Tom asked. "What's the matter, can't wait to get back to your friend? Is that it?"

Jody lowered his head. "It's not like that."

"You can cut out anytime, you know? I can get along without your help."

"Don't say that, Tommy. Jesus Christ, I'm doing my best. I'm trying to be what you want. I'm trying to be a good brother."

"Yeah, well."

There was a brief silence.

Jody sighed again and shifted position. "I only wanted to know what was going to happen next. That's all. I was just wondering when we'd be able to start living a normal life again."

Tom didn't even know what a normal life was anymore. Didn't Jody understand that? Could the two of them really go off someplace and be happy like other people? Even after all that had happened?

Even after the boys?

But all that was too scary to think about right now. He shook his head. "No, we're not gonna kill him yet. That would be too easy. He has to suffer first. Just like he made us suffer."

"Maybe. I guess so. But what are we going to do?"

"I don't know yet. We'll work on it. But for now, let's get out of here before the bastard turns up." They started for the door.

Tom saw a fat Magic Marker lying on the table next to the mail. He smiled as an idea struck him and picked it up.

Jody, standing by the door, watched. "What're you doing?"

"Leaving a message for my friend, the pig. Just for old time's sake." He leaned close to the wall and printed the words in big purple letters.

When he was finished, he recapped the marker carefully and put it into his shirt pocket.

129

They went back to the car and sat there, waiting. Jody ran out once to the store on the corner for some beers and hero sandwiches.

It was hot.

Finally, late in the afternoon, a bright red and yellow Jeep squealed to a stop and a man jumped out.

It had been a long time, but Tom recognized Kowalski immediately. He was a little heavier, with a moustache that hadn't been there before and a bit less hair on top, but it was him, all right.

Tom didn't know what he had expected to feel at that moment, but it couldn't have been the deep cold that was filling him now. There was the man who had ruined his life, dragged him away from home and Jody, sent him to ten years of hell. Tom thought he should have wanted to rage. But all he could do was watch as Kowalski disappeared into the building.

"You okay?" Jody asked.

Tom realized that he was gripping the beer can with both hands, crushing it.

"Tommy?"

He shook his head to clear it. "I'm okay," he said. "I'm okay. But let's get out of here. Back to the motel."

Jody started the car.

"We have to hurt him," Tom said suddenly. "I don't even care so much about killing him. Just so long as we can make him hurt. Hurt bad."

He threw the squashed beer can out the window.

130

Chapter 25

IT was a nice day for a funeral.

There is a myth in some circles that a murderer will sometimes show up at the burial of his victim. Because of that belief, cops will often attend such services. In Spaceman's experience, no one had ever once caught a killer that way. Myths, though, die hard.

Not many people turned out to see Peter Lowe laid to rest. A young black minister said the words and almost sounded as if he meant some of them. Listening were the representative of the cemetery, a reporter from the *Times* (young, brash, and new to the police beat, who was there hoping that the cops would put the drop on the killer right at the graveside, and she'd have an exclusive), Spaceman, and Blue.

That, at least, was the main group. Three others hung on the periphery. One was an old woman dressed all in black. Spaceman knew her. Her hobby was attending funerals and she cried very nicely.

Second was a young boy wearing dark shades that hid most of his face.

Finally, and hovering so far back that he might have been waiting for another service, was a fat man.

The old lady didn't interest Spaceman and Blue. The boy did. Most of all, the fat man caught their attention. Even myths had to have some truth to them, Spaceman thought.

The coffin and flowers must have cost a bundle; it certainly wasn't your hum-drum potter's field burial. Perhaps impressed by the cost of the thing, the minister put all he had into the service. He read a poem about children dying that Spaceman had never heard before.

131

As the brief service ended, Spaceman moved toward the boy, and Blue trailed the fat man, hoping to get his license number.

The boy was nervous. Or maybe he just didn't like funerals much. Spaceman offered him a cigarette, which he accepted with alacrity and smoked quickly; his movements seemed jerky, desperate. He was hurting bad.

"You knew Pete, did you?" Spaceman asked.

The boy nodded.

"Tell me about it. Starting with your name."

"Martin." That was all, not even any way of telling whether it was his first name or his last. Maybe it was neither. But Spaceman didn't press the subject; he knew that it probably didn't matter. "I just knew him, that's all. You know people, don't you?" Even his smartass tone had a listless quality to it.

"Yeah, I know people. Mostly I know other cops. You two in the same line of work, were you?"

Martin seemed to be looking at him, but there was no way of knowing for sure behind the glasses. "Hell, no. That's not my bag."

Spaceman wished he could see the boy's eyes, but it wasn't that important. Martin was trying to play it cool, but he was strung out. The kid would probably be buried himself within three months. "You have any idea who might have wanted Pete on ice?"

"Nope, nope." He jiggled nervously. "Hey, you know, man, I just felt bad about him buying it like that. I seen in the paper that he was getting stuck in the ground today, and I thought that maybe somebody who knew him should - be here." The speech wore him out; he took a deep breath. "Pete was okay. He was okay, that's all."

"He was a user, right?"

A quick glance around. "Pills is all. Not the hard stuff. He didn't even smoke. Made him sick, he always said."

Spaceman saw Blue approaching. There wasn't anything

else to be learned from Martin. He did manage to squeeze the address of a downtown crashpad out of him, supposedly a place where he might be reached, should the necessity arise. Spaceman wouldn't have bet the rent money on that, but he let the boy go.

Martin started away, then paused long enough to watch the sod being replaced over the grave. He shook his head and walked away quickly. It would have been nice if the sight made him think a little bit about his own fragile mortality, but Spaceman knew it wouldn't. Pete was already a part of history, except that for Martin, like for so many others in this city, there was no such thing as a past. There was just the future. Martin would keep looking ahead, never back, and still he wouldn't see disaster coming. Until it was too late.

Blue reached the spot where Spaceman was standing. "Nothing?"

"*Nada*. Of course." Spaceman turned to look at him. "Believe it or not, Martin was just a good buddy. He thought Pete ought to have one standing by." He shrugged. "Sometimes even the creeps of this world will do something nice.

"Well, maybe our plump friend felt the same way. Maybe he just wanted to do something humane."

"You run the license?"

"The car is registered to a guy named Donelli. Managed to find out that he owns a drugstore in Westwood."

"A drugstore?"

Blue nodded as they turned and headed back toward the car.

"Martin just told me that young Peter's single vice was pills. He liked to take them."

"That's interesting."

"I think so."

It wasn't until they were in the car and headed for Westwood that Spaceman mentioned the message he'd found scrawled on the wall of his apartment the previous day. " 'You'll be sorry,' it said. That's all, in big purple letters."

Blue frowned. "What was taken?"

"Not a damned thing. Except the purple pen." He shrugged. "Probably just kids."

"You think so?"

"Sure. What else?"

"Maybe you have a secret enemy out there somewhere."

Spaceman snorted. "I have a lot of enemies, but not many of them are subtle enough for this kind of thing. Most of them would just lay a two-by-four alongside my head if they wanted to make a point."

Blue hesitated before speaking again. "If I say something personal you won't take it wrong, will you?"

"I might. Say it anyway."

"You think maybe it could have been your son?"

"Robbie?" The possibility hadn't even occured to him.

"Well, I just thought he might be really pissed about something," Blue explained quickly. "That might explain why he ran away and this could be just more of the same."

Spaceman wondered if maybe he should blow up at a suggestion like that. But as he thought about it, and about what he'd learned the last few days, he was forced to consider the idea seriously. "I don't think Robbie would have done it," he said. "But who the hell knows? I never thought he'd steal or shack up with some rich bitch, either."

If Blue was surprised by the revelations, he didn't show it. "Well, it probably wouldn't hurt to keep your eyes open for the next few days. Just in case."

"Just in case. So I can fight off the flying two-by-fours, right?"

The drugstore had a sleek façade, fitting the image of the greenery-bedecked mall in which it was located. Not exactly the kind of place a street kid like Pete would be expected to feed his pill habit. They spotted the car from the cemetery parked nearby. As they sat there, a steady stream of customers moved in and out of the store. None of them looked like anything but straight Republican ticketers. "Well," Spaceman said finally, "shall we converse with Mr. Donelli?"

They got out of the car and walked into Donelli's. Spaceman loosened his tie as he moved. The chic store was stocked with trendy greeting cards, best-selling paperbacks, and all the other necessities of life in the fast lane.

Donelli himself was at the back, manning the pharmacy counter. He had shed the dark sport coat he'd worn to the funeral, wearing instead a lime green smock over his shirt and tie. They waited patiently until he finished filling a prescription for an old lady bent and twisted with age, and then Spaceman leaned across the counter. "We need to talk, Donelli," he said quietly.

The man looked up and saw them. A faint but visible shudder passed through his body. He had a beer gut that shook. "I'm busy," he said, trying to sound brusque, but coming off scared.

"Get unbusy. Or we can go downtown, if you'd rather."

He blanched. "Come into my office." He released the hidden catch on the gate and they passed through. "Dinah, take over out here, please."

A young woman in a matching smock appeared from somewhere and nodded. "Sure thing, Mr. D."

Donelli led them into his office, closed the door firmly, then turned to look at them. "It was really stupid of me."

"What was?" Spaceman asked.

"You know. Going to that damned funeral."

"Why did you?"

Donelli sat behind a cluttered desk. They could almost see his mind clicking behind the thick glasses he wore. "I went," he said finally, "because I knew the boy. That's no crime."

"Depends. How did you know him?"

"What do you mean, how?"

Spaceman sat in a chair facing Donelli. Blue remained standing by the door. "I mean this. Pete was a street hustler. He lived by having sex with men and getting paid for it. Nobody can work all the time, though, and Pete had a hobby. His hobby was swallowing pills. It just seems a little curious to me that somebody like him would number among his acquaintances a man like you. Successful businessman. Married, I'll bet, with a couple of kids."

Donelli nodded miserably. "Three," he said.

"There you go. Just like I figured, the perfect American family."

"Except for one thing," Blue put in. "The simple fact that it isn't enough for you. Maybe you need more. Maybe you need something only a kid like Pete can give."

The man's face was by now almost the same shade of green as his smock. "You have no right to say things like that. You have no proof of anything. I knew Pete, but it was nothing like that. We just knew each other. Go away, please, and leave me alone. Before I call my lawyer."

Spaceman nodded. "You're right. We can't prove a thing, so I guess you're off the hook. But humor me. How about if I just theorize a little?" When Donelli didn't respond, he glanced at Blue.

"I don't mind," Blue said cheerfully. "Theorize to your heart's content."

"Thank you. The way I see it is, Donelli here likes to have his kicks with boys. Young boys. Now, I'm not in the business of passing moral judgment, no matter how sick and disgusting anyone might be. Different strokes, you know?"

"That's a nice liberal attitude," Blue said.

"Thanks again. Anyway, Pete liked pills, all the pretty little bits of color that made him feel good...and maybe made what he did with creeps like Donelli here a little more bearable. So I figure they had what is known as a reciprocal relationship. Sex for pills. Or pills for sex, depending on how you look at it."

Donelli was staring at the top of his desk. "You can't prove anything," he repeated dully.

"True. But we can make your life very unhappy from now on, and I think we will."

Donelli made a gagging sound which was followed by a silence that lasted for minutes. Then he sighed deeply. "Pete was supposed to meet me downtown," he said in a whisper. They had to strain to hear him. "The night he died, we were supposed to get together at the bus station. He called that afternoon to set it up."

"Where was he calling from?"

"At the beach someplace, that's all I know."

"How was he going to get downtown to meet you?"

"I suppose the same way he got everywhere. Hitch. But he never showed up. I waited over an hour, but he never came." Donelli was starting to cry, but Spaceman figured the tears were for himself, not for Peter Lowe. "I shouldn't have gone today. It was stupid. But Pete was a nice boy."

They didn't answer, and in a few more minutes, they were ready to go. There was nothing they could do to Donelli, except warn him to shape up, but Spaceman felt a grim satisfaction as they departed. The fat pig would think twice the next time he paid some kid to get on his knees in front of him.

They spent several hours cruising the streets that night, talking to the kids and the crazies, bluffing a little, making some threats and spreading some petty cash. It all added up to nothing.

Spaceman also flashed Robbie's picture around, but that netted him no more than did their questions about the murdered boys.

It was after midnight by the time they gave up and

137

parted company. Spaceman didn't feel like facing his apartment alone, so he went to Mandy's. She was having a party and most of the guests still lingered, working on the last of the wine and the joints. They all knew Spaceman and knew he was a cop. He went first into the bedroom to shed his jacket and hide the gun. It bugged Mandy when he did that; she said it was like accusing her friends of being criminals or something. He never bothered to debate the issue with her.

Turned for the moment at least into a civilian, he joined the circle sitting on the living room floor. Someone handed him a Dixie cup filled with cheap red wine and someone else passed the joint. He drank first, then inhaled noisily. In only a few minutes he had started to relax.

They were heatedly arguing the merits of some French movie that he hadn't seen and didn't want to see, so he felt no obligation even to listen. Instead, he stretched out on the rug to let the pot, the wine, and Mandy's massaging hands do their job. He could almost forget the case and Robbie.

Which was why he kept coming back.

That and the sex.

One of the jerks kept giving him dirty looks. Maybe he had figured on scoring with Mandy tonight. Too bad, Spaceman thought airily as Mandy ushered everyone else out, including the disappointed Romeo. Too bad.

When they were alone, Mandy led him by the hand to the waterbed. He was too whacked to do much more than just lie there and enjoy the touch of her hands and mouth roaming over his body. He concentrated on the stars overhead.

Stars. Like the ones on Hollywood Boulevard. Like the galaxies Pete probably saw when he swallowed the pills. Better make-believe constellations than the reality of Donelli.

Stars. Poor Chris, who probably would have sold his

soul to have his name on the Boulevard, and who died in futile pursuit of that dumb dream.

It was all too much for Spaceman and he stopped thinking about it, concentrating instead on what Mandy's mouth was doing. It got better and better; he built and built until everything came together perfectly.

The universe exploded in his head.

Blue was having a hard time getting to sleep, so he sat in the dark, drinking. He knew the reason: This was the anniversary of his father's death. Some things hung on a lot longer than they should have. It wasn't exactly an act of mourning that kept him awake. Not the mourning of his old man's death anyway. Maybe it was just the sense of loss and failure that had been their relationship.

Like the hunting trip when he was twelve.

Hank Maguire was a man of action and he loved hunting. Probably it was that very lust for action that made him the success he was in business. He wanted his son to take after him in that. So when he ordered, Blue took the rifle and donned the clothes, and into the woods they went.

But when push came to shove, when Blue had the deer within his sights, he couldn't pull the trigger.

"You lack the killer instinct," his father said in a cold and distant voice. "No man can be a success in this world without the goddamned killer instinct." Then he killed the deer himself.

He had the right instincts.

Blue poured another shot and smiled into the darkness. Too bad the old man hadn't been able to see him in Nam. It would have made him proud the way his boy learned to kill.

Unfortunately, by the time Blue got out of the POW camp and home, Hank Maguire was dead, so Blue never knew what his father thought about it all.

Blue was disgusted with himself. All this maudlin thought was pointless. He needed to go to bed and get some sleep, so that tomorrow he could be sharp. They had to find out who was killing kids.

He dumped the rest of the drink down the drain, rinsed the glass carefully and went to bed.

Spaceman woke up sometime in the blackest part of the night. He went to the john, then hunted for his cigarettes, in his jacket pocket. Instead of the cigarettes, he pulled out the creased memo from Lompoc. Why the hell was he still carrying that around?

He crumpled the paper to throw it away.

Then, instead, he shoved it back into his pocket. Forgetting the cigarette, he went back to bed.

Chapter 26

JODY didn't like what they were doing.

"It's too fuckin' dangerous," he complained for the hundredth time that day. They were sitting in the newly acquired car, parked outside a drug rehab center on Spring Street. Kowalski and a man who was probably his partner were inside.

"We have to take a few chances," Tom said. "Or else we'll never get anywhere. Risks are necessary."

"I don't even know what the hell we're supposed to be doing besides following Kowalski all over the damned city." He was slumped against the car door, the *Times* in his lap.

"I know."

"Do you really, Tommy? For sure? Have you actually thought this thing through?"

Tom smiled. "Sure. I've had ten years to think it through. After all, I didn't have a job and a lot of friends to keep me busy. There was just me and my thoughts."

Jody sighed, but didn't say anything. His head was pounding again, and he realized that the headache had been there since the night Tom got out of the hospital.

That seemed like a disloyal thought, and he squelched it immediately.

Jody knew for damned sure that he, himself, hadn't thought any of this through. In the beginning, all he wanted was to have Tom out of that place. He'd done enough time. But now Jody was finding out that there was a lot of difference between visiting his brother for an hour or so every few months, and being around him all the time.

141

He used to think that having his brother with him would make life better.

Better.

Shit, what a joke that was. Nothing was working out the way he'd planned. Now he had a headache all the time, he was scared, and he was a killer.

He shoved that thought away, too.

Life before had been good. After all the rough years, things had finally fallen into place. He liked working in the bookstore. He liked the little house that was almost in the country. And he especially liked living with Jerry.

Jerry. What must he be thinking? Was he hurt by the way things had happened? Jody hoped not. Maybe someday he could explain it all to him. Maybe someday he could go back to the funny little house and his life there.

But for right now, he was stuck. He owed Tommy.

Jody sighed and lifted the paper again.

Tom kept his eyes on the door of the shabby building. He didn't want to take a chance of missing his prey. Not much chance of that happening, of course, with them riding around in that fancy car.

He knew that Jody was getting restless and he heard the sigh. It bothered him, made him think that maybe Jody was slipping away. He reached out to rub his brother's arm. "Hey, it's gonna be okay."

"Yeah, if you say so, Tommy."

"I say so." He glanced down at the newspaper and Kowalski's name seemed to jump off the page at him. "What's that about?"

Jody read quickly. "It's about Pete and Chris," he said softly. "About what happened to them in the park."

"No shit? It's in the paper?"

"Yeah. A small story."

"Kowalski's on the case?"

"Seems to be. He had no comment, but a spokesman

142

said they have a number of strong leads and an arrest is imminent."

Tom laughed. "Hell, he doesn't have nothing. That's just bullshit for the press." He shook his head, still chuckling. "You know, it's pretty ironic. That's what it is, ironic. Him being the one on this thing."

Jody didn't laugh. "He caught you once before. What makes you so sure it can't happen again?"

Tom straightened. "I was just a kid then. What did I know? He won't be so lucky this time." An idea started to take form, ever so slowly, in Tom's mind. "Besides," he said thoughtfully, "maybe he won't have the chance to catch me this time. Maybe we'll catch him first."

"What the hell does that mean?"

He wasn't sure yet; it was all still too vague, but he was starting to get a little excited anyway. "Maybe we'll snatch him."

"Terrific." Jody sounded sarcastic. "And then do what?"

Tom smiled again. "Whatever we want."

It got boring following the two cops in their fancy car, so when they stopped for lunch at a place on Melrose, Tom told Jody just to keep driving. There was no risk. He knew, now, that he could reach out and put the drop on Kowalski whenever he wanted. They drove to a Pizza Hut and shared a large pepperoni and a pitcher of beer.

When the pizza was gone and they were working on the last of the beer, Jody leaned closer and spoke in a low voice. "Were you serious about what you said before?"

"About what?"

"Snatching the cop."

Tom glanced around, but the lunch rush was over and no one was sitting near them. "I think so. I think I was real serious."

"Kidnapping is a bad rap, you know."

He just looked at Jody, who finally realized the

143

absurdity of what he'd said, and shrugged. "Anyway," Tom went on, "I'm crazy, right? They've been saying for years that I'm off the wall. So I'm not responsible."

"What about me?"

"Maybe you're crazy, too."

Jody blinked, but didn't say anything.

Tom emptied the last of the beer from the pitcher into his mug. "The thing is, something like this takes planning." His mind was racing too fast, and he lighted a cigarette to help calm himself down a little. "First of all, we need to find a place. Someplace private, where nobody would think to look. That'll be our headquarters."

"What kind of place?"

"Hell, I don't know. Use your imagination, why don't you? I can't do all the thinking."

They left the restaurant and got back into the car. Jody inserted the key (this driver had been more considerate than most) and then he just sat there.

"What's wrong?" Tom asked.

"I know a place," he said. "But maybe it's not right."

"What place?"

Jody shook his head. "I'd rather show you."

"Okay. Show me."

They headed east out of the city, and then north. Tom was curious about where they were going, but he didn't ask. Jody's face was closed and secretive; it was clear that he was on some dangerous edge, and the last thing Tom needed or wanted was for Jody to fall.

They finally left the freeway, turning onto a narrower highway and then sometime later onto a dirt road. "How'd you ever find a place way out here anyway?"

"Came out here once," was all Jody said. "Before it closed down."

At last, a sign appeared. Weathered and in danger of falling, it was still readable. HOLLY POINT AMUSEMENT PARK.

144

Jody stopped the car and stared at the sign. "It was a nice place," he said. "But the people running it went broke. They couldn't compete."

Tom wondered when Jody had come out here, and with whom, but again he decided not to ask. Instead, he just opened the car door. "Let's check it out. See if we can get in."

That proved to be no problem. A few strikes with a rock and the padlock snapped open.

Once inside, it was easy to see why the park hadn't been able to survive in a *Star Wars* world. Holly Point was an old-fashioned place, with a merry-go-round, ferris wheel, and a few other rides, as well as several buildings.

There was a sense of sadness about the place, but Tom liked it.

He walked around for almost an hour, sizing things up, his mind filled with possibilities. The whole plan seemed to fall into order now.

"This is perfect, Jody," he said, meaning it. He gave his brother a tight hug.

Jody didn't say anything, but he returned the hug.

Jody stopped to take a deep breath before going through the door. The name of the bar was the Sweatshop. It was Tom's idea to come here and meet somebody to party with, instead of just picking a boy up on the street.

His reasoning was clear, at least to him. By changing the way they worked, they could confuse the cops. Shake old Kowalski up a little. Also, nobody much cared about street kids, so the case was only worth a small story in the *Times*. By picking somebody more important, they could up the stakes.

Jody thought it sounded pretty stupid, but he didn't have the strength to argue, so here he was. It had been a long time since he'd hit the bar scene, not since meeting Jerry, and Jody wasn't sure he could still hack it.

Music assaulted his ears as he entered. The place was crowded with customers, mostly young college and professional types. Jody, in his good slacks and a clean shirt, fit right in. He made his way to the bar and ordered a beer. It wasn't long before somebody slid onto the neighboring stool.

"Hi," a voice said.

"Hi," Jody said, glancing sideways. The guy looked about his own age, and he wasn't a hustler. Or at least he wasn't cheap. His clothes were expensive and there was gold around his neck, on both wrists, and on several fingers.

"I'm Steve," he said.

"Jody."

They talked for about twenty minutes, the kind of bar chatter that passed for sociability in this world. Steve, it turned out, was a music student at UCLA. Classical stuff mostly; he was working on a symphony of his own now. He wasn't into the bar scene—he laughed when he said that, adding, "Who is? But here we all are anyway, right?"

Right, Jody thought. All of us here and wondering why.

Steve lived in Santa Monica with someone named J.P. They had this really great relationship. But J.P. was a lot older and liked a quiet kind of life. Luckily, he was also very understanding and didn't mind if Steve went out alone.

Jody didn't say much beyond what was necessary to keep Steve talking. At last, weary of it all, he spoke up. "My car is right outside," he said. "How about going out there for a few minutes?"

He'd decided that a fast trip outside was all that Steve would agree to. Anything else might smack too much of emotional involvement, and he was true, in his way, to the missing and tolerant J.P.

After the obligatory hesitation, Steve agreed, and he even picked up Jody's tab.

Only Jody saw Tom duck out of sight as they approached the car. When he opened the door, an arm emerged and the knife was at Steve's throat before he could react. He lost most of his tan.

"What the hell is going on?" he managed to say. There was a croak in the words.

Tom smiled. "A party is going on. You're the guest of honor." He pulled until Steve was inside the car and they were sitting side by side in the back seat.

Jody got behind the wheel. "His name is Steve," he said flatly.

"Nice name. You like good times, Steve?" Tom held the knife so that its point pressed lightly at Steve's throat.

"You want money? There's almost two hundred dollars in my wallet. Take it. Take the chains. The watch."

Tom shook his head. "That makes me feel bad, Steve. You must think we're just a couple of punks. Is that what you think?"

Steve didn't say anything.

Tom studied him and then frowned. "He's a little old."

"Shit, Tommy, you're the one who sent me into the bar. There weren't any kids in there."

"Okay, okay. He'll do."

"Don't hurt me," Steve whispered. "Please. Please."

"We only want to have a good time. Play along with us and nothing will happen to you."

His lips moved silently; maybe he was praying.

"Let's go to the beach," Tom said. He knew they couldn't risk the park again. Besides, he liked the beach. A good place for a party.

They killed him, of course. Once he was dead, Tom decided that not to take the money would be really dumb. He might have taken the jewelry, too, but Jody got stubborn about that.

They left the body in the shadows of an old hot dog stand.

147

Instead of going straight back to the motel, Tom ordered Jody to detour to Vermont Avenue. It was very late and all the lights were off in Kowalski's apartment. Tom hunted through the glove compartment until he found an old envelope. Then he took out the purple pen. He kept the note brief and to the point.

Jody took it inside and slipped it under Kowalski's door.

Driving back to the motel, Jody seemed disgusted. "You like this, don't you?" he said. "It's all just a big game to you, and you're having fun."

"Maybe," Tom said. His eyes were closed. "But maybe I figure it's my turn."

Chapter 27

SPACEMAN found the note just before dawn.

He didn't usually get up that early, of course. But as he was finding out lately, the old bladder didn't operate with quite the same efficiency as it had in earlier years. A beer too many before bed and he paid the price.

Standing in the bathroom, he decided he was thirsty. It was as he detoured to the kitchen for a glass of orange juice that he saw the paper.

It didn't register at first. His mind, the small part of it that was awake, was on the cold juice. If not for the fact that he'd impulsively straightened the living room before calling it a night, the paper could have escaped his attention completely. But because the floor was relatively clean, the square of gleaming whiteness caught his eye in the pale morning light.

He walked over and picked it up.

At first, all that struck him was the purple ink, and he felt a nervous tightening in his stomach. If Blue's theory was right, this might be another message from Robbie.

But then he read the note and he knew differently. The tight feeling became a dull ache. There wasn't much on the paper. A crudely drawn map, an arrow pointing, and a few words: "Dear Kowalski, this ones for you. See you soon and then you'll be SORRY."

It wasn't signed.

Spaceman found an envelope in a drawer and carefully slid the message into it. He knew what would be waiting for him at the spot marked by X on the map. Another body.

He called Blue and once he was sure the other man was awake, told him about the note. He was quiet for a moment after hearing the news. "What the hell is going on here?" he said finally.

"Do I fucking know?" Spaceman said.

"Could be a hoax. Maybe somebody just saw your name in the paper. There are all kinds of crazies out there." Blue paused. "And if it is a hoax, Robbie could still be behind it."

Spaceman shrugged silent and unseen agreement. None of what Blue was saying eased the pain in his gut. "Pick me up," he said.

"We're going out there on our own?"

"Yeah, we are. I am anyway."

Blue sighed over the line. "I'll be there as soon as I can."

"Thanks."

"Hell," he said lightly. "What's a partner for?"

Spaceman was waiting on the sidewalk when the Porsche pulled up a short time later. He got in without a word, and Blue kept quiet, too. The only noise was the soft chatter of the police radio. It was a slow morning in Los Angeles.

"Heard they finally got those fires under control," Blue said at last. When there wasn't any response, he said, "Maybe it's an omen. Maybe it means that the weather is going to break, and we're going to bust these creeps."

"Maybe."

Blue gave up.

There was no more conversation, not even when they had reached their destination, and were standing poised on the top of a steep bank, looking down upon a ramshackle hot dog stand. Finally, they went down toward the shack, Spaceman in the lead, making his way clumsily through the sand in slick-soled loafers. Blue moved more easily in his Pumas.

They saw the body at the same moment; no real attempt

had been made to hide it. The bloody form of a young man was sprawled in the shadow of the building. The other killings had been bad enough, but what had been done to this human being made the taste of bile rise in Spaceman's throat. He turned away and swallowed hard.

Blue wavered a little.

"Damn," Spaceman said. "Damndamndamn."

Gaining control of himself, Blue bent down and poked carefully through the pile of clothes. He came up with a wallet and flipped it open. "Steven Lawrence," he said, glancing quickly at the face of the dead man and comparing it to the image on the driver's license. "A shitload of credit cards. No money. That's the first time they took the money."

"It's the first time there was any money. Pete had a dollar and Chris just a couple of bucks. This guy probably had a bundle. Check out the shiny stuff he's wearing. Wonder why they left that."

Blue was still flipping through the wallet. "He's a student at UCLA. Member of the auto club and some private health spa. A real solid citizen. Not like Pete and Chris."

Spaceman nodded glumly. "That might be what got him killed."

Blue handed him the wallet and started back toward the car to radio in.

Spaceman was mad. The case, bad enough to begin with, had taken an even nastier turn. He felt, stupidly, responsible. And he didn't like the feeling that maybe all these people were dead because of him.

It was several hours later before they were able to get away from the beach and into the office. McGannon was waiting. He sat behind the desk and surveyed them sourly. "So?"

Spaceman sat; again, Blue remained standing by the door. "So what?" Spaceman said.

"The stiffs seem to be piling up."

"They do."

"And I hear the killers are sending you mash notes." McGannon held up a Xerox of the note; the original was already in the lab. "Interesting."

"Maybe you think so."

"And what do you think?"

Spaceman shrugged.

"That's a great answer."

"What the hell do you want me to say?"

"How about that you've got the crazies that are doing this?"

Blue stepped forward. "Maybe the perps are somebody he busted before."

"Maybe," McGannon agreed. "I guess somebody should start going through his files."

"Somebody already is. It doesn't take a damned college degree to figure that out."

Blue accepted that with a nod and stepped back to his place by the door.

McGannon put both hands behind his head and stretched. "So what are you plans for the rest of this glorious summer day?"

"To backtrack Lawrence."

"Do you think that will gain you any more than tracking down the first two did?"

"Maybe not," Spaceman said, "but do you have a better idea?"

McGannon smiled. "That's the pleasure of command. I don't have to have a better idea. I just get to tell you when your ideas suck. But I won't do that right now." He relaxed. "Come up with something pretty soon, will you? I've already had calls from a couple of the angrier gay groups in town. They're wondering if this case is being pursued with full enthusiasm."

"Screw them. I like their sudden social concern. Why

didn't they do something for Peter and Chris before it was too late?"

McGannon shrugged. "I didn't ask."

"Ask next time."

They stopped at the diner for some breakfast before setting out in quest of Steven Lawrence. Joe was behind the counter, of course, and he already knew about the latest killing. He offered up some encouraging words with the under-cooked eggs and over-done sausage, but they didn't feel much encouraged.

The standard *To Be Notified In Case of Accident* in Lawrence's wallet was a Joseph P. Kilbane, and the address was in a posh part of Santa Monica.

They went to the top floor of the very first-class apartment building. Their feet sank into the thick carpeting as Spaceman rang the muted bell.

The door was opened quickly. Spaceman figured that money could deal best with money, so he let Blue take it. There was no doubt that the man facing them was loaded. His clothes were the kind of casual designer things that cost plenty. And Blue, even unshaven and dressed in jeans, seemed to have class. They could relate to each other, probably.

Blue had his shield case in hand. "Mr. Kilbane? We're Detectives Kowalski and Maguire. May we talk with you, please?"

There was no hint of emotion on the finely-chiseled features as Kilbane's eyes swept over the ID and then raised to study Blue's face. "Is it very bad?" The voice sounded like New England.

Blue hesitated. "If we could step in?"

"Yes, of course."

He turned and led the way into a vast living room, furnished with antiques. Everything gleamed. The low table in front of the sofa held a silver tray with a coffee pot and one china cup. Kilbane sat down. "Coffee?" he said automatically.

Blue shook his head. "Mr. Kilbane, you are acquainted with Steven Lawrence? He lives here?"

"Yes."

"I'm afraid we have some bad news for you."

"I knew something had happened when he didn't come home. Is he dead?"

"Yes. Murdered."

The man took a careful sip of the steaming coffee. "Steven never stayed out all night. I hoped that perhaps it was merely an accident of some kind. I hoped..." He shut up and shook his head.

"Did he have any family that should be notified?"

"Not as far as I know. He never mentioned any family." Kilbane stood again and walked across the room to a picture window that looked out over the Pacific. "We lived together almost three years, but I don't know anything about his background."

"Yet you took him in?" Blue glanced around at the artwork decorating the room.

"We got along well. He was a very talented musician, with an astounding future. What a waste." He might have been discussing a stranger.

"We have reason to believe that Steven was killed by the same people who murdered two young boys this week."

Kilbane glanced at him. "The boys in the park, you mean?"

Blue nodded.

"But how can that be? As I understand it, they were both hustlers."

"They were. What about Lawrence?"

"That's absurd." He spoke firmly, yet without heat. It didn't seem possible that anything could stir him to emotion. "Steven was a music student. He did not go with men for money." Now it was Kilbane's turn to look at the

154

room and consider all that it signified. "He didn't need money."

"What was he doing when you met him?"

Kilbane sighed. "I suppose this is necessary."

"We want to catch the killers."

"Yes. The lust for revenge must be satisfied. It won't bring Steve back, of course."

"No," Blue said. "But it might keep others from dying."

Kilbane nodded. "When I met him, he was a music student. The only difference was that then he was a poor student. After we met, he was a very well-off student. He was not, then or now, a cheap hustler."

Spaceman, who was standing somewhat awkwardly in the middle of the room, afraid he might break something, cleared his throat. "Do you know how he might have met the killers?"

There was the briefest silence. "Sometimes he went into the bars. He was young."

"You didn't mind?"

A smile. "Of course I minded. But that was my own private problem."

"Do you have any idea where he might have gone last night?"

"None. We never discussed it."

They asked a few more questions, hoping to fill in some gaps, but nothing new was revealed by Kilbane's answers. As they were leaving, he walked them to the door. "Will there be any problem about the arrangements? I can claim the body?"

"Shouldn't be a problem," Blue said. "Unless some next-of-kin shows up."

"That is unlikely, I think."

They promised to let him know when the body could be claimed and he closed the door.

"Cold fish," Spaceman said.

Blue shrugged.

155

From behind the closed door there was a sudden crash and the sound of china breaking.

"Hell," Blue said.

There was a message from Karen on his desk when they got back to the office. He ignored it. The problem of Robbie was eating away at him, but there was just no time now to think about it. There was also a message from Sharon Engels. Her best guess (guess?) was that Lawrence had not been a willing participant in the sex acts that preceded his death. He was apparently raped, her note said. Repeatedly, including with one or more foreign objects, including a bottle.

So.

There was a pile of other papers in his basket and while waiting for Blue to return from the lab, Spaceman plowed through the accumulation. There was still no picture of the dead boy in Lompoc. He frowned. Probably he should still call up there and check that out, even if he felt sure Robbie was just screwing around with Becky Whatsherface.

One paper marked urgent caught his eye. It was several days old. Typical. He reached for a cigarette and started to read.

As the words penetrated his brain, he forgot the cigarette and about calling Lompoc. He kicked the metal wastebasket that sat beside his desk, sending it flying across the room. It crashed against the water cooler. Petrie, who was standing there drinking from a paper cup, jumped two feet into the air. Water spilled down the front of his shirt and pants. "Shit!" he yelled.

Spaceman was on his feet now. "Goddamn son of bitching motherfuckers! Why the hell doesn't anybody ever tell me anything in this fucking place?"

"Maybe," Petrie suggested, wiping at his clothes with a handkerchief, "because you're never in this fucking place."

"Hell."

156

Spaceman started for McGannon's office. Halfway there, he ran into Blue, literally. Without a word, he grabbed the slender man by one arm and dragged him along.

McGannon looked up, startled, as they burst through the door. "What?"

"You won't believe what I just found on my desk," Spaceman said, releasing his grip on Blue and waving the paper in McGannon's face.

"I suppose you're going to tell me."

Blue watched curiously.

"This is an APB from the Highway Patrol. They thought I might like to know that Thomas Hitchcock escaped last week from that hospital up north."

McGannon appeared to run his mind back over the years. Then he swore softly. "The knife, right?"

"For starters. And a lot of other things."

"Yeah, that was a strange one." McGannon obviously didn't like thinking about the Hitchcock case.

"Kinky is what it was," Spaceman said.

"Somebody want to tell me what the hell is going on?" Blue said.

Spaceman lowered himself into a chair. "Tom Hitchcock. I busted him about ten years ago. The court decided he was looney tunes and sent him up for treatment." He glanced at McGannon. "I don't think it worked."

"Apparently not."

"What'd he do?"

Spaceman grimaced. "Killed his parents. He used a butcher knife on both of them. Bloodiest damned thing I ever saw. At least, until this morning."

"You said kinky?"

"Yeah. The best story we could ever get down was that this Hitchcock and his brother were involved in some closer-than-usual sibling activities."

157

"Incest?"

The very word caused McGannon to sigh; he flicked away some invisible dust on the top of his desk.

"Right," Spaceman went on. "The parents found out and blamed him. The brother was just a kid, like twelve or so. I guess the shit really hit the old fan. They were going to have Tom sent away, arrested or something. He flipped out and filleted them both."

"Jesus. And now he's killing boys."

"Like I said, kinks upon kinks." He waved the paper in the air like a banner. "According to this, Tom used a knife on an aide up north and more or less walked out."

"Well, that would explain the personal angle," Blue said.

Spaceman nodded.

"Whatever happened to the brother?"

"Don't know. What the hell was his name anyway?" He closed his eyes and thought back. "Jody. Jody Hitchcock."

"Tom has a sidekick, right? Two killers. You think it's possible?"

"I think we better see whatever happened to Jody."

"Good idea," McGannon said. "And fast."

Spaceman crumpled the paper and walked out of the office.

Blue followed him.

158

Chapter 28

IT proved surprisingly easy to follow the trail left by Jody Hitchcock over the past ten years. Spaceman remembered him only vaguely, as a skinny little kid with huge dark eyes. The first time he saw Jody was on the night of the murders. He was sitting on the couch, wearing only the bottom half of some thin summer pajamas, when Spaceman came into the room. He was curled into a tight ball, pale but quiet. No tears or hysterics, as might have been expected.

Spaceman, thinking of his own son, knelt beside the couch. "Hey, Jody," he said.

The eyes struggled to focus on him.

"You okay, are you?"

Jody nodded.

"Everything's going to be all right now. You don't have to be scared." A stupid thing to say. How could a child have seen the hacked-up bodies of his parents and not be terrified?

But Jody didn't look terrified. More bewildered. "Don't hurt him," he said in a whisper.

Spaceman leaned closer. "What?"

"Don't hurt Tommy, please. He's my brother."

Spaceman's mouth went dry. "You mean your brother did that?"

Jody nodded. Then a stricken look appeared in his eyes and the first tears began to roll down his face. "I didn't mean to snitch. Forget what I said. It wasn't true." The childish voice was edged with a very grown-up sense of desperation. "It wasn't Tommy," he said. "It was...it was a big Chinaman. That's who did it. A big Chinaman with a knife."

159

Spaceman glanced up at another cop. "Put out an APB on the older son."

Jody grabbed at his sleeve. "Don't hurt him."

Spaceman patted the seemingly fragile hand. "We won't, Jody."

"I shouldn't have told. It's my fault."

Later that night somebody drove the boy over to juvenile hall, and it was there that the paper trail began, a trail that ten years later they could still follow.

Jody was never adopted or even farmed out to a foster family; there were no relatives willing to take him. He stayed in the county home until age seventeen, when he graduated high school. He was an average student, a loner. Once he left the care of the county, his path became a little harder to follow, but with the help of social security it was possible. They found that he'd held a string of jobs, moving around the area restlessly for nearly a year. Then he started working in a small bookstore out in Azusa. He was now a partner in the store, and also in the ownership of a house nearby. Theoretically, he should still be happily in residence there.

Spaceman wouldn't have put much money on that likelihood, however.

It was an odd little house that made Spaceman think, for some reason, of a saltine cracker box. The white paint and blue trim gleamed in the bright sunshine, and flowers covered most of the small front yard.

"I'm in the back," a voice called in answer to the doorbell's chime. "Come on around. Unless you're selling something."

They followed the sound of the voice around the house.

A young man, thirty or so, was pulling weeds from a vegetable patch. He was thin almost to the point of gauntness, starting to turn red from the sun beating down on him, with sandy hair and horn-rimmed glasses. As they

160

approached, he leaned back onto his heels and shaded his eyes with one hand.

"Excuse us," Blue said. "We're trying to locate Jody Hitchcock."

"The whole world is," he replied shortly. Then he grinned sheepishly and wiped at the sweat rolling down his face. "Weeding is damned hard work, isn't it? I don't usually go in for this kind of thing."

"Somebody does. It's a terrific garden," Blue said.

He stood, wiping both hands on his denim shorts. "Yeah, well."

"Jody usually takes care of that, does he?"

"Uh-huh. Who are you anyway? Why are you looking for Jody?"

They introduced themselves. His name was Jerry Potter, and he didn't know where Jody was, either.

"I can't understand it," he said a few minutes later. They were in the house, sitting at the kitchen table, drinking the lemonade he'd offered. It was too sweet.

"So what happened between you and Jody before he left?" Spaceman asked, trying to swallow the sticky drink.

"Nothing. Absolutely nothing." Potter used a paper napkin on his face; he was going to have a hell of a burn. "We have the bookstore and this place. I mean, it's nothing fancy, but it's enough. Things were just fine." He was quiet for a moment, frowning thoughtfully, rubbing the damp napkin back and forth on the table. "I've been thinking, though. I guess it was about three months ago that Jody started to get uptight. Not about us; things were fine there. It was like an attack of nerves. He..." Potter paused again, seeming to search for the right words. "It was like he was always looking over his shoulder. As if he were afraid of being surprised by something."

"Or someone," Blue said.

"Yeah. Then one day he just announced that he had some 'business' to take care of. I wasn't to worry and he'd be back as soon as possible." Potter shrugged, but the darkness in his hazel eyes belied the casual tone of his words. "Then he climbed into his truck and took off."

They exchanged a look; it was thought that Tom Hitchcock had made his getaway in a truck.

"Does Jody have a violent streak?" Spaceman asked. Sitting in this sun-dappled, red-and-white kitchen, it sounded like a ridiculous question.

Potter seemed to think so, too. "Jody? Of course not. He's a quiet guy. A little moody, maybe, but good-natured. Gentle."

"What do you know about his past?"

"Not much. I know he spent a lot of time in an orphanage. His parents died when he was about twelve, I think."

"You know how?"

Potter shook his head. "I know it was traumatic for him."

Blue was quiet, studying the pattern of the tablecloth.

"Did Jody ever mention his brother?"

"Tom? Yes, but only once, just to say that he existed. I always sort of thought that maybe he was in jail or something. But I never pressed Jody about it. It wasn't important to me."

Spaceman lit a cigarette and looked for an ashtray.

Potter got a saucer from the cupboard and gave it to him. "There were letters, I know. But we just didn't talk about the past."

Spaceman scooted the saucer closer. "Jerry, Tom Hitchcock broke out of a hospital for the criminally insane last week."

Beneath the sunburn, his face went ashen. "My god, you're kidding."

"And we think Jody helped him escape. Is still helping him."

162

Potter took a quick gulp of lemonade. "That's very serious, isn't it? I mean, Jody could get into trouble?"

"Yes. A lot of trouble."

"But it was for his brother. Jody's very loyal."

"When Tom Hitchcock was seventeen, he murdered their parents," Spaceman said bluntly.

Potter was speechless now. He just shook his head helplessly.

Blue leaned forward. "Jerry, it gets worse."

He set the glass down very carefully. "Tell me." He sounded like a man clinging to a sinking raft.

Instead of answering directly, Blue pulled a newspaper from his pocket and flopped it open on the table. The faces of Chris and Pete looked up at them.

Potter seemed mesmerized. He ran a fingertip over the images. "You think Jody and his brother did these terrible things?"

Blue nodded.

"Oh God." He took a deep shuddering breath, then met Blue's gaze. "It's Tom's fault, you know. Jody wouldn't do anything like that on his own. His brother must be forcing him."

"Maybe. But we won't know that until we find them."

Potter must have had a store of personal strength. His jaw firmed. "Jody will need me. Will you call me when you find them?"

"You're pretty loyal, too."

"Jody is family. We have a good thing going here and I won't give up on it without a fight."

All three stood. "If you hear from him," Spaceman said, "let us know immediately. That's his best chance."

"I know. I'll call."

They left him standing in the kitchen.

163

Spaceman kicked a tree.

"Feel better?" Blue asked mildly.

"No, damnit, I don't feel better. I think I broke my fucking toe."

"Occupational hazard."

Spaceman leaned against the car. "I just wish I didn't feel like this is all my fault."

"Your fault? How do you figure that?"

"Maybe all these people are dying so that Thomas Hitchcock can get back at me."

"You know that's a load of shit, don't you?"

Spaceman didn't say anything.

Blue sighed. "I think we're going to beat this case, Spaceman."

"You do, huh?"

"Sure. Frankly, I think we make a pretty good team."

Spaceman looked at him for a moment. "Maybe," he admitted grudgingly. "But I keep getting the feeling that I'm playing Jack Klugman to your Tony Randall."

After a moment, Blue grinned. He lightly punched Spaceman on the arm. "Well, come on, then, Oscar. Let's go catch a crazy."

Spaceman limped around to the other side of the car and got in.

Tom watched as they drove off. He let them go and thoughtfully finished a cigarette, then tossed the butt out the window.

It annoyed him to see Kowalski and his partner talking and smiling like they were. Kowalski didn't have a right to be happy, to have friends. Another idea was beginning to edge into his mind, but Tom set it aside for the moment. There was something else he had to do first. He got out of the car.

This was the place where Jody lived. The fact that
Kowalski was here meant they were onto him. How the
hell. . .?

Then Tom told himself that it didn't matter. The plans
were rolling now and nothing the cops would do could stop
him. Still, to know that Kowalski was getting so close
rankled.

Tom reached the house and peered in through the front
window, glad that Jody had stayed out at Holly Point to
get things cleaned up. He couldn't see anything through the
window, so he walked around the house. Through the
back door, he could see a tall thin figure bent over the sink.
The man was splashing water in his face.

Tom opened the screen door and stepped in quietly.

Not quietly enough, though. Some faint sound must
have alerted the man because he turned around quickly.
He squinted near-sightedly across the room. "Jody?" he
said hesitantly. Then he fumbled for the glasses on the
counter.

"No," Tom said softly. "It's not Jody." He kept one
hand in his pocket.

"My God. You're Tom, aren't you?"

"Yes."

"Where's Jody?"

"He's safe, if it's any of your business."

The skinny creep held out a hand. "Please, Tom, turn
yourself in. Let Jody turn himself in. Before it's too late.
You don't want to see him hurt, do you?"

"You're a real chickenshit faggot coward, ain't you?
We're not scared of the cops."

"Can I talk to Jody? If I could just talk to him we might
be able to fix things."

Tom realized that as the man was talking, he was edging
toward a drawer. That made him angry. "You better stop
right there," he warned.

165

Instead, the man lunged at him, empty-handed.

The first knife thrust was almost an accident. Tom pulled back quickly and stepped away. The man was staring at him, clutching at his stomach. Blood leaked out between his fingers, and he was crying. It was too bad, but the guy had brought it on himself. Besides, Jody didn't need him anymore.

"Please. . . help me." He fell to his knees.

Tom stabbed him again and he toppled over. He was still breathing, but quiet. Blood began to form a puddle on the shiny floor.

Tom walked out of the kitchen. It was a nice little house. Maybe he and Jody could live here later, when this was all over. The living room had a lot of books, as well as a big color television. He walked closer to the set to look at the framed photo on top. Jody and the other guy were standing in front of the house, holding onto a SOLD sign, and smiling. He wondered who had taken the picture.

There was one bedroom, small and tidy, the big bed neatly made up with a colorful patchwork quilt. Tom stared at the bed for a long time. He was angry again, suddenly, without knowing why. Stupid to get angry at a damned bed.

But he was. He knelt on the quilt and used the bloody knife to make long gashes in the mattress. Again and again he stuck the blade in and ripped. So caught up was he in the frenzy of the attack, that he was hardly aware of the rush of heat and the explosive climax until it was over.

He slid to the floor and huddled there, gasping for breath.

It was a noise from the kitchen that brought him back to reality. He straightened, listening, then jumped up and went back into the kitchen.

The man was crawling slowly toward the door. He left a vivid red trail as he moved.

Tom sighed. Some people just didn't know when they

were dead. In two steps he was across the room and a few seconds later the guy knew for sure that he was finished.

Tom cleaned up in the bathroom and left the body there on the kitchen floor.

He was very glad to get back to Holly Point. Jody had the Humpty Dumpty Fun Palace practically gleaming. It felt like home. Just like their bedroom when they were kids, this place belonged to them.

They sat on the floor, eating salami sandwiches. Tom didn't think anymore about the house in Azusa or the dead man.

Chapter 29

It was nearly two a.m. when the phone rang.

Spaceman swore groggily, reached out, swept the receiver up. Someday, he thought with a fuzzed corner of his mind, someday I'm actually going to sleep all the way through the night without this damned machine waking me up.

Actually, this time he didn't mind so much being disturbed, because his dreams hadn't been all that terrific. He kept seeing faces of people he thought he should recognize, but didn't. The people were all dead, and he seemed to see blame in their wide-open, staring eyes.

So he was almost glad when the phone wrecked his sleep.

He made a sound into the receiver, signifying that he was ready to talk.

"Is this Kowalski?" The voice was muffled, as if it were being filtered through a handkerchief.

"Yeah, so?"

"You're looking for your son, right?"

He sat up. "Who is this?"

"Never mind that. I'll do the talking. I might be able to help you find him."

"How could you do that?"

"Maybe I know where he is."

Spaceman fumbled for his cigarettes on the nightstand. "Either you know or you don't. If you know anything, I strongly suggest you tell me."

The voice chuckled. "Okay, I'll tell you. For a price."

"How much?"

"Gee, ain't it hard to know how much your son is worth?"

168

Spaceman flicked ashes toward the empty coffee cup, just missing. "How much?" he asked again.

"One hundred bucks. And cheap at that, right?"

"Fine. Give me your name and address. If the dope pans out, I'll mail the money."

"Whaddaya think I am, anyway?"

"I don't think you want to hear that, do you?"

"Fuck you. We do it my way or not at all."

"What's your way?"

There was the sound of a deep breath being taken. "That's better. Okay. There's an empty grocery store near Lincoln and Olympic."

He visualized a map. "Yeah, okay."

"Come there. Now. Bring the dough and be here in thirty minutes or the deal is off. Got that?"

Spaceman sighed, exhaling toward the ceiling. "I got it."

"Good." The connection was broken with a click.

He didn't get up right away. Instead, he finished the cigarette and replayed the phone conversation in his mind. It was probably nothing. Still, he had to take the chance. He rolled from the bed.

After some scrounging, and by raiding his poker stash, he managed to scrape up the hundred dollars. Then he dressed quickly.

It was fifteen minutes past the appointed time when he pulled up in front of the empty storefront. LoPressi and Sons read the fading sign over the door. The street was almost empty, except for an occasional car passing, and one old man pushing a shopping cart. He went from trash can to trash can, stopping by each one to paw through the contents, sometimes removing a new treasure to add to the pile already in the cart.

It didn't look like such a bad way to spend your life.

He got out of the car and walked to the front door, which was boarded up. He ducked into the alley and went around to the rear. The back door was ajar, and he stepped through, into complete darkness. After two steps, he stopped.

"You're late," the same voice said, this time without benefit of handkerchief.

Spaceman didn't answer.

The room was suddenly flooded with light.

The boy standing there looked vaguely familiar, but maybe that was because he was just another punk, and they were all pretty much the same. He stared at Spaceman through barely opened eyes. "You bring the bread?"

"You have the dope?"

"Well, not exactly."

There was a sudden movement behind Spaceman, and the door slammed shut. He looked around, not really surprised to see three more kids standing there. He didn't think any of them were friends of Robbie's, but he couldn't be sure.

"This is real cute," he said.

"Hand over the money, and nothing bad has to happen here," the leader said.

"Where's Robbie?"

"Who the hell knows?" He laughed nastily. "Who the hell cares? He's a creep."

Spaceman had been a cop too long for a crack like that to bother him. Much. "Well, I guess our business is finished, then, isn't it?" He stepped to the side and toward the door. The boys blocked his way, four of them, staring him down. "This is pretty fucking stupid," Spaceman said.

"We don't think so. We think you're the stupid one."

That was a valid point. Spaceman sighed and held up one hand, like a traffic cop. "Why don't we end this right now, before you boys get into a lot of trouble?" He was starting to get mad.

"Give us the cash."

"Fuck you," Spaceman said shortly. He took another step toward the door.

One of the punks flashed a switchblade. "Maybe you need a little persuading," he said in a TV tough guy voice. Something snapped inside Spaceman. Maybe it was seeing the knife that did it. Over the last several days, he'd had too much experience with just how much damage a blade could inflict on the human body. Maybe he was just tired. Or scared. Without even thinking about what he was doing, Spaceman shoved one hand inside his jacket; when the hand came out again, it held his gun. "Anybody moves even a hair, he's liable to end up in a lot of little pieces," he said tightly. "Any of you creeps ever see what a gun this size can do to a person's face?"

The boys froze. "Hey, man, cool it," the leader said. "It was just a joke, that's all. Can't you take a goddamned joke?"

"Am I laughing?"

"We didn't mean nothing."

"Do you know anything about where Robbie is?"

"No. I just heard that he'd split and you was looking for him."

"So you vermin thought you'd cash in on somebody else's troubles, is that it? You make me sick."

They were nervously watching the gun. "Look, man, why don't you just forget it? You go, we'll go. Pretend it never happened."

"I should blow you all away, and save the world a lot of trouble." Spaceman realized that he almost meant it. The amount of anger and hatred he felt for these kids scared him. He really wanted to kill the bastards, and maybe he'd do it.

"You're crazy, man," one of them said.

"Sure. Why shouldn't I be crazy? Everybody else in the fucking world is crazy. Why not me?"

One of the boys made a sudden move, probably trying to get away, and Spaceman lunged, jamming the gun barrel into his ribs. "I said, don't move!" he screamed in a voice that didn't sound like his own.

The boy began to cry.

The insane tableau remained intact for almost two minutes. Then, as suddenly as it had fled, his reason returned. He pulled the gun back. "Get the hell out of here," he said wearily. "If I ever see any of you again, I'll bust you. No matter if you're innocent as a virgin. I'll think of something dirty and I'll make it stick. Got that, creeps?"

They all nodded, without saying anything. Nobody moved for yet another moment; then, as one, they bolted through the suddenly opened door, and were gone.

Spaceman leaned against the wall and closed his eyes. Sweat made his whole body feel clammy. He wiped at his face with his sleeve.

It was a long time before he had the strength to leave the building and walk back to his car.

Chapter 30

BLUE wondered what the hell was bugging his partner.

Besides the case, of course, and the additional fact that his son was missing. Just those things were enough to make anybody crazy, but Blue decided that there was something else weighing on Spaceman. He came into the squadroom looking like a thing that had been warmed over once too often before being served.

Despite his curiosity, however, Blue hadn't been Kowalski's partner even this long without learning a few things along the way. He didn't ask why the man was the color of old yogurt or why his clothes looked even more than usually as if they'd been slept in.

They were still in the office when a report came in that Steven Lawrence's car had been found parked outside the Sweatshop. Although it seemed as if Spaceman had no interest at all in pursuing the matter, they drove over to the bar.

It was too early for the Sweatshop to be open, but the door was unlocked. A sign in the foyer proclaimed that auditions were being held. A crowd of about ten young men, apparently lured by the promise of a job and maybe fame, were waiting in line for a chance to show their stuff, whatever that might be.

Spaceman and Blue worked their way through the crowd and into the bar itself. "Excuse us," Spaceman said, raising his voice a little so he'd be heard over the conversation and muted rock music. "We're looking for D.C. Brigham?"

A woman at the end of the bar raised her head. "You found her, honey."

She wasn't exactly what they'd been expecting. For one

173

thing, she was a she, or the best damned imitation Blue had ever seen. Brigham looked like somebody's maiden aunt, wearing a well-cut and obviously expensive linen suit, with a rope of pearls that Blue knew had to be real. The eccentricity was expressed in the Billy Squier tee shirt worn with the suit, and in the vivid orange hair. Even with the hair, she was a good-looking woman.

She waved a long cigarette holder in their direction. "Come on over, dear, but I'll say right now, you're too old and rotund for the job. No offense." She squinted to look beyond Spaceman. "Blondie there, you might make it. Depends on what your body looks like out of that ice cream suit you're wearing."

Blue felt a flush of red flood his face as he stepped forward. "We're police officers," he said flatly, showing his badge. "Detectives Kowalski and Maguire."

"So sorreee," she said airily. "What brings you two down here?"

"One of your customers got himself killed the other night."

"I heard." Her face, all angles and not hiding her fifty years, but still attractive, grew serious. "He wasn't the first to die lately, was he? You people have to do something to stop all the pretty young men in this town from getting killed."

"We're trying," Spaceman said. "Did you know Lawrence?"

"Know him?" Her gaze flickered toward the small stage, where one of the hopeful waited, wearing only jeans and a smile. The smile was strained, but determined. "Well, not to speak of. Not much beyond the amenities. He was a pretty regular customer."

"Came in a lot, did he?"

"Once a week, maybe."

"And I suppose he left with a lot of different men?"

"He never left with anybody, as far as I know."

174

"He didn't?" Spaceman said skeptically.

She looked at him, seeming amused. "No. Oh, he might slip into the backroom or out into the parking lot for a little fun, but I think he always left alone."

"Except that night," Blue said. "Since his car was still in the lot."

She only shrugged.

"Did you see who he left with?"

"No."

"How about someone else?"

"I don't think so. Mick was off that night. Flu. So it was just Karl and me behind the bar. There was a big crowd in here. We were both too busy to pay much attention. Prince Charles could have left here with Henry Kissinger, and we wouldn't have noticed. Sorry. If I could help, I would, believe me."

They believed her, but that didn't make them any happier. Blue nodded their thanks, and they walked toward the door.

"Okay, sweet thing," they heard her say to the young man waiting on the stage. "Drop those jeans and let me see what you've got."

Neither of them turned around.

They were no sooner in the car than a message came in from McGannon. He wanted to see them immediately. Spaceman sighed and leaned his head back against the seat. "Maybe I'm getting too old for this kind of work."

"Shit," Blue replied.

There was a silence, then: "I almost killed some kids last night."

So. That was the problem. "What happened?"

Spaceman told him about the phone call and the events in the empty store. "I came so close to pulling the trigger, to blowing one of the bastards away," he said. "It scares me to think about it."

175

"They had a knife on you, right?"

Spaceman waved away the knife and its implications. "I screwed up, man. Lost fucking control."

"It happens to everybody once in a while."

Spaceman turned his head to look at him. "Yeah? When was the last time it happened to you? Shit, I doubt you ever even put your deodorant to the test."

Blue watched the traffic. "The last time I blew it," he said, "was a few years ago. A Vietcong colonel was asking me questions and he wasn't crazy about my answers. Blew me out of my frigging skull. So I know all about going crazy, partner. I could probably give lessons."

He parked and got out of the car quickly, without even waiting to see if Spaceman was following him.

"Jerry Potter is dead."

McGannon's words hung in the air for a long time.

Spaceman turned and hit the wall with his open hand and Blue sat down quickly.

McGannon gave them the moment, then said, "It must have happened just after you spoke to him. The cops out there found your card and called us just a little while ago. A knife was used on him."

Blue thought about the bright, sunny kitchen and the terrible lemonade. "Damn," he said. "It isn't fair."

McGannon shrugged. "John Kennedy once said that life isn't fair. Then he got his head blown off, so maybe he knew what he was talking about."

Spaceman turned around. "Was it Hitchcock?"

"Seems to have been. They got a description. From a passing birdwatcher, if you can believe that. Fits what we have on him."

Blue felt sick. "Was it both of them?" he asked. He couldn't believe—didn't want to believe, anyway—that Jody would have done this to someone who so obviously cared about him.

176

"No. The witness says only one man."

Spaceman was leaning against the wall. "Hitchcock must have trailed us out there. We led him right to Potter."

"Looks that way."

Spaceman shook his head. "Jesus, Maguire, we're a couple of real fuck-ups."

Then he walked out.

McGannon looked at Blue. "How's it going with you two?"

"Fine."

"No hassles?"

"We get along."

"Nobody else has been able to do that. Maybe he's mellowing in his old age."

Blue shrugged and left the office, too.

They spent most of the rest of the day talking back and forth with the Azusa cops. Facts were skimpy. One killer had apparently stabbed Jerry Potter to death. There was no evidence of sexual activity. Nothing seemed to be missing, although the bed was cut to shreds.

When quitting time finally came, they went across the street for a drink. They had that one and then another and then two more. Blue finally remembered that he had a late date. Sharon Engels was coming to his place for dinner after finishing work. He paid for the last round and left Spaceman still sitting at the table.

Chapter 31

SPACEMAN made his way very carefully up the steps to Mandy's apartment. Knowing just how much he'd consumed in the bar, he knew he had to be drunk. He didn't feel drunk, but that was undoubtedly just a joke that the gods were playing on him. Trying to give him a false sense of security, so that one wrong step would lead to a fall and a broken neck.

He walked with precise attention up the steps and tapped softly on the door.

Mandy was glad to see him. She always was. They went into the kitchen and she put a pan of water on for coffee. Waiting for the water to boil, she jiggled nervously around the room in panties and tee shirt. "Guess what," she said finally.

He was sitting at the table, not much feeling like guessing games. "What?" he said.

"I have a job."

"Terrific."

"The new road show of *A Chorus Line*." She put a cup down in front of him. "It means I'll be gone for at least six months."

He hadn't thought about that. He frowned and took a sip of the coffee. "Six months? Shit."

"I'll miss you, of course, but my career has to come first."

"I guess."

She bent down and gave him a quick hug. "I knew you'd understand. We've had some great times, but we both knew it couldn't be permanent."

"Sure. I understand."

178

"How about some supper?" She opened the freezer and began to rummage through the ice-shrouded contents.

Spaceman didn't understand anything at all. How could she just take off like this? What about him? What about their so-called relationship? The world had turned into a pretty shitty place if a broad could just take off and go running around the country for months at a time, without giving a thought to anyone else.

She emerged from the freezer finally, holding a package of lasagna. "This be okay?"

He nodded sullenly.

Maybe he could find a girl who knew how to make a decent cup of coffee. At least this gave him something to think about besides Jerry Potter's murder.

Blue had to stop at the liquor store for a bottle of special wine, so by the time he got home, he was already running twenty minutes behind schedule. And he wanted the meal with Sharon to be special.

He left the car in the driveway and stopped at the mailbox to pull out a handful of envelopes: bills, some bank statements, invitations to a couple gallery openings. He thumbed through the collection indifferently as he started for the house.

There was a slight noise in the bushes that lined the drive.

Maybe Merlin, his peripatetic tabby, had returned from his latest bout of wanderlust. He'd been gone almost a month this time. Blue half-turned. "Merlin? That you? Have you finally come home, you horny old bastard?"

The blow across the back of his head knocked him down. Dazed, but conscious, he fell forward into the grass. His face was pressed to the ground, and above him were voices.

"You hit him pretty hard. He's not dead, is he?"

179

"Of course not, dummy. Can't you see he's still breathing?" A foot nudged at his ribcage.

Blue waited for the punks to grab his wallet. Mugged in his own driveway. Shit. Some hotshot cop he was. They'd probably take his ring and the goddamned $3000 watch that was just a month old. Shit.

And his gun.

Double shit.

He kept his eyes closed. Someone knelt next to him and rough hands patted him down. The gun was lifted. Blue swore to himself, thinking about the paperwork ahead. Losing his weapon was bad news. Maybe he ought to do something, make some noise, try to fight them off.

The thought was there, but the body wouldn't or couldn't follow through. The brain couldn't make the arms or legs move.

"Get his feet," one of the voices said.

Hands grabbed him and tied his legs together with heavy rope. What the hell was going on? Since when did muggers tie their victims up? His hands were bound, too, behind his back. Blue started to get groggily worried. Something was happening, and he didn't think it was going to be good.

When he was effectively trussed up, the foot nudged him again, harder this time. "God, what stupid jerks these cops are. Get the car, Jody."

Jody. It all fell into place. Blue swallowed down a sudden rush of bile. For the first time in a long time, he felt as if dying were much too close.

The lasagna was crummy. The cheese on top was charred and the middle was still cool. But at least the food and a couple more cups of coffee sobered Spaceman up. He didn't feel any better, but he could see straight. Whether he liked what he was seeing was a different story.

He stretched out on the couch while Mandy did the dishes, half-sleeping through some made-for-TV movie about a crazed rapist stalking Las Vegas. There was always something vaguely cheering about watching stories with crime set in some other city. He could watch without feeling responsible.

The last thing he needed on this particular night was something else to feel guilty about. The Jerry Potter killing had hit him hard; he couldn't stop thinking about the quiet gentleman they had spoken to. Neither could he stop feeling like people were dead because of something he, Kowalski, had done or failed to do. People kept dying and he wasn't one goddamned step closer to stopping it.

Mandy turned off the light in the kitchen and joined him on the couch. She was up emotionally, excited about the job, obviously ready for some heavy-duty fucking to celebrate.

Spaceman wasn't in the mood.

He should have been out there someplace trying to stop Tom Hitchcock. Or trying to find Robbie. There were victims to be avenged and it was his job to be sure they were. Instead, here he was, trying to work his hand into the blue silk panties of a twenty-year-old girl.

Where the hell were his priorities?

He knew that it wouldn't be any use to try talking to Mandy about it all. Rule number one was that he not talk about his work. He sighed and kept his hand where it was.

For the second time recently, he was almost glad when the phone rang. Not that he would admit it. "Sometimes," he said to McGannon, "your timing really sucks."

"There's a problem," McGannon said.

"What else? I didn't think you called just to wish me sweet dreams."

"Sharon Engels just called me. She was supposed to have dinner with Maguire at his place tonight."

"So? He got lucky."

"Maybe not. When she got there, no Maguire. His car was in the drive, there was mail all over the ground, and the house was dark."

181

Spaceman massaged his left temple wearily. "So what do you think?"

"I don't think anything yet. Except that maybe you should go over there and have a look around."

"Yeah, sure."

"That's a pretty classy neighborhood. Maybe somebody broke in and Blue caught them."

"I guess that's possible."

"Call me."

"I will."

He hung up.

The house was still dark when he got there. He checked the car quickly, but nothing seemed amiss. Spaceman collected the mail that was scattered across the lawn, then crouched down to examine the flattened grass. It looked to him as if something heavy had rested there. Half-crawling, he followed a faint trail through the yard. The object apparently had been dragged from its resting place to the curb. Spaceman stood there on the same curb, staring up and down the dark street for a few moments.

At last, he turned and walked to the house, pausing only long enough to pick up a bottle of wine that was lying in the grass. The front door was secure, so he walked around to the rear, climbing a few steps to the redwood balcony. The sliding glass door had been jimmied. He pushed it open easily and went in. Nothing in the living room seemed out of place, so he walked up the winding stairs to the loft bedroom. The bed was made; there was a single silk tie draped over a chair. Nothing else was out of order, as far as he could tell.

The house was very quiet.

Spaceman glanced into the bathroom before going back downstairs. He didn't really know what he was looking for, but it was in the front hall that he found it, written on the wall in a familiar bright purple.

"This little piggy is missing. One more for you, Kowalski."

Spaceman read the words again and then once more. It didn't help. He sank down onto the couch, so tired all of a sudden that his legs wouldn't hold him.

"Shit," he said, without emotion.

Then he reached for the telephone.

Chapter 32

HE had never really known how long twenty-four hours could be. The day and night following Maguire's disappearance dragged unbelievably, and not because he didn't have enough to do.

He was in charge of the team that canvassed the neighborhood, setting up roadblocks and knocking on doors to find out if anyone had seen something that might give them even a vague hint of where to go. Nobody had. They might have been living in palaces instead of slums, but the people around here didn't seem any more observant than the inner-city folks.

The press had finally jumped on the case and they were playing it for all the thing was worth. On the front page of the *Times* was a rehash of the murders ten years ago of the elder Hitchcocks, the story updated to include Tom's hospitalization and escape. Each of the current murders was discussed at length, with heart-rending quotes from Chris Blair's aunt. The Lowe family was "unavailable for comment." Steven Lawrence was named as having "no known relatives." Lovers, apparently, didn't count in the obits.

Jerry Potter's sister had nothing to say.

The least space of all was devoted to the missing cop, but they hadn't had much time on that angle yet. Spaceman knew what would happen when they found out that Maguire was not only a cop, but a millionaire several times over as well.

He tossed the paper aside with a grunt of disgust and looked up to see McGannon standing next to his desk.

"You need to get away from here for a while," McGannon said.

"Yeah, you're right. Maybe I'll take a trip to Mexico. Lie on the beach; swim some. Take in a bullfight. Fuck a few señoritas."

"Go home and sleep for a few hours."

"Oh, that's what you meant."

"That's what I meant. Go."

"You want to know something?" Spaceman searched for a cigarette and realized that he was all out. "I feel like I've been sleeping all day. Like this is just some kind of dream. The whole world seems kind of vague." He then realized that he was talking nonsense and shut up.

"Go home," McGannon said again. "Consider that an order, if it helps."

"Yes, sir." Spaceman saluted.

He left the office and walked around the corner to the diner. Joe gave him change for the cigarette machine, and for once, was mercifully out of good advice. While Spaceman was tearing into the cigarettes, the door opened again and Sharon Engels came in.

"I was looking for you," she said.

"Well, you found me. Why don't you become a detective? I can never find anybody."

"Can we talk? Just for a minute. I'll buy you a cup of coffee."

He smiled. "Sweetheart, if you knew how much caffeine is already coursing through my fucking veins, you'd withdraw that offer." Nevertheless, he sat down. "Gimme a glass of oj," he said to Joe.

"Better choice," the old guy approved.

Sharon slid onto the stool next to his. "Any word on Blue?"

"No."

"What do you think?"

"What do I think?" His shaking fingers finally got the

185

cigarettes open. He offered her one, which she refused, and then lighted one for himself. "I think Maguire's in a hell of a mess."

"Is he alive?"

Spaceman shrugged, picking up the glass Joe had set in front of him.

"Just a shrug? What kind of an answer is that?"

"It's the best goddamned answer I have right now." He downed the juice in one long drink, then set the empty glass back on the counter. "You and Maguire have a little something going, is that it?"

"We're friends." She sounded fierce. "Damn it, there hasn't been time yet for anything else. There might be more, if we have the time."

"I hope you do. Nothing would make me happier."

Sharon looked at him; her eyes were very dark. "You don't sound like you care at all."

"I care. Sure I do."

"Well, no one could tell by looking at you."

"Sorry about that. What should I be doing? What would satisfy your sense of propriety? Should I throw a chair through the goddamned window over there? Or maybe I should shed a few tears about how rotten it all is?"

After a moment, she patted his arm. "I'm an idiot. Sorry."

"Don't mention it," he said. "I have to go."

Instead of going directly home, Spaceman drove slowly up Hollywood Boulevard, looking for his son. Twice he parked the Jeep and trudged to the sidewalk to show the snapshot to groups of young freaks.

Nobody knew anything.

Inside his apartment, he pulled off the sweat-stinking suit and dropped it into a heap on the floor. He was standing in the kitchen, drinking a glass of Alka-Seltzer, when there was a knock on the door.

He sighed, too tired even for despair, and went to answer it in his shorts.

Karen was standing in the hall, but not for long. As soon as the door opened, she pushed by him, and then she was standing in his living room. "You bastard," she said in a small, tight voice.

He shook his head a little, hoping to clear away some of the cobwebs, but it didn't help much. "What?"

"I've been calling and calling, and you haven't answered one of my messages. You haven't called or anything!" She paused and inhaled deeply, obviously trying not to cry. "Where is Robbie? Why haven't you been looking for my son?"

"My son, too," he said. Unable to stay on his feet any longer, he almost fell into a chair. "And I have been looking."

"In your spare time, right?"

"Whenever I goddamned could. Karen, have you seen a paper or watched the news? Do you have any idea at all what's going on in this city?"

She shook her head.

"There happens to be a madman out there. A madman who kills people." He tried to tally the number, including the hospital aide, excluding Blue. "At least five in the last couple of weeks."

"I don't care about that. I want my son." She pushed one hand through her hair helplessly, glaring at him. "You never change, do you? Always have to be the hero. Always have to save the world. Well, what about your own son? Can't you care as much for him? Can't your heart bleed a little for Robbie?"

"He ran away, damn it. Robbie is not a little boy. He ran away of his own free will, and from what I've been able to find out, he's probably shacked up with his girlfriend right now."

She was pale. "Where did you hear that?"

187

"I heard. But I'm still looking."

"Find him then!" She was screaming now.

"I will. But right now I have to find that maniac." He didn't raise his voice, mostly because he didn't have the energy.

"Let somebody else do that."

"It's my case. He's killing these people because I put him away ten years ago. Now he's out again, killing again, and I have to stop him." He touched his chest with one finger. "Me."

"Not you."

"He's kidnapped my partner." Maybe, just maybe, he's even killed my son. Spaceman thought the words, wanted to scream them at her. But he didn't.

Karen turned and walked into the kitchen. He watched as she searched for a clean glass, managed to find one, and swallowed a pill. "I don't know how much more of this I can take," she said, walking back into the living room.

"I'm still looking for Robbie," he said wearily. "But I have these other things to do, too. Please, Karen. If I don't get some sleep soon, I'm gonna crack up. Then I won't be any good to anyone. Go home."

"Maybe I should hire a private detective."

"Fine. Do that. Call me tomorrow, and I'll give you a couple names."

She stood there for another moment, then turned and left, slamming the door.

Spaceman stayed where he was and finished the flat Alka-Seltzer.

When he finally got into bed, he couldn't sleep. He stared at the ceiling for a long time, then switched on the radio and listened to the news.

In the middle of a report on a new fire outbreak in the hills, Spaceman finally lost consciousness.

Chapter 33

BLUE forced himself to wake up.

For a long time, it had been easier just to stay asleep. That way he couldn't feel the pain from the ropes still holding him, or from the kicks inflicted on his body. But part of him finally accepted that crawling into a hole and trying to pretend that none of this was happening wouldn't help at all. He had to get a grip on things.

So he opened his eyes.

A giant green dragon leered down at him.

He closed his eyes again. Careful, man, he thought. Careful, you don't want to blow it now. Hold onto a little bit of sanity. He took a couple of deep breaths and opened his eyes again. The dragon was still there. Blue shook his head slightly, refuting the absurdity of it all.

"There really is a dragon," a voice said suddenly. "It isn't your imagination."

Blue managed to turn his head slightly, enough to see the young man sitting just a few feet away. "Hello, Jody," he said, although it wasn't easy to talk with a tongue that felt about twice as big as it should have.

Jody looked surprised. "How'd you know my name?"

"I know all about you, Jody. Except for one thing."

"What?"

"How the hell did you ever get yourself into such a mess?"

The face went blank, shutting out Blue and what he was saying. "I better tell Tommy you're awake."

"Oh, yes. Tell Tommy. He's the boss around here, right?"

Jody didn't say anything.

"Can you at least tell me where the hell I am? And why there are dragons and elephants watching me?"

"You're in the Humpty Dumpty Fun Palace," Jody said shortly. He started out of the room, then paused. "But I don't think it's going to be much fun," he said. Strangely, there wasn't any hint of sarcasm or even threat in the words. There was only a sort of weary resignation.

"He's awake."

Tom was sitting outside, reading a paperback western. He looked up at Jody's words. "For real this time? No more drifting?"

Jody shook his head. "No more drifting."

"Good." Tom stood, stretched. "Too fucking hot." Then he went inside.

After a moment, Jody followed. Tom was standing over Maguire, not saying anything when Jody joined them. "Well," he finally said, drawling the words out like a cowboy. "Whattaya think?"

Maguire met his gaze. "I think it's funny that you don't look like a fucking maniac."

Tom's foot moved swiftly, colliding yet again with the tied man's ribs. Maguire grunted, but didn't say anything. "We have a real smartass pig here," Tommy said. "A regular funny guy." He kicked again. "How funny do you feel now?"

Maguire's face was pale and bright with sweat. "Not terribly," he gasped out.

"Good. Glad to hear it. Nothing makes me sicker than a cop cracking jokes."

"Could I have a drink of water? Please?"

"Nice manners. You say please."

Maguire seemed to speak through gritted teeth. "Miss Puddingham would be proud of me."

Tom was running the toe of his foot up and down Maguire's ribcage lightly. "Who the hell is that?"

190

"The mistress of the Puddingham School of Deportment for Young Ladies and Gentlemen. I graduated with honors when I was seven."

"Which were you? A young lady or a gentleman?"

"Ha, ha."

Tommy just shook his head. "You're the crazy one here. I could kill you just as easily as look at you. Why don't you act like a man that close to dying?"

Maguire didn't say anything.

Jody didn't like the way things were going. He stepped closer. "Tommy?"

"What?"

Jody wiped his sweaty hands on the front of his shirt. "You can't kill him now. We need him for bait. Isn't that what you said before?" He tried not to sound as desperate as he felt.

Tommy frowned, then nodded. "For the moment." He took a needle out of his pocket. "But I don't need to keep listening to his big mouth."

Jody watched as Tommy injected more of a knock-out drug into Maguire.

"That should keep you quiet for a while," he said with satisfaction. Then he turned to Jody. "I'm going to buy a paper," he said. "You stay with funny man here, and if he tries anything, why just tap him." It was much more than a tap that his shoe applied to Maguire's ribs. He winked at Jody and left. A moment later they could hear the sound of a car engine.

Jody sat on the floor again, staring at Maguire.

The cop's eyes were only half open, but he was still awake enough to talk. "Can ya' tell me somethin'?" he said in a thick voice.

"What?"

Maguire seemed to be making a great effort to speak. "I don't pretend to understand any of this," he said slowly. "But what I don't understand most is Potter."

191

Jody bit his lip, tasting blood. "How do you know about Jerry?"

Maguire's eyes opened just a little. "We talked to him."

Jody leaned forward eagerly. "You did? Is he okay?"

"You don't even know, do you?"

"What?"

Instead of answering, Maguire shook his head. "I need a drink."

Jody got up and went into the other room. He could see himself reflected over and over in the distorted mirrors that lined the walls; the effect made him dizzy. He poured some bottled water into a Dixie cup. There was a small flicker of fear inside, but he tried not to think about it.

He took the cup to Maguire, holding it while the other man drank. "What about Jerry?" he asked then.

"Tom killed him."

The words fell like lead balls. Jody's fingers crushed the cup involuntarily. "What?"

"Tom went into the house and stabbed Jerry to death. Just like you stabbed the others. Jerry's dead."

"No, please." It was an anguished groan. Jody tried to fight against the great trembling darkness threatening to swallow him. "You can't say that."

Maguire's eyes suddenly closed and his head fell forward.

"No," Jody said again. "You're lying." He grabbed Maguire by the shirt and shook him. "Tell me it was a lie."

But Maguire was out cold.

Jody dropped him. He stood shakily and walked out of the building. His legs felt like they were going to fold under him. He took deep gulps of the heavy humid air.

Maguire's words had to be a great big lie. Tommy wouldn't....Jody wiped his mouth with the back of one hand. Oh God...Oh shit....

Jody ran across the compound through the front gate, to

192

the phone booth just beyond. There was no sign of the car returning. Jody dug through his pockets for change, and when he found it dialed without thinking about what he would say.

All he needed was to hear the familiar voice on the other end of the line, and he would hang up.

"Hello?" It was a woman's voice.

"Who is this?" Jody asked, although he thought he should know.

"Lainie Potter. Who's this?"

Jerry's sister. She lived in Malibu and came out to see them every so often. Jody had always liked her. "Let me talk to Jerry, please."

There was a silence. "Haven't you heard? Jerry is dead."

Jody sagged against the wall of the phone booth.

"Who is this? Who's calling?" Then Lainie's voice broke. "Jody? Is this you? Oh, Jody, how could you do it? Jerry loved you and you killed him."

Jody's hand lost its strength suddenly and the phone fell. He leaned forward out of the booth and threw up, heaving again and again, until there was nothing left inside him, as his body shook with violent efforts to expel the knowledge.

After a long time, he straightened and retrieved the dangling phone. "I'm sorry," he whispered. "I'm sorry, I'm so sorry."

Lainie's voice sounded calmer when she spoke again. "Where are you, Jody? Tell me, please."

"I can't." He was quiet, staring back into the park and into his memory. "Remember that time we had the picnic?" he said.

"Picnic?"

"Yeah. On my birthday, three years ago. God, that was such a good day for me."

"For Jerry, too," she said softly.

Jody felt a sob breaking free inside his chest. He hung up the phone quickly. Tommy would be back anytime

193

now, and he would expect to find Jody inside with Maguire.

There wasn't any time to cry for Jerry right now.

Chapter 34

"Is this Robbie Kowalski's father?"

"Yes. Who's this?"

The question was ignored. "Is it true what I heard?"

"What?"

"That him and Becky Malloy ran off together?"

Spaceman was drinking a beer for breakfast. "Could be. Why should you care?"

"I seen Becky last night. I know where it is she's staying."

"Did you see Robbie?"

"Nope. But if you figure they're together..."

He sighed and took another gulp of the warmish beer. "I suppose that now you want to make a deal with me."

"A deal?" The voice, youthfully sexless, giggled. "Oh, no, sir. I don't want money."

"Then why are you telling me this? Pure altruism, I suppose?"

"Al who?"

He shook his head. "Never mind. Look, kiddo, I've already been shafted once. Why are you suddenly coming forward to help?"

"You want the absolute truth?"

"That would be a nice change."

The caller took a deep breath. "I just want to get back at that snooty Becky Malloy. She's a rich bitch, thinks she's a fucking queen or something. I want to see her in trouble. This should settle her case pretty good. Don't you think?"

Nothing like good healthy hatred as a motivation. "I think. So where did you see her?"

"She was carrying a box of Kentucky Fried Chicken into the Sleepy Time Motel, on Ocean Boulevard. Room seventeen."

"You're sure it was Becky?"

"Hey, I know the bitch. We've been in school together since fucking kindergarten. It was her, all right. For sure."

"Well, thanks for calling."

"She's gonna get it now, right?"

"Without doubt."

There was a sigh of exquisite pleasure from the other end of the line.

Spaceman hung up. He leaned against the counter and finished the beer. The few hours sleep he'd finally managed to get hadn't done anything except make him feel worse. His eyes felt like they were full of sand, and he had a headache that ran through his entire body.

He didn't want to bother with this now. If Robbie and the bitch were screwing around in the Sleepy Time, it was a pretty stupid thing for them to be doing, but it wasn't exactly going to shake the foundations of the world. He had to keep trying to find Maguire. If it wasn't too late already.

But if he got this settled, he could concentrate on more important things than a couple of horny kids. Also, he could forget about the dead boy in Lompoc.

He reached for the phone again and dialed the office, asking for McGannon. "What's the word?" Spaceman said when the other man got on the line.

"Nothing," he said, sounding tired. "I suppose that's good in a way."

"Good?"

"Well, we haven't found a body yet." The words were flat, hopeless. Cop words.

Spaceman pitched the empty beer can across the room. It just missed the wastebasket, which figured. "Okay," he said, giving briskness a try and missing with that, too. "I'll be in as soon as I can. There's a stop I have to make first."

"Oh?"

"I got a tip on where my son might be. I need to check it out."

"Good luck."

"I'm about due."

He hung up and headed for the bathroom.

The air outside was heavy and sluggish. Spaceman could see a thin line of dark clouds moving in from the west. Maybe there would be some rain, please God, and the damned grip of heat would be broken. According to the radio news, the authorities were hoping for rain, too, to help with fighting a new rash of fires.

The Sleepy Time Motel was about what he had expected it would be. Fifteen dollars a night and no questions asked. He went into the small office. The young black man behind the desk was reading one of the underground sex papers and watching *The $25,000 Pyramid*. "Room seventeen," Spaceman said.

The clerk was barely interested. He glanced at a register open on the desk. "Mr. and Mrs. Jones," he said. He licked a fingertip and turned the page of the paper.

"What do they look like?"

"Beats me."

"You didn't check them in?"

"Maybe. Maybe not. But even if I did, I don't know what they look like."

Spaceman reached out and pushed the newspaper down so that he could see the man's face. "You're not a very observant type, is that it?"

"I don't get paid to be observant."

"And you earn every penny you make," Spaceman said. He turned and walked out.

He went to room seventeen. On another day, he would

have used a little finesse on this kind of thing. But he was hot and tired and worried. And mad. He pounded the door with the heel of his hand. "Open up."

"Who is it?" The voice was female, tentative.

"Police. Open the door, please."

There was a flurry of soft, unintelligible conversation. Then: "Go away." It was a deeper voice, but no less tentative.

Spaceman swore. He judged the strength of the door carefully and decided that it was nothing but flimsy plywood covered with veneer. Cheap. He took two steps back and threw himself against the door. There was a cracking sound, but the damned thing held. He leveled his shoulder against it again and this time the wood shattered.

Spaceman stumbled into the room.

A young blonde girl, wearing only the top half of a pair of man's pajamas, was sitting on the bed. She was eating a Mounds bar and drinking a can of Diet-Rite. *The $25,000 Pyramid* seemed to be a popular show, because she was watching it too, or had been. Now she was staring at Spaceman.

The man standing by the bed wasn't Robbie. He was tall, built like an ex-jock, about forty years old. At the moment, he was looking sort of sick. "Oh, shit," he said.

"Becky Malloy?" Spaceman asked, rubbing his shoulder gingerly. He'd have a bruise there tomorrow.

She smiled at him smugly. "Becky Rostow," she said, waving the hand that still held a half-eaten candy bar. The third finger wore a thin gold band. "We went to Vegas and got married."

"Congratulations," Spaceman said shortly. "Who the hell are you?"

"Al Rostow," the bridegroom said in a low voice.

"She's underage, you know."

He nodded.

"And you did it anyway?"

"We love each other," the girl said fiercely. "We've been in love for over a year." She was looking at Rostow; Spaceman wondered what the hell she saw. It certainly wasn't the half-naked middle-aged man with the thinning hair and emerging gut who stood there. "He was my history teacher."

"A teacher," Spaceman repeated.

"Yes," Rostow said. Then he smiled weakly. "Until now."

"You got that right, I think." Spaceman shook his head. "You people have really fucked up."

They looked like they knew it.

It took him over an hour to get the whole mess straightened out. Becky seemed to have a better grip on things than did Rostow. She only shrugged when Spaceman said he'd have to call her parents. "I knew the honeymoon would have to end sometime," was her only reply.

Spaceman asked her about Robbie.

It wasn't very nice, what she had to say. While Rostow, pants on by then, sat to one side and listened, Becky told Spaceman how she had used Robbie as a cover. Pretending to like him and going out with him only so her parents wouldn't suspect the truth about the affair with Rostow.

Before they went to Vegas, she told Robbie the truth. How did he react, Spaceman wanted to know. She shrugged. That was all.

Spaceman felt hurt for his son.

He finally called the Malloys, told them where Becky was, and left the newlyweds to await whatever befell them next. He almost felt a little sorry for Rostow; he didn't stand a chance in hell, caught between the Malloy women.

McGannon handed him a sheaf of messages as they passed in the hall. Spaceman sat at his desk and thumbed through them quickly. Most of it was worthless. Karen had

199

called three times. He jotted down a reminder to himself to call her about the private dicks.

The jerks in Lompoc sent another memo, still trying to find out if anybody had a missing person who fit the ID of the dead boy, but although the memo said "see attached photo," there was no picture attached. Spaceman swore. He had to call them.

Another note caught his attention. Someone by the name of Lainie Potter had called a short time earlier. The message was to call her back as soon as possible. He picked up the phone and dialed the number.

"Hello?"

"Miss Potter? This is Detective Kowalski. You called me?"

"Yes, I thought you should know."

"About what?"

"Jody called here early this morning."

"What? Are you sure?"

"Quite sure. I spoke to him myself."

"What did he say?"

Her voice held the same tone of quiet calm that Jerry Potter's had. "He asked for my brother. I don't think he knew that Jerry was dead. When I told him, he became very upset." She paused. "I don't understand. The police here told me that Jody and his brother were responsible for the recent murders."

"Yes. For the others. But it looks like your brother was killed by Tom Hitchcock alone. Jody seemed to have nothing to do with it."

She sighed deeply. "Well, that's something."

"Is it?" He found himself wondering what the person who went with the pleasant voice looked like.

"It's a lot, in fact. The thought that Jody could have done that to Jerry broke my heart. At least my brother didn't have to face that before he died."

200

Spaceman thought he understood. "Did Jody give you any idea where he was calling from?"

"No. He just asked for Jerry, and I told him. He got very upset. I think he threw up. Then he came back on the line. He talked about a picnic."

"A picnic?"

"Yes. Three years ago, on his birthday. Jerry, Jody, a friend of mine, and I all had a picnic."

"Why would he mention that?"

"It was a very...a very nice day. He said it was the first time he'd ever been on a picnic."

"Where?"

"Where was the picnic, you mean?"

Spaceman realized that he was sitting on the edge of his chair. He forced himself to relax. "Yes."

She was quiet for a moment. "I don't remember exactly. Some amusement park."

"Disneyland, you mean? Knott's Berry Farm?"

"No, not one of those. This was a small, family-run place. Out in the country somewhere."

"You can't be more specific?"

"I'm afraid not. Is it important?"

"Probably not. But if it comes to you, call me back, would you, please?"

"Sure, of course."

He cleared his throat. "I'm very sorry about your brother."

"So am I. Jerry was a very nice guy."

Spaceman hung up thoughtfully. An amusement park was not a good place to hide, at least right in the middle of the summer season. Still, it couldn't hurt to snoop a little. And he sure as hell didn't have anything better to hang his hopes on.

He opened a drawer and started looking for a map.

Chapter 35

BLUE woke again. It was even harder this time than it had been the last. He rolled over onto his back and stared at the ceiling. The faces of the dragons and other creatures still looked down on him. There was no way of knowing how long he'd been here. Not that he cared much. His hands and feet were getting numb, leading to unpleasant thoughts of gangrene. He'd seen that a couple times in Nam. It wasn't pretty.

What the hell kind of cop could he be with no hands or feet?

For that matter, what the hell kind of cop was he now?

Before he was forced to pursue that line of thought, Jody came in, carrying a paper plate and cup. "I brought you some food," he said dully. "Are you hungry?" Jody seemed to have grown years older in the time Blue had been here. His face was pale and lined, and his hands shook.

Blue opened his mouth to speak, but his throat was so dry that all that emerged was a croak. He mustered up a little moisture and swallowed before trying again. "Yeah. But I can't eat like this."

"I know." Jody set the plate and cup down and knelt beside him. "I'll untie your hands. You won't try anything stupid, will you?"

"No. Cross my heart and hope — " He broke off.

Jody stared at him for a moment, then shook his head and went to work on the knots.

Blue closed his eyes briefly at the cramping pains that ran through his arms as the rope was removed. He tried to shake some feeling into his hands. "Thanks," he said. "But are you sure Tom won't mind?"

"He's asleep." Jody moved the food within Blue's reach. Blue managed to get his fingers working. There was a salami sandwich and some potato chips on the plate. He took a sip from the cup and found Kool-Aid. It all tasted wonderful.

Jody was across the room, sitting with his back against the mirror. His eyes, although they watched Blue, did so without interest.

Blue didn't speak until the sandwich was half-gone. He took a sip of the sweet drink. "Did you ask him why?" he said.

Jody blinked. "What?"

"Tom. Did you ask him why he killed Jerry?"

"No." It was a whisper. "I didn't say anything about it."

"Why? Are you afraid of him?"

"Tommy wouldn't ever hurt me."

Blue crunched a stale chip thoughtfully. "You say Tommy wouldn't hurt you. What the hell was he doing when he stabbed Jerry Potter to death? Doesn't that hurt you?"

Jody was chewing on a fingernail. He nodded.

"Doesn't that hurt even more than if he'd put the knife in you?"

"Yes." He bent forward suddenly, clutching at his stomach.

"Well, then, don't you want to know why?"

"I can't ask him. He's my brother."

"Is that why you helped him kill the others?"

"I guess so. Maybe. Who knows. It was just something I got caught up in. The...excitement. It just sort of took me over." He shook his head. "Probably you can't understand that."

Blue felt a little dizzy suddenly. The past intruded upon him with a fierce vengeance. The dirty little villages, one

203

after another, the sound of gunfire, the smell of blood. He could remember the vicious surge of adrenaline that filled him, that kept his finger on the trigger of the damned M-16.

"Maybe I understand more than you think," he said.

"Well, then." Jody made a helpless gesture with one hand, then went back to chewing on the nail. "Besides, I owe him."

"Why?"

"Because. . . because it was all my fault." He ducked his head. "It was because of me he killed them. They deserved to die. Those people should not have been allowed to bring children into the world."

"Tom did what he did. You're not at fault for the deaths of your parents."

Jody shook his head again. "I was the one who told the police. I told them Tommy did it and they locked him up." He smiled bitterly. "They should have given him a fucking medal for wasting those two, but they called him crazy and locked him up."

"But what about the boys?"

"I feel bad about them. I felt bad all along." He was quiet for a moment. "I feel worse now."

"Why?"

"Because it hurts so much. The ones who died must have had people who cared about them."

"Like you cared about Jerry."

"Yes. And it hurts." He shrugged.

"Jody, it's not to late to stop this. We can get Tom back into the hospital where he belongs. You can still make a life for yourself."

He smiled faintly. "You think so? When the hell did they start teaching cops to bullshit?"

"I'm not trying to bullshit you. It wouldn't be the life you had before, but you could make something of it."

"I already started life over again," Jody said. "Twice.

204

Once when I was thirteen and then again when I met Jerry. I'm too tired to try again."

"Christ, man, you're only twenty-three years old."

"Yeah, I know. Hell of a thing, isn't it?"

They were quiet for a moment. Blue finished off the last of the Kool-Aid. "Would you like to know something?"

"What?"

"The last thing Jerry said to us. That we should be sure to call him when we found you. He knew that you would need his help. He said that you two were a real family, and that he was willing to fight for what you had."

Jody shook his head, as if willing him to shut up.

"It was probably about five minutes after he said that when Tom came in. And killed him. Jerry never had a chance."

"Enough. Please. For god's sake, give me a break. Are you finished eating?"

"Yeah. But I need to take a leak."

"Use the cup."

Blue shrugged. "Forget it then."

"Up to you." Jody crossed the room and bent down to retie the rope around Blue's wrists.

Blue didn't let the opportunity go; as his old man always said, a chance might come by just once, so you damned well better grab for it. That philosophy had made Maguire senior a very rich man. Blue hoped that the same kind of thinking might now save his life.

He crashed an elbow into the side of Jody's head, sending him sprawling. Before Jody could regain his balance, Blue butted him in the stomach. As Jody fell, his head struck the wall and he was still.

Blue instantly began to work on the knot at his feet, cursing his still awkward fingers. At last, though, he managed to get free. He tried to stand, but his legs just wouldn't work, so he crawled to the entranceway and peered into the next room. He could see Hitchcock stretched out on top of a sleeping bag, apparently asleep.

Blue edged out into the hallway. The floor seemed to tilt suddenly and he scrabbled for a hold. His reflection bounced around the hall. He stopped to take a deep, steadying breath. Fun house, shit, this was a torture chamber.

Once when he was just a kid, maybe four, the old man took him to a carnival with a place like this. All mirrors and slanting floors. Blue could remember the feeling of utter panic that seized him then, as he ran in helpless circles, crying and trying to find his way out.

Finally one of the attendants came in and rescued him. Outside, the whole crowd, except for his father, was laughing. The old bastard just shook his head and took him home. Blue knew, even then, that he'd failed somehow to be what he should have been.

He tightened his lips. This time he couldn't let himself fail. Besides, it was easy to find the way out, because the door had been left propped open, probably in an attempt to catch whatever stray breeze might appear. Blue headed for that open door. He moved slowly, both to cut down on the chance of noise, and because his body just wouldn't go any faster.

It seemed to take forever, but at last he reached the exit. Half-crawling and half-rolling, he made it down the slight ramp that led into the building. The ramp had a metal handbar running its length, where eager customers must have once lined up to gain admittance. Using that bar, he managed to get himself pulled into a standing position.

He rested for just a few seconds, breathing heavily from the effort, and wondering just how long Jody would be out. The blow to the head hadn't been that hard. As he started across the compound toward the entrance of the park, the thought came to him that maybe Jody hadn't been unconscious at all, but only faking it. Maybe Jody wanted him to get away.

When Blue got closer to the gate, he could see the phone booth just beyond. His cramped legs eased and his gait speeded up. He reached the booth and leaned against it as a hand lifted the receiver.

Only then did it occur to him that he needed a dime; this wasn't one of those up-to-date models that you could get the operator with, even without money. Blue searched his pockets quickly. Nothing, not a damned thing. He closed his eyes for a moment. Shit.

"Need a dime?" The voice was mocking.

He opened his eyes and stared into the face of Tom Hitchcock. "Yeah. Will you lend me one? I'm good for it."

"You're a real bastard, aren't you?"

"Yeah, maybe so. But I'm fun at parties." He looked beyond Tom and saw Jody standing there, rubbing his head. There was no way of telling if the look of pain he wore was real or faked.

Hitchcock pulled him out of the booth, twisting both arms behind him again. Blue thought, fleetingly, about putting up a fight, but his better judgement prevailed. "Don't be no hero," his old sergeant used to say.

Tom dragged him back across the compound and into the building, where he threw Blue down like something he was getting very tired of. "Tie him again," he ordered in an angry voice. "And try to do it right this time."

As Jody started to work on the ropes again, Tom pulled the needle out of his pocket. "I'm gonna be sure you don't give us no more trouble. This is some very special stuff that I've been saving. This stuff used to give me dreams all in color."

"I always dream in color," Blue said tightly. "So I'll pass, if you don't mind."

"I do mind, in fact. You've got no choice."

Jody didn't skimp on the knots this time. When he was finished, he stepped back as Tom bent down and jabbed Blue's arm with the needle. He depressed the plunger all the way. "Sweet dreams, piggie," he whispered, his lips right next to Blue's ear.

Blue tried to pull away. Tom laughed softly.

When they were gone, Blue didn't even try to struggle. He just rested there on the floor and let whatever Tom had shot him full of take over. It was so easy to do, lazy, and not bad. The slow curtain of darkness that was descending seemed almost comforting.

Dimly, coming from the other room, but seeming to be from another planet, Blue could hear their voices.

"I'm sorry about messing up, Tommy."

"Never mind. It happens, and no harm was done."

"How long is this going to last?"

"I don't know. As long as it takes. Why? Are you still in a hurry to get home?"

"No. I don't want to go back there. Ever."

"Good. You'd rather stay with me, right?"

"Whatever."

"You okay? You seem kinda down."

"I'm all right."

"Maybe we could have a little party, just you and me. Come here...isn't that better? Feels good, huh?"

"Sure. It feels fine."

Blue tried to stop listening, but the sounds from the next room got all mixed up with the dreams in his mind. He couldn't tell which was real and which fantasy. It didn't seem to matter much anyway.

Chapter 36

"SHIT."

Spaceman folded the map and pushed it aside. Joe refilled the coffee cup. "Problem?"

"I was trying to follow up on something. A hunch. But I guess it's a bust." He added sugar and milk to the coffee, hoping that this third cup would give him a burst of energy.

"What?" Joe pressed. "I know this city, this whole area, better than anybody else you're likely to meet."

"Yeah, sure," Spaceman muttered. After a moment, when he realized that he had no idea, not one, about where to go next or what to do, he said again, "Shit."

Joe was still standing there, polishing some glasses.

"Somebody mentioned an amusement park," Spaceman said finally, half-angrily. "The perp went there a couple years ago, and I just thought that might be where they're hiding now. But that's stupid. Who could hide in the middle of an amusement park?"

Joe frowned. "Unless it ain't open anymore."

"I thought of that. But nothing seems to fill the bill, not anywhere within a reasonable distance of the city."

Joe finished with the glasses and tucked the polishing rag into his belt loop. "Holly Point," he said succinctly.

"What?"

"Holly Point Park. Used to take my kids out there, years ago. Heard it closed down."

"It's not on my map."

"Hell, it was just a small place. And if it's a new map, it wouldn't be there anyway." Joe opened the map again, searched for a moment, then pointed. "Right there is where Holly Point used to be."

Spaceman looked. It was a couple hours from the city, close to where Potter and Jody had lived. "You say it's closed down now?"

"For a couple years, I think."

"I wonder. . ." Spaceman folded the map again, quickly this time. "Thanks, Joe. Catch me on the coffee later."

"Forget it. Good luck, Kowalski."

He went back to the office and shoved the map back into the drawer, at the same time taking out some extra rounds for his gun. Then he picked up the phone and dialed, but Potter's number was busy. To hell with it, he decided, just as easy to stop there and check with her in person. Besides, it would give him a chance to see what she looked like.

Spaceman realized that he was excited, the way he sometimes felt when a big case took the right turn. Holly Point was a long shot, but at least it was a shot, and better than anything else he'd come up with so far. Until now, Hitchcock had made things go all his way. But not now.

He was operating on the thesis that Maguire was still alive. What would be served by killing him this early in the game? Alive, he could at least serve as some sort of bargaining chip. Dead, he was just so much baggage.

Such thinking made sense to Spaceman.

Of course, he wasn't a homicidal maniac and maybe if he were, he'd figure things differently. But a man had to have hope.

McGannon passed him in the hallway. "What's up?"

"Probably nothing," he hedged.

The lieutenant eyed him. "You will let the rest of us in on it, won't you? If it turns into something?"

"Sure," he said.

Which was a lie, of course.

Too many people had died already because of him. All

they had to do now was hit the place with a SWAT team, or half the damned department, and Maguire would be a dead man before anybody got close. Maybe he didn't like the idea of having a partner, damn it, but he did have one and no bastard like Tom Hitchcock was going to kill him. Like old Sam Spade said: "When a man's partner is killed, he's supposed to do something about it." Except that Spaceman was going to do something beforehand. And he was going to do it alone.

This was a one man show and he was the fucking star.

Lainie Potter had the same coloring and slender form as her brother. She was about thirty-five, with a few lines around her soft eyes. A real grown-up woman that Spaceman thought might be worth knowing.

She answered the door wearing tight jeans and a man's shirt with the sleeves rolled up. Her hair was tucked under an old baseball cap and she was surprised to find another cop at her door.

She showed him into the living room, where boxes were sitting everywhere, half-filled. "Sit down, please. I've just been...sorting through things. Mostly just killing time." She grimaced. "That's a horrible phrase, isn't it? Anyway, the funeral is tomorrow, and I'm sort of at loose ends. No more family left." She looked around the room, almost as if to keep from looking at him. "This was always such a nice place."

"Miss Potter, does the name Holly Point mean anything to you?"

"Lainie, please." She sat cross-legged on a large leather hassock. "Sure. Now I remember. Holly Point is the place we had the picnic. We all piled into Jody's old truck and drove out there. Spent the whole day acting like a bunch of kids. It was all very dumb and very wonderful." She laughed softly at the memory and her eyes seemed lighter. "What a day. When Jody called before, he said it was such

211

a good day. I think Jerry probably felt the same way. I never saw him smile so much." Her fist clenched suddenly, and she pounded it against the arm of the chair. "Why do things have to get so horrible?"

"I don't know, Lainie."

Without warning, she was crying. "He was so good. So sweet. I don't understand why this had to happen to Jerry."

He sat awkwardly for a moment, then moved to put a careful arm around her, not saying anything, but just holding on.

After several minutes, the quiet crying ended. She pulled a wadded Kleenex out of her pocket and used it. "Damn. Sorry about that."

"You're entitled." He glanced at his watch. "Lainie, I'm going out to Holly Point now. I think that may be where Jody and his brother are."

"You're going alone?"

"Yes." He moved away again, sitting on the couch edge. "I'm just so damned tired of the dying. This whole thing is between Tom Hitchcock and me, and it's going to end now. Now, damn it."

"You're taking a dangerous chance."

He shook his head. "Not such a chance. Surprise is on my side. And besides, I won't be all on my own. I've got a back-up."

"Where?"

"Right here."

She looked around. "What?"

"You. At nine o'clock, if I haven't been in touch, call headquarters and ask for Lieutenant McGannon. Tell him where I've gone and why. Will you do that? I know damned well I've got no right to ask, but it would help."

"Of course I'll do it. I'm glad to know that the hero is alive and well in America."

He shook his head. "If you want heroes, watch television. I'm just a tired cop."

She walked to the door with him. "You'll be careful, won't you, Detective Kowalski?"

"Spaceman," he corrected. "And I'm always careful."

Chapter 31

BLUE dreamed that he fell through a time warp.

He fell and when he stopped falling, he was back in the camp in Nam. The end of it all, the coming home, the being a cop and all the rest he'd thought was real was nothing but fantasy.

The fucking VC guards came to look at him occasionally, once brought him food, but he couldn't eat. He just huddled in the corner and tried to stay sane. Sometimes he made faces at himself, wondering as he did when the hell they'd put mirrors all over the hut. Didn't make much sense, but he could dig it.

Suddenly, without warning, there was the crash of artillery fire very near by. The guards were all gone, probably in the shelter, and he was left all alone. There was another, even closer explosion.

Blue began to scream.

"What the hell is wrong with him?" Tommy complained. "He scared of a little thunder?"

Jody had soaked a handkerchief in the bottled water and he rubbed it on his face in an effort to cool off. "I think he's out of it. Whatever you gave him in the last shot."

"Yeah, maybe so." Tommy smiled and ruffled Jody's hair. "Almost over now. First thing in the morning I call Kowalski and set up a meet."

"How do you know he'll come?"

"He'll show. You think he wants his partner dead? If the pig thinks he can save Maguire by doing what I say, he'll do it. Kowalski is right in the palm of my hand." Tommy crushed the beercan he was holding.

Jody moved away, going to stand in the open doorway. "It won't help, will it?"

"What?"

"You're going to kill him anyway, right?" He spoke flatly.

"Sure. Have to. But not until Kowalski is here to watch. That's the fun part."

Jody was staring out into the early night sky, watching the boiling clouds. "Then what?" he said.

"What?"

"After you're all finished with Kowalski, then what the hell do we do next?"

"Whatever we want."

"What if there's nothing I want?"

Tommy walked over and stood behind him. "You're acting funny, Jody. Is anything wrong?"

"Is anything wrong? Are you serious?" Jody felt a sudden sadness sweep over him. He shook his head. "I think it's gonna rain any minute," he said. "Hope to hell it cools things off."

"Yeah." Tommy began to massage Jody's back. "Hey, you're all tense." He laughed softly. "Bet I know how to untense you."

Jody jerked away. "Not now," he said.

"Okay, sure." Tommy sounded surprised. His hands began to rub again. "Maybe you're right. We'll wait until this is all finished and then we'll have a big party. We'll find us a couple of nice kids and go to the beach. How about that?"

Jody was still watching the approaching storm. It was very close now. He thought he saw some headlights way down the road, but then decided it was only lightning. He raised his eyes to the sky again. "Why did you kill Jerry?"

The words were soft, said into the night, and he was surprised that they'd come from his mouth. He had been

215

silently screaming the question ever since he'd found out. Now the words were said.

Tommy's hands stopped rubbing, but stayed where they were. "How'd you find out? Did that bastard in there tell you?"

"It doesn't matter how I found out. What difference does it make?" Jody turned to face his brother. "Why, that's the question, why? Jerry was a good person. He loved me, that's all, and for that you killed him."

Tommy slapped him across the face. "Shut up. I did what I had to do. What right do you have to question it?"

Jody rubbed his cheek, staring at him. For the first time in his life, he didn't like the feelings he was having toward Tommy. It scared him to feel this way. He couldn't hate his brother, because Tommy was a part of him.

But Tommy killed Jerry.

Jody wanted just to turn and run into the darkness and hope that the storm would swallow him up. He wanted to disappear.

But he didn't.

Tommy pulled him into a tight hug. "I'm sorry if I did the wrong thing. I didn't mean to make you mad." He spoke softly into Jody's ear, the words falling like gentle touches. "I'm sorry."

Jody stood there for an endless moment and then he returned the hug. He did it because he felt like a man falling into a bottomless pit and he had to hold onto something.

He held onto Tommy because Tommy was there.

Spaceman left the car some distance from the park entrance. As he walked closer, he took the gun from its holster and held it loosely in one hand. The rain which had been threatening finally broke just as he reached the gate and slipped through. The skies opened up and let loose.

Perfect, he thought. Just fucking perfect.

216

So heavy was the rain that he couldn't see more than a foot in any direction. He kept moving anyway, toward the dimly defined shapes ahead.

He had a sudden flash of *déjà vu:* 1966. Nam. The fucking jungle in the rainy season. Some fun. A sharp crack of thunder made him jump, then he swore. Battle nerves. Killed a lot of grunts, nerves like that. Well, they weren't going to kill Spaceman Kowalski.

He wiped water from his eyes and peered straight ahead. Was that a light in the large building to the left? He decided it was, and moved in that direction. His hand, shoved into his jacket pocket now, was still wrapped around the gun.

By the time he reached the side of the building and pressed himself against it, Spaceman felt as if he'd spent a month in the monsoon. He edged toward the door. Through the crack of the opening, he could see a narrow shaft of light.

Spaceman stood very still for a moment, considering. He was going on a hunch, nothing more than that. Nothing less than that too, he reminded himself. Who the hell else would be out here in the middle of nowhere on a night like this?

It had to be Hitchcock in there and now was the time for action. Act first, think about it later.

He took a deep breath, said a prayer to whoever might be listening, and kicked the door open with his foot. He jumped in, landing on one knee, the gun raised. "Freeze," he screamed.

Spaceman's vision blurred as he saw his own image come back at him dozens of times. Then a shot sounded, very close by, and one of the images shattered. Spaceman fell to the floor and rolled until he hit the wall. He tried to focus, but the room was still filled with wavery reflections, and he didn't know where to fire. "Give it up, Hitchcock!" he yelled helplessly.

"Fuck you!" came the reply. The words were followed by another shot and more glass shattering.

Spaceman hugged the floor. He stayed there, trying to orient himself. Suddenly the light went out and he could hear the sound of fast-moving feet. After a moment, he started to crawl, hoping he was going in the right direction. Actually, he discovered that it was easier in the dark. The distorting mirrors no longer added their confusion.

He bumped into a wall, angled off slightly and kept going.

After only a couple of centuries of crawling, he made it to the door again. He pushed it open and slid down the wet ramp on his stomach. The rain had let up, and a sudden flash of lightning outlined three figures running across the compound. Actually, two were running and the third, bound hand and foot, was being dragged along.

"Stop!" Spaceman yelled again, but the word was swallowed up by the wind and rain. He started after them, slipping and stumbling in the mud.

They were already gone from sight, except for the pale glow of a flashlight. Then even that disappeared and Spaceman was alone.

He stood still and waited, not even breathing, until another flash of lightning illuminated the three figures again. They weren't running now, they were climbing. Already they were about halfway up the side of the ferris wheel, moving slowly from one car to the next, dragging Maguire behind.

Spaceman headed that way. When he was right underneath them, he looked up. "You can't get out that way, Hitchcock."

It sounded like Hitchcock said something in reply, but Spaceman couldn't make out the words. He just stood, waiting.

After threatening for so long and hitting so brutally, the storm seemed to have spent itself quickly. The rain just stopped and some light began to show through the clouds. Instead of cooling things off, however, all it seemed to have done was make the world steam. Everything took on a dirty yellow glow.

Spaceman stepped back a little so he could see them better. They had climbed into a car. "This won't help, Tom," he said. In the sudden stillness, the words carried well. "Do you want to get yourself and your brother killed?"

"We're not scared. You make one move I don't like, and your partner'll do a swan dive. *Comprendé?*"

"Killing a cop is dumb, Tom."

"Fuck you."

Spaceman peered up through the pale light. "Blue? You okay?"

If there was an answer, he didn't hear it.

Spaceman tried another tactic. "Jody? Why don't you quit this now before it's too late? He killed Jerry, do you know that?"

"He knows. He doesn't care. Tell him that you don't give a damn, Jody."

Jody didn't say anything.

"I talked to Lainie, Jody. She wants it to work out okay for you. She knows that you didn't have anything to do with what happened to Jerry."

"Shut up!" Tom screamed suddenly. "Shut the fuck up, or I'll push this bastard over the side." He shoved Blue a little and the tied man swung precariously out of the car, held only by the rope in Tom's hand. Then he was yanked back into the seat.

"Stop!" Jody seemed to have finally found his voice. "Stop, Tommy, please. No more dying. I can't stand anymore dying."

"You siding with the pigs now, Jody? Turning against your own brother? You forgetting everything I've done for you?"

219

"I just want it to end. Now."

"It'll end when I say so."

Spaceman watched the small car move back and forth high in the air. "They're burying Jerry tomorrow, Jody. I think he'd like to have you there."

Above there was only silence. He could make out Jody and Tom, staring at one another.

"Frag the mutha' fuckers!" Blue yelled suddenly. "Frag the slanty-eyed mutha' fuckers!"

Tom, startled by the unexpected noise, dropped the rope. Instantly, Blue moved. There was only one way to go and he went. Over the side. He climbed out of the car and dangled there, holding onto the side with both hands.

"Hang on, Blue!" Spaceman yelled, stupidly.

"What the fuck else can I do?" Blue sounded drunk.

Tom was trying to pull Blue back into the car. Exasperated, he yanked out a gun and leaned over the side to press the barrel against Blue's head. "You bastard."

Spaceman was watching Tom. He never saw Jody move. Neither did his brother until it was too late. It was such a quick moment, just a shove, and it was done.

Tom screamed once sharply on the way down.

He hit against the concrete piling at the bottom of the ferris wheel. Then he was still.

Spaceman ran over and dropped to his knees beside the body, but there wasn't a thing he could do for Thomas Hitchcock. His neck had snapped. Spaceman stared at him for a moment, feeling a certain sense of justice inside. One part of him knew he shouldn't feel that way, but he did.

He jumped up and moved back out to where he could see the car overhead again. While Blue struggled to climb back into the violently rocking metal box, Jody was standing, one leg slung over the restraining bar.

Spaceman knew what was going to happen next. For one split moment, he wanted to let it just happen. That would make a nice tidy end to this whole mess. Everybody could be done with it, except of course, for those in mourning. But then he knew he couldn't let it just happen. "Don't jump, Jody. Please." He was sick and tired of death, too. "Let me go," Jody pleaded, as if someone were actually holding him back. "It doesn't matter. Just let it be done." "It matters to me. Enough, already. No more dead bodies."

Jody shook his head.

Blue was still trying to pull himself back into the car. "Jody," he said breathlessly. "Help me, please. I don't think I can make it."

"Let me die."

"Help me."

After another moment, Jody pulled his leg back. Then he reached over the side and helped Blue up into the car. Spaceman was already on his way up. After several treacherous minutes on the rain-slippery metal, he reached the car and managed to squeeze in. Nobody was getting out of the thing without help.

Blue was still dopey; his face was pale and his eyeballs kept disappearing. Still he managed a wobbly thumbs up.

Jody was between them, crying. "I'm sorry," he whispered. "I'm so sorry."

Spaceman didn't say anything. In the distance, he could hear the wail of sirens and see flashing lights. Lainie had come through.

He relaxed into the gentle rocking of the car.

Chapter 38

"I SHOULD lift your shield," McGannon said. "For being such a stupid asshole."

It was one of the milder things he had said in the last forty minutes. Spaceman, wearing a sweatsuit from his locker, just nodded. He'd been sitting across from the infamous desk, nodding, for a long time.

McGannon seemed to run out of steam suddenly. "Get the hell out of here," he said wearily. "Before I lose my temper."

Spaceman got up and shuffled to the door. It was already well into the next day and he hadn't had any sleep.

"Spaceman —"

"Huh?"

"Good work."

He lifted his hand a few inches in acknowledgement and left. He didn't know whether he should turn right or left. He tossed a mental coin, dropped it, and went left. He stood outside the interrogation room. Through the one-way window, he could see Jody, his head resting on the table. With him was a broad from the public defender's office. She wasn't having any better luck with Jody than had Spaceman or the other detectives. He had just clammed up, withdrawn into his own private hell.

Spaceman sighed and shook his head. Later for Jody. He turned in time to see Blue enter the room. Dressed in jeans and a tee shirt, Maguire was still white and his hands seemed to be shaking a little, but he smiled faintly in greeting.

"You hanging tough?" Spaceman said.

"Oh, sure." He inclined his head toward the window. "Sad."

"Yeah, maybe." Spaceman was tired of sad. "You sure that you don't belong in the hospital?"

"I'm sure. The doc cleared me. He suggested a cup of tea and bed. I suggested a couple drinks and bed. We compromised. One drink and bed."

"Okay. I'm buying."

They started out.

"Kowalski!" It was McGannon's voice.

Spaceman sighed. "Shit, I thought he was done with me for a while." He turned. "Yeah?"

"Into my office."

They both started in. McGannon stopped Blue. "This is personal for Kowalski," he said, not rudely.

Blue and Spaceman glanced at each other. Spaceman shrugged. "Maguire's okay," he said.

McGannon just nodded and went behind his desk. "It's about your son," he said.

Spaceman's stomach did a minor flip-flop; that was all he could manage at the moment. "What about him?"

McGannon seemed fascinated by the grain of the wood in the top of his desk. "Kowalski, he was arrested this morning."

"Busted? What for?" Spaceman closed his eyes and rubbed the bridge of his nose.

"Seems like he's the one been setting the fires in the hills. Some county guys caught him in the act, and he apparently confessed to the whole thing. They're holding him at Parker Center."

Spaceman didn't say anything for several long moments. Then he stood. "Okay. Thanks for telling me. Come on, Maguire, I owe you a drink."

They walked out of the building and across the street without saying anything. Not until they were sitting in the back of the Lock-up, with drinks in front of them, did Spaceman break the silence. "What the fuck am I gonna do?" he said.

Blue took a careful sip of the drink, testing the booze, or maybe his own ability to handle it. "What do you want to do?"

"Something. Kill the little son of a bitch. Yell. Something."

"Yelling would be fine, I guess. A real fatherly thing to do."

Spaceman hit the table suddenly, with the palm of his hand. "Why the hell would he do something like this?"

Blue felt way out of his depth; what did he know about trying to raise a kid? All he had to go by was the example of his own father. "I don't know, Spaceman," he said. "I suppose he felt like he had reasons."

"Reasons? What kind of reasons can there be for something like this? Shit." Briefly, he was sullenly quiet. Then he said, "Well, it's his mess, damn it. To hell with it. I'm tired. Let his mother do the handholding."

"You don't mean that."

"Don't I?"

"He's your son. Give him a chance."

But Spaceman shook his head.

Blue frowned, but kept his mouth shut.

At last, Spaceman sighed deeply and rubbed his eyes. "I better haul my ass down to Parker," he said. "See the boy."

"Yeah, I think that sounds like a good idea," Blue said carefully.

"You get home okay?"

"No problem. I'll see you later."

Spaceman glanced at his watch and seemed just barely

224

able to make out the time. "The Potter funeral is at three. I want to make that."

"Any special reason?"

He shook his head. "No good reason. I just want to be there. The sister might like to have somebody there."

Blue looked at him. "Okay. Pick me up. I'll go along."

"Whatever." Spaceman was quiet again for a moment. "Do me a favor," he said then.

"Sure."

"Call the Lompoc department and find out about the boy up there. I'd like to know who he was." A fleeting smile crossed Spaceman's face. "No good reason for that, either." No matter what Karen said, he couldn't seem to stop hurting, to stop bleeding. And no matter what she thought, he bled for his own son as much as all the others.

"I'll do it," Blue said. "I'll find out about the boy."

"Thanks." Spaceman stood, and Blue waited, thinking the other man had more to say. But then he just shook his head a little and left the bar.

When he finally did get home, Blue couldn't sleep. He sat in front of the window, looking out over the city and drinking a glass of flat ginger ale. Behind him, the police radio chattered on softly. There wasn't much going on, which suited him fine.

The damned cat had returned, and was even deigning to keep him company for the moment. Pretty soon, he'd have to stir himself and get dressed for the funeral, but for right now, he was free to sit and do nothing.

It wasn't a bad way to spend some time.

...lar merged spellings such as
...from much earlier, is no reason for
...ple still find it unacceptable in

...sometimes used in place of
...American English. In British English the
... quite distinct: **alternative** means
...sibility or choice', as in *some European*
...*ative approach* **Alternate** means 'every
...*n alternate Sundays*, or 'each following
...attern', as in *alternate layers of potato and*
...**nate** to mean **alternative**, as in *we will*
...*urces of fuel*, is common in North America,
...ries now record it as equivalent in this
...ve. In British English, however, it is not
... style.

... can be replaced by **though**, the only
...at **although** tends to be more formal than

...**ther** and **all together** do not mean the same
...**er** means 'in total', as in *there are six bedrooms*
...reas **all together** means 'all in one place' or 'all at
...*as good to have a group of friends all together; they*
...ether.*

...mes from Latin, and refers to an ex-student of a
...niversity or similar educational establishment.
...**s alumni**. The technically correct form for a female
...is **alumna**, the plural of which is **alumnae**. **Alumni** is
...o use when referring to groups including both sexes,
...**nae** when they are exclusively female. Although

---

changes in hundreds of other words which have long been
accepted without comment.

ago

When **ago** is followed by a clause, the clause should be
introduced by **that** rather than **since**, e.g. *it was sixty years ago*
that I left this place, but you could avoid **ago** by writing *it is sixty*
years since I left this place.

agreement

Agreement (also called *concord*) is the correct relation of
different parts of a sentence to each other: for example,
the form of a verb should correspond to its subject: *the*
***house was** small, and its **walls were** painted white*; again,
the gender and number (singular or plural) of a pronoun
should conform to those of the person or thing it refers to:
*he had never been close enough to a **girl** to consider making*
***her** his wife*. As English has lost many inflections over
centuries of use, problems of agreement only arise in the
two cases just mentioned. This article deals with noun-verb
agreement. Discussion of pronoun agreement and other
aspects of verb agreement is dealt with under individual
entries: see AND, ANY, AS WELL AS, EACH, EITHER, GENDER-NEUTRAL
LANGUAGE, HALF, KIND, NONE, NUMBER, OR, SORT, and THEY.
Here are some typical difficulties that people have in
making verbs agree with noun subjects.

1 Sentences, especially long ones, in which the verb is
separated from its singular subject by intervening words in
the plural can make the speaker or writer put the verb in
the plural, but these examples are incorrect: *the*
***consequence** of long periods of inactivity or situations in*
*which patients cannot look after themselves **are** often quite*
*severe and long-lasting; **copyright** of Vivienne's papers **are***
in the keeping of the Haigh-Wood family.
In the first example there are three options: ▶

change *consequence* to *consequences*, change *are* to *is*, or (probably best) recast the sentence more simply, *e.g. Long periods of inactivity . . . can often have quite severe and long-lasting consequences.*

2 Two nouns joined by **and**: these normally form a plural subject and require a plural verb: *speed and accuracy are what is needed*; *fish and chips are served in the evening.* But when the noun phrase is regarded as a singular unit, it can take a singular verb: *fish and chips is my favourite meal*; *wine, women, and song was the leitmotiv of his lifestyle.* This can extend to concepts that are distinct in themselves but are regarded as a single item in a particular sentence: *a certain cynicism and resignation comes along with advancing years.*

The last convention is very old, with evidence dating back to Old and Middle English. Clearly there will be borderline cases, and then it is what sounds natural that matters: *the hurt and disbelief of parents' friends and families **is/are** already quite real.*

3 Two or more nouns can be joined by words other than **and**, e.g. *accompanied by, as well as, not to mention, together with,* etc. These noun groups are followed by a singular verb if the first noun or noun phrase is singular, because the addition is not regarded as part of the grammatical subject: *even such a very profitable company, along with many other companies in the UK, **is** not prepared to pay even a reasonable amount*; *Daddy had on the hairy tweed **jacket** with leather elbow patches which, together with his pipe, **was** his trademark.*

4 When a subject and a complement of different number (singular/plural) are separated by the verb *to be* (or verbs such as *become, seem,* etc.), the verb should agree with the number of the subject, not that of the complement:

- (singular subject and plural complement) *the only **traffic** is ox-carts and bicycles; the **view** it obscured **was** pipes, fire escapes, and a sooty wall* ▶

19th century, while other sim
altogether and **already** date
denouncing it, but many pe
formal writing.

alternative

The adjective **alternate** is
alternative, especially in
two words continue to b
'available as another pos
countries follow an altern
other', as in they meet
the other in a regular p
sauce. The use of **alte**
need to find alternate s
and many US diction
meaning to **alternati**
yet considered good

although

The form **althoug**
difference being t
though.

altogether

Note that **altog**
thing. **Altoget**
altogether, whe
once', as in it v
came in all tog

alumnus

Alumnus c
particular u
The plural
ex-student
the form
and **alun**

alb

1 Al
is u
cont
unwe

2 It shou
Standar

3 Even thou
keep going
albeit with
he was not in
is that **albeit**
already contai

alibi

The word **alibi**, wh
since the 18th cent
or she was elsewhere
originally in the US, o
natural extension of th
accepted in standard En
some people.

alright

There is no logical reason fo
and should always be written
word forms such as **altogethe**
The fact that **alright** is not rec

alumnus is a masculine noun in Latin, it is sometimes used to refer to a female ex-student in contexts where the feminine form might sound overacademic: *she's touted as the number one alumnus of Southern Methodist University*. **Alumnus** is pronounced /uh-**lum**-nuhs/. **Alumni** is generally pronounced as /uh-**lum**-nI/, and **alumnae** as /uh-**lum**-nee/.

Alzheimer's disease

This condition is often incorrectly spelled with a letter **t** inserted before the **z**, reflecting its pronunciation. Some German names used in English expressions do contain **tz**, such as *Hertz* and *Helmholtz*, but **z** in **Alzheimer's** is pronounced /-ts-/ anyway: /**alts**-hI-muhz/.

a.m.

As an abbreviation of Latin **ante meridiem**, meaning 'before noon', **a.m.** is pronounced as two letters and written with two full stops in the form **8.15 a.m.** (in American English **8:15 a.m.**). Note that **12.00 a.m.** is midnight and **12.00 p.m.** is midday, but because of the uncertainty these designations cause, the explicit forms **12 midnight** and **12 noon** or **12 midday** are clearer. The abbreviation is sometimes used informally as a noun: *I arrived here this a.m.*, but this use is not acceptable in any kind of formal writing.

American Indian

The term **American Indian** has been steadily replaced in the US, especially in official contexts, by the more recent term **Native American** (first recorded in the 1950s and becoming prominent in the 1970s). Some people prefer **Native American** as being a more accurate and respectful description as well as avoiding the stereotype of cowboys and Indians in the stories of the Wild West. **American Indian** is still widespread in general use even in the US, however, perhaps at least partly because it is not normally regarded as offensive by American Indians themselves. Nevertheless, since the category **American Indian** is very broad, it is preferable,

a

where possible, to name the specific people, e.g. **Apache**, **Comanche**, or **Sioux**.

amount

It is always correct to use **amount** with nouns with a singular meaning, such as *money*, *time*, and *energy*. With nouns which have a plural form or meaning, it is always right to use **number**: *the number of people*, *the number of patients*, *the number of accidents*, etc. But quite often people use **amount** instead of **number** with plural nouns, as in *the amount of nutrients available*; *the amount of bribes*; *the amount of calls at night*. This use has a long tradition and is broadly forgivable in speech, but it is best avoided in writing: people with tidy grammatical minds may be as irritated by it as they are by the use of *less* when *fewer* is correct, as in *customers with less than five items*.

an

Opinions differ over whether to use **a** or **an** before certain words beginning with **h-** when the first syllable is unstressed: *a historical document* or *an historical document*; *a hotel* or *an hotel*. The uncertainty arises for historical reasons: **an** was common in the 18th and 19th centuries, because the initial **h** was often not pronounced in these words. Nowadays, use of **a** or **an** varies in both writing and speaking. Only older speakers are likely to pronounce words such as **hotel** and **historic** with the silent **h**; nevertheless, *an hotel* and *an historic event* are often heard and are equally correct.

In writing, there are many examples in the Oxford English Corpus of **an** being used with **habitual**, **historian**, **historic(al)**, **horrendous**, and **horrific**, albeit less often than **a**.
Remember that whether you use **a** or **an** depends on the sound at the start of the following word, however it is spelled. For instance, although the letter **u** normally represents a vowel, the words **unique** and **uniform** start with a **y** sound, which is a consonant, and it is therefore correct to write and say *a unique feature* and *a uniform approach*. This also applies to abbreviations where the initials are pronounced as the names of letters, such as *EU* and *SAS*. The names of the letters **E** and **S** are

said as /ee/ (a vowel sound) and /ess/ (also starting with a vowel sound), so you would say and write both *an EU ruling* and *an SAS unit*.

analogous

Strictly speaking, **analogous** should not be used merely as a supposedly stylish synonym for *similar*. It means 'comparable in certain respects', especially where the analogy makes the nature of the things compared clearer: *they saw the relationship between a ruler and his subjects as analogous to that of father and children.* As in the example just shown, the preposition to use with **analogous** is **to**, rather than **with**.

Analogous is pronounced with a hard **g**.

and

1 Many people believe that conjunctions such as **and**, **but**, and **because** should not be used to start a sentence. They argue that a sentence starting with a conjunction expresses an incomplete thought and is therefore incorrect. Writers down the centuries, from Shakespeare to David Lodge, have ignored this advice, however, typically for rhetorical effect: *What are the government's chances of winning in court? And what are the consequences?*

2 For the expression **try and do something**, see TRY AND.

3 For information about whether it is more correct to say *both the boys and the girls* or *both the boys and girls*, see BOTH.

4 Where items in a list are separated by **and**, the following verb needs to be in the plural: see OR.

antidisestablishmentarianism

Antidisestablishmentarianism is almost never found in genuine use and is most often merely cited as an example of a very long word. Other similar curiosities are *floccinaucinihilipilification* and *pneumonoultramicroscopicsilicovolcanoconiosis*, the second being generally reckoned to be the longest word in any dictionary. The longest word to be encountered in Britain is the Welsh place name

a

Llanfairpwllgwyngyllgogerychwyrndrobwllllantysiliogogogoch,
which is generally abbreviated to Llanfair PG; this name was
created in the 19th century.

antisocial

On the difference in use between **antisocial**, **unsocial**, and
unsociable, see UNSOCIABLE.

anxious

Anxious and **eager** both mean 'looking forward to something',
but they have different overtones. **Eager** suggests enthusiasm
about something and a positive outlook: *I'm eager to get started
on my vacation*. **Anxious** implies worry about something: *I'm
anxious to get started before it rains*. This is a useful distinction
to maintain.

any

When used as a pronoun, **any** can be used with either a singular
or a plural verb, depending on the context. If **any** refers to a
singular uncountable noun, the verb is always singular: *we needed
more sugar but there **wasn't any** left*. Uncertainty occasionally
arises, however, when the noun referred to is plural, especially
in questions and hypotheses: *are **any** of the above suitable? if **any**
of them **escape**, notify the police*. The general tendency is to
use the verb in the plural, especially in conversation. If you
use the verb in the singular, you are presupposing that
only one person or thing is being referred to, as in *if **any** of
them **inspires** the public*... Otherwise, use with a singular
verb is likely these days to sound stilted or affected.
See also AGREEMENT.

anyone

The one-word form **anyone** is not the same as the
two-word form **any one**, and the two forms cannot be used
interchangeably. **Anyone** means 'any person or people',
as in *anyone who wants to can attend*. **Any one** means 'any
single (person or thing)', as in *no more than twelve new
members are admitted in any one year*.

apostrophe

This insignificant-looking mark is the loose cannon of the punctuation world, responsible for more howlers than any other punctuation mark. So, it may be helpful to refresh your memory about its two very distinct functions. It is also useful to be on the lookout for the obvious traps apostrophes can lay for you, as explained under **four pitfalls to avoid**, below.

- Apostrophes stand for letters that have been missed out.

- They show that someone or something owns something.

1 Missed out letters

In speaking we often leave out sounds from certain words, particularly verbs: we tend to say *I'm going*, not *I am going*. In other cases, we run two words together: *I shan't go* instead of *I shall not go*.
The apostrophe shows where we have left out these sounds:
won't = will not
can't = cannot
she's = she is; she has
you're = you are
In a few other words, often rather old-fashioned or poetic ones, apostrophes also show letters missed out:
o'er (= over); *ne'er-do-well*; *rock 'n' roll*.

2 Ownership

- The apostrophe indicates that someone owns something, or shows a relationship between the things mentioned:
  Jack's new mountain bike
  the parrot's cage
  the book's cover

- To help you decide if the apostrophe comes before or after the letter **s**, first try rephrasing your sentence using the word **of**. Then look carefully at the final ▶

a

letter of the relevant word as it now appears. The correct place to put the apostrophe is immediately after that letter. For example *in a week's time* becomes *in the time of a week*, which shows that the apostrophe goes after the letter **k**. But *in three weeks' time* becomes *in the time of three weeks*, proving that the apostrophe should come after the letter **s**.

3 Four pitfalls to avoid

- Never use an apostrophe to show the plural of a word when there is no ownership involved. You will often see this mistake on shop signs or on grocers' stalls: *apple's and pear's*, which should be *apples and pears*. The same rule applies to plurals which are abbreviations: *MPs, QCs, DVDs*. See also the entry for *'s*.

- Remember the difference between **it's** and **its**. The first one shows that a letter has been left out: *it's on the trolley*. The second indicates ownership, but in spite of that has no apostrophe: *the kitten licked its paws*. **Its** in this meaning is the same type of word as *ours*, *yours*, *his*, and *hers*, where it is clear that no apostrophe is required.

- **Who's** and **whose** are often confused. Remember those corny old jokes that go *Knock, knock!—Who's there?* In that case, ***who's*** is obviously short for *who is*. **Whose** is like **its**: although it shows ownership, it needs no apostrophe: *that's the man **whose** son got married to my cousin.*

- **You're** and **your** are very easy to muddle up when writing at speed. The first indicates a missing letter: *you're late again* = you are late again. The second is like **its** and **whose**—ownership, but no apostrophe: *is this **your** wallet, Bob?*

appendix

Appendix has the plural form **appendices** when referring to
parts of books and documents, and **appendixes** when referring
to the bodily organ. For more information on the plural of Latin
words, see LATIN PLURALS.

appraise, apprise

The verb **appraise** is frequently confused with **apprise**.
Appraise means 'to assess', as in *a need to appraise existing
techniques*, or 'to value', as in *have the gold watch appraised by
an expert*. **Apprise** means 'to inform' and is often used in
the construction **apprise someone of something**, as in
psychiatrists were apprised of his condition. People often
incorrectly use **appraise** rather than **apprise**, as in *once appraised
of the real facts, there was only one person who showed any
opposition*.

aristocrat, aristocratic

There are two ways of pronouncing **aristocrat**. You can
emphasize either the first syllable (/**a**-ris-tuh-krat/) or the second
(/a-**ris**-tuh-krat/). The first pronunciation is still the standard one
in British English. The second is the standard American
pronunciation, but is fast gaining ground in Britain too,
particularly among transatlantic academics and pundits.
Interestingly, it was once the standard in Britain, so it could be
seen as a revival rather than an intrusion. **Aristocratic** is normally
pronounced emphasizing the fourth syllable in British English
(/a-ris-tuh-**kra**-tik/) and emphasizing the second in American
English (/a-**ris**-tuh-kra-tik/).

around

1 On the difference in use between **round** and **around**, see ROUND.

2 It is curious how some words become so popular that they oust
the ones people routinely used before. **Around** is such a word.
It is now, arguably, overused as an all-purpose preposition,
generally to show the relationship between two abstract ideas:
I think there's a misconception around that, somehow; we would

like some flexibility around that implementation; there are
concerns around the following issues. *While there is no objection
in principle to using **around** in the ways shown, it comes laden
with the heavy baggage of bureaucracy or of the caring
professions. It seems to have expanded from its core use in the
common phrase **issues around**, through similar contexts to
general use, willy-nilly. Prepositions such as **over** and **about**
could replace it in all the examples above with absolutely no
loss of meaning, and with a considerable gain in freshness
or sincerity.*

artefact

Artefact, 'a product of human art or workmanship' comes from
the Latin *arte factum*, 'made by art'. The spelling with the letter
e is much the more common in British English. In American
English, **artifact**, corresponding to pronunciation rather than
etymology, is the preferred form, but would be looked on
unfavourably in most of the circles in Britain in which such
a word would be used.

as

1 For a discussion of whether it is correct to say:
he's not as shy as I rather than *he's not as shy as me*
or
I live in the same street as she rather than *I live in the same street
as her*
see PERSONAL PRONOUN.

2 For more information on when **as** is preferable to **like**, see LIKE.

ascribe

Ascribe and **subscribe** are sometimes confused. If you **ascribe**
a quality **to** a person or group of people, you think it is typical
of them, as in *tough-mindedness is a quality commonly ascribed
to top bosses*. If you **subscribe to** a belief, view, or idea, you
agree with it: *we prefer to subscribe to an alternative explanation*.
It is wrong to give this meaning to **ascribe to**, as in *which
theory do you ascribe to?*

as far as

Using **as far as** to specify something, as in the phrase, *as far as the money, you can forget it*, is well established in American usage and is a useful shorthand for the older **as far as ... is/are concerned**. Nevertheless, many more conservative British speakers are likely to object to it, so it is best avoided with a British audience.

Asian

In Britain, **Asian** is used to refer to people who come from (or whose parents came from) the Indian subcontinent, but in North America it is used to refer to people from the Far East.

Asiatic

The standard and accepted term when referring to individual people is **Asian** rather than **Asiatic**, which can be offensive. However, **Asiatic** is standard in scientific and technical use, for example in biological and anthropological classifications.

assurance

In life insurance, a technical distinction is made between **assurance** and **insurance**. **Assurance** is used of policies under whose terms a payment is guaranteed, either after a fixed term or on the death of the insured person; **insurance** is the general word, and is used in particular of policies under whose terms a payment would be made only in certain circumstances (e.g. accident or death within a limited period).

asterisk

Asterisk should be pronounced with an /-isk/ sound at the end, to match the spelling, and not as though it were spelled -**ix**. **Asterix** is a character in a cartoon strip.

as well as

A verb following **as well as** should be singular if the noun or pronoun that precedes **as well as** is singular: *their **singing*** *as well as acting **is** exemplary*. This is because the addition (here, the phrase *as well as acting*) is regarded as an aside and not as part of the main sentence. This is in contrast to what would happen if **as well as** were replaced by **and**. For more information see AND and OR.

aural

The words **aural** ('relating to the ears or the sense of hearing') and **oral** ('spoken rather than written') are both pronounced as /**aw**-ruhl/ in Received Pronunciation, which is sometimes a source of confusion. However, although a distinctive pronunciation for **aural** has been proposed, namely /**ow**-ruhl/, it is very little used.

Australoid

The term **Australoid** belongs to a set of terms introduced by 19th-century anthropologists attempting to categorize human races. Such terms are associated with outdated notions of racial types, and so are now potentially offensive and best avoided. See MONGOLOID.

author

Some people object to the verb **author** as in *she has authored several books on wildlife*. It is well established, though, especially in North America. See also VERBS FORMED FROM NOUNS.

averse

On the confusion of **averse** and **adverse**, see ADVERSE.

awhile

The adverb **awhile** as in *we paused awhile* should be written as one word. The noun phrase, meaning 'a period of time', should be written as two words, especially when preceded by a preposition: *Margaret rested for a while*; *we'll be there in a while*.

backward

1 In their adverbial uses **backward** and **backwards** are interchangeable in meaning: *the car rolled slowly backward* and *the car rolled slowly backwards*. **Backward** is mainly used in

US English, but even there **backwards** is more common, as the Oxford English Corpus reveals. As an adjective, on the other hand, the standard form is **backward** rather than **backwards**: uses such as *a backwards glance* would generally be considered incorrect.

2 To describe a person with learning difficulties as **backward** is nowadays offensive.

bacterium

Bacteria is the plural form, from Latin, of **bacterium**. Like any other plural it should be used with the plural form of the verb: *the **bacteria** causing salmonella **are** killed by thorough cooking*, not *the **bacteria** causing salmonella **is** killed by thorough cooking*. However, general unfamiliarity with the form **bacterium** means that **bacteria** is often mistakenly treated as a singular form, as in the second example above. For other examples of this kind of mistake, see NOUNS, SINGULAR AND PLURAL.

balk, baulk

However this verb is spelled, it is usually pronounced so that you can hear the letter **l** (/bawlk/). Some older British speakers may pronounce it without the **l**. The spelling without **u** is now the more common one in all varieties of English.

Bantu

The word **Bantu** became a strongly offensive term under the old apartheid regime in South Africa, especially when used to refer to a single individual. In standard current use in South Africa the term **black** or **African** is used as a collective or non-specific word for African peoples. The term **Bantu** has, however, continued to be accepted as a neutral 'scientific' term outside South Africa to refer to the group of languages and their speakers collectively.

barbecue

Barbecue is often spelled **barbeque**. It is easy to see that this is because of how the word is pronounced and because of the informal abbreviations **BBQ** and **Bar-B-Q**. The spelling **barbeque** is now accepted in standard English.

barely

Barely, like **scarcely**, should normally be followed by *when*, not *than*, to introduce a subsequent clause: *he had barely reached the door when he collapsed*.

basis

It is very common for **basis** to be included in phrases describing how often something happens: *on a daily basis, on a weekly basis*, and so forth. Unless the word is really required in a technical context, e.g. *inspection of the facility is carried out on the basis of a weekly rota*, ordinary time adverbs such as **weekly** or **daily**, or a phrase such as **every week** can easily and more economically be used instead: *I do it weekly*.

bated breath

It is a common mistake to write **baited breath** instead of **bated breath**. The first written example of the original phrase is in Shakespeare's *The Merchant of Venice*, and **bate** is a shortened version of **abate**. About a third of all examples of this phrase in the Oxford English Corpus are with the incorrect spelling.
For more information, see FOLK ETYMOLOGY.

baulk

See BALK.

BC

BC is normally printed in small capitals and placed *after* the year, as in *72 BC* or *the 2nd century BC*. This position is logical since BC stands for 'before Christ'; compare with AD. It is not written with full stops after each letter.

bear

Until the 18th century **borne** and **born** were simply variants of the past participle of **bear**, used interchangeably with no distinction in meaning. By around 1775, however, the present distinction in use had become established. **Borne** became the standard past participle for the transitive verb: *she has borne you* *another son*; *the findings have been borne out*. **Born** became the standard, neutral way to refer to birth: *she was born in 1965*; *he was born lucky*; *I was born and bred in Gloucester*. The most common mistake is to write **born** instead of **borne**, as in the incorrect *his suspicions have not been born out*.

because

1 When **because** follows a negative construction the meaning can be ambiguous. In the sentence *he did not go because he was ill*, for example, it is not clear whether it means 'the reason he did not go was that he was ill' or 'being ill was not the reason for him going; there was another reason'. Some usage guides recommend using a comma for the first interpretation (*he did not go, because he was ill*) and no comma for the second interpretation, but it is probably wiser to avoid using **because** after a negative altogether; one way would be to turn the sentence around: *because he was ill, he didn't go*.

2 As with other conjunctions such as **but** and **and**, it is still widely held that it is incorrect to begin a sentence with **because**. It has, however, long been used in this way in both written and spoken English (typically for rhetorical effect), and is quite acceptable.

3 On the construction **the reason ... is because**, see REASON.

beg

The original meaning of the phrase **beg the question** belongs to the field of logic and is a translation of Latin *petitio principii*, literally meaning 'laying claim to a principle', i.e. assuming something that ought to be proved first, as in the following sentence: *by devoting such a large budget to Civics, we are begging the question of its usefulness*. For some people this is still the only correct meaning. However, over the last 100 years or so another, more general use has arisen: 'invite an obvious question', as in *some definitions of mental illness beg the question of what constitutes normal behaviour*. This is by far the commoner use today and is widely accepted in modern standard English.

b

behalf

Behalf is used in the phrase **on behalf of** and the rare variant **in behalf of**, the second used in American English. It can mean either 'in the interests of', as in *he campaigned on behalf of the poor*, or 'as a representative of', as in *I attended on her behalf*. It is increasingly being used to express responsibility for something, as in *this was a mistake on behalf of the government*, where **on the part of** is the appropriate phrase. This use is generally considered incorrect and should be avoided in writing.

beholden, behove

If you are **beholden** to someone for something, you owe them something in return for favours or services that they have done you: *politicians who are beholden to big business*. In formal language, if **it behoves you** to do something, it is your responsibility or duty to do it: *it behoves the House to assure itself that there is no conceivable alternative*. The form 'behoven' created by combining the two words is occasionally used instead of **beholden** but is not yet acceptable in standard English.

beside, besides

1 Both **beside** and **besides** have the meaning of 'apart from'. Some people claim that only **besides** should be used in this meaning: *he commissioned work from other artists besides Minton* rather than *he commissioned work from other artists beside Minton*. Although there is little logical basis for such a view, in standard English it can be clearer to use **besides** in this meaning, because **beside** can be ambiguous: *beside the cold meat, there are platters of trout and salmon* could mean either 'the cold meat is next to the trout and salmon' or 'apart from the cold meat, there are also trout and salmon'.

2 **Besides** is the correct form to use as an adverb meaning 'as well', as in *I'm capable of doing the work, and a lot more besides* or *besides, I wasn't sure*.

best

See WELL.

better

In the verb phrase **had better do something** the word **had** acts as an auxiliary verb and in informal spoken contexts is often dropped, as in *you better not come tonight*. In writing, the **had** may be contracted to **'d**, but it should not be dropped altogether.

between

In standard English it is correct to say *between you and me* but incorrect to say *between you and I*. There is a very good reason for this. A preposition such as **between** is correctly followed by object pronouns such as *me*, *him*, *her*, and *us* rather than subject pronouns such as *I*, *he*, *she*, and *we*. It is therefore correct to say *between us* or *between him and her* and it is clearly incorrect to say *between we* or *between he and she*.

People mistakenly say *between you and I* through confusing what follows a preposition and what ordinarily comes at the beginning of a sentence. They know that it is not correct to say *John and me went to the shops* and that the correct sentence is *John and I went to the shops*. They therefore assume that 'and me' should be replaced by 'and I' in all cases. For more information see PERSONAL PRONOUN.

bi-

1 The meaning of **bimonthly** and other similar words such as **biweekly** and **biyearly** is ambiguous. Such words can either mean 'occurring twice a month/week/year' or 'occurring every two months/weeks/years'. The only way to avoid this ambiguity is to use alternative expressions like 'every two months' and 'twice a month'.

2 **Biennial** means 'taking place every two years': *congressional elections are a biennial phenomenon*. A *biennial plant* is one that lives a two-year cycle, flowering and producing seed in the second year. **Biannual** means 'twice a year': *the solstice is a biannual event*. To avoid confusion, rephrasing is often the best option.

b

biceps

The form **biceps** works as both a singular and plural noun: *the biceps on his left arm*; *a pair of bulging biceps*. The singular 'bicep' is a back-formation and is generally viewed as incorrect, as is the plural 'bicepses'. See also NOUNS, SINGULAR AND PLURAL.

billion

The older meaning of **billion** in British English was 'a million million'. However, this meaning has now been almost entirely superseded by the meaning 'a thousand million'.

bipolar disorder

This term is increasingly being used as a more neutral way of referring to what was previously known as **manic depression.** For more information see MANIC DEPRESSION.

black

Evidence for the use of **black** to refer to African peoples (and their descendants) dates back at least to the late 14th century. Although the word has been in continuous use ever since, other terms have been favoured in the past. In the US **coloured** was the term adopted in preference by emancipated slaves following the American Civil War. **Coloured** was itself superseded in the US in the early 20th century by **Negro** as the word preferred by prominent black American campaigners such as Booker T. Washington. In Britain, on the other hand, **coloured** was the most widely used and accepted word in the 1950s and early 1960s. With the civil rights and Black Power movements of the 1960s, **black** was adopted by Americans of African origin to signify a sense of racial pride, and it remains the most widely used and generally accepted term in Britain today. It has been written with a capital letter—**Black**—as a way of indicating that it is a racial description rather than just a colour, but that is not now considered necessary. See also AFRICAN AMERICAN.

blatant

Blatant, a word invented by Spenser in the 16th century, generally refers to bad behaviour which is done openly: *a blatant lie* is one which is very obviously a lie.

Flagrant also refers to behaviour which is obviously bad or immoral, and is often applied to concrete breaches of laws, rules, and regulations: *a flagrant violation of school rules*. Nowadays there is considerable overlap in meaning between them, with **blatant** often applied to such breaches, though purists will maintain the distinction. The adverb **blatantly** (unlike **flagrantly**) has developed a weakened meaning, especially in youth slang, as a stock form of intensifier like **absolutely** and **extremely**: *this song is blatantly subtle*.

blind

It is better to avoid using *the blind* to refer to people in society with sight problems. Instead you should refer to *visually impaired people* or *blind or partially sighted people*.

blond, blonde

The alternative spellings **blond** and **blonde** correspond to the masculine and feminine forms in French, but in English the same distinction is not applied, and either form is therefore correct. Thus, **blond woman**, **blonde woman**, **blond man**, and **blonde man** are all used, though overall **blonde** is the commoner of the two spellings. American usage since the 1970s has generally preferred **blond**, thereby making it gender-neutral.

bona fide, bona fides

Bona fide is an adjectival phrase meaning 'in good faith' and hence 'genuine': *a bona fide tourist*. **Bona fides** is a noun phrase meaning 'good faith' and hence 'sincerity and honesty of intention': *he was at pains to establish his liberal bona fides*. Be careful not to spell them 'bone fide' or 'bone fides'. The pronunciation is /**boh** nuh **fI**-dee(z)/.

bored

The normal construction for **bored** is **bored by** or **bored with**. More recently, **bored of** has emerged (probably by analogy with other construction, such as **tired of**), but **bored of**, though common in informal English, is not yet considered acceptable in standard English.

b

born, borne

On the difference between **born** and **borne**, see BEAR.

both

When **both** is used in constructions with **and**, the structures following each should be symmetrical in well-formed English. Accordingly, *studies of lions, both in the wild and in captivity* is better than, for example, *studies of lions, both in the wild and captivity*. In the second example, the symmetry of 'in the wild' and 'in captivity' has been lost.

brackets

The word **brackets** is often applied generally to types which have more specific names: () are **round brackets** or **parentheses**; [] are **square brackets**; {} are **curly brackets** or **braces**; <> are **angle brackets**. When editing or describing documents it may be confusing if you use the general word when you mean a specific type of bracket. In particular, it is useful to remember that in US English **brackets** often means 'square brackets'.

Britain, Great Britain, the British Isles, England

The way these terms are used can be confusing. Some of them have an exact political or legal status, while others are used more loosely.

1 **The British Isles** is the traditional geographical term for the group of islands consisting of Great Britain and Ireland and the smaller islands around them, such as the Hebrides, Orkney, Shetland, the Scilly Isles, the Channel Islands, and the Isle of Man. Nowadays, many people, especially the Irish, prefer the term **Britain and Ireland**.

2 **Great Britain** refers to the largest island in the British Isles, divided between England, Scotland, and Wales. Politically, it means these three countries (since ▶

the Act of Union of 1707), but excludes Northern Ireland, the Isle of Man, and the Channel Islands.

3 **The United Kingdom** is a political term, short for **the United Kingdom of Great Britain and Northern Ireland**. It includes those two countries but not usually the Isle of Man or the Channel Islands.

4 **Britain** is a term with no official status. Sometimes it is used to mean the same as **Great Britain**. Government and media often use it to mean the **United Kingdom** (i.e. including Northern Ireland). While the word **British** has no defined legal status, it is often used as a shorthand for matters relating to the whole United Kingdom, as in *British government, British troops, the British public,* and so forth.

5 **England** strictly refers to a single political division of Great Britain, excluding Wales and Scotland. Less enlightened English people frequently and lamentably say or write **England** when they mean **(Great) Britain**, and using the word in this way can be rather offensive to the Welsh and Scots. This incorrect shorthand is very often used by English-speakers outside the British Isles, and by speakers of other languages. The same is true of the word **English**.

6 To refer in general to a citizen of the United Kingdom, **Briton** is the normal word in British English, and **Britisher** in American English.

broadcast

The verb **broadcast**, by analogy with **cast**, does not change in its past form and past participle: *the programme will be broadcast on Saturdays.* The form 'broadcasted' is not generally considered correct.

bruschetta

If you want to refer to this topped slice of Italian rustic bread approximately as an Italian would, pronounce it /broo-**sket**-uh/, with a short pause before the **t** sound, and spell it with -*sch*- not

b

-*sh*- in the middle. However, so many people pronounce it as
/broo-**shet**-uh/ that this seems likely to be the pronunciation
that will establish itself.

bullet points

People are often not sure how to write and punctuate text
which uses bullet points. As bullet points are relatively
recent, it is hardly surprising that there are no hard-and-fast
rules. Also, much depends on each person's visual
sensibility, the medium in which bullet points are being
used, and the intended audience. The following advice is
offered merely as a rule of thumb. If the text of the bullet
point is not itself a full sentence, it need not begin with
a capital letter and should not finish with a full stop, e.g.

- annual review of capital gains issues

If you prefer to punctuate your list, you should finish each
point that is not a complete sentence with a semi-colon,
and put a full stop after the last one, e.g.

- annual review of capital gains issues;
- outstanding inheritance tax issues;
- changes in tax regulations.

If the bullet point is a complete sentence, a full stop at the
end is technically correct, but might look a bit fussy, e.g.

- This will involve a review of the whole procedure.

You should bear in mind that in an electronic
presentation, where you may have few complete sentences,
punctuation at the end of bullet points may clutter the look.
In other written material you should consider the overall
look of the document, the number of bullet points, and
their length. You will also need to gauge your audience:
lecturers in an English department might be fussier about
punctuation than other audiences.

burned, burnt

Both **burned** and **burnt** are used for the past tense and
past participle of **burn** and are equally correct. **Burned** is
much more common for the past tense, e.g.: *she burned her
hand on the kettle*; *the church burned down in 1198*. As a
past participle, **burned** and **burnt** are equally common in
British English, e.g.: *she had burned herself on the wax*; *the
place was burnt to a crisp*, but **burned** is found elsewhere.
When the participle is used as an adjective, however, **burnt**
is somewhat commoner in all varieties of English: *walls of
burnt brick*.

b
c

but

For advice about using **but** and other conjunctions to begin
a sentence, see AND.

caesarean

The spelling **caesarean**, ending with **-ean** (or **cesarean** in
the US), is now much more commonly used than **caesarian**
with an **i** and is the generally accepted form.

cafe

There are two ways of pronouncing **cafe**. Americans generally
stress the second syllable (/ka-**fay**/) and British English speakers
the first (/**ka**-fay/). British English speakers who stress the second
syllable run the risk of sounding bizarre or affected. Omitting
the accent over the letter **e** is nowadays perfectly legitimate,
and is the spelling recommended by Oxford dictionaries.
Nevertheless, not all dictionaries recognize that spelling and
some people may consider it a mistake to leave out the accent.

can

People are often unclear whether there is any difference
between **may** and **can** when used to request or express
permission, as in *may/can I ask you a few questions?* It is
still widely held that using **can** for permission is somehow
incorrect, and that it should be reserved for expressions to
do with capability, as in *can you swim?* Although using **can** to

request or give permission is not regarded as incorrect in standard English, there is a clear difference in formality between the two verbs: **may** is a more polite way of asking for something and is the better choice in more formal contexts.

candelabrum

If we stick religiously to the Latin forms, the correct singular is **candelabrum** and the correct plural is **candelabra**. But **candelabra** has taken on a new life as the more common singular form, with its own plural **candelabras**.

cannot

Both the one-word form **cannot** and the two-word form **can not** are correct, but **cannot** is far more common in all contexts; in the Oxford English Corpus, there are 25 times more examples of **cannot** than of **can not**. The two-word form is recommended only when **not** is part of a set phrase, such as 'not only … but (also)': *Paul can not only sing well, he also paints brilliantly.*

Caribbean

The word **Caribbean** can be pronounced in two different ways. The first, which is more common in British English, puts the emphasis on the **-be-** (/ka-ri-**bee**-uhn/), while the second, heard in the US and the Caribbean itself, emphasizes the **-ri-** (/kuh-**ri**-bee-uhn/).

Caucasian

In the racial classification developed by Blumenbach and others in the 19th century, **Caucasian** (or **Caucasoid**) included peoples whose skin colour ranged from light (in northern Europe) to dark (in parts of North Africa and India). Although the classification is outdated and the categories are now not generally accepted as scientific (see MONGOLOID), the term **Caucasian** has acquired a more restricted meaning. It is now used, especially in the US, as a synonym for 'white or of European origin', as in *the police are looking for a Caucasian male in his forties.*

Celtic

Celt and **Celtic** can be pronounced with the first letter **c** sounding like either **k-** or **s-**, but the normal pronunciation is with a **k-**, except in the name of the Glaswegian football club.

C

censure, censor

Censure and **censor**, although quite different in meaning, are frequently confused. To **censure** means 'to express severe disapproval of' (*the country was censured for human rights abuses*), while to **censor** means 'to examine (a book, film, etc.) and suppress unacceptable parts of it': *the letters she received were censored*. Avoid writing **censure** when you mean **censor**, as in the incorrect *the film was censured*.

cervical

Cervical means 'relating to the cervix' (the neck of the womb). With the advent of cervical screening and cervical smears the word has become part of general language. Its pronunciation in general use tends to be /ser-vi-k'l/ and in medical circles /suh-**vl**-k'l/.

chair, chairman, chairwoman, chairperson

The word **chairman**, which combines connotations of power with grammatical gender bias, was a key word in feminist sensitivities about language. **Chairwoman** dates from the 17th century, but it was hardly a recognized name until the 19th century, and even then it did not solve the problem of how to refer neutrally to a **chairman**/**chairwoman** when the gender was unknown or irrelevant. Two gender-neutral alternatives emerged in the 1970s: **chairperson** and **chair**, although **chair** was already in use to mean 'the authority invested in a chairman'. **Chair** seems to be more popular than **chairperson**, partly because it seems less contrived and less obviously gender-neutral. See also -PERSON.

chaise longue, chaise lounge

Chaise longue comes from French, literally 'a long chair', with *longue* being the feminine form of the French adjective *long*.

c

Since it has a very un-English spelling and pronunciation, it has been transformed by folk etymology into the logical **chaise lounge** in the US, where it is the accepted and dominant form. See also FOLK ETYMOLOGY.

challenged

The use with a preceding adverb, e.g. **physically challenged**, was originally intended to give a more positive tone than words such as **disabled** or **handicapped**. It arose in the US in the 1980s and quickly spread to the UK and elsewhere. Despite the originally serious intention the word rapidly became stalled by uses whose intention was to make fun of the attempts at euphemism and whose tone was usually clearly ironic: mocking examples include *cerebrally challenged*, *conversationally challenged*, and *follicularly challenged*. See also DISABLED.

chastise

Chastise is correctly spelled -*ise*, never -*ize*.

cherub

Cherub has the Hebrew plural **cherubim**, pronounced /**che**-ruh-bim/, when referring to angelic beings, and **cherubs** when referring to adorable children. Since **cherubim** is already plural, the form 'cherubims' is unnecessary. The adjective **cherubic** is pronounced /chuh-**roo**-bik/.

Chicano

The term **Chicano** (borrowed from Mexican Spanish and derived from the Spanish word *mejicano*, meaning 'Mexican'), and its feminine form **Chicana**, became current in the early 1960s, first used by politically active groups. **Chicano** and **Chicana** are still in frequent use but have become less politicized. However, Mexican-Americans with less militant political views might find the words offensive. **Hispanic** is a more generic word denoting people in the US of Latin-American or Spanish descent. See also HISPANIC.

chimera

The recommended spelling for this word for a mythological
being, an illusory hope or a genetic mix is **chimera** not **chimaera**,
and the recommended pronunciation is /ky-**meer**-uh/.

chord, cord

1 There are two distinct words spelled **chord**: (1) in music, a group
of notes sounded together to form the basis of harmony, and
(2) a technical word in mathematics and engineering,
meaning 'a straight line joining the ends of an arc, the leading
and trailing edges of an aircraft wing, etc.' The idiom **to strike
a chord** derives, somewhat surprisingly, from the technical
meaning.

2 The word **cord** meaning 'string, rope, etc.' is used in **spinal cord**,
umbilical cord, **vocal cord**, etc. The anatomical meaning is
often spelled **chord**, particularly in the phrase **vocal chords**,
but this spelling is not recommended.

chorizo

Chorizo is a word English has borrowed from Spanish to describe
a kind of highly spiced pork sausage. British and American
dictionaries suggest the pronunciation (/chuh-**ree**-zoh/) as the
standard. You can also pronounce the **z** as an **s**: /chuh-**ree**-soh/.
Some people, including famous cooks, pronounce the **z** as in
pizza: /chuh-**ree**-tsoh/. If you wish to impress by mimicking
the pronunciation of the language from which a word comes,
it is wise to make sure you choose the right language.

Christian name

In recognition of the fact that English-speaking societies
have many religions and cultures, not just Christian ones,
the term **Christian name** has largely given way, at least in
official contexts, to alternative terms such as **given name**,
first name, or **forename**.

circumcise

Circumcise is correctly spelled *-ise*, never *-ize*.

classic, classical

Traditionally, **classic** means either 'outstanding', as in *a classic novel*, or 'very typical and representative of its kind', as in *a classic little black dress*, *a classic example*. **Classical** generally means 'relating to Greek or Roman antiquity' or 'relating to serious or conventional music': *the museum was built in the classical style*; *he plays jazz as well as classical violin*. Often **classical** is mistakenly used when **classic** is more appropriate: *a classical example* would be one taken from Greek or Latin whereas *a classic example* is the most typical example of its kind.

cleft lip

Cleft lip is the standard accepted term and should be used instead of **harelip**, which is likely to cause offence.

cliché

See OVERUSED WORDS.

climactic, climatic

Climactic means 'forming a climax', as in *the film's climactic battle sequence*. **Climatic** means 'relating to climate', as in *a wide range of climatic conditions*. **Climactic** is sometimes incorrectly used when **climatic** is meant, as in *harsh climactic conditions*. **Climacteric** is a different word again, a rarely used noun meaning 'the period of life when fertility and sexual activity are in decline' or a 'critical period or event'.

clique

Clique, 'a small group of people who spend time together and do not let others join them', is among the thousands of English words purloined from French. If English speakers use French words a lot, they usually alter the pronunciation: it would be very affected indeed to pronounce **clairvoyant** as the French do. But it is better to say **clique** with the French-like pronunciation /kleek/, rather than /klik/, to avoid confusion with **click**.

co-

1 In modern American English, the tendency increasingly is to write compound words beginning with **co-** without hyphenation, as in *costar*, *cosignatory*, and *coproduce*. British usage generally shows a preference for the hyphenated spelling, but even in Britain the trend seems to be in favour of less hyphenation than in the past. In both the US and the UK, for example, the spellings of *coordinate* and *coed* are encountered with or without hyphenation, but the more common choice for either word in either country is without the hyphen.

2 **Co-** with the hyphen is often used to prevent a mistaken first impression (*co-driver*—because *codriver* could be mistaken for *cod river*, and *coworker* initially looks like something to do with a cow), or simply to avoid an awkward spelling (*co-own* is clearly preferable to *coown*). There are also some relatively less common words, such as *co-respondent* (in a divorce suit), where the hyphenated spelling distinguishes the word's meaning and pronunciation from that of the more common *correspondent*.

cohort

The earliest meaning of **cohort** is 'a unit of men within the Roman army'. From this it developed the meanings of 'a group of people with a shared characteristic', e.g. *the Church in Ireland still has a vast cohort of weekly churchgoers*. From the 1950s onwards a new meaning developed in the US, meaning 'a companion or colleague', as in *young Jack arrived with three of his cohorts*. Although this meaning is well established (it accounts for most of the uses of this word in the Oxford English Corpus), there are still some people who object to it on the grounds that **cohort** should only be used for groups of people, never for individuals.

coleslaw

The first part of this word is correctly spelled *cole-*, not *cold-*. **Cole-** is from Dutch *kool* 'cabbage'. It has been replaced by *cold* through a process of FOLK ETYMOLOGY.

c

collective noun

A **collective noun** is a singular noun which refers to a group of people, such as **family**, **committee**, **government**, **BBC**, **NATO**. Collective nouns can be used with either a singular or a plural verb: *my **family was** always hard-working*; *his **family were** disappointed in him*. With a singular verb you are emphasizing the group; with a plural verb, the individuals in the group. Generally speaking, in the US it is more usual for collective nouns to be followed by a singular verb. Bear in mind that any following pronouns or adjectives must be singular or plural like the verb: *the government **is** prepared to act, but not until **it** knows the outcome of the latest talks* (not . . . *until they know the outcome* . . .); *the family have all moved back into their former home.*

coloured (US colored)

The use of **coloured** to refer to skin colour is first recorded in the early 17th century and was adopted by emancipated slaves in the US as a term of racial pride after the American Civil War. In Britain it was the accepted term until the 1960s, when it was superseded (as in the US) by **black**. The term **coloured** lost favour among blacks during this period and is now widely regarded as offensive except in historical contexts. In South Africa, the term **coloured** (also written **Coloured**) has a different history. It is used to refer to people of mixed-race parentage rather than, as elsewhere, African peoples and their descendants. In modern use in this context the word is not considered offensive or derogatory.

communal

Americans tend to stress the second syllable (/kuh-**myoo**-n'l/) and British English speakers the first (/**ko**-myoo-n'l/). The American pronunciation is rapidly gaining ground in Britain, but still grates on the ears of many.

compact

Compact as an adjective can be stressed on the first or second syllable: /**kom**-pakt/ or /kuhm-**pakt**/. Both are correct, but there is a preference for the first in the phrase **compact disc**.

C

comparable

Although the traditional pronunciation of **comparable** in standard British English is with the emphasis on the first syllable rather than the second (/**kom**-pruh-b'l/), an alternative pronunciation with the emphasis on the second syllable (/kuhm-**pa**-ruh-b'l/) is gaining in currency. Both pronunciations are used in American English.

comparatively

The use of **comparatively** in contexts such as *there were comparatively few casualties* has been criticized in the past on the grounds that there is no explicit comparison being made. Even so, there is an implicit one, even if very vague: for instance, in the example above, the comparison is presumably with other incidents or battles. **Comparatively** has been used like this since the early 19th century and to use it in this way is acceptable in standard English.

compare

1 People are sometimes unclear about whether there is any difference between **compare with** and **compare to**, and, if so, whether one is more correct than the other. There is a slight difference. It is usual to use **to** rather than **with** when describing the resemblance, by analogy, of two quite different things, as in *Shall I compare thee to a summer's day?* In the other sense, 'to make a detailed comparison of', it is traditionally held that **with** is more correct than **to**, as in *schools compared their facilities with those of others in the area*. However, in practice the distinction is not clear-cut and both **compare with** and **compare to** are used in either context.

2 In intransitive uses, e.g. *but of all these friends and lovers, there is no one compares with you* (The Beatles, *In My Life*) **with** is the usual preposition in British English, whereas in the US it is **to**, as exemplified in *nothing compares to you*.

complacent, complaisant

Complacent and **complaisant** are two words which are similar in pronunciation and which both come from the Latin verb

complacere 'to please', but which in English do not mean the
same thing. **Complacent** is the commoner word and means
'smug and self-satisfied'. **Complaisant**, on the other hand,
means 'willing to please', as in *the local people proved
complaisant and cordial*.

complement, compliment

Complement and **compliment**, together with **complementary**
and **complimentary**, are frequently confused. Pronounced in
the same way, they have quite different meanings. As a verb
complement means 'to add to something in a way that
enhances or improves', as in *a relaunched website will
complement the radio programmes*. To remember that this
meaning has an **e** before the **m** it may help if you think of
complete, to which it is related. **Compliment** means 'to admire
and praise someone for something', as in *he complimented her on
her appearance*, and is often wrongly used where **complement**
is the correct spelling. **Complimentary** means 'expressing
a compliment' as in *he made lots of complimentary remarks
about her*. From this meaning comes the sense of 'given free'
as in *honeymooners receive complimentary fruit and flowers*.

complete

On the question of whether you should say *very complete*,
more complete, etc., see UNIQUE.

compliment

Compliment and **complimentary** are quite different in meaning
from **complement** and **complementary**. See COMPLEMENT.

compound

The verb **compound** in its meaning 'to make something bad
worse', as in *this compounds their problems*, has an interesting
history. It arose through a misinterpretation of the legal phrase
compound a felony, which, strictly speaking, means 'not to
prosecute a felony, in exchange for money or some other
consideration'. This led to the use of **compound** in legal contexts
to mean 'make something bad worse', which then became
accepted in general usage as well.

comprise

1 **Comprise** mainly means 'consist of', as in *the country comprises twenty states*. It can also mean 'constitute or make up a whole', as in *this single breed comprises 50 per cent of the Swiss cattle population*. Sentences like the first example can be put in the passive—*the country is comprised of twenty states*—and this is standard English. However, the construction **comprise of**, as in *the property comprises of bedroom, bathroom, and kitchen*, is regarded as incorrect.

2 For a comparison of **comprise** and **include**, see INCLUDE.

concerned

The idiomatic expression **as far as … is/are concerned** is well established and is a useful way of introducing a new topic or theme or of stating your opinion, especially in conversation. But it can also sometimes be unnecessary or long-winded: for example, *the punishment does not seem to have any effect so far as the prisoners are concerned* could be more economically expressed as *the punishment does not seem to have any effect on the prisoners*.

conjoined twins

The more accurate and correct term **conjoined twins** has supplanted the older term **Siamese twins** in all contexts other than informal conversation.

connote

Connote does not mean the same as **denote**. **Denote** refers to the literal, primary meaning of something, while **connote** refers to other characteristics suggested or implied by that thing. So, you might say that a word like *mother* **denotes** a woman who is a parent but **connotes** qualities such as protection and affection.

consummate

Consummate is pronounced /**kon**-syoo-mayt/ as a verb, e.g. *the marriage was never consummated*. As an adjective meaning 'complete, perfect', e.g. *a consummate liar; consummate*

elegance it was traditionally pronounced /kuhn-**sum**-uht/, with
the emphasis on the second syllable, but the pronunciation
/**kon**-syuu-muht/, with the emphasis on the first syllable,
is now standard.

contagious

In practice, there is little or no difference in meaning between
contagious and **infectious** when applied to disease: both mean,
roughly, 'communicable'. There is, however, a difference in
emphasis or focus between the two words. **Contagious** tends
to be focused on the person or animal affected by the disease
(*precautions are taken with anyone who seems contagious*), while
infectious emphasizes the agent or organism which carries the
disease: there are, for example, plenty of examples in the Oxford
English Corpus of *infectious agent* but none of *contagious agent*.

continual, continuous

There is some overlap in meaning between **continuous** and
continual, but there is also a useful distinction between them.
Both can mean roughly 'without interruption' (*a long and
continual war*; *five years of continuous warfare*), but **continuous**
is much more prominent in this sense. Also, unlike **continual**,
it can be used to refer to space as well as time, as in *the
development forms a continuous line along the coast*. **Continual**,
on the other hand, typically means 'happening frequently,
but with intervals between', as in *continual breakdowns,
continual arguments*. Overall, **continuous** occurs much more
frequently than **continual** (around six times more often in the
Oxford English Corpus) and is found in many technical and
specialist uses ranging from grammar and education to
mathematics.

contribute

In British English there are two possible pronunciations of
the word **contribute**, one which emphasizes the first syllable
(/**kon**-trib-yoot/) and one which emphasizes the second
(/kuhn-**trib**-yoot/); /kuhn-**trib**-yoot/ is held to be the standard,
correct pronunciation, even though /**kon**-trib-yoot/ is older.

controversy

There are two possible pronunciations of the word
controversy in British English: /**kon-**truh-ver-si/ and
/kuhn-**trov**-uh-si/. The latter, though common, is still widely
held to be incorrect in standard English.

convince

Using **convince** with an infinitive as a synonym for **persuade** first
became common in the 1950s in the US, as in *she **convinced** my
father to branch out on his own*. Some traditionalists deplore the
blurring of the distinction between **convince** and **persuade**.
They maintain that **convince** should be reserved for situations
in which someone's belief is changed but no action is taken as
a result (*he **convinced** me **that** he was right*), while **persuade**
should be used for situations in which action results (*he
persuaded me rather than he convinced me to seek more advice*).
In practice, **convince someone to do something** is well
established, and few people will be vexed by its use.

cord

On the confusion between **cord** and **chord**, see CHORD.

could

For a discussion of the use of **could of** instead of **could have**,
see HAVE.

councillor, counsellor (US councilor, counselor)

Confusion often arises between the words **counsellor** and
councillor. A **counsellor** is a person who gives advice or *counsel*,
especially on personal problems (*a marriage counsellor*),
whereas a **councillor** is a member of a city, county, or other
council (*she stood as a Labour candidate for city
councillor*).

covert

In British English, **covert**, meaning 'secret, disguised', is
traditionally pronounced like *cover* (/**kuv**-ert/), although the US

pronunciation like *over* (/**koh**-vert/) is gaining ground in Britain and elsewhere.

credible, creditable

Confusion often arises between the words **credible** and **creditable**. **Credible** chiefly means 'convincing' (*few people found his story credible*), while **creditable** means 'praiseworthy' (*their 32nd placing was still a creditable performance, considering they had one of the smallest boats*).

creep

The past tense and past participle of **creep** can be either **crept** or **creeped**, but **crept** is much more often used for both. **Creeped** occurs most commonly in US English.

crescendo

Crescendo in Italian means literally 'growing', and was originally a musical term for a gradual increase in loudness, building to a climax. It has since developed further to mean the resulting state and is widely used to mean 'peak' or 'climax': *demands for a public inquiry rose to a crescendo last week*. Some traditionalists are against this extension of its meaning, but it is now well established.

cripple

The word **cripple** has long been in use and is recorded in the *Lindisfarne Gospels* as early as AD 950. It has now acquired offensive connotations and has been largely replaced by broader terms such as 'person with disabilities'. Similar changes have affected **crippled**; see DISABLED.

criterion

The traditional singular form (following the original Greek) is **criterion**, and the plural form is **criteria**. It is a common mistake, however, to use **criteria** as if it were a singular, as in *a further criteria needs to be considered*, and this use is best avoided. For other examples of this kind of mistake, see NOUNS, SINGULAR AND PLURAL.

critique

Critique is pronounced with emphasis on the second syllable,
/kri-**teek**/, and means 'a detailed critical essay or analysis'
especially of a literary, political, or philosophical theory: *Kant's
Critique of Pure Reason*. Although it may not be liked by some,
critique is now also regularly used as a verb, especially in the
arts world, in a general sense of 'to review' or even just 'to
criticize', as in *my writing has been critiqued as being too academic*.
For further examples, see VERBS FORMED FROM NOUNS.

dangling participle

A **participle** is a form of a verb ending in **-ing**, **-ed**, etc., such as
arriving or *arrived*. A **dangling participle** is one which is left
'hanging' because, in the grammar of the clause, it does not
relate to the noun it should relate to. In the sentence ***Arriving**
at the station, **she** picked up her case*, the construction is correct
because the participle *arriving* and the subject *she* relate to each
other (*she* is the one doing the *arriving*). But in the following
sentence, a **dangling participle** has been created: ***Arriving** at
the station, **the sun** came out*. We know, logically, that it is not
the sun which is arriving, but grammatically that is exactly the
link which has been created. Such errors are frequent, even
in written English, and can give rise to genuine confusion.

data

In Latin, **data** is the plural of **datum** and, historically and in
specialized scientific fields, it is also treated as a plural in English,
taking a plural verb, as in *the **data were** collected and classified*.
In modern non-scientific use, however, it is treated as a mass
noun, similar to a word like *information*, which cannot normally
have a plural and which takes a singular verb. Sentences such
as ***data was** collected over a number of years* are now the norm
in standard English and are perfectly correct.

deaf mute

In modern use **deaf mute** has acquired offensive connotations
(implying, wrongly, that such people are without the capacity

for communication). It should be avoided in favour of other
terms such as 'deaf without speech'.

decade

1 There are two possible pronunciations for **decade**: one puts
the emphasis on the first syllable (/**de**-kayd/) while the other
puts it on the second syllable (/di-**kayd**/, like *decayed*). The
second pronunciation is disapproved of by some traditionalists
but is now regarded as a standard, acceptable alternative.

2 It is good style not to write individual decades with an
apostrophe: *during the eighties* or *the 80s*, not *the 'eighties*
or *the '80s*.

deceptively

Deceptively belongs to a small set of words whose meaning is
rather ambiguous. It can be used in similar grammatical
contexts to suggest either one thing or its complete opposite.
This happens because people use **deceptively** in two rather
different ways. For example, is *a **deceptively** smooth surface*
smooth or not? The answer is that it *appears* to be smooth, but in
reality is not. So, in this case **deceptively** means something like
'apparently' or 'misleadingly'. But this is the reverse of its use,
beloved by estate agents, in phrases such as *a **deceptively**
spacious room*. If we follow the logic of the first example, this
would mean that the room *looks* spacious, but in fact isn't.
And that is the exact opposite of the meaning intended. We
can all easily understand what is meant in this sort of example
without going to the trouble of analysing it. But often what
is being stated really is rather unclear. If you describe a
person as *deceptively complex*, is he complex while seeming
straightforward, or straightforward while seeming to be
complex? To avoid confusion, it is probably best not to use
deceptively at all when it may be ambiguous, as in the last
example.

defining relative clauses

See RELATIVE CLAUSES.

d

definite, definitive

Definitive is often used, rather imprecisely, when **definite** is actually intended, to mean simply 'clearly decided'. Although **definitive** and **definite** have a clear overlap in meaning, **definitive** has the additional meaning of 'having an authoritative basis'. A *definitive decision* is one that is not only conclusive but also carries the stamp of authority or is a benchmark for the future, but a *definite decision* is simply one that has been made clearly and is without doubt.

defuse

On the potential confusion between **defuse** and **diffuse**, see DIFFUSE.

deliver

Deliver is often used to mean 'provide something that you have promised or that people expect of you' as in *the failure of successive governments to deliver economic growth* or *if you can't deliver improved sales figures, you're fired*. While this meaning is well established and was once a lively metaphor, it now runs the risk of being hackneyed and vague. Words you could use instead include **provide** and **supply**. Or you could rewrite your sentence to be more precise and specific about what you mean.

denote

For an explanation of the difference between **denote** and **connote**, see CONNOTE.

depends

In informal use, it is quite common for the *on* to be dropped in sentences such as *it all depends how you look at it* (rather than *it all depends on how you look at it*), but in well-formed written English the *on* should always be retained.

dependant, dependent

Until recently, the only correct spelling of the noun in British English was **dependant**, as in *a single man with no dependants*. However, in modern British English (and in US English), **dependent** is now a standard alternative. The adjective is always spelled **-ent**, never **-ant**, as in *we are dependent on his goodwill*.

deprecate, depreciate

The similarity in spelling and meaning of **deprecate** and **depreciate** has led to confusions in their use, with **deprecate** being used simply as a synonym for **depreciate** in the meaning 'disparage or belittle'. This use is now well established and is widely accepted in standard English. In particular, the phrases **self-deprecating** and **self-deprecatory** are far more common than the alternatives **self-depreciating** and **self-depreciatory**.

derisory

Although the words **derisory** and **derisive** share similar roots, they have different core meanings. **Derisory** usually means 'ridiculously small or inadequate', as in *a derisory pay offer* or *the security arrangements were derisory*. **Derisive**, on the other hand, is used to mean 'expressing contempt'. The proper reaction to a *derisory salary increase* is a *derisive laugh*.

descendant, descendent

In British English, the only way to spell the noun meaning 'a person descended from a particular ancestor' is with the ending **-ant**, as in *property is inherited by descendants of the original owner*. In US English you can spell it that way, or with a final **-ent**.

dice, die

Historically, **dice** is the plural of **die**, but in modern standard English **dice** is both the singular and the plural: *throw the dice* could refer to either one or more than one dice.

different

Different from, **different than**, and **different to**: many people wonder if there is any distinction between these three phrases, and whether one is more correct than the others. In practice, **different from** is by far the most common structure, both in the UK and North America, while **different than** is almost exclusively used in North America. **Different to** is also correct, but is not used as often as either **different from** or **different than**. Since the 18th century, **different than** has been singled out by critics as incorrect, but it is difficult to sustain the view in modern standard English that one version is more correct than the others. There is little difference in meaning between the three, and all of them are used by respected writers.

d

differently abled

Differently abled was first proposed in the 1980s as an alternative to **disabled**, **handicapped**, etc. on the grounds that it gave a more positive message and so avoided discrimination towards people with disabilities. The term has gained little currency, however, and has been criticized as both over-euphemistic and condescending. The accepted word in general use is still **disabled**. See also DISABILITY, THE LANGUAGE OF.

diffuse, defuse

The verbs **diffuse** and **defuse** sound similar but have different meanings. **Diffuse** means, broadly, 'to disperse', while **defuse** means 'to reduce the danger or tension in'. Sentences such as *they successfully diffused the situation* are wrong, while *they successfully defused the situation* is correct. The literal meaning of **defuse**, that is 'taking out (**de-**) the fuse' may help you remember the distinction.

dilemma

At its core, a **dilemma** is a situation in which a difficult choice has to be made between equally undesirable alternatives. Informally, it can be used of any difficult situation or problem (as in *the insoluble dilemma of adolescence*), and some people regard this weakened meaning as unacceptable. However, the usage is recorded as early as the first part of the 17th century and is now widespread and becoming far more acceptable, although it is best avoided in formal contexts.

diphtheria, diphthong

In the past, **diphtheria** was pronounced with an f sound representing the two letters ph (as in *telephone*, *physics*, and other '*ph-*' words derived from Greek). Today the most common pronunciation is with a p sound, and it is no longer considered incorrect in standard English . A very similar shift has taken place with the word **diphthong**, which is now also widely pronounced /**dip-**/ rather than /**dif-**/.

d

disability, the language of

The language that is now generally considered suitable to describe and refer to people with different kinds of physical or mental disabilities is very different from what it was a couple of decades ago. The changes are due partly to the activity of the organizations which promote the interests of particular groups with disabilities, and partly to increased public sensitivity to language that might perpetuate stereotypes and prejudices. Just as most people studiously avoid previously established sexist or racist uses of language, so they are more sensitive to the appropriate way in which to talk about people with disabilities.

If you want to use appropriate language you not only need to avoid words which have been or are being superseded, such as *mongolism* or *backward*, and which are listed below with their more neutral equivalents. You should also try to:

- avoid using *the* + an adjective to refer to the whole group, as in *the blind*, *the deaf*, and so forth. The reasoning behind this is twofold: because the humanity of people with a disability should not be circumscribed by the disability itself ('the disability is not the person'); and that talking about people with a given disability as a group diminishes their individuality. The preferred formulation these days is 'a person with . . .' or 'people with . . .' as in *people with sight problems*, *people with asthma,* or *people with disabilities*.

- avoid using words such as *victim*, *suffer from*, and *wheelchair-bound* which suggest that the person concerned is the helpless object of the disability. ▶

Suitable alternatives to *suffer from* are *have*, *experience*, and *be diagnosed with*. Instead of talking about *victims* you can talk about people who have a particular disability; and instead of *wheelchair-bound* you can say *who use(s) a wheelchair*.

d

■ avoid using words which once related to disabilities and which have now become colloquial, especially as insults, such as *mongoloid*, *mong*, *spastic*, *psycho*, *schizo*, and so forth.

Some of the terms below are better established than others, and some groups with disabilities favour specific words over others. These lists are offered only as a general guide.

OLDER TERM	NEUTRAL TERM
able-bodied	non-disabled
asthmatic (noun)	person with asthma
backward	having learning difficulties, having a learning disability
blind	partially sighted, visually impaired
cripple	person with a disability, person with mobility problems
deaf aid	hearing aid
deaf-and-dumb	deaf without speech
deaf-mute	deaf without speech
diabetic (noun)	person with diabetes
disabled	having a disability
handicapped	having a disability
harelip	cleft lip
to help	to support
invalid	person with a disability
mongol	person with Down's syndrome
spastic	person with cerebral palsy
stone-deaf	profoundly deaf

d

disabled

The word **disabled** came to be used as the standard term in referring to people with physical or mental disabilities from the 1960s onwards, and it remains the most generally accepted term in both British and US English today. It superseded words that are now more or less offensive, such as *crippled*, *defective*, and *handicapped*, and has not been overtaken itself by newer coinages such as *differently abled* or *physically challenged*. Although the usage is very widespread, some people regard making the adjective a plural noun (as in *the needs of the disabled*) as dehumanizing because it tends to treat people with disabilities as an undifferentiated group, defined merely by their capabilities. To avoid offence, a more acceptable term would be 'people with disabilities'.

disassociate

Disassociate is slightly older than its variant **dissociate**, which is first recorded in 1623. **Disassociate** is, however, regarded by some people as an ignorant mistake, being formed regularly like **disassemble**, and it is therefore occasionally best avoided.

disc, disk

Generally speaking, the preferred British spelling is **disc** and the preferred US spelling is **disk**, although there is much overlap and variation between the two. In particular, the spelling for meanings relating to computers is nearly always **disk**, as in *hard disk, disk drive*, and so on. In *compact disc*, however, the spelling with a *c* is more usual.

discomfit, discomfort

The words **discomfit** and **discomfort** are historically unrelated but in modern use their principal meanings as verbs have collapsed into one ('to make someone feel uneasy').

discreet, discrete

The words **discrete** and **discreet** are pronounced in the same way and share the same origin but they do not mean the same thing. **Discrete** means 'separate', as in *a finite number* *of discrete categories*, while **discreet** means 'careful and circumspect', as in *you can rely on him to be discreet*.

disinterested

Nowhere are the battle lines more deeply drawn in usage questions than over the difference between **disinterested** and **uninterested**. According to traditional guidelines, **disinterested** should never be used to mean 'not interested' but only to mean 'impartial', as in *the judgements of disinterested outsiders are likely to be more useful*. Following this view, only **uninterested** means 'not interested', but the 'incorrect' use of **disinterested** is widespread. Nevertheless, in careful writing it is advisable to avoid using it to mean 'not interested' as many people will judge it to be incorrect.

dissociate

For a comparison of **dissociate** and **dissasociate**, see DISASSOCIATE.

distribute

The word **distribute** is pronounced either as /dis-**trib**-yoot/, with the emphasis on the second syllable, or as /**dis**-trib-yoot/, with the emphasis on the first. Until recently, /**dis**-trib-yoot/ was considered incorrect in standard British English, but now both pronunciations are standard.

dive, dove

In British English the standard past tense is **dived**, as in *he ran past us and dived into the water*. In the 19th century **dove** (rhyming with *stove*) occurred in British and American dialect and it remains in regular use. It is more frequent than **dived** in the US and Canada. In Britain it should still be avoided in careful writing.

double negative

According to standard English grammar, it is incorrect to use a **double negative,** i.e. two negative words to express a single negative idea, as in *I don't know nothing*. The rules dictate that the two negative elements cancel each other out to give an affirmative statement, so that *I don't know nothing* would be interpreted as 'I know something'.

In practice this sort of double negative is widespread in dialect and other non-standard usage and rarely gives rise to confusion as to the intended meaning. Double negatives are standard in other languages as diverse as French, Russian, and Afrikaans, and they have not always been unacceptable in English, either. They were normal in Old English and Middle English and did not come to be frowned upon until some time after the 16th century, when attempts were made to relate the rules of language to the rules of formal logic.

Modern (correct) uses of the double negative give an added subtlety to statements: saying *I am **not un**convinced by his argument* suggests reservations in the speaker's mind that are not present in its supposedly logical equivalent, *I am convinced by his argument*.

dove

For the use of **dove** as the past tense of **dive**, see DIVE.

Down's syndrome

Of relatively recent coinage, **Down's syndrome** (or, increasingly frequently, **Down syndrome**) is the accepted term in modern use, and former terms, such as **mongol** and **mongolism**, should be avoided as they are highly likely to cause offence. A person with the syndrome is best called exactly that, a **person with Down's syndrome**.

downward, downwards

The only correct form for the adjective is **downward** (*a downward spiral*, *a downward trend*), but **downward** and **downwards** are both used for the adverb, e.g. *the floor sloped downward/downwards*, with a marked preference for **downwards** in British English and **downward** in American English.

dream

For the past tense and past participle of **dream**, **dreamt** and **dreamed** are both used and are both correct. **Dreamed** is pronounced /dreemd/ (and occasionally /dremt/) and **dreamt** is pronounced /dremt/. For the past tense in British English **dreamt** and **dreamed** are equally common, but in US English **dreamed** is more often used. For the past participle, **dreamed** is used more often in Britain and the US.

due

Using **due to** to mean 'because of', as in *he had to retire due to an injury*, has been condemned as wrong on the grounds that **due** is an adjective, and should therefore refer to a noun or pronoun, e.g. *an illness due to old age*. According to this view, it should not refer to a verb, such as *retire* in the first example above; **owing to** is often recommended as a better alternative. However, the use with a verb, first recorded at the end of the 19th century, is now common in all types of literature and is regarded as part of standard English.

dumb

Although 'not able to speak' is the older meaning of **dumb**, it has been so overwhelmed by the newer meaning of 'stupid' that using it in the first meaning is now almost certain to cause offence. Alternatives such as 'having a speech disorder' are more appropriate.

dwarf

In the meaning 'an abnormally small person', **dwarf** is normally considered offensive. However, there are no accepted alternatives in the general language, since terms such as **person of restricted growth** have gained little currency.

each

People are sometimes confused about whether verbs and possessives following **each** should be singular or plural. **Each** is treated as singular when it comes before a singular noun (*each house stands on its own*), when it is followed by

of and a plural noun (***each** of the houses **stands** on its own*), and when it stands by itself as a pronoun: *a series of interconnecting courtyards, each with its own character*. When **each** follows and qualifies a plural noun or pronoun, e.g. ***they** each **carry** several newspapers; the voices **each have** slight differences in note-lengths*, it is treated as a plural. This is because it is the noun or pronoun and not **each** that determines if the sentence is singular or plural.

ebullient

Ebullient is pronounced /i-**bul**-yuhnt/, with the second syllable as in *bulb*, not as in *bull*.

economic, economical

People sometimes describe something as **economic** when they mean **economical**. **Economic** means 'concerning economics': *he's rebuilding a solid economic base for the country's future*. **Economical** means 'thrifty, avoiding waste': *small cars should be inexpensive to buy and economical to run*.

effect

For an explanation of the difference between **effect** and **affect**, see AFFECT.

egregious

Egregious is an unusual word because its original meaning of 'remarkably good, distinguished' has been ousted by the exact opposite, 'outstandingly bad, shocking'. The word comes from Latin *grex* meaning 'flock', and originally meant 'towering above the flock', i.e. 'prominent'. Now it means 'prominent because bad': *egregious abuses of copyright*.

either

1 In good English writing style, it is important that **either** and **or** are correctly placed so that the structures following each word balance and mirror each other. Accordingly, sentences such as ***either** I accompany you **or** I wait here* and *I'm going to buy **either** a new camera **or** a new video* are correct, whereas sentences

such as *either I accompany you or John* and *I'm either going to
buy a new camera or a video* are not well-balanced sentences
and should not be used in written English.

2 **Either** can be pronounced /**I**-thuh/ or /**ee**-thuh/: both are correct.

Electronic English

Over the last decade or more our lives have been
transformed by electronic communication; arguably our
language has been transformed as well. Electronic
communication includes several different forms: email,
chatrooms, newsgroups, weblogs, and SMS (Short
Messaging Service) messages between mobile phones, or
'texts'. In fact, it is probably more accurate to talk about
'Electronic Englishes', since different groups in
cyberspace have different jargons and conventions.
English in general constantly evolves, and the influence of, for
instance, TV and films on the language can be very rapid: take
'*am I bothered?*', which became a catchphrase in Britain in
2005. The difference with electronic communication is that
a word can be invented and then spread immediately round
the world.

Electronic communication is an extremely fertile source of
new words, which enter the mainstream if what they refer to
takes root. For example, a *blog* (short for *weblog*, a personal
website on which someone records or writes about topics of
interest to them), of which there are now estimated to be at
least twenty million worldwide, is now a well-established
word, though only a few years ago it was a completely
unknown concept to most people. Similarly, *podcasts*
(digital recordings of a radio broadcast or similar
programme, made available on the Internet for
downloading to a personal audio player) were little
known in 2004 but are now part of mainstream media. In
the same way, *to google* is in the process of ▶

becoming a generic term for 'to look for information on the web'.

Older forms of communication are renamed to distinguish them from the electronic version, so that *snailmail* refers to traditional postal mail, and *dead tree edition* refers to articles, books, and so forth published on paper rather than in electronic format.

Not only are new words created at a vast rate, new 'dialects' come into being. There has been talk of *globish* and *globespeak*, which are pared down versions of traditional English, with severely limited vocabularies, designed to make it easier for people with different mother tongues to communicate. Similarly, *Leetspeak* is a language which emerged from online gaming communities and users of bulletin boards. It works with a cipher system, such as replacing letters with numbers, transposing letters, and modifying existing words in other ways, so that, for instance 'hacker' can be written as 'haxxor' or 'haxor'.

Apart from producing hundreds of new words every year, 'Electronic English' has also affected the conventions governing the way we write. If we send an email for business purposes, we are likely to be more informal in the way we write it and address the recipient than we would be in a letter or memo. Certain abbreviations which are widely used in text messaging, chatrooms, and so forth are now being widely used in advertising and marketing: *event starts @ 8 o'clock 2moro*, *gr8* (= great), *l8r* (= later), *specially 4 U*, and so forth. Even electronic message signs on motorways will flash up *R U 2 close?* Another effect is that capital letters are less favoured in titles, brand names, and so forth, lower-case letters possibly being seen as less distant and authoritarian, and as establishing a more personal connection with the consumer or customer.

elicit

Elicit is sometimes confused with **illicit** because both words are pronounced the same way (/i-**liss**-it/). **Elicit** is a verb meaning 'to extract (an answer, admission, etc.)' whereas **illicit** is an adjective meaning 'unlawful, forbidden', as in *illicit drinking*.

eminent

Some people write **eminent danger** when what they probably mean is **imminent danger**. They may do this because they pronounce the **e** and the **i** at the beginning of the two words similarly. If it means anything at all, 'eminent danger' would be great danger. **Imminent danger** is a danger that will arise very soon.

emotive

The words **emotive** and **emotional** are similar but are not the same. **Emotive** means 'arousing intense feeling', while **emotional** tends to mean 'characterized by intense feeling'. An *emotive issue* is, therefore, one which is likely to arouse people's passions, while an *emotional response* comes from your feelings, not your thoughts.

empathy

Empathy is often used in contexts where **sympathy** would be more appropriate. **Empathy** means 'the ability to understand and share the feelings of another', as in *both authors have the skill to make you feel empathy with their heroines*. **Sympathy** means 'feelings of pity and sorrow for someone else's misfortune', as in *they had great sympathy for the flood victims*.

endear

To **endear** someone **to** someone else means 'to make someone popular with or liked by someone'. The meaning is easy to grasp, but some people get into a bit of a muddle with the grammar. You can **endear yourself to** other people: *she endeared herself to all who worked with her*. Alternatively, a quality someone has, or an action on their part, can **endear** them **to** other people: *Flora's spirit and character endeared her to everyone who met her*.

But to say *his attitude endeared me to him*, when you mean 'made ME like HIM', is to describe who likes whom back to front; it should be *his attitude endeared him to me*.

end of the day

At the end of the day is one of the less attractive clichés of the 20th century. It is first recorded in 1974 and means no more than 'eventually' or 'when all's said and done'. It is now wildly overused in speech as a 'filler' and tends to creep into almost any conversation. It is not good style to use it in writing.

England

For inappropriate use of **England** to mean **Britain**, see BRITAIN, 5.

enormity

Enormity traditionally means the 'extreme scale or seriousness of something bad or wrong', as in *his time in prison has still not been long enough to allow him to come to grips with the enormity of his crime*, but it is not uncommon for it to be used to mean 'hugeness' or 'immensity', as in *the enormity of French hypermarkets*. Many people regard this use as wrong, arguing that as the word originally meant 'crime, wickedness' it should only be used in a negative way, but the newer use is now broadly accepted in standard English.

enquire

Usage guides have traditionally drawn a distinction between **enquire** and **inquire**, suggesting that, in British English at least, **enquire** is used for general meanings of 'to ask', while **inquire** is reserved for uses meaning 'to make a formal investigation'. In practice, however, there is little difference in the way the two words are used, although **enquire** and **enquiry** are more common in British English while **inquire** and **inquiry** are more common in US English.

ensure

On the difference between **ensure** and **insure**, see INSURE.

enterprise

Enterprise in modern use is always spelled *-ise*, not *-ize*.

enthuse

The verb **enthuse** was formed by shortening the noun **enthusiasm**. Like many verbs formed from nouns in this way, especially those from the US, traditionalists regard it as unacceptable. It is difficult to see why: forming verbs from nouns is a perfectly respectable means for creating new words in English: verbs like **classify**, **commentate**, and **edit** were also formed in this way, for example. **Enthuse** itself has now been in English for over 150 years. For further information, see VERBS FORMED FROM NOUNS.

e

envelop, envelope

Envelop, pronounced /in-**vel**-uhp/, is a verb, meaning 'to wrap up, surround, etc.', while **envelope**, pronounced /**en**-vuh-lohp/ (or, increasingly rarely, /**on**-vuh-lohp/), is a noun, meaning 'a container for a letter, etc.'.

equal

It is widely held that adjectives such as **equal** and **unique** should not be modified and that it is incorrect to say **more equal** or **very unique**, on the grounds that these are adjectives which refer to a logical or mathematical absolute. For more information on this question, see UNIQUE.

equally

The construction **equally as**, as in *follow-up discussion is equally as important*, rather than ... *is equally important*, is relatively common but is condemned on the grounds that it says the same thing twice. Either word can be used alone and be perfectly correct, e.g. *follow-up discussion is equally important* or *follow-up discussion is as important*.

equidistant

To refer to something being the same distance from two other points or places, **equidistant** is traditionally used with

from, as though it were 'equally distant from': *equidistant from Aberdeen and Inverness*. The use of **between** instead, though quite widespread, would be considered incorrect by many people.

erratum

In Latin, the word **erratum** is singular and its plural form is **errata**. In English, this distinction is maintained. It is therefore incorrect to use **errata** as a singular, as in *it was not intended to print an errata*. Similarly, it is wrong to create the form *erratas* as the plural: *to check out the erratas of the book* should be *to check out the errata of the book*. For other examples of this kind of mistake, see NOUNS, SINGULAR AND PLURAL.

escalate

To **escalate** has gained a novel, transitive meaning, which is 'to refer an issue to a manager or superior': *in the event that you need to escalate an issue, our technical staff are ready to help*. It is part of the jargon of IT and call centres, and best avoided outside those rarefied environments.

Eskimo

In recent years, the word **Eskimo** has come to be regarded as offensive (partly through the associations of the now discredited folk etymology 'one who eats raw flesh'). The peoples inhabiting the regions from the central Canadian Arctic to western Greenland prefer to call themselves **Inuit** (see INUIT). The word **Eskimo**, however, continues to be the only term which can be properly understood as applying to the people as a whole and is still widely used in anthropological and archaeological contexts.

especially

Especially and **specially** overlap in use and meaning. Broadly speaking, both words mean 'particularly', and the preference for one word over the other is linked with particular conventions of use rather than with any deep difference in meaning. For example, there is little to choose between *written especially for Jonathan* and *written specially for Jonathan* and neither is more correct than the other. On the other hand, in sentences such as *he despised them all, especially Sylvester*, **specially** is used instead in informal speech but should not be used in written English, while in *the car was specially made for the occasion* **especially** would be somewhat unusual. Overall, **especially** is by far the commoner of the two, occurring more than thirteen times as frequently as **specially** in the Oxford English Corpus.

e

espresso

The often-occurring variant spelling **expresso** is incorrect and was probably formed by analogy with **express**.

-ess

The suffix **-ess** has been used since the Middle Ages to form nouns denoting female persons, using a neutral or male form as the base (such as **hostess** from **host** or **actress** from **actor**). In the late 20th century many of these feminine forms came to be seen as old-fashioned, sexist, and patronizing, and the 'male' form is increasingly being used as the 'neutral' form, where the gender of the person concerned is simply unspecified because irrelevant. Some *-ess* forms have all but vanished (e.g. **poetess**, **authoress**, **editress**), but some persist in varying degrees, many falling into these categories:

- they denote someone very different from the male 'equivalent' (e.g. **mayoress**, the wife of a mayor, not a female mayor; **governess**, not a female governor; **countess** if she is the wife of an earl; **manageress**, who might manage a restaurant but not a football team, or **hostess**, who could not be the presenter of a television programme
- they are fixed titles (e.g. **princess**)
- the male equivalent word is rather different in form (e.g. **abbess**, **duchess**, **mistress**)
- in a few cases where there has been a completely different expression for the male equivalent, both have given way to new neutral forms; for instance, **air hostesses** and **stewards** are now generally both called **flight attendants**.

e

estimate

How you should pronounce **estimate** depends on whether you are using it as a noun or a verb. As a noun, as in *our first estimates were too low*, **estimate** is pronounced /**e**-sti-muht/. As a verb it is pronounced /**e**-sti-mayt/, giving the final vowel its full value. Quite often you hear the verb pronounced /**e**-sti-muht/, like the noun, but this is incorrect.

et cetera (also etcetera)

A common mispronunciation of **et cetera** involves replacing the **t** in **et** with a **k**: /ik-**set**-ruh/ instead of /it-**set**-ruh/. This follows a process known technically as 'assimilation' by which sounds become easier for the speaker to make, but careful speakers will tend to avoid pronouncing the word that way.

ethnic

In recent years, **ethnic** has begun to be used in a euphemistic way to refer to non-white people as a whole, as in *a radio station which broadcasts to the ethnic community in Birmingham*. Although this usage is quite common, especially in journalism, it is considered by many to be inaccurate and mealy-mouthed and is better replaced by words such as 'black', 'Asian', etc.

-ette

The use of **-ette** as a feminine suffix for forming new words is relatively recent: it was first recorded in the word **suffragette** at the beginning of the 20th century and has since been used to form only a handful of well-established words, including **usherette** and **drum majorette**, for example. Nowadays, when the tendency is to use words which are neutral in gender, the suffix **-ette** is not very common and new words formed using it tend to be restricted to the deliberately flippant or humorous, as, for example, **bimbette**, **punkette**, and **ladette**.

euphemism

Euphemism is the use of a milder or vaguer word or phrase in place of one that might seem too harsh or direct in a particular context, and **a euphemism** is such a word or phrase, e.g. *to pass away* for 'to die'.

The few examples of common euphemism below give an idea of the richness of this area in English.

lavatory	bog, comfort station, convenience, little boys' room, little house, loo, restroom (N. Amer.), washroom (N. Amer.), water closet
urinate	have a tinkle, pass water, relieve oneself, spend a penny, take a leak
prostitute	call girl, fallen woman, lady of the night, street-walker, working girl
die	depart this life, give up the ghost, kick the bucket, pass away, pass on
kill	do away with, remove, take out, terminate

The most productive subjects for euphemism in English are bodily functions, sexual activity, death, politics, and violence. In the past, religion and god were rich sources of euphemism and gave English many disguised versions of oaths, such as *crikey* (instead of *Christ*) and *gosh* (instead of *God*). Nowadays business, politics, and warfare create a lot of euphemisms, such as *downsizing*, *rationalization*, *restructuring*, *slimming down*, etc., instead of the more direct 'redundancy'; *strategic alternatives* for 'potential sale'; *ethnic cleansing* instead of 'mass expulsion or extermination of ethnic minorities'; *collateral damage* for 'accidental destruction of non-military areas'; *friendly fire* for 'killing of soldiers on one's own side'; and *extraordinary rendition* for 'handing over terrorist suspects for interrogation and possible torture'.

One area of euphemism that advertisers are particularly fond of is taking a feature of their product that might seem to be a disadvantage and turning it into something neutral or even ▶

positive. For instance, a product that is basic may be described as *standard* or one that is small as *compact*. A small quantity of a product may be described as a *handy version* or *fun size*, and a long-standing design as *traditional* or *classic*.

Euphemism is not confined to single words. Examples of phrases which are in themselves euphemistic are: *helping the police with their inquiries* (= under interrogation and facing imminent arrest), and *tired and emotional* (= drunk).

Eurasian

In the 19th century the word **Eurasian** was normally used to refer to a person of mixed British and Indian parentage. In its modern uses, however, the word is more often used to refer to a person of mixed white-American and South-East-Asian parentage.

everybody

Everybody, along with **everyone**, was traditionally followed by a singular possessive adjective or pronoun: *everybody must sign **his** own name*. Because the use of **his** in this context is now commonly perceived as sexist, a second option has become popular: *everybody must sign **his or her** own name*. But **his or her** is often awkward, and many people feel that the plural simply makes more sense: *everybody must sign **their** own name*. Although this violates strict grammar, pairing a singular subject (*everybody*) with a plural possessive determiner (*their*), it is in fact standard in British English and increasingly so in US English. Indeed, in some sentences, only **they** makes grammatical sense: *everybody agreed to convict the defendant, and they voted unanimously*.

everyday

The adjective **everyday**, 'relating to every day; ordinary', is correctly spelled as one word (*carrying out their everyday activities*), but the adverbial phrase **every day**, meaning 'each day', is always spelled as two words: *it rained every day*.

everyone

The pronoun **everyone**, meaning 'every person', is
correctly spelled as one word: *everyone had a great time at
the party*. The two-word expression **every one** means 'each
individual of a group', as in *every one of the employees got a
bonus at the end of the year*. The word **everybody** could be
used in the first example but not in the second example.
See also EVERYBODY.

everyplace

Everyplace is a modern American English synonym of
everywhere: *they seem to be everyplace we go*. It is thought
to be more 'logical' than *everywhere*, mirroring expressions
such as *everybody* and *every time*—on the grounds that we
don't say *everywho* or *everywhen*!

extraordinary

In British English, **extraordinary** is traditionally pronounced
/ik-**stror**-duhn-ri/ as four syllables, the -**a**- being merged into
the following -**or**- to form one syllable. The pronunciation as
/eks-truh-**or**-din-ri/ is being increasingly heard, based on US
pronunciation.

extrovert

The original spelling **extravert** is now rare in general use
but is found in technical use in psychology.

farther, farthest

On the difference in use between **farther** and **further**, see
FURTHER.

faze

Faze means 'to disconcert or disturb' and is often used
informally with a negative word: *the prospect of going on stage
for forty minutes does not seem to have fazed her*. In origin it is a
19th-century American English variant of the ancient verb *feeze*
'to drive off, to frighten away' and has nothing to do with the

ordinary verb **phase**. The spelling **phase** is now quite common, but it should be avoided in writing.

feasible

The core meaning of **feasible** is 'possible and practical to do easily or conveniently', as in *the Dutch have demonstrated that it is perfectly feasible to live below sea level*. Some traditionalists object to its use to mean 'likely' or 'probable', as in *the most feasible explanation*, on the grounds that it derives from an Old French word meaning literally 'doable'. If English were restricted to the 'literal' or 'original' meanings of words, our vocabulary would probably be halved at a stroke. This use has been in English for centuries, first recorded in the mid 17th century and supported by 'considerable literary authority', according to the *Oxford English Dictionary*. However, it can be advisable to avoid it in formal contexts.

February

To pronounce **February** 'the way it is written' is not easy. It requires the separate pronunciation of both the **r** following the **Feb-** and the **r** in -**ary**, with an unstressed vowel in between: /**feb**-ruu-uh-ri/. As a result, the **r** following **Feb-** has been replaced by a y sound: /**feb**-yuu-ri/. This is now the norm, especially in spontaneous speech, and is fast becoming the accepted standard. (The process that made this happen is technically called 'dissimilation', which means that when identical sounds are close to each other, one of them is replaced by a different sound.)

-fest

-fest is a now well-established suffix derived from the German word *Fest* meaning 'festival, celebration'. It occurred first in American English in the late 19th century in the word **gabfest** meaning 'a gathering for talking' and spread rapidly to produce other words. It is now very freely used and produces words such as **slugfest**, **lovefest**, and **ladyfest**.

fetus

The spelling **foetus** has no etymological basis but is recorded from the 16th century and until recently was the standard British spelling in both technical and non-technical use. In technical usage **fetus** is now the standard spelling throughout the English-speaking world, but **foetus** is still quite commonly found in British English outside technical contexts.

fewer, less

Strictly speaking, the rule is that **fewer**, the comparative form of **few**, is used with words referring to countable things, including people: *fewer books*; *fewer than ten contestants*. **Less**, on the other hand, is used with things which cannot be counted: *less money*; *less music*. In addition, **less** is normally used with numbers when they are on their own, e.g. *less than 10,000*, and with expressions of measurement or time: *less than two weeks*; *less than four miles away*. To use **less** with countable things, as in *less words* or *less people*, is widely regarded as incorrect in standard English. It is a well-known usage point in English—so much so that an upmarket British store chain was forced by public demand to change the check-out signs in its food supermarkets from 'Less than five items' to 'Fewer than five items'.

fictional, fictitious

The distinction between **fictional** and **fictitious** is quite subtle but worth maintaining. **Fictional** means 'occurring in fiction', i.e. in a piece of literature, whereas **fictitious** means 'invented, not genuine'. So *Oliver Twist* is a **fictional** name when it refers to Dickens' character, and a **fictitious** name when someone uses it as a false or assumed name instead of their own. Similarly, events are **fictional** when described in a work of fiction, and **fictitious** when invented in ordinary life.

first, firstly

Some people maintain that when listing a sequence of points or topics you should introduce the first item with **first**, not **firstly**, although you can follow it with **secondly**, **thirdly**,

fourthly, etc. The reason for this is that **first** early on had a role as an adverb, and the use of **firstly**, though established by the 17th century, has been felt to be an unnecessary affectation, derided by, for instance, De Quincey as 'your ridiculous and most pedantic neologism of firstly.' Today this rule seems little more than a superstition, and various sequences are in use:

- *first, . . . , secondly, . . . , thirdly, . . .*
- *firstly, . . . , secondly, . . . , thirdly, . . .*
- *first, . . . , second, . . . , third, . . .*

The one option that is not acceptable is:

- *firstly, . . . , second, . . . , third, . . .*

first name

For **first name** see CHRISTIAN NAME.

fish

The normal plural of **fish** is **fish**: *a shoal of fish*; *he caught two huge fish*. The older form **fishes** is still used to refer to different *kinds* of fish: *freshwater fishes of the British Isles*.

fit

1 For **fit** as a verb, the past tense and past participle in British English are **fitted** in all meanings: *the dress fitted well; the dress fitted her well; we've fitted a new lock to the front door*. In some parts of the US, **fit** can be used in the first two of these three meanings and is perfectly acceptable in US English: *his head fit snugly into his collar; I tried on several jackets, but none fit me*.

2 The British English use of **fit** to mean 'sexually attractive' is still rather slangy. It is therefore best avoided in any kind of language which is not slang. It is also potentially ambiguous in contexts such as *she is really fit*, which many speakers will understand to mean 'she is in peak physical condition'.

flaccid

The pronunciations /**flak**-sid/ and /**flass**-id/ are both standard. /**Flak**-sid/ is the older and more traditional one and enjoys support on the grounds that it follows the rule for other words

containing -**cci**- or -**cce**- (*succinct*, *access*, etc.) except those
derived from Italian (*cappuccino* etc.).

flagrant

For a comparison of **flagrant** and **blatant**, see BLATANT.

flammable

The words **flammable** and **inflammable** paradoxically mean
the same thing: see INFLAMMABLE.

flaunt

Flaunt and **flout** may sound similar but they have different
meanings. **Flaunt** means 'to display ostentatiously', as in *visitors
who liked to flaunt their wealth*, while **flout** means 'to openly
disregard', as in *new recruits growing their hair and flouting
convention*. It is a common error, recorded since around the
1940s, to use **flaunt** when **flout** is intended, as in *the young
woman had been flaunting the rules and regulations*. Around
20 per cent of the uses of **flaunt** in the Oxford English Corpus
are incorrect in this respect.

fleshy, fleshly

Fleshy relates to flesh in its physical sense and means primarily
'plump, fat' (e.g. *fleshy hands*, *fleshy fruit*) whereas **fleshly**
relates to the more metaphorical meanings of flesh, and means
'carnal, sensual, sexual', as in *fleshly desires*, *fleshly thoughts*.
To use **fleshly** to mean 'plump' or 'fat' will generally be
considered incorrect.

floccinaucinihilipilification

Floccinaucinihilipilification, supposedly meaning 'the action
or habit of estimating something as worthless', is one of a
number of very long words that occur very rarely in genuine
use. See also ANTIDISESTABLISHMENTARIANISM.

flounder

For the difference between **flounder** and **founder**, see FOUNDER.

flout

Flout and **flaunt** do not mean the same: see FLAUNT.

foetus

On the spelling of this word, see FETUS.

f

folk etymology

Folk etymology is the name given to the process by which people modify a strange or unfamiliar word or phrase so that they can relate it to a word or phrase they already know. It has produced the modern forms of many words we now take for granted and is still a dynamic process in the development of English, as can be seen from the modern examples below.

There are three main reasons for the modification of the word to take place.

1 The form is foreign, and so is altered to resemble a more familiar or natural-sounding English word or root. Examples of this are: *crayfish*, from the Middle English and Old French form *crevice*, where the second syllable has been interpreted as 'fish'; *chaise lounge*, the very common form, especially in the US, of the *chaise longue*; and *cockroach*, which used two English words, cock and roach, to turn the odd-sounding *cacarootch* into something more native.

2 Part of the word or phrase has dropped out of use altogether, or has become rather rare, so its meaning is not understood. It is then replaced by a more familiar word which sounds or looks similar.

This happened, for instance, to *bridegroom*, in which 'groom' has nothing to do with horses. The Old English word was *brideguma*, meaning 'bride-man', and over time the second part was re-interpreted. Current examples of this process are the replacement of *moot point* by *mute point*, and *damp squib* by *damp squid*. A related process, which is not strictly speaking folk etymology, is when the spelling of a word or phrase changes because the words are divided ▶

differently from their original form. Classic examples of this
are *an adder* from *a naddre*, and *a newt* from *an ewt*. A
modern example of this process in operation is the phrase *to
all intensive purposes* for *to all intents and purposes*.

3 One element of the word or phrase is interpreted as a
different word which sounds exactly the same. Examples of
this are *free reign* for *free rein* and *just desserts* for *just deserts*.

Some modern folk etymologies are now so widespread that
they are likely to become the dominant and accepted form.
The list below shows some of the most frequent, and how
often they occur relative to their traditional forms in the
Oxford English Corpus.

TRADITIONAL FORM		FOLK ETYMOLOGY	
sleight of hand	85%	slight of hand	15%
fazed by	71%	phased by	29%
home in on	65%	hone in on	35%
a shoo-in	65%	a shoe-in	35%
bated breath	60%	baited breath	40%
free rein	54%	free reign	46%
chaise longue	54%	chaise lounge	46%
buck naked	53%	butt-naked	47%
vocal cords	51%	vocal chords	49%
just deserts	42%	just desserts	58%
fount of knowledge	41%	font of knowledge	59%
strait-laced	34%	straight-laced	66%

following

Following has long been used as an adjective qualifying a noun,
as in *for the following reasons*, or as a noun, as in *the following are
my reasons*, where the 'reasons' are what is doing the 'following'
and are therefore the logical subject of the verb **follow**. From
this has developed a use of **following** as a preposition, as in *used
car prices are going up, following the Budget*, where 'follow' has
no logical subject. This use has been criticized in cases where

it merely means 'after' rather than 'as a result of'. In such cases **after** would do equally well, and **following** may sound somewhat pompous. In the example just given there is a strong element of cause and effect, and so the use of **following** is justified. This is not true of *members are invited to take tea in the Convocation Coffee House following the meeting*.

forename

See CHRISTIAN NAME.

former

Traditionally, **former** and **latter** are used in relation to pairs of items: either the first of two items (**former**) or the second of two items (**latter**). The reason for this is that **former** and **latter** were formed as comparatives, adjectives which are correctly used when referring to just two things. In practice, **former** and **latter** are now sometimes used just as synonyms for **first** and **last** and are routinely used to refer to a contrast involving more than two items. Such uses, however, are not good English style.

formidable

There are two possible pronunciations of **formidable**: /**for**-mi-duh-b'l/ with the emphasis on the first syllable and /for-**mid**-uh-b'l/ with the emphasis on the second. /for-**mid**-uh-b'l/ is now common in British English, and the traditional pronunciation /**for**-mi-duh-b'l/ is rarely heard nowadays. Both pronunciations are acceptable in modern standard English.

fortuitous

The traditional, historical meaning of **fortuitous** is 'happening by chance': *a fortuitous meeting* is a chance meeting, which might turn out to be either a good thing or a bad thing. Today, however, **fortuitous** tends to be often used to refer only to fortunate outcomes, and the word has become more or less a synonym for 'lucky' or 'fortunate': *the ball went into the goal by a fortuitous ricochet*. Although this usage is now widespread, it is still regarded by some people as being rather informal and not correct.

founder, flounder

It is easy to confuse the words **founder** and **flounder**, not only because they sound similar but also because the contexts in which they are used tend to be similar. **Founder** means 'to fail', as in *the scheme foundered because of lack of organizational backing*. **Flounder**, on the other hand, means 'to be in difficulties', as in *new recruits floundering about in their first week*.

fragmentary

Fragmentary should be pronounced with the emphasis on the first syllable: /**frag**-muhn-tri/.

free rein

The image behind the phrase **give free rein** (to somebody) is from horse-riding, and the **rein** referred to is the strip of leather used to control a horse's (or child's) movements. Nowadays the spelling **free reign**, with an image taken from kingship, is almost as frequent, particularly in the US. In the Oxford English Corpus, 46 per cent of examples have the second spelling. Nevertheless, many people would consider the first spelling correct. For more information, see FOLK ETYMOLOGY.

-ful

The combining form **-ful** is used to form nouns meaning 'the amount needed to fill' (**cupful**, **spoonful**, etc.). The plural of such words is **cupfuls**, **spoonfuls**, etc., with the words joined together. *Three cups full* would mean the individual cups rather than a quantity measured in cups: *on the sill were three cups full of milk*, but *add three cupfuls of milk to the batter*.

fulsome

The modern, generally accepted meaning of **fulsome** is 'excessively complimentary or flattering' as in *a long and fulsome forty-seven page dedication to Princess Caroline*, but it is also often used to mean simply 'abundant', especially in uses such as *the critics have been fulsome in their praise*. Although this is in line with its earliest use, first recorded in the 13th century, some people consider it to be incorrect.

fun

The use of **fun** as an adjective meaning 'enjoyable', as in *we had a fun evening*, is not fully accepted in standard English and should only be used in informal contexts. There are signs that this situation is changing, though, given the recent appearance in US English of the comparative and superlative forms **funner** and **funnest**, formed as if **fun** were a normal adjective.

further, furthest

In some contexts **further** and **farther** are completely interchangeable: *she moved further/farther down the train*. The two words share the same roots and are equally correct when the meaning is 'at, to, or by a greater distance'. **Further** is a much commoner word, though, and is used in various abstract and metaphorical contexts, for example referring to time, where it would be unusual to use **farther**, e.g. *without further delay*; *have you anything further to say?*; *we intend to stay a further two weeks*. The same distinction is made between **farthest** and **furthest**: *the farthest point from the sun*, but: *this first team has gone furthest in its analysis*.

gay

Gay meaning 'homosexual' became established in the 1960s as the word preferred by homosexual men to describe themselves. It is now the standard accepted term throughout the English-speaking world. As a result, the centuries-old other meanings of **gay** meaning either 'carefree' or 'bright and showy' have more or less dropped out of natural use. The word **gay** cannot be readily used unselfconsciously today in these older meanings without suggesting a double entendre. **Gay** in its modern use typically refers to men, **lesbian** being the standard word for homosexual women, as in *the owners of a gay and lesbian bookstore*, but in some contexts it can be used of both men and women.

gender

The word **gender** has been used since the 14th century primarily as a grammatical term, referring to the classes of noun designated as masculine, feminine, or neuter in Latin, Greek, German, and other languages. It has also been used for just as long to refer to 'the state of being male or female', but this did not become a common standard use until the mid 20th century. Although the words **gender** and **sex** both mean 'the state of being male or female', they are typically used in slightly different ways: **sex** tends to refer to biological differences, while **gender** tends to refer to cultural or social ones.

g

gender-neutral language

In English, gender is explicit in nouns which refer exclusively to males or females, such as *businessman* and *actress*, and in the third person singular personal pronouns and adjectives *he, she, it, his, hers, its*, etc. Nowadays it is often very important to use language which implicitly or explicitly includes both men and women and makes no distinction between them. For more information on how to do this with nouns, see SEXIST LANGUAGE. What follows here is a discussion of how to be gender-neutral as regards pronouns such as *he* and determiners such as *his*.

1 From earliest times until about the 1960s people unquestioningly used the pronoun *he* (and *him, himself*, and *his*) when talking in general about one or more people of either sex. This most often happened:

- after indefinite pronouns and determiners such as *anybody, anyone, each, every*, etc., e.g. *anybody who really sets his heart on it*;
- after gender-neutral nouns such as *person, individual, speaker, student, researcher*, etc., e.g. *a researcher has to be completely objective in his findings*;
- in fixed expressions such as *every man for himself*.

2 Thanks to the feminist movement most people are now much more sensitive in these areas of language, ▶

and there are alternative ways of expressing these same ideas.

- When a gender-neutral pronoun is needed, the options usually adopted are *he or she* (or *his or her*, etc.), or the plural forms *they, their, themselves*. etc.

- Using *he or she*, etc., can be rather cumbersome, as in *each client should take the advice of his or her estate agent*, so there is a preference for using the plural form: *each client should take the advice of their estate agent*. Similarly *anyone who involves himself or herself in such issues does so for his or her own sake* is rather long-winded and better as *anyone who involves themselves in such issues does so for their own sake*.

- This use of plural pronouns following a singular subject is not new, but a revival of a practice dating from the 16th century. Nevertheless, some people object to it as ungrammatical. If you want to avoid it, an alternative strategy is to rephrase the sentence, generally by couching the whole thing in the plural. Recast in this way, the first example above becomes *clients should take the advice of their estate agents*.

3 Artificial devices, including the use of composite forms such as *s/he, hesh, wself*, etc., have not found general currency, partly because they are only possible in writing. A reflexive pronoun *themself* is occasionally used. This may become more common, but at present it is non-standard: *it is not an actor pretending to be Reagan or Thatcher, it is, in grotesque form, the person themself*; *someone in a neutral mood can devote themself solely to problem-solving*.

genealogy

The correct spelling is with the letter **a** before the ending **-logy**. Because most nouns referring to a branch of study end in **-ology**—*astrology, sociology*, etc.—people often write and say **geneology**, but this is incorrect.

genius

Genius used to be exclusively a noun, but is now quite often used as a sort of adjective: *I think it's a genius idea*. This use still has a tang of slang about it, and is best avoided in more formal writing.

geriatric

Geriatric is the normal, semi-official term used in Britain and the US when referring to the health care of old people (*a geriatric ward*; *geriatric patients*). When used outside such contexts, it typically carries overtones of being worn out and decrepit and can therefore be offensive if used to refer to people, as in *the photographer's bemused, bright-colour studies of the geriatric residents of San City*. In fact it may be seen as insulting to old people if used of anything else, e.g. *the US is full of geriatric coal-fired power stations*.

get

The verb **get** is one of the most common verbs in the English language. Nevertheless, despite its high frequency, there is still a feeling that almost any use containing **get** is somewhat informal. This may stem from the fact that many people were told at school not to write **get** at all, even though that was really only justifiable in relation to informal uses such as *I got a bike for my birthday*, and not standard expressions such as *he fought to get his breath back*.

girl

Few words are capable of raising some women's hackles as much as **girl** when used to refer to an adult woman. Conservatives may say that using it in this way is usually harmless and jokey; feminists might argue, in contrast, that it is disempowering and infantilizes women. It is certainly true that there is often a huge difference between the connotations of **girl** and those of **boy** when applied to adults: *his boyish charm* vs. *the film is a bit girlie*; *boys will be boys* vs. *he's a big girl's blouse*.

Since it is such a contentious word, it is better to be extremely cautious about making use of it.

Avoid using nouns which include it, such as *newsgirl*, *weathergirl*, *working girl*, *girl Friday*, and *career girl*, ▶

and use a neutral word: *newsreader*, *weather forecaster*, *working woman* or *sex worker*, *office assistant*, and *working woman* or *professional woman*.

Avoid using it to refer to any woman in a job or role, for instance *the woman who helps us out in the shop* rather than *the girl*...

Although the word is still used informally by some women to refer to exclusive groups of women (*a night out with the girls*; *Come on girls! Let's show them we are more than cheerleaders with sticks*), not all women are happy with this use of it.

The one area where it still seems to be used consistently is in the popular press, in expressions such as *glamour girl*, *page-three girl*, *cover girl*, and so forth.

given name

See CHRISTIAN NAME.

glamorous

Both **glamor** and **glamour** are acceptable spellings in US English, but only the second is standard in British English, and is much commoner even in the US. Some people mistakenly suppose that **glamorous**, dropping the **u**, is an American spelling only. In fact, it is the correct spelling on both sides of the 'pond', while **glamourous** is universally a mistake. See also HUMOROUS.

Google

When referring to the Internet search engine itself, or the organization that owns it, **Google** should be written with a capital **G**. As a noun the name is a registered trademark, as a verb it is not. So, when using the word as a verb, you should write it with a small first letter: *I was idly googling two of my favourite words*. In that respect, you can treat it exactly like other verbs derived from trademarks, such as *to hoover* and *to xerox*.

gotten

Gotten and **got**, the past participles of **get**, both date back to Middle English. The form **gotten** is not generally used in British English but is very common in North American English, though even there it is often regarded as non-standard. In North American English, **got** and **gotten** are not identical in use. **Gotten** usually implies the process of obtaining something, as in *he had gotten us tickets for the show*, while **got** implies the state of possession or ownership, as in *I haven't got any money*. **Gotten** is also used in the meaning of 'become', as in *she's gotten very fat this last year*.

g

gourmand

The words **gourmand** and **gourmet** are similar but not identical in meaning. Both can be used to mean 'a connoisseur of good food' but **gourmand** is more usually used to mean 'a person who enjoys eating and often eats too much'. In other words, there is a hierarchy of finesse: *I am a gourmet, you are a gourmand, he is a glutton*.

graduate

The original use of this verb is **be graduated from**, i.e. as a transitive verb, used passively: *she will be graduated from medical school in June*. However, it is now much more common to say **graduate from**: *she will graduate from medical school in June*. A different transitive use, as in *he graduated high school last week*, is becoming increasingly common, especially in speech, but is considered incorrect by many editors.

graffiti

The word **graffiti** comes from Italian, and in Italian is a plural noun which has a singular form **graffito**. Traditionally, the same distinction was maintained in English, so that **graffiti** was used with a plural verb: *the graffiti were all over the wall*. Similarly, the singular would require a singular verb: *there was a graffito on the wall*. Today, this distinction survives in some specialist fields such as archaeology but sounds odd to most native

speakers. The most common modern use is to treat **graffiti** as
a singular and not to use **graffito** at all. In this case, **graffiti** takes
a singular verb, as in *the graffiti was all over the wall*. Such uses
are now widely accepted as standard, and may be regarded
as part of the natural development of the language, rather
than as mistakes. For more information, see NOUNS, SINGULAR
AND PLURAL.

Great Britain

g

See BRITAIN.

grievous

This word has two syllables, /**gree**-vuhss/, and should not be
pronounced as if it had three, /**gree**-vee-uhss/, since there
is no letter **i** after the **v**.

grisly, grizzly

The words **grisly** and **grizzly** are quite different in
meaning, though often confused. **Grisly** means 'gruesome',
as in *grisly crimes*, whereas **grizzly** chiefly describes a kind
of large American bear, but can also mean 'grey or
grey-haired'.

grow

Although **grow** is typically used intransitively, as in *he would
watch Nick grow to manhood*, using it as a transitive verb
has long been standard in contexts which refer to growing
plants and one's hair (*more land was needed to grow crops; she
grew her hair long*). Recently, however, **grow** in its transitive
meaning has become popular in business jargon:
entrepreneurs who are struggling to grow their businesses.
This is still a relatively new usage, and it is perhaps better
to avoid it in formal contexts. It irritates certain people
beyond measure.

gymnasium

The preferred plural form for this is **gymnasiums**. See also LATIN
PLURALS.

h

Pronouncing the letter **h** at the beginning of words like *house, home,* and so on, has long been regarded as a yardstick of correct pronunciation in standard British English. Not pronouncing it, known as *dropping one's aitches*, is, conversely, considered to mark the speaker as regional or uneducated. So, it seems like a strange paradox that the exact opposite applies to how the letter itself is said. To pronounce it **aitch** is considered standard; to pronounce it **haitch**, non-standard (though it is the usual pronunciation in certain parts of the United Kingdom). But things have changed. While many people still regard the **haitch** pronunciation as anathema, it seems to be rapidly becoming the normal pronunciation for younger people, and carries no social stigma as far as they are concerned.

halcyon

The phrase **halcyon days**, referring to an idyllically happy period of time, is occasionally incorrectly turned into 'halcyonic days'.

half

People are sometimes not sure whether to use a singular or plural verb in phrases with **half**. When **half** is followed by a singular noun (with or without *of* between), the verb is also singular, and when the noun is plural the verb is plural: *half of the country is employed in agriculture*; *half the people like the idea*; *half that amount is enough*. Occasionally, when **half (of)** is used with a collective noun, the plural can correctly be used: *nearly half (of) the population lose at least half their teeth before they reach the age of 40*.

handicapped

The word **handicapped** is first recorded in the early 20th century to refer to a person's mental or physical disabilities. In British English it was the standard term until relatively recently, but like many terms in this sensitive field its prominence has been short-lived. It has been superseded by more recent terms such as **disabled**, or, when referring to mental disability, **having**

learning difficulties or learning-disabled. In American English,
however, handicapped remains acceptable.

hang

In modern English **hang** has two past tense and past participle
forms: **hanged** and **hung**. **Hung** is the normal form in most
general uses, e.g. *they hung out the washing*; *she hung around for
a few minutes*; *he had hung the picture over the fireplace*, but
hanged is the normal form to refer to execution by hanging: *the
prisoner was hanged*. The reason for this distinction is a complex
historical one: **hanged**, the earlier form, was superseded by
hung sometime after the 16th century; it is likely that the
retention of **hanged** for the execution meaning has to do with
the tendency of archaic forms to live on in the legal language of
the courts.

harass

There are two possible pronunciations of the word **harass**: one
emphasizing the first syllable, /**ha**-ruhs/, and the other, the
second: /huh-**ras**/. /**Ha**-ruhs/ is the older one and is regarded by
some people as the only correct one, especially in British English.
However, the pronunciation /huh-**ras**/ is very common and is now
accepted as a standard alternative.

hardly

1 Words such as **hardly**, **scarcely**, and **rarely** should not be
used with negative constructions. It is correct to say *I can hardly
wait* but incorrect to say *I can't hardly wait*. This is because
adverbs such as **hardly** are treated as if they were negatives,
and it is a grammatical rule of standard English that double
negatives (i.e. in this case having **hardly** and **not** in the same
clause) are not acceptable. Words such as **hardly** behave as
negatives in other respects as well, as for example in combining
with words such as **any** or **at all**, which are normally only
used where a negative is present: standard usage is *I've got
hardly any money*.

2 See also DOUBLE NEGATIVE.

harelip

Use of the word **harelip** can cause offence and should be avoided; use **cleft lip** instead.

hash

In British English this is the normal name for the symbol #, for example on a telephone keypad. In the US and elsewhere it is called either the **number sign**, in contexts such as *question #2*; or the **pound sign**, on telephone keypads or when used as a symbol for pounds of weight, e.g. *2# of sugar*. You may impress your friends briefly by telling them that the technical name for this symbol is the **octothorp**, but that name is not widely used.

hashtag

This refers to the use of the hash symbol # in front of a word or phrase on social media sites such as Twitter, to identify messages on a specific topic.

have

1 **Have** and **have got**: there is a great deal of debate on the difference between these two forms. A traditional view is that **have got** is chiefly British, but not correct in formal writing, while **have** is chiefly American. Actual usage is more complicated: **have got** is in fact also widely used in US English. In both British and US usage **have** is more formal than **have got** and it is more appropriate in writing to use constructions such as **do not have** rather than **have not got**.

2 A common mistake is to write the word **of** instead of **have** or **'ve**: *I could of told you that* instead of *I could have told you that*. The reason for the mistake is that the pronunciation of **have** in unstressed contexts is the same as that of **of**, and people confuse the two in writing. The error was recorded as early as 1837 and, though common, is unacceptable in standard English.

3 Another controversial issue is the insertion of an unnecessary **have** referring to a hypothetical situation introduced by **if**, as for example *I might have missed it if you hadn't* **have** *pointed it out* (rather than the standard . . . *if you hadn't pointed it out*). This construction has been around since at least the

15th century, and there has recently been speculation among grammarians and linguists that it may represent a kind of subjunctive and is actually making a useful distinction in the language. However, it is still regarded as an error in standard English.

he

1 For a discussion of *I am older than he* versus *I am older than him*, see PERSONAL PRONOUN.

2 At one time, **he** was used uncontroversially to refer to a person of unspecified sex, as in *every child needs to know that **he** is loved*. Nowadays, this use has become problematic and is a hallmark of old-fashioned or sexist language. **They** as an alternative to **he** (*everyone needs to feel that **they** matter*) has been in use since the 18th century, in contexts where it occurs after an indefinite pronoun such as **everyone** or **someone**. Despite objections by some, it is now widely accepted both in speech and in writing. Another alternative is **he or she**, but this can become tiresomely long-winded when used frequently. See also GENDER-NEUTRAL LANGUAGE.

her

For a discussion of *I am older than her* versus *I am older than she*, or *it's her all right* rather than *it's she all right*, see PERSONAL PRONOUN.

hers

There is no need for an apostrophe: the spelling should be **hers** not **her's**.

him

For a discussion of *I could never be as good as him* versus *I could never be as good as he*, see PERSONAL PRONOUN.

Hindustani

Hindustani was the usual term in the 18th and 19th centuries for the native language of NW India. The usual modern term is

Hindi (or **Urdu** in Muslim contexts), although **Hindustani** is
still used to refer to the dialect of Hindi spoken around Delhi.

Hispanic

In the US **Hispanic** is the standard accepted term when
referring to Spanish-speaking people living in the US. Other,
more specific, terms such as **Latino** and **Chicano** are also
used where occasion demands.

historic, historical

1 On the use of *an historic moment* or *a historic moment*, see AN.

2 **Historic** and **historical** are used in slightly different ways.
Historic means 'famous or important in history', as in *a(n)
historic occasion*, whereas **historical** means 'concerning history
or historical events', as in *historical evidence*. An *historic event*
is one that was very important, whereas an *historical event* is
something that happened in the past. Confusing the two
is something careful writers avoid.

hoard

The words **hoard** and **horde** are similar in meaning and are
pronounced the same, and so they are sometimes confused.
A **hoard** is 'a secret stock or store of something', as in *a hoard
of treasure*, while a **horde** is sometimes a disparaging word for
'a large group of people', as in *hordes of fans descended on the
stage*. Instances of **hoard** being used instead of **horde** are
not uncommon: around 10 per cent of the uses of **hoard** in
the Oxford English Corpus are incorrect.

hoi polloi

1 **Hoi** is one of the Greek words for the definite article *the*; the
phrase **hoi polloi** thus translates as 'the many'. This knowledge
has led some traditionalists to insist that it should not be used in
English with *the*, since that would be to state the word *the* twice.
However, the fact is that, once established in English,
expressions such as **hoi polloi** are treated as a fixed unit and
are subject to the rules and conventions of English. Evidence
shows that use with *the* has now become an accepted part
of standard English usage.

2 Hoi polloi is sometimes used to mean 'upper class', i.e. the exact opposite of its normal meaning. This is not recommended, for the obvious reason that you could be completely misunderstood.

home in, hone in

If you **home in on** something you focus all your attention on it: *we've homed in on the products that are most sought after*. For some reason, people very often say and write **hone in on** to express this meaning. **Hone** may become a perfectly acceptable variant in future; for the time being, it is still generally considered a mistake.

homogeneous

This word meaning 'uniform, alike' is correctly spelled **homogeneous** with an **e** before the **ou**, and pronounced /hom-uh-**jee**-ni-uhs/, but it is frequently spelled **homogenous** and pronounced /huh-**mo**-ji-nuhs/. This rarely matters, but it is good to be aware that **homogenous** is a different word, an albeit dated term used in biology.

hopefully

The traditional meaning of **hopefully**, 'in a hopeful manner', has been in use since the 17th century. In the second half of the 20th century a new use, commenting on the whole sentence, arose, meaning 'it is to be hoped that', as in *hopefully, we'll see you tomorrow*. This second use is now very much commoner than the first use, but it is still widely believed to be incorrect. This is somewhat illogical. People do not criticize other similar adverbs, e.g. **sadly** (as in *sadly, her father died last year*) or **fortunately** (as in *fortunately, he recovered*). Part of the reason is that **hopefully** is a rather odd adverb of this kind: while many others, such as **sadly**, **regrettably**, and **clearly**, may be paraphrased as 'it is sad/regrettable/clear that . . .', this is not possible with **hopefully**. Nevertheless, it is clear that use of **hopefully** has become a test case of 'correctness' in the language—even if the arguments on which this is based are not particularly strong—and it may be wise to avoid its use in formal or written contexts.

horde

The words **hoard** and **horde** are quite distinct; see HOARD.

hotel

The normal pronunciation of **hotel** sounds the **h-**, which means that you should write and say *a hotel*. However, the older pronunciation without the **h-** is still sometimes heard, in which case *an hotel* would be appropriate. For a discussion of this, see AN.

Hottentot

Hottentot is first recorded in the late 17th century and was a name applied by white Europeans to the Khoikhoi group of peoples of South Africa and Namibia. It is now regarded as offensive when referring to people and should always be avoided in favour of **Khoikhoi** or the names of the particular peoples, such as the Nama. The only acceptable modern use for **Hottentot** is in the names of animals and plants, such as the *Hottentot cherry*.

however, how ever

If you use **ever** for emphasis after **how** or **why**, you should write it as a separate word. It is correct to write *how ever did you manage?* rather than *however did you manage?* In contrast, **however** is written as one word in the following cases: when it is equivalent to 'but' (*when the film opened in 1923, however, audiences stayed away in droves*); when it means 'in whatever way' (*take that however you like*); and when it means 'to whatever extent' (*he is exempt from any rule , however clearly stated it is*). But, with other words such as **what**, **where**, and **who**, the situation is not clear-cut: people write both **what ever** and **whatever**, and so on, and neither is regarded as particularly more correct than the other.

humanitarian

Humanitarian means 'concerned with or seeking to promote human welfare', so it is rather loosely used in sentences such as *this is the worst humanitarian disaster this country has seen*, where it just means 'human'. This use is quite common, especially in journalism, but is not generally considered good style.

humankind

Humankind is often used as a non-sexist replacement for **mankind**. See also MAN.

humorous

Though **humor** is the standard US spelling for British **humour**, it is a mistake to suppose that only Americans write **humorous**. It is the correct spelling on both sides of the Atlantic, while **humourous** is a mistake everywhere. See also GLAMOROUS.

hypercorrection

Hypercorrection is an incorrect use of language because, in an attempt to be correct, one is following a rule that does not apply. There are common hypercorrect forms in the areas of grammar, spelling, and pronunciation.

- A grammatical example is *between you and I*, instead of the correct *between you and me*, caused by people's belief that *you and me* is always wrong, not just as the subject of a sentence, as in *you and me could go to the cinema*.
- *Glamourous* is a hypercorrect spelling, based on the belief that because *glamor* is the US spelling equivalent to the British *glamour*, *glamorous* must be a US spelling too.
- Hypercorrect pronunciations are very often of foreign words, for instance that of pronouncing *machismo* with -k- in the middle, thinking that -ch- is too English a sound to be in a foreign word.

hyphenation

Hyphenation is an area in which practice is somewhat fluid, since it varies between different types of English and different house styles, and evolves over time. As H. W. Fowler wrote in his *Modern English Usage* (1926): '...its infinite variety defies description'. He did, however, also say that the hyphen 'is not an ornament but an aid to being understood', and that laudable aim often governs its use, as illustrated below.

The primary function of the hyphen is to indicate that two or more words should be interpreted together as a single unit of meaning, and the examples below use that as the basis to show why it is necessary in some cases and unnecessary in others. There are also cases where its use varies according to context. Nouns are dealt with separately, since they raise questions of their own.

h

Necessary uses

- in many, but not all, compound adjectives of various sorts, e.g. (noun + adjective) *accident-prone*, *sports-mad*, *sugar-free*, *carbon-neutral*, *time-poor*, *camera-ready*; (noun/ adjective + participle) *computer-aided*, *custom-built*, *good-looking*, *quick-thinking*, *slow-moving*; (noun + ing/ed) *stress-busting*, *muddle-headed*; (adjective + noun (+ ed)) *seventh-century*, *double-breasted*, *short-sighted*. NB: it is important to use hyphens in adjectives referring to ages and durations, since leaving them out can create ambiguity: compare *250-year-old trees* and *250 year old trees*; in the second the trees could be merely a year old.

- in compound adjectives formed from adverb + past participle, e.g. *well-equipped*, and in adjectives based on phrases, e.g. *in-your-face*, *top-of-the-range*, which are hyphenated when they come before the noun but   ▶

not when they follow it: *this is a top-of-the-range model*, but *this model is top of the range*.

- in many verbs formed from nouns: *they booby-trapped the door; he was body-searched*
- to separate certain prefixes, especially those derived from classical languages, e.g. *anti-intellectual, co-driver, ex-directory, extra-large, over-intellectual, pro-life, post-coital*

  NB: in American usage, words in the last group are often written without a hyphen.

- to separate pairs of vowels or consonants which could otherwise be misread or sound awkward: *co-opt* (*coopt* could be read as /koopt/), *pre-eminent* (which could look like preem-), *drip-proof*
- to distinguish *re-cover* (= 'cover again') from *recover*; *re-sort* (= 'sort again') from *resort*, etc.
- to separate a prefix from a name, designation, or date: *post-Aristotelian; ex-husband; pre-1960s*
- with *odd* when used with a number, e.g. *thirty-odd people* ('approximately thirty people'), as opposed to *thirty odd people* ('thirty people who are odd').

Use varies according to context

As noted above, if an adjective such as *top-of-the-range* or *up-to-date* comes before the noun it is hyphenated, but otherwise it is not: *an up-to-date account*, but *I like to keep up to date*.

Mid in compounds before nouns is hyphenated, e.g. *a mid-nineteenth century forgery*, but otherwise it functions as an adjective in its own right and is not hyphenated, e.g. *in the mid nineteenth century*.

The suffixes *-less* and *-like* need a hyphen if the root word ends with *-ll*: *cell-less, thrill-less, doll-like, shell-like*.

Unnecessary uses

Hyphens are superfluous in:

- phrasal verbs: *to give up the fight*, not *to give-up the fight*
- adjective phrases formed from an adverb ending in *-ly* and a participle, as in *a poorly understood condition* ▶

(not poorly-understood), *a widely held view* (not a widely-held view)

Nouns

Compound nouns consisting of two words can in principle be written in one of three different ways: e.g. *air fare*, *air-fare*, or *airfare*. In practice, however, the use of hyphens in compound nouns is generally decreasing. Usage in the US tends towards writing the two nouns as one, and usage in Britain tends towards writing them separately, as is the case with *air fare* etc. Otherwise there are few hard-and-fast rules, but a few tendencies can be detected, e.g.:

- Compounds of which the first element has only one syllable are some of the most likely to be written as one word, e.g. *website*, *spyware*, *blockbuster*, *playgroup*, as opposed to *bottle bank*, *filling station*, *regime change*.
- If the first element is an adjective, the compound tends to stay as separate words, e.g. *virtual reality*, *black box*.
- Compounds tend to stay as two words if joining them up would produce an awkward or misleading result, as with *wood duck*, *binge drinker*.
- Hyphens are used in well-established multiword nouns, such as *stick-in-the-mud*, *ne'er-do-well*, *jack-in-the-box*.
- They are also used with most nouns derived from phrasal verbs, such as *build up*, *warm up*, *carry on*, *walk through*. A few very common ones are written predominantly as one word, e.g. *handout*, *breakthrough*, *pickup*, but usage varies a great deal.

I

It is incorrect to say *between you and I* instead of *between you and me*. See BETWEEN. It is also incorrect to say *John and me went to the shops* instead of *John and I went to the shops*. On this point and whether it is correct to say *she's much better than me* or *she's much better than I*, see PERSONAL PRONOUN.

-i

Many nouns that are derived from a foreign language retain their foreign plural, at least when they first enter English and particularly if they belong to a specialist field. Over time, however, it is quite normal for a word in general use to acquire a regular English plural. This regular plural may coexist with the foreign plural (e.g. **cactus**, plural **cactuses** or **cacti**) or, more commonly, especially over time, oust it (e.g. **octopus**, plural **octopuses** rather than **octopodes**). The plural ending **-i** is more persistent that many other foreign plural endings, probably because it is a better-known one—so well known, in fact, that it is sometimes applied to words which never had it in the first place, as with the spurious *octopi*.

if

If and **whether** are more or less interchangeable in sentences like *I'll see if he left an address* and *I'll see whether he left an address*, although **whether** is generally regarded as more formal and suitable for written use.

ignoramus

The correct plural of **ignoramus** is **ignoramuses**. This may sound odd, considering the word is from Latin, leading one to think the plural ought to be *'ignorami'*. However, it was never a noun in Latin, only a verb, meaning literally 'we do not know', and the English word derives from the name of a character in George Ruggle's play *Ignoramus* (1615), a satirical comedy exposing lawyers' ignorance. For more information on the plural forms of Latin words, see LATIN PLURALS.

ilk

Nowadays, **ilk** is used in phrases such as *of his ilk*, *of that ilk*, to mean 'type' or 'sort'. This use arose out of a misunderstanding of the earlier, Scottish use in the phrase **of that ilk**, where it means 'of the same name or place'. For this reason, some traditionalists regard the modern use as incorrect. It is, however, the only common current use and is now part of standard English.

illegal, illicit

Something that is **illegal** is against the law, as in *illegal drugs*, *illegal immigrants*. **Illicit** traditionally covers things that are forbidden or disapproved of but not against the law, as in *an illicit love affair*, but it is commonly used to mean the same as **illegal**.

imminent

For the mistaken use of **eminent** to mean **imminent**, see EMINENT.

impact

The verb **impact on**, as in *when produce is lost, it always impacts on the bottom line*, has been in the language since the 1960s. Many people disapprove of it, despite its relative frequency, saying that **make an impact on** or other equivalent wordings should be used instead. They may object partly because new forms of verbs from nouns (as in the case of **impact**) are often regarded as somehow inferior. Also, since the use of **impact** is associated with business and commercial writing, it has the unenviable status of jargon, which makes it doubly disliked. For further information, see VERBS FORMED FROM NOUNS.

imply

Imply and **infer** do not mean the same thing and are not interchangeable: see INFER.

important, importantly

Both **more/most important** and **more/most importantly** are used as written asides, e.g. *a non-drinking, non-smoking, and, more importantly, non-political sportsman*. It is sometimes maintained that the only correct form in this use is **important**, on the grounds that it stands for 'what is more/most important'. However, **importantly** used in this way is perfectly well established and acceptable in modern English.

impracticable, impractical

Although their meanings are similar, **impracticable** and **impractical** should not be used in exactly the same way.

Impracticable means 'impossible to carry out' and is normally used of a specific procedure or course of action, as in *poor visibility made the task difficult, even impracticable*. **Impractical**, on the other hand, tends to be used in a more general way, often to mean simply 'unrealistic' or 'not sensible': *in windy weather an umbrella is impractical*. It is good style to avoid using **impracticable** in such contexts.

improvise

Improvise is always spelled *-ise* not *-ize*.

include

Include has a broader meaning than **comprise**. In the sentence *the accommodation comprises 2 bedrooms, bathroom, kitchen, and living room*, the word **comprise** implies that there is no accommodation other than that listed. **Include** can be used in this way too, but it is also used in a less restrictive way, implying that there may be other things not specifically mentioned that are part of the same category, as in *the price includes a special welcome pack*.

Indian

The native peoples of America came to be described as **Indian** as a result of Christopher Columbus and other voyagers in the 15th and 16th centuries believing that, when they reached the east coast of America, they had reached part of India by a new route. The terms **Indian** and **Red Indian** are today regarded as old-fashioned and inappropriate, recalling, as they do, the stereotypical portraits of the Wild West. **American Indian**, however, is well established. See also AMERICAN INDIAN and NATIVE AMERICAN.

Indigenous Australians

See ABORIGINAL, ABORIGINE.

infectious

On the differences in meaning between **infectious** and **contagious**, see CONTAGIOUS.

infer

Infer and **imply** mean different things. In the sentence *the speaker implied that the General had been a traitor*, **implied** means that something in the speaker's words **suggested** that this man was a traitor (though nothing so explicit was actually stated). However, in *we inferred from his words that the General had been a traitor*, **inferred** means that something in the speaker's words enabled us to **deduce** that the man was a traitor. So, the two words **infer** and **imply** can describe the same event, but from different angles. Mistakes occur when **infer** is used to mean **imply**, as in *are you inferring that I'm a liar?* (instead of *are you implying that I'm a liar?*). The error is so common that some dictionaries record it as a more or less standard use: over 20 per cent of examples for **infer** in the Oxford English Corpus are a mistaken replacement for **imply**. Nevertheless, many people still regard the use of **infer** for **imply** as an error.

inflammable

The words **inflammable** and **flammable** mean the same thing, 'easily set on fire'. This may seem surprising, since the prefix **in-** normally negates the adjective that follows it, as in *indirect* and *insufficient*, so you might expect **inflammable** to mean the opposite of **flammable**, i.e. 'not easily set on fire'. The reason that it means the same as **flammable** is that **inflammable** is formed using a different Latin prefix **in-**, which means 'into' and here has the effect of intensifying the meaning. **Flammable** is a far commoner word than **inflammable** and is less likely to confuse people.

innit

The word **innit** arose as an informal way of saying 'isn't it', especially in questions in spoken English where the speaker is seeking confirmation of a statement, as in *weird that, innit?* More recently, however, **innit** has also started serving as *don't I?*, *can't you?*, *aren't we?*, etc., either when there is a genuine seeking of confirmation or merely for emphasis, as in *we're all friends, innit?* This extended use is especially common among young people and is often satirized. (Interestingly, many other languages have just one expression equivalent to all these English ones: *n'est-ce pas?* in French, for example, or *nicht wahr?* in German.) From this confirmation-seeking or emphatic use, **innit** has further developed into a general-purpose 'filler', conveying very little actual content, as in *some MCs just MC but they don't really know what's going on, on the road innit… but we know innit*. In this type of context, it is much like *you know* or *sort of*.

input

As a verb, **input** has the past tense and past participle **input** and **inputted**, both of which are correct, though **input** is more often used. See also VERBS FORMED FROM NOUNS.

inquire

On the difference between **inquire** and **enquire**, see ENQUIRE.

insurance

There is a technical distinction between **insurance** and **assurance** in the context of life insurance: see ASSURANCE.

insure

Insure and **ensure** are related in meaning and use. In both British and US English the main meaning of **insure** is the commercial meaning of providing financial compensation in the event of damage to property; **ensure** is not used at all with this meaning. For the more general meaning of 'to make sure', **ensure that** is at least 50 times more common in the Oxford English Corpus than **insure that**, as in *the system is run to ensure that a good quality of service is maintained*. In similar examples to the last one, **insure that** is sometimes used but is likely to be regarded as a mistake.

integral

There are two possible pronunciations for **integral** as an adjective: /**in**-ti-gruhl/ and /in-**teg**-ruhl/. /In-**teg**-ruhl/ is sometimes frowned on, but both are acceptable as standard.

intense, intensive

Intense and **intensive** are similar in meaning, but they differ in emphasis. **Intense** tends to relate to subjective responses—emotions and how we feel about something—while **intensive**, in the meaning of 'very thorough, vigorous', tends to be an objective description. So, *an intensive course* simply describes the type of course: one that is designed to cover a lot of ground in a short time. On the other hand, in *the course was intense*, **intense** describes how someone felt about the course. *Intense negotiations* are ones where there is a lot of tension and emotional excitement, while *intensive negotiations* are very thorough and probably concentrated into a short period of time. **Intensive** is sometimes used where **intense** is meant, as in *an intensive love of Tolkien*, but this should be avoided in writing.

interface

The word **interface** has existed as a noun since the 1880s. The metaphorical meaning, 'a place or means of interactions between two systems, organizations, etc.', to which many people object, was first used before the literal, computing meaning. It has become widespread in this extended use as both a noun and a verb in all sorts of spheres. Some people object to it on the grounds that there are plenty of other words that could be used instead. Although it is now well established as a part of standard English, if you wish to avoid it in certain contexts you could use *interaction*, *liaison*, *dialogue*, *contact*, etc., and their related verbs. See also VERBS FORMED FROM NOUNS.

in terms of

In terms of is to be treated with extreme caution. Widely criticized for being overused and vague, it is often abused as an all-purpose way of cobbling together fuzzy ideas, as this example from the business world illustrates: *the effect would be significant in terms of potential impact on earnings*. The problem with this sentence is that it says the same thing twice. It should be cut down to size as *the effect on potential earnings would be* *significant*. And the same is true of many sentences where it is used as a connector like this. Assess any sentence in which you write it with a critical eye. Does it make your point easier to understand—or merely long-winded? **In terms of** is also often used at the start of a clause, to announce the topic: *there were also benefits in terms of reducing fixed costs, he said*. While it can be a useful hook on which to hang your thoughts when speaking, in writing preferable alternatives for this use are **as for**, **as regards**, or, more forcefully, **when it comes to**.

Inuit

The peoples living in the regions from the central Canadian Arctic to western Greenland prefer to be called **Inuit** rather than **Eskimo**, a broader term including peoples living elsewhere in the Arctic region, notably Siberia. **Inuit** now has official status in Canada. It is also used as a synonym for **Eskimo** in general, usually in an attempt to be politically correct, but is best avoided in that meaning, for the reason just mentioned. See also ESKIMO.

irregardless

Irregardless means the same as **regardless**, but the negative prefix **ir-** merely duplicates the suffix **-less**, and is completely unnecessary. The word dates back to the 19th century, and may be a confusion of **regardless** with **irrespective**. It is regarded as incorrect in standard English, and most people would regard it as a non-word.

-ise

There are some verbs which must be spelled **-ise** and are not variants of the **-ize** ending. Most reflect a French influence, and they include **advertise**, **compromise**, **enterprise**, **improvise**, and **televise**. For more details, see -IZE OR -ISE.

issue

Many people object to the overuse of the word **issue** referring to emotional and psychological difficulties, or to problems in providing a service: *emotions and intimacy issues that were largely dealt with through alcohol; a small number of users are experiencing* *connectivity issues*. In both contexts, the word is clearly a euphemism. In the first case, by avoiding the word **problem**, it casts the person concerned in a less negative light. However, in this use it often has an aura of psychobabble about it. In the second case, **issue** is meant to imply that a solution will be found, and that everything is under control. While the intention behind using the word in these ways may be praiseworthy, overuse has turned it into a cliché, beloved of politicians and pundits. If you want an alternative, you may have to call a spade a spade and use a word which is rapidly becoming taboo: **a problem**.

its

A common error in writing is to confuse the possessive **its** (as in *turn the camera on its side*) with the contraction **it's** (short for either **it is** or **it has**, as in *it's my fault*; *it's been a hot day*). The confusion is understandable since the possessive forms of singular nouns do take an apostrophe + **-s**, as in *the girl's bike*; *the President's smile*.

-ize or -ise

The main difficulties people encounter with words ending in **-ize** and **-ise** are:
- which words have alternative spellings and which don't?
- where there are alternative spellings, which is the correct one?

This article gives guidance on both these aspects, as well as commenting on some relatively recent words ending in *-ize*.

1 The reason there is a choice in many cases between *-ize* and *-ise* is historically complex. The *-ize* ending ultimately derives from the Classical Greek verbal ending *-izo*, whether or not the English verb existed in Greek in the same form. Many words with alternative endings in *-ize/-ise* have come to English via Latin and French sources, but in French the ▶

spelling has been adapted to *-ise*. The first *-ize* word recorded in English is *baptize*, from the 13th century. In French it is written *baptiser*, and a large proportion of English writers and publishers followed suit by writing the word as *baptise*.

2 There is a small group of words which are only ever written *-ise*, in all varieties of English, including American English, and they are listed below. It may help to remember that *-ise* is obligatory where it forms part of a larger word element, such as *-cise* in *excise*, *-mise* in *compromise*, *-prise* in *surprise*, and *-vise* in *supervise*. *-ise* is also obligatory in verbs closely related to nouns with **-s-** in the stem, such as *advertise* (compare *advertisement*) and *televise* (which is actually derived from *television*).

advertise
advise
apprise
arise
chastise
circumcise
comprise
compromise
demise
despise
devise
dis(en)franchise
disguise
enfranchise
enterprise
excise
exercise
franchise
improvise
incise
merchandise
prise (open)
reprise

▶

revise
supervise
surmise
surprise
televise

3 Words where there is a choice of ending such as *authorize/
authorise*, *civilize/civilise*, *legalize/legalise* may be correctly
spelled with either *-ize* or *-ise* throughout the English-speaking
world, except in America, where *-ize* is always used.

In other cases the choice is a matter of house style.
However, Oxford University Press and many other
publishing houses prefer the spelling in *-ize*.
British English writers are generally aware of the
choice but often mistakenly regard the *-ize* ending
as an Americanism. They tend to be particularly
reluctant to use the *-ize* form in words which have
other forms in which the letter *s* features, such as *criticize*
(*criticism*), *hypnotize* (*hypnosis*), and *emphasize* (*emphasis*).

4 Adding *-ize* to a noun or adjective has been a standard
way of forming new verbs for centuries, and verbs such
as *characterize*, *terrorize*, and *sterilize* were all formed in this
way hundreds of years ago. For some reason some people
object to recent formations of this type: during the 20th
century, objections were raised against **prioritize**, **finalize**,
and **hospitalize**, among others. There does not seem to be
any coherent reason for such objections, except that verbs
formed from nouns tend, in general and for no clear reason,
to be criticized. Despite objections, it is clear that *-ize* forms
are an accepted part of the standard language.

judgement

In British English the traditional spelling in general contexts is
judgement, though **judgment** without the **-e-** is also often
found. However, the spelling **judgment** is the standard
spelling in legal contexts, and in all contexts in North
American English.

Kaffir

The word **Kaffir** is first recorded in the 16th century (as **Caffre**) and was originally simply an innocuous descriptive term for a particular ethnic group. Although it survives in the names of a few plants, such as the *Kaffir lily*, it is always a racially abusive and offensive term when used of people, and in South Africa its use is actionable.

Khoikhoi

To refer to the indigenous peoples of Namibia and parts of South Africa, **Khoikhoi** should be used in preference to **Hottentot**, since the latter is likely to cause offence: see also HOTTENTOT.

kilometre (US kilometer)

There are two possible pronunciations for **kilometre**: /**kil**-uh-mee-tuh/ and /ki-**lom**-i-tuh/. The first is traditionally considered correct, with a stress pattern similar to other units of measurement such as *centimetre*. The second pronunciation, which originated in US English and is now also very common in British English, is still regarded as incorrect by some people, especially in British English.

kind

The use of **kind** sometimes causes difficulty, as in *these kind of questions are not relevant*, where the plurals *these* and *are* are used with the singular *kind*. With *this* or *that*, speaking of one kind, use a singular construction: ***this kind** of question **is** not relevant; **that kind** of fabric **doesn't** need ironing*. With *these* or *those*, speaking of more than one kind, use a plural construction: *we refuse to buy **these kinds** of books; I've given up **those kinds** of ideas*. The ungrammatical *these kind* has been used since the 14th century, but although often encountered today it should be avoided. The same point applies to the noun **sort** used in a similar way.

koala

Koalas, the bear-like Australian marsupials, are widely called **koala bears** in everyday language. Zoologists, however, regard this form as incorrect on the grounds that, despite appearances, koalas are completely unrelated to bears.

kudos

Kudos comes from Greek and means 'praise'. Despite appearances, it is not a plural word. This means that there is no singular form **kudo** and that the use of **kudos** as a plural, as in the following sentence, is incorrect: *he received many kudos for his work* (correct use is *he received much kudos for his work*).

Lapp

Although the word **Lapp** is still widely used and is the most familiar term to many people, the indigenous people referred to by this name consider it somewhat offensive: the better term to use is **Sami**. The name **Samiland** for the area they inhabit has yet to fully establish itself.

last, lastly

When introducing points or topics in sequence it is good style to be consistent in your choice of words. If you use **firstly**, **secondly**, and so on, **lastly** fits better than **last**. On the other hand, if you introduce your first point with **first**, **last** at the end is perfectly acceptable; see also FIRST.

Latin plurals

Many relatively common words in English have been borrowed directly from Latin. Sometimes their plurals are formed following English rules, by adding a letter **s**, and sometimes following Latin rules; often there are two different plural forms for the same word, as in *referendum, referendums/referenda*.

As a rule of thumb, the Latin-style plural is appropriate in scientific, technical, or very formal language, and the English plural in all other contexts. So, telling your friends about the different 'aquaria' you have visited (rather ▶

than the different 'aquariums') might make them titter or guffaw, whereas for a marine biologist to talk about 'aquaria' would be entirely fitting.

Plurals which are more common than their singular counterparts, such as *criteria* and *bacteria*, are frequently used with a singular meaning, as in *we didn't have a set criteria when we started working*. Such uses are not good style, and will be considered completely wrong by some people. The lists below show the different forms, and also highlight some common mistakes to avoid.

Forming plurals

SINGULAR	PLURAL
-um	**-ums** or **-a**
addendum	addendums or addenda
aquarium	aquariums or aquaria
crematorium	crematoriums or crematoria
gymnasium	gymnasiums or gymnasia
maximum	maximums or maxima
memorandum	memorandums or memoranda
minimum	minimums or minima
moratorium	moratoriums or moratoria
referendum	referendums or referenda

Most of the words above have both English-style and Latin-style plurals, and the guidance given earlier holds good. Note that *stratum* only has the plural *strata*.

SINGULAR	PLURAL
-us	**-uses**
bonus	bonuses
callus	calluses
caucus	caucuses
focus	focuses
f(o)etus	f(o)etuses
ignoramus	ignoramuses
lotus	lotuses
octopus	octopuses
phallus	phalluses

▶

prospectus	prospectuses
sinus	sinuses
surplus	surpluses
virus	viruses

For all of these, if you make the plural by adding **-es** you will not go wrong, and in many cases there is no plural in **-i**. In the Oxford English Corpus, *syllabi* is about twice as common as *syllabuses*, while *narcissi* is much preferred over *narcissuses*.

SINGULAR	PLURAL
-a	**-ae**
amoeba	amoebas
larva	larvae

Amoebae is often used in scientific writing, and *amoebas* more generally. The plural of *larva* is always *larvae* (**lar**-vee).

Antenna has alternative plural forms with different meanings: strictly speaking, an insect has *antennae*, while *antennas* are telecommunications aerials, although these are quite often called *antennae* as well.

Formulae traditionally come up in science and maths, and *formulas* are solutions to general problems. Though this distinction is often blurred, it is wise to stick to the first in scientific contexts.

SINGULAR	PLURAL
-x	**-xes** or **-ces**
apex	apexes or apices
appendix	appendixes or appendices
codex	codexes or codices
cortex	cortexes or cortices
crux	cruxes or cruces
helix	helixes or helices
index	indexes or indices
vortex	vortexes or vortices

As these words are mainly used in technical or scientific texts, the Latinate forms such as ▶

apices are commoner. Note that the plural of *crux* is generally *cruxes*.

Appendix and *index* have alternative plural forms with different meanings. *Appendixes* may require an operation, while *appendices* are to be found at the end of some books; following them you may find *indexes*, while *indices* measure things.

Watch out for:

Addenda, *bacteria*, *criteria*, *errata*, and *strata* are often used with a singular meaning, which is a mistake to avoid in writing. The correct forms are *addendum*, *bacterium*, *criterion*, *erratum*, and *stratum*.
Octopi and *ignorami* as plurals are grammatically mistaken, even though they sound authentic: *octopuses* and *ignoramuses* are correct.

latter

You should avoid using **latter** when mentioning more than two people or things. For an explanation, see FORMER.

lay

Some forms of the verb lay are often used instead of the appropriate forms of **lie**. For instance, it is incorrect to say: *why don't you lay on the bed* (the correct form is **lie**); *she was laying on the bed* (the correct form is **lying**). The form **laid**, the past participle of **lay**, is also quite often mistakenly used instead of **lain**, which is the correct past participle of **lie**. So, *he had lain on the floor for hours* is correct, while *he had laid on the floor on the floor...* is not. Finally, it is incorrect to use **lie** followed by an object, as in *she was lying her head on his shoulder*, where the correct use is *she was laying her head...*

layman

To avoid sounding unintentionally sexist you could consider replacing **layman** with **layperson** in the singular and **laypeople** in the plural: *in layperson's terms*; *scholars and educated laypeople alike*. See also MAN and SEXIST LANGUAGE.

lean

Though the forms **leant** and **leaned** for the past tense and past participle are equally acceptable, **leaned** is markedly more common in all varieties of English.

leap

Though the forms **leapt** and **leaped** for the past tense and past participle are equally acceptable, **leapt** is markedly more common in all varieties of English.

learn

Learn is one of the small group of verbs which have alternative forms for the past tense and past participle. Usage varies according to the variety of English you speak. The Oxford English Corpus shows that in British English and many other varieties **learnt** is relatively common both as the past participle and the past tense: *I've really* learnt *a lot from TV*, *painters* learnt *their craft the hard way*. In North American English, however, these uses are rather uncommon. Using the form ending in **-ed** is therefore always a safe choice.

learning difficulties

The phrase **learning difficulties** covers a range of conditions, including Down's syndrome as well as cognitive or neurological conditions such as dyslexia. In emphasizing the difficulty experienced rather than any perceived 'deficiency' it is less discriminatory and more positive than older terms such as **mentally handicapped**. It is the phrase you should use to avoid the risk of causing offence and is the standard term in Britain in official contexts. **Learning disability** is the equivalent in North America, but in Britain that tends to refer specifically to conditions in which IQ is impaired.

lend

Lend is not a noun in standard English, where **loan** is the correct word to use. Though used informally in a number of dialects and varieties, as in *can I have a lend of your pen?*, it should be avoided in writing.

-less

When you are adding the ending **-less** to a word that already ends in a letter **-l** there is a simple rule to follow. If the first word ends in a *single* letter **-l** you do not need a hyphen, as in *soulless newbuild housing estates*; if it ends in **-ll** , you need a hyphen: *a small, wall-less town*. See also HYPHENATION.

less

In standard English, **less** should only be used with uncountable things (*less money*, *less time*). With countable things it is incorrect to use **less**; strictly speaking, correct use is *fewer people* and *fewer words*. For more information, see FEW.

lest

Lest remains one of the very few words in English with which (in good style) the subjunctive is used, as in *she was worrying lest he be attacked* (not *lest he was . . .*) or *she is using headphones lest she disturb anyone* (not *. . . lest she disturbs anyone*). It is also used with a conditional, as in *she is using headphones lest she should disturb anyone*, but in the Oxford English Corpus the subjunctive is ten times more common. See also SUBJUNCTIVE.

libel

Libel refers to a written untrue statement that is damaging to someone's reputation, while **slander** refers to the spoken expression of similar sentiments. Though the two are often used interchangeably it is useful to preserve the distinction in writing.

licence, license

It is easy to get confused about when to write **licence** and when **license**. Which spelling you choose depends on whether you are using the word as a noun or a verb, and whether you are following British usage or not. Spell the word with **c** in British

English when using it as a noun, as in *driving licence*, *off-licence*, *poetic licence*. When using it as verb, you should spell it with an **s**, as in *licensed premises*. Other varieties of English often follow this rule, except United States English, where the **-s-** is much more common in both the noun and the verb.

lie

Some forms of the verb **lie** are often confused with forms of the verb **lay**. See LAY.

life assurance, life insurance

There is a technical distinction between **life assurance** and **life insurance**: see ASSURANCE.

light

This is one of a small group of verbs which have alternative forms for the past tense and past participle. Both **lighted** and **lit** can be used in all varieties of English, but **lit** is much more common for the two forms mentioned. When you want to use the past participle before a noun, however, the two forms work differently. **Lighted** tends to be used when the verb is not modified in any way, as in *lighted windows*; *a lighted match*. When you modify the verb with an adverb, **lit** is much the more common form: *a brightly lit office*; *pleasantly lit corridors*.

lightning

The form **lightning** developed as a contracted form of *lightening* (the old spelling *light'ning* shows this process), but the two forms are now distinct words. In the meaning of *thunder and lightning* and *lightning speed*, the spelling is always **lightning**. When it means 'making or becoming lighter' the spelling is always **lightening**.

-like

When writing words ending in **-like** which are well established, such as *childlike*, *businesslike*, *dreamlike*, and *ladylike*, it is correct not to use a hyphen, even though you may come across such words written with one. In contrast, where the combination is a one-off or not fully established, you should insert a hyphen: *flu-like*, *Zen-like*, *needle-like*. For hyphen use with other adjectives, see HYPHENATION.

like

1 In the sentence *he's behaving like he owns the place*, **like** is a conjunction meaning 'as if', and it is best to avoid using it in written British English. Although **like** has been used as a conjunction in this way since the 15th century by many respected writers, it is still considered unacceptable in formal British English, where you should use **as if** instead.

2 Another use of **like** as a conjunction which many people object to is: *like I said, it's not possible*. This use is quite common in speech, but is likely to be considered incorrect in writing, where it is better to write *as I said, ...*

lit

For the use of **lighted** and **lit**, see LIGHT.

literally

In one of its meanings, **literally** is used to show that a metaphor or idiom is to be interpreted in its real, physical meaning, as in *literally too tired to move*. This use can lead to nonsense, as in *we were literally killing ourselves laughing*, so you should only use it in this way when you are sure that your audience will not take *you* literally.

loath, loathe

Loath and **loathe** are often confused in writing. **Loath** is an adjective meaning 'reluctant or unwilling', as in *I was loath to leave*, whereas **loathe** is a verb meaning 'feel intense dislike or disgust for', as in *she loathed him on sight*. **Loath** is occasionally written **loth**, which is also correct, even though it appears in fewer than five per cent of examples in the Oxford English Corpus. **Loath** and **loth** are pronounced the same, rhyming with *oath*.

locate

Locate is an 18th-century Americanism that still has a transatlantic flavour for some people, especially in its intransitive use (that is, without an object) as in *numerous industries have located in this area*. In both British and American English, **to be located** is a synonym for 'to be situated'—*the supermarket is located near a park*—but may cause disquiet among British purists.

lot

1 **A lot of** and **lots** of are very common in speech and writing, but they still have a somewhat informal feel and are generally not considered acceptable for formal English, where you should use alternatives such as *many* or *a large number of* instead.

2 If you do use **a lot** in writing, it is incorrect to write it as one word, although you may come across this spelling. For other words often written as one when they should be separated see TWO WORDS OR ONE.

luxurious, luxuriant

Luxurious and **luxuriant** are often confused, especially in marketing and promotional material. **Luxurious** means 'very comfortable, elegant, and involving great expense', as in *a luxurious hotel*, whereas **luxuriant** means 'lush', referring to vegetation, as in *acres of luxuriant gardens*. To speak of *luxuriant comfort* or *luxuriant four-poster beds*, for instance, would be considered incorrect by many people.

machinations

The **-ch-** in this word can be pronounced either as a **k** or as in *machine*, and both are acceptable.

machismo, macho

The **-ch-** in **machismo** can be pronounced either as a **k** or as in *church*, and both are acceptable, though the second is closer to the original Spanish. In **macho**, the **-ch-** is always pronounced as in *church*.

majority

Strictly speaking, **majority** should be used with countable nouns to mean 'the greater number', as in *the majority of cases*. Using it with uncountable nouns to mean 'the greatest part', as in *I spent the majority of the day reading*, is not considered good written English by purists, although it is common in informal contexts. It is still a cliché, and **the majority** is best replaced by **most**.

man, -man

There are two uses of **man** which many people may find objectionable nowadays. The first is when it refers to all human beings, as in *that's one small step for a man, one giant leap for mankind*, and the second is the use of **-man** in words denoting roles and activities, such as *fireman*.

Traditionally the word **man** was used to refer not only to adult males but also to human beings in general, regardless of sex. In Old English the principal meaning of *man* was 'a human being', and the words *wer* and *wif* were used to refer specifically to 'a male person' and 'a female person' respectively. Subsequently, **man** replaced *wer* as the normal term for 'a male person', but at the same time the older meaning of 'a human being' remained in use. Nowadays, this generic use of **man** will generally be regarded as sexist— or at best rather old-fashioned.

Similarly, since women are just as likely as men to be involved in all professions and activities, words for occupations and roles ending in -man, such as *fireman*, *layman*, and *chairman*, are increasingly being replaced by gender-neutral words: *firefighter*, *layperson*, and *chair* or *chairperson*.

In order to avoid being considered either an unreconstructed sexist or incorrigibly last-century it is therefore advisable to use alternatives to the more traditional words when the gender of the person concerned is not relevant. If the person referred to is a man, however, it is in general perfectly acceptable to use the word ending in -man: *he was a keen sportsman*.

▶

Below is a list giving suitable alternatives—some more
established than others—for some of the most commonly
used terms.

Generalizing

OLDER USAGE	NEWER USAGE
man	human beings, the human race
manhour	hour, person-hour
mankind	humankind, the human race, humanity
the man in the street	the person in the street, the average person, ordinary people, laypeople, people in the street

In one or two cases, such as *manpower* and *to man*, there
are many alternatives, depending on the exact context,
such as *staff*, *employees*, *people*, etc. and *to staff*, *to operate*,
etc., respectively.

Professions

OLDER USAGE	NEWER USAGE	PLURAL
barman	bartender	bartenders, bar staff
businessman	businessperson	businesspeople
*chairman	chair, chairperson	chairpersons
clergyman	vicar, priest	the clergy
fellow countryman	compatriot	compatriots
fireman	firefighter	firefighters
freshman	fresher	freshers
layman	layperson	laypeople, the laity
policeman	police officer	police officers
salesman	salesperson	sales staff
spokesman	spokesperson	spokespeople
sportsman	sportsperson	sportspeople, sportsmen and sportswomen

*For referring to the head of a company, *chairman* is still
the correct word.

manageress

See -ESS.

manic depression

Though terms that many people are familiar with, **manic depression** and **manic depressive** are sometimes felt to be negative by people experiencing the condition and those working with them. A less loaded term which is being increasingly used in medical and psychiatric circles is **bipolar disorder**, or **bipolar affective disorder**. People with the condition can be referred to simply as **bipolar**, or as **having bipolar disorder**.

man in the street

For a gender-neutral alternative, see MAN.

mankind

On the use of **mankind** versus that of **humankind** or **the human race**, see MAN.

m

masterful

Many people strive to maintain a distinction between **masterful** and **masterly**, using **masterful** to mean 'powerful and able to control others'—*a masterful tone of voice*—and **masterly** to mean 'with the skill of a master'—*a masterly performance*. In practice, the two words overlap considerably in this second meaning, and in the Oxford English Corpus most uses of **masterful** mean 'with the skill of a master'. But, if you are writing for a well-educated audience, maintaining the distinction will stand you in good stead.

maximum

Maximum is one of those Latin-derived words which have two plurals: the Latinate **maxima** and the English **maximums**. For guidance on when to use which, see the entry on LATIN PLURALS.

may

1 **May** and **might** are two ways of expressing that the truth of an event is unknown at the time of speaking or writing. Traditionalists insist that you should distinguish between **may** (present tense) and **might** (past tense): *I may have some dessert if I'm still hungry*; *she might have known her killer*. However, this distinction is rarely observed today, especially in informal usage, and **may** and **might** are generally acceptable in either case: *she may have visited yesterday*; *I might go and have a cup of tea*.

2 Whether you use **may have** or **might have**, though, is a different matter. If at the time of speaking or writing the truth is still not known, then either is acceptable: *by the time you read this, registration may have been received*; *I think that might have offended some people*.

3 However, if the event referred to did not in fact occur, it is best to use **might have**: *the draw against Arsenal might have been a turning point, but it didn't turn out like that*. **May have** is wrong in this example: *if they had been left the alternative verdict to consider, they may have focused their minds on it*.

4 On the difference in use between **may** and **can**, see CAN.

m

me

There are four cases where the choice between **me** and **I** can be problematic.

1 **I** should be used as the subject of the sentence, together with other people: *Trisha and I went out for a few months*; *he and I don't get on*. Though phrases such as *Trisha and me . . .*, *him and me . . .* are quite often used in speaking, they are grammatically wrong, and should be avoided.

2 **Me** should be used instead of **I** after a preposition, or as the object of a verb: *this letter is for you and me*, *they gave Jane and me a fantastic send-off*. Problems arise because people often think that it is correct to use **I** whenever other people are involved, as in the examples above. But this rule only applies to the subject of the sentence.

When you are referring to other people and yourself as the object of a verb or after a preposition, you need to replace **I** with **me**. So, it is not correct to write *a couple of guys flew from Germany to meet Tom and I at a convention*: it should be *Tom and me*. If you are in any doubt, try removing the other names from the sentence you are writing and it should then be clear whether **I** or **me** is appropriate. In the example just given you would not say: *a couple of guys flew from Germany to meet I at a convention*. Similarly, a concern to be correct often leads people to say *between you and I*, whereas *between you and me* is grammatically correct.

3 For advice on whether you should say *you have more than me* or *you have more than I*, see PERSONAL PRONOUN.

4 There is also some confusion over whether it is correct to say, for instance, *it was me that decided* or *it was I that decided*. The second is markedly more formal: it would, for instance, be very pompous indeed when announcing yourself to say *it is I* rather than *it's me*.

m

media

The word **media** comes from the Latin plural of **medium**. The traditional view is that it should therefore be treated as a plural noun in all its meanings in English and be used with a plural rather than a singular verb: *the media have not followed the reports* (rather than 'has'). In practice, in the meaning of 'television, radio, and the press collectively', it behaves as a collective noun (like *staff* or *clergy*, for example). This means that it is now acceptable in standard English to use it with either a singular or a plural verb, and few people are likely to object to its use with the first. See also COLLECTIVE NOUN.

memento

A **memento** of an occasion is something to remember it by. It comes from Latin, and means literally 'remember'. Although the variant spelling **momento** exists, many people will think you wrong if you use it. Think of all the letters **e** in **remember**, and it may help you to remember to put them in **memento** as well.

mental

Yesterday's euphemisms sometimes become today's insults, and **mental** is a case in point. Its use in compounds such as *mental hospital* and *mental patient* is first recorded at the end of the 19th century and became the normal accepted term in the first half of the 20th century. Now, however, it is regarded as certainly old-fashioned, if not offensive. The most usual acceptable alternative is *psychiatric*, which has already generally replaced it in official use. The particular terms **mental handicap** and **mentally handicapped**, though widely used a few decades ago, have fallen out of favour in recent years and have been largely replaced in official contexts by less demeaning terms such as **learning difficulties**.

merchandise

Merchandise and words derived from it, such as *merchandising*, are always correctly spelled with an s, not a z.

meter, metre

Meter is the normal spelling in both British and American English for the measuring or recording instrument, such as a *gas meter*. It is also the American English spelling for the unit of length and for 'rhythm in poetry', which in British English are both spelled **metre**.

might

On the distinction between **might** and **may**, see MAY.

militate

The verbs **militate** and **mitigate** are often confused. See MITIGATE.

millennium

The correct spelling is **millennium** with -**ll**- and -**nn**-. It may help you if you remember that the first part of the word means 'a thousand' in Latin, as in *millipede*, and is ultimately the basis for the word *million*. The second part is closely related to the word *annual*.

minimum

For information on which plural form to use, see LATIN PLURALS.

minuscule

The standard spelling is **minuscule** with a **u** in the second syllable rather than **miniscule**, with an **i**. The second form is a very common one, and appears in almost half the citations for the term in the Oxford English Corpus. It has been in use since the late 19th century, and arose by analogy with other words beginning with *mini-*, where the meaning is similarly 'very small'. It is now so widely used that it can be considered as an acceptable variant, although it should be avoided in formal contexts.

minutiae

Since **minutiae** is a word more often seen than heard, it can be hard to remember exactly how to pronounce it. The recommended pronunciation is /my-**nyoo**-shee/.

mischievous

Mischievous is a three-syllable word, pronounced /**miss**-chi-vuhs/. It should not be pronounced /miss-**chee**-vi-uhs/ with four syllables, as though it were spelled 'mischievious' (with an extra **i**), which is also wrong.

misspell

There are two possible forms for the past tense and past participle of this verb, **misspelled** and **misspelt**. Both are correct, although **misspelled** is much more common, while **misspelt** is rarely used at all outside British English.

mitigate

The verbs **mitigate** and **militate** do not mean the same thing, but their similarity leads to them often being confused. **Mitigate** means 'to make less severe', as in *drainage schemes have helped to mitigate this problem*. **Militate** is nearly always used in constructions with *against* to mean 'be a powerful factor in preventing', as in *these disagreements will militate against the two communities coming together.*

mongol, mongolism

The term **mongol** was adopted in the 19th century to refer to a person with **Down's syndrome** (and **mongolism** for the condition itself), owing to the supposed similarity of some of the physical symptoms of the disorder with the normal facial characteristics of East Asian people. In modern English these terms are offensive and have been replaced in scientific as well as in most general contexts by **Down's syndrome** (first recorded in the early 1960s), and related expressions such as *a person with Down's syndrome, a Down's baby*, etc.

Mongoloid

The terms **Mongoloid**, **Negroid**, **Caucasoid**, and **Australoid** were introduced by 19th-century anthropologists attempting to classify human racial types, but today they are recognized as having very limited validity as scientific categories. Although occasionally used when making broad generalizations about the world's populations, in most modern contexts they are potentially offensive, especially when used of individuals. The names of specific peoples, nationalities, or regions of the world should be used instead wherever possible.

m

moot

It is quite common to come across a debatable point being described as *'a mute point'*. This is a logical but mistaken adaptation of the old-established phrase **a moot point** and is generally not considered good style.

mouse

Unless we are very young children, we all know that we use **mice** to refer to more than one of these lovable rodents. But when we want to refer to more than one computer **mouse**, is it correct to say **mice** or **mouses**? You may sometimes hear **mouses**, but people seem to prefer the standard **mice**.

Muslim

Muslim is the preferred spelling for 'a follower of Islam' and 'relating to Islam', although the form **Moslem** is also used. The terms **Muhammadan** and **Mohammedan** are archaic and are likely to sound deliberately offensive.

mute

1 To describe a person without the power of speech as **mute**, especially as in **deaf mute**, is today regarded as outdated, and it is highly likely to cause offence. However, there is no direct, acceptable alternative, but *profoundly deaf* is used to imply that someone has not developed any spoken language skills. Compare DUMB.

2 For the phrase 'a mute point', see MOOT.

myself

There are two ways of using **myself** which nobody will object to, and two which some people will criticize. The innocuous uses are:

1 to show that the recipient of the action is the same as the speaker: *I hurt myself quite badly*.

2 to emphasize the word **I**: *I myself have no objection; I did it myself*.

The uses to which some people object are:

1 when **myself** is the subject of a verb: *the wife and myself had a wonderful time*.

2 when **myself** is the object of a verb: *they hauled Barry and myself in for questioning*.

Both these uses are perfectly acceptable in conversation. In more formal writing they should be avoided. In the case of 1 above, use **I**; and in the case of 2, use **me**. See also ME, YOURSELF.

Nama

The **Nama** people are one of the **Khoikhoi** peoples of South Africa and SW Namibia. They have in the past been called **Hottentot** (actually a somewhat broader term), but that is

m
n

now obsolete and **Nama** is the standard accepted term.
See HOTTENTOT.

native

In contexts such as *a native of Boston* the use of the noun
native is quite acceptable. But when used as a noun without
qualification, as in *this dance is a favourite with the natives*, it is
more problematic. In modern use it can refer humorously to the
local inhabitants of a particular place: *New York in the summer
was too hot even for the natives*. However, it is likely to sound
offensive if used to refer to any area of the world that has been
under colonial rule, in which it was the standard term for
indigenous people as opposed to their foreign masters.

Native American

Native American is now the current accepted term in most
contexts, particularly in the US, for a member of any of the
indigenous peoples of the United States, but see also AMERICAN
INDIAN.

need

1 In modern English you can use the verb **need** followed by
another verb in two different ways when asking a question or
making a negative statement. One way is with *do* as in *I don't
need to go just yet* and *do you really need to go?* The second way is
without *do*, as in *I needn't go just yet* and *need you really go?* The
two constructions are equally correct, but the construction using
do is more common. In questions, the form without *do* is used
especially in rhetorical questions: *need I say any more?, need I
elaborate?*
When making a negative statement using **need** without *do*,
the thing to remember is not to add on a letter s in the third
person: *he need not worry*.

2 The two constructions in *that shirt needs washing*
(verb + present participle) and *that shirt needs to be washed*
(verb + infinitive and past participle) have more or less the same
meaning. Both are acceptable in standard English, but a third
construction, *that shirt needs washed* (verb + bare past

participle), is restricted to certain dialects of Scotland and North America and is not considered acceptable in standard English.

3 The phrase **if need be** has a long historical pedigree and is still widely used today. Traditionalists are likely to object to the form with the plural: *if needs be*.

Negro

The word **Negro** was adopted from Spanish and Portuguese and is first recorded in the mid 16th century. It remained the standard term from the 17th to the 19th century and was even used by prominent black American campaigners such as W. E. B. DuBois and Booker T. Washington in the early 20th century. Since the Black Power movement of the 1960s, however, when the term **black** was promoted as an expression of racial pride, **Negro** (together with related words such as **Negress**) has dropped out of use and is now likely to seem offensive in both British and US English.

Negroid

The term **Negroid** belongs to a set of terms introduced by 19th-century anthropologists attempting to categorize human races. Such terms are associated with outdated notions of racial types, and so are now potentially offensive and best avoided. See MONGOLOID.

neither

1 The use of **neither** with another negative, as in *I don't like him neither* or *he's not much good at reading neither* is recorded from the 16th century onwards, but is not good English. This is because it is an example of a **double negative**, which, though standard in some other languages such as French and Spanish and found in many dialects of English, is not acceptable in standard English. In the sentences above, **either** should be used instead. For more information, see DOUBLE NEGATIVE.

2 When **neither** is followed by **nor**, it is important in good English style that the two halves of the structure mirror each other: *she saw herself as neither wife nor mother* rather than *she*

neither saw herself as wife nor mother. *For more details, see* EITHER.

3 It is equally correct to pronounce **neither** as /**nl**-*thuh*/ or /**nee**-*thuh*/.

nerve-racking, nerve-wracking

Both spellings are used in British and American English and are correct, although in British English there are more examples of the spelling with a **w**.

neuron

In scientific material the standard spelling is **neuron**. The spelling **neurone** is found only in non-technical contexts.

nevertheless

It is quite common to find **nevertheless** spelled 'never the less'. Although this is how it was written many centuries ago, the standard modern spelling is as one word. For more information, see TWO WORDS OR ONE.

n

niggardly

Niggardly has no historical connection whatsoever with *nigger*, but because it sounds similar, and probably because it has a negative meaning—'ungenerous with money, time, etc.' or 'mean'—it is wise to avoid it outside literary contexts. Politicians, both in the US and the UK, have been severely embarrassed by having used it.

nigger

The word **nigger** was first used (as an adjective, in fact) to denote a black person in the 17th century, and it has long had derogatory overtones. However, it has not been seen as generally offensive for as long: Bertie Wooster, in a P. G. Wodehouse novel of 1934, refers to 'a troupe of nigger minstrels', and Guy Gibson, the leader of the 'Dambusters' in the Second World War, called his black dog Nigger, and that name was used in the film made in 1954. The scenes in which it is referred to are edited out of some showings nowadays, as the word is now possibly the single most offensive word in English. It is true that it is sometimes used by black people themselves to refer to other black people, but in any other context it is unacceptable.

noisome

Noisome is a relatively uncommon word meaning 'harmful, noxious' and has nothing to do with the word **noise**. It comes from a Middle English word **nay**, related to **annoy**. Purists will object to its being used to mean 'noisy'.

non-

For a comparison of the prefixes **non-** and **un-**, see UN-.

non-defining relative clauses

See RELATIVE CLAUSES.

none

Some language purists maintain that **none** can only take a singular verb, never a plural one: *none of them* is *coming tonight* rather than *none of them* are *coming tonight*. There is little historical or grammatical justification for this view. **None** comes from Old English *nan* meaning 'not one' and has been used for around a thousand years with both a singular and a plural verb, depending on the context and the emphasis needed. see also AGREEMENT.

nonetheless

It is quite common to find **nonetheless** spelled 'none the less'. Although this is how it was written many centuries ago, the standard modern spelling is as one word. For more information see TWO WORDS OR ONE.

non-flammable, non-inflammable

The adjectives **non-flammable** and **non-inflammable** mean the same; see FLAMMABLE.

nonplussed

In standard use **nonplussed** means 'surprised and confused',
as in *she was nonplussed at his eagerness to help out*. In
North American English a new use has developed in recent
years, meaning 'unperturbed'—more or less the opposite of its
traditional meaning—as in *he was clearly trying to appear
nonplussed*. Although the use is common it is not yet
considered standard. Similarly, many people would not
consider spelling this word with a hyphen, **non-plussed**, to
be good style.

non-restrictive relative clauses

See RELATIVE CLAUSES.

non-white

Many people object to the term **non-white** on the grounds
that it assumes that the norm is white. It is difficult to find
a widely acceptable and accurate alternative: *person of colour*
is rather stilted, and *ethnic* too euphemistic for many, but
'black or Asian' is an effective substitute in Britain (see ASIAN).
If you are talking about a person or number of people from
only one racial group, it is simpler to refer to that group.

n

normalcy

Normalcy has been criticized as an uneducated alternative to
normality. The Oxford English Corpus shows that in the United
States and Canada it is as common as **normality**, and it is the
preferred form in Indian English. Elsewhere it is less common and
has a distinctly American flavour, which purists, especially in
Britain, are likely to object to.

noun

A **noun** is a word that names a person, animal, or thing.
Common nouns name persons, animals, or things of which there
is not just one example (*bridge, girl, sugar, unhappiness*), whereas
proper nouns name specific people, places, events, institutions,
magazines, books, plays, and so forth, and are written with initial
capital letters (*Billy, Asia, Easter, Hamlet*). Concrete nouns refer
to physical things and living beings (*bread, woman*), and abstract

nouns to concepts (*greed*, *unhelpfulness*). Some nouns are concrete and abstract in different meanings, e.g. *cheek* is concrete when it refers to a part of the face and abstract when it means 'impertinence'.

nouns, singular and plural

No language stays still, least of all English. Among the myriad changes which take place over the course of time, some words change 'number': some which were singular become plural, and vice versa. Our modern **pea** was formed from *pease*. Once the singular, based directly on the French, its -**s** sound at the end was interpreted as a plural, and so a new singular was created. **News**, on the other hand, was for many centuries plural as well as singular, so that Shelley could write *There are bad news from Palermo*.

With some loanwords (words 'borrowed' from other languages), there is uncertainty over which form is the singular, and which the plural. In the past many of these nouns came from Greek and Latin; when those two languages were widely studied, it was expected that people would be familiar enough with their grammar to know that, for instance, **criterion** was a singular form in Greek and its plural was **criteria**. Nowadays, however, most people have little or no knowledge of either language and many make perfectly reasonable assumptions about them which happen to be wrong historically. If someone does not know Latin, it is perfectly sensible for them to think that **addenda** is a singular, like *agenda*, and give it a plural **addendas**.

PLURALS USED AS SINGULAR	SINGULAR FORM IN ORIGINAL LANGUAGE
addenda	addendum
bacteria	bacterium
bijoux (as adjective)	bijou
cherubim	cherub

▶

n

criteria	criterion
errata	erratum
panini	panino
phenomena	phenomenon
strata	stratum
tableaux	tableau

All of these plurals used as a singular would be regarded as mistakes, except **panini**, which is now established in English as the singular form, with **paninis** as an acceptable plural. Other such 're-pluralizations', made by adding an English plural ending, are not acceptable, e.g. *'cherubims'*, *'criterias'*, and *'stratas'*.

By contrast, a loanword whose singular form looks like an English plural, such as **biceps**, may well be altered to produce a 'proper-looking' singular. This has produced *'bicep'* meaning one biceps muscle, but it is considered incorrect. To compound the confusion, *biceps*, being singular, sometimes has an English plural ending added, just to make sure, as it were, producing *'bicepses'*. Neither *bicep* nor *bicepses* is recommended.

Some loanwords mislead people into using spurious foreign plurals: **addenda**, as mentioned above, is already a plural, but is sometimes mistakenly turned into *'addendae'* on the grounds that many Latin nouns ending in -*a* become -*ae*, e.g *alga, algae*. This can also happen to **agenda**. *Octopus* is often mistakenly given the plural *'octopi'* because many Latin nouns ending in -*us* change to -*i*, but **octopus** is from Greek. **Ignoramus** comes from the name of a 17th-century fictional character and was never a noun in Latin, so the correct plural is *ignoramuses*, not *'ignorami'*. **Kudos** is an interesting case. It is traditionally used as an uncountable singular noun, like **fame**, with only a singular form: *he earned a lot of kudos for his resistance*. However, many people seem to be using it to mean an award, point, or congratulation for something well done. As a result, a singular *'kudo'* has been created, as well as the plurals *'kudoses'* and, almost inexplicably, *'kudi'*.

n

number

The construction **the number of** + plural noun should be used with a singular verb, as in *the number of people affected remains small*. This is because it is the noun **number** rather than the noun **people** which is taken to agree with the verb. In contrast, the similar construction **a number of** + plural noun is used with a plural verb: *a number of people remain to be contacted*. In this case the verb agrees with the noun **people**. This is because **a number of** works as if it were a single word, such as **some** or **several**.

numerals

The main question about numbers is whether to write them as figures or as words. The following are some basic guidelines.

In general, numerals are used in more factual or statistical contexts and words are used (especially with numbers under a hundred) in more descriptive material: compare *I have lived in the same house for twelve years* with *the survey covers a period of 12 years*.

It is usual to use words rather than figures at the beginning of sentences: *Sixty-four people came to the party*.

Words are used in idiomatic expressions such as *I must have told you a hundred times; thousands of people swarmed through the gates*.

Separate objects, animals, ships, persons, etc. are not units of measurement unless they are treated statistically: *the peasant had only four cows; a farm with 40 head of cattle*.

Whether written as figures or words, plurals of numbers are written without an apostrophe: *the 1970s, a man in his thirties, they come in twos*.

With numerals consisting of four or more figures,   ▶

n

commas should be used to divide off the thousands, e.g. *3,096, 10,731*.

When specifying ranges of numbers, use as few figures as possible, e.g. *31–4*; *1923–6*. But dates BC should be written in full: *432–431* BC (since *432–31* BC and *432–1* BC represent different ranges).

More detailed information will be found in *New Hart's Rules*, published in 2005 by Oxford University Press.

obtuse

Obtuse and **abstruse** are often confused. Someone who is **obtuse** is rather stupid, as in *she's about as obtuse as they come*. Something which is **abstruse** is rather obscure and difficult to understand. To use **obtuse** in the meaning of 'obscure, difficult', though often done, is not considered good style, and conservatives will consider it a rank mistake.

occurrence

The letter **u** in **occurrence** is normally pronounced like the **u** of **cut**. Some people pronounce it in the same way as in the verb (/uh-**ker**-uhns/), but this is wrong.

octopus

The standard plural of **octopus** in English is **octopuses**. The word comes from Greek, but the Greek plural **octopodes** is almost never used genuinely (i.e. outside writing about the plural of **octopus**). The plural form **octopi**, formed according to the rules of Latin plurals, is incorrect. See also LATIN PLURALS.

of

It is a mistake to use **of** instead of **have** in constructions such as *you should have asked* (not *you should of asked*). For more information, see HAVE.

off

The compound preposition **off of** is sometimes used interchangeably with the preposition **off** in a context such as *she picked it up off of the floor* compared with *she picked it up off the floor*. The use of **off of** is recorded from the 16th century, was used commonly by Shakespeare, for example, and is logically parallel to **out of**, but is not accepted in standard modern English. Today **off of** is restricted to dialect and informal contexts, particularly in the US.

offence, offense

The spelling **offence** with a letter **c** is standard in nearly all varieties of English, except in the US, where **offense** with an **s** is the norm. To use this second spelling in a non-US context is therefore likely to be considered incorrect.

offspring

The meaning of **offspring** covers both an individual child and several children, though the latter meaning is the more common. As a result, the word does not need the plural form *'offsprings'* with an **-s** which is sometimes encountered.

oftentimes

Though somewhat rare outside the US, and likely to sound archaic to a British ear, **oftentimes** is a perfectly acceptable and standard alternative to **often**, as in: *oftentimes the dialogue has an unnatural ring*.

on-board, on board

Should you write **on-board** or **on board**? It depends on the meaning. If you are talking about passengers on a ship or plane, you would say they are **on board**: *the plane crashed with twenty people on board*. You also write **on board** in non-literal phrases like *to take something on board* and *to bring someone on board*. You write **on-board** with a hyphen if you are talking about a piece of equipment or computer fitted into a car, boat, plane, or other vehicle: *on-board DVD players for the kids*.

one

1 One is used as a pronoun to mean 'anyone' or 'me and people in general', as in *one must try one's best*. In modern English it is generally only used in formal and written contexts, outside which it is likely to be regarded as pompous or over-formal.

In informal and spoken contexts the normal alternative is **you**, as in *you have to do what you can, don't you?*

2 When **one** means 'anyone', British and American English use different pronouns to refer back to it. In British English another **one** or **one's** always follows: *one should be especially careful if one already uses prescription anti-coagulants*. In American English this pattern is possible, but it is also common to use **he**, **she** (or **they**, to avoid gender problems), and **his**, **her**, and **their**: *I like to believe one can be honest and sincere and committed in what he's doing.*

3 When using phrases such as *one in ten people* or *one out of every six people interviewed*, you need to be careful with the following verb. It should be singular, not plural, when it refers back to **one**: *only one in ten men affected **is** seeking treatment*, not *one in ten businesses **are** owned by ethnic minorities*. See also AGREEMENT.

online

Is it correct to write **online** or **on line** to describe things you do over the Internet? The first thing to think about is how exactly you are using the word. Does it relate to a noun, as in *online shopping, online banking,* and *online dating*? Or does it relate to an adjective or verb: *now available online; you can register online*? In the first case, there is no choice: you should write **online** as one word. In the second case, you could in principle write it either way. However, people write it as one word much more often than as two, and Oxford Dictionaries Online show it in this form.

only

The traditional view is that the adverb **only** should be placed next to the word or words whose meaning it restricts: *I have seen him only once* rather than *I have only seen him once*. The argument for this, a topic which has occupied grammar experts for more than 200 years, is that if **only** is not placed correctly the emphasis may be wrong, and could even lead to ambiguity. But in normal, everyday English the impulse is to state **only** as early as possible in the sentence, generally just before the verb. The result is, in fact, hardly ever ambiguous. Few people would be confused by the sentence *I have only seen him once*, and the supposed 'logical' meaning often emerges only if there is further clarification, as in *I've only seen him once, but I've heard him many times*.

onto

The preposition **onto**, meaning 'to a position on the surface of', as in *they fell off their stools onto the rough stone floor*, has been widely written as one word (instead of **on to**) since the early 18th century. Some people, however, still do not wholly accept it as part of standard English (unlike **into**, for example). In US English, **onto** is more or less the standard form and this is likely to become the case in British English before long.

Because of the increasing tendency to write the two words as one, it is important to remember never to write **on to** as one word when it means 'onwards and towards', as in *let's go on to the next point*.

or

1 Where a verb follows a list separated by **or**, the traditional rule is that the verb should be singular, as long as the things in the list are individually singular, as in *a sandwich or other snack is included in the price* (rather than *a sandwich or other snack are included in the price*). The argument is that each of the elements agrees separately with the verb precisely because they are alternatives. The opposite rule applies when the elements are joined by **and**: here, the verb should be plural, *a sandwich and a cup of coffee are included in the price*. These traditional rules should be observed in good English writing style but are often disregarded in speech.

2 On the use of **either ... or**, see EITHER.

oriental

The term **oriental** has an out-of-date feel when used to refer to people from the Far East. It tends to be associated with a rather offensive stereotype of the people and their customs as exotic and inscrutable. In US English, **Asian** is the standard accepted term in modern use; in British English, where **Asian** tends to denote specifically people from the Indian subcontinent, it is better to use precise terms such as **Chinese**, **Japanese**, and so forth.

ought

The verb **ought** is a *modal verb*, which means that it does not behave grammatically like ordinary verbs. In particular, the negative is formed with the word **not** alone and not with auxiliary verbs such as **do** or **have**. Therefore the standard construction for the negative is *he ought not to have gone*. The alternative forms *he didn't ought to have gone* and *he hadn't ought to have gone*, formed as though **ought** were an ordinary verb rather than a modal verb, are found in dialect from the 19th century but are not acceptable in standard modern English.

ours

There is no need for an apostrophe: the spelling should be **ours** not **our's**.

ourself

The standard reflexive form corresponding to **we** and **us** is **ourselves**, as in *we can only blame ourselves*. The singular form **ourself**, first recorded in the 15th century, is sometimes used in modern English, typically where 'we' refers to people in general. This use, though logical, is uncommon and not generally accepted in standard English. Compare THEMSELF.

o

out

The use of **out** as a preposition rather than the standard prepositional phrase **out of**, as in *he threw it out the window*, is common in informal contexts but is not widely accepted in standard British English.

output

The past tense and past participle of **output** as a verb can be either **output** or **outputted.** The first is more common and the second may strike a jarring note for more traditional speakers. See VERBS FORMED FROM NOUNS.

outside

There is no difference in meaning between **outside** and **outside of** as in *the books have been distributed outside Europe* and *the books have been distributed outside of Europe*. The use of

outside of is much commoner and better established in
North American than in British English.

overly

The use of **overly** in place of the prefix **over-**, e.g. *overly confident*
instead of *over-confident*, although not uncommon and well
established in British usage, is still likely to be regarded as an
Americanism by more conservative speakers and could well
strike a jarring note.

oversimplistic

Many language purists would argue that **oversimplistic** is
an unnecessary word, and that it says the same thing
twice, since **simplistic** already means 'over-simple'. It is
therefore best to avoid it in formal contexts.
See also SIMPLISTIC.

overused words

Some words and phrases are trotted out over and over
again, unthinkingly and without proper regard to their
context, so that any lustre they may have once had is soon
worn away through overhandling. They can be loosely
grouped into the twin categories of (a) clichés proper and
(b) modish technical words and phrases in general use.
In both cases it is worth asking yourself:

- what exactly the word or phrase adds to what you are trying
  to say
- whether it expresses what you really want to express
- whether removing it would detract from the meaning you
  want to communicate.

Clichés

The French word *cliché* means a stereotype printing block,
which produces the same page over and over again. It was
first used in this meaning in English, before acquiring ▶

its modern meaning in 1892. A cliché is a phrase that has become meaningless with overuse, or, as the *Oxford Dictionary of English* pithily defines it, 'a phrase or opinion that is overused and betrays a lack of original thought'. For instance, it is now almost meaningless to wish someone *Have a nice day* because the once sincere intention has become an empty formula.

Clichés range from once striking metaphors, such as *the tip of the iceberg*, to conversational formulas, such as *not to put too fine a point on it*, and stereotyped combinations of words, as in *to unveil plans*, *a robust defence*, *to open a dialogue with*, etc.

In everyday language it would probably be rather difficult to communicate without occasional recourse to what some critics would regard as clichés: *when all's said and done*, the aim in ordinary conversation is not originality but getting your message across. However, most authorities suggest that, when it comes to original writing, clichés should be used sparingly: 'Yesterday's daring metaphors are today's clichés,' as Arthur Koestler put it. Clichés are often the refuge of the journalist with a deadline and the politician in a tight corner. No doubt we all have our own list of most irritating overworked phrases, and what follows is just a short list of some typical ones:

at this moment/point in time
by and large
conspicuous by one's absence
constructive dialogue
draw a line under
explore every avenue
full and frank exchange of views
I hear what you're saying
in the 21st century
keep a low profile
last but not least

o

put your head above the parapet
take something on board
take your eye off the ball

Technical terms

Technical terms are terms which are used by people in a
particular field of activity and have a very precise meaning.
They often pass into mainstream use (*mainstream* itself
being a case in point), and this is one of the standard ways
in which English is enriched through metaphors. Classic
examples are *to be in the limelight*, from the intense white
light produced by heating lime which was used in Victorian
theatres, and *the acid test*, from the test for gold using
nitric acid. Problems occur when a technical term is used
incorrectly or in a way which attempts to blind the reader
with science. Some very visible examples are:

crescendo
exponentially
factor (as noun and verb)
interface (as noun and verb)
leading-edge
learning curve
order of magnitude
product
profile
think outside the box
zero-sum game

o

p

owing

For an explanation of the difference between **owing to** and
due to, see DUE.

panini

See NOUNS, SINGULAR AND PLURAL.

participle

There are two kinds of participle in English: the present
participle ending with **-ing**, as in *we are going*, and the past
participle, generally ending with **-d** or **-ed** for many verbs
and with other letters in other verbs, as in *have you
decided?*; *new houses are being built*; *it's not broken*.
Participles are often used in writing to introduce
subordinate clauses that relate to other words in a
sentence, e.g. *her mother, **opening** the door quietly, came
into the room*, where it is *her mother* who is opening the
door. Other examples are: ***hearing** a noise I went out to
look*; ***having been born** in Rochdale, he spent most of his life
in the area*.

1 Participles at the beginning of a sentence, as in the last
two examples, are perfectly acceptable grammatically,
but when they are overused they can produce a poor
style. They are especially poor style when the clause they
introduce has only a weak logical link with the main
clause: ***being** blind from birth, she became a teacher
and travelled widely*. It is therefore advisable in your
writing to make sure that any participles you use at
the beginning of a sentence are strongly linked to what
follows them.

2 A worse stylistic error occurs with so called
'dangling participles'. Participles 'dangle' when the
action they describe is not being performed by the
subject of the sentence. Interpreted very literally, the
sentence *recently converted into apartments, I passed
by the house where I grew up* implies that the person
writing has recently been converted into apartments.
Here is another example: *driving near home recently,
a thick pall of smoke turned out to be a bungalow well
alight*. Although we know exactly what these two
examples mean, unattached participles can   ▶

p

distract and sometimes genuinely mislead the reader and
are best avoided.

3 A small group of participles, which include *allowing
for*, *assuming*, *considering*, *excepting*, *given*, *including*,
provided, *seeing* (*as/that*), and *speaking* (*of*) have
become prepositions or conjunctions in their own
right, and their use when unrelated to the subject of
the sentence is now standard and perfectly acceptable,
as in *speaking of money, how much did this
all cost?*

peak, peek

The word meaning 'to look quickly or furtively' and 'a quick or
furtive look' is written **peek**, not **peak**: *the sun peeks out only
intermittently*; *a sneak peek at what's in store*.

pence

Both **pence** and **pennies** have existed as the plural of **penny**
since at least the 16th century. Nowadays, the two forms tend
to be used for different purposes: **pence** refers to sums of money
(*five pounds and sixty-nine pence*) while **pennies** refers to the
coins themselves (*I put pennies in my piggy bank*). In recent
years, **pence** rather than **penny** has often sometimes been
used in the singular to refer to amounts of one penny: *the
Chancellor will put one pence on income tax*. The coin itself is
stamped **penny**, not **pence**, and this singular use of **pence** is
not standard English.

peninsula

The spelling of the noun as **peninsular** instead of **peninsula**
is a common mistake; around 20 per cent of examples in
the Oxford English Corpus are for the incorrect spelling.
The spelling **peninsula** should be used when a noun is
intended (*the end of the Cape Peninsula*), whereas
peninsular is the spelling of the adjective (*the peninsular
part of Malaysia*).

penny

On the different uses of the plural forms **pence** and **pennies**, see PENCE.

perceive

The core meaning of **perceive** is 'to become aware of or notice something', especially through your senses: *she perceived that all was not well; I perceived a change in his behaviour*. Used with that meaning it is rather formal in tone. But it is far more widely used with a different meaning, as a high-falutin' way of saying **see**, **consider**, or **regard**: *some geographers perceive hydrology to be a separate field*. When used that way it is arguably somewhat pretentious, not to mention laden with psychological baggage. The alternatives mentioned above work as well, or better, in most cases.

perfect

The traditional pronunciation of **perfect** as an adjective is with an **i** sound in the second syllable: /**pur**-fikt/, as Lou Reed famously sang in his anthemic *Perfect Day*. There is now a widespread tendency to pronounce the second syllable as in **bed**, perhaps under the influence of the 'speak as you spell' school of thought. Only time will tell if the older pronunciation eventually becomes extinct, but currently the chances of its survival are not looking good.

perpetrate, perpetuate

The words **perpetrate** and **perpetuate** are sometimes confused. **Perpetrate** means 'to commit a harmful, illegal, or immoral action', as in *a crime has been perpetrated against a sovereign state*, whereas **perpetuate** means 'to make something continue indefinitely', as in *a monument to perpetuate the memory of those killed in the war*.

p

-person

The use of -**person**, instead of -*man*, as a gender-neutral suffix denoting occupations, began in the 1970s with *chairperson* (see CHAIRMAN). Although coining these words was in principle a laudable attempt to reduce sexism enshrined in the language, their use in practice, as demonstrated by the Oxford English Corpus, has spread rather more slowly than might have been expected. One reason for this may be that people are reluctant to adopt forms that, while more politically correct, are linguistically more awkward or cumbersome. In some cases they sound almost fundamentalist or are deliberately contrived or ironic, as in *fisherperson*, *clergyperson*, *henchperson*, or *snowperson*. One solution has been to use a different word, such as *firefighter* instead of *fireman* or *fireperson*, and *police officer* instead of *policeman* or *policewoman*. People are also finding other ways of expressing the professions and roles concerned: for instance, instead of referring to someone as a *barman* or *barperson* (let alone *barmaid*), one hears *a member of the bar staff* or that someone *works behind the bar*.

It is also interesting that the most widely used forms according to the Corpus, namely *spokesperson* and *chairperson*, come from the area of public life and are often used in official and news documents. Even so, *spokesperson* in the Corpus is about a quarter as frequent as *spokesman*, and slightly less frequent than *spokeswoman*, but this could be because these terms are commonly used of a particular person, when there is felt to be less need to be gender-neutral.

The list below gives the 'top ten' from the Corpus, starting with the most frequent, and their year of coinage, where known. As can be seen, most of them are 1970s creations.

spokesperson   1972
chairperson   1971

salesperson	1971
layperson	1972
sportsperson	
businessperson	
foreperson	1973
craftsperson	1976
congressperson	1972
tradesperson	1886

The substitution of *person* for *man* in other ways, e.g. in *personhandle*, *personpower*, and *gingerbread person*, still shows little sign of being taken seriously.

personally

Personally has two unobjectionable uses, illustrated by:
- *the decision was made by the president personally* ('by the president and no one else'), and
- *he took the criticism personally* ('in a personal manner').

Some people, however, object to **personally** being used to mean 'for myself, for my part', as in *personally, I don't approve of such behaviour*. Although using the word in this way is a very useful way of emphasizing your own view, it is best restricted to informal contexts. In many cases it can be simply omitted, or replaced by the more formal *for my part*. Less acceptable is using the word in this meaning when the 'person' is not referred to at all, as in *personally, that would be nice*.

P

personal pronoun

1 The correct use of personal pronouns is one of the trickier areas of English usage. **I**, **we**, **they**, **he**, and **she** are known technically as **subjective** personal pronouns because they are used as the subject of a sentence, often coming before the verb (*she lives in Paris*; *we are leaving*). **Me**, ▶

us, **them**, **him**, and **her**, on the other hand, are called **objective** personal pronouns because they are used as the object of a verb, or following a preposition (*John hates me; his father left him; I did it for her*).

The distinction made above explains why it is incorrect to say either *John and me went to the shops* or *John and her went to the shops*: the personal pronoun is in subject position, so it must be **I** not **me**, and **she** not **her**. Using the pronoun alone makes the incorrect use obvious: *me went to the shops* is clearly not acceptable.

This analysis also explains why it is incorrect to say *he came with you and I*: the personal pronoun follows the preposition **with** and is therefore objective, so it must be **me** not **I**. Again, a simple test for correctness is to use the pronoun alone: *he came with I* is clearly not acceptable. (See also BETWEEN.)

2 Where a personal pronoun is used alone without a verb or a preposition, however, the traditional analysis starts to break down. Traditionalists sometimes argue, for example, that *she's younger than me* and *I've not been here as long as her* are incorrect and should be *she's younger than I* and *I've not been here as long as she*. Their argument is based on the assumption that **than** and **as** are conjunctions and so the personal pronoun is still subjective even though there is no verb; they argue that there is an implied verb, i.e. *she's younger than I am*. Yet the supposed 'correct' form does not sound natural at all to most speakers of English and is almost never used in speech.

It might be more accurate to say that in modern English those personal pronouns listed above as being **objective** are used 'neutrally'—i.e. they are used in all cases where the pronoun is not explicitly **subjective**. From this it follows that it is standard and perfectly acceptable English to use any of the following: *who is it? it's me!; she's taller than him; I didn't do as well as her*. Those who would consider these last examples as wrong are attempting to dictate the grammar of English, using the grammar of Latin as their yardstick.

p

perspective

Perspective is well established in the meaning of 'point of view', as in: *from our perspective this is a sensible proposal*. Nowadays it is increasingly common to encounter phrases where **perspective** is replaced by **prospective**: *from our prospective this is a sensible proposal*. Though there are historical precedents for **prospective** being used in this way, it is best to avoid doing so, as many people, especially British speakers, will regard such a use as a mistake.

peruse

Peruse is a rather formal word with the very specific meaning 'to read something in a very thorough and careful way': *he has spent countless hours in libraries perusing art history books*. Many people mistakenly think it means 'to read something through quickly', as in *documents will be perused rather than analysed thoroughly*. To use it in this way is not only wrong, but may also confuse your listener or reader.

phenomenon

The word **phenomenon** comes from Greek, and its plural form is **phenomena**, as in *these phenomena are not fully understood*. You will quite often come across **phenomena** used as a singular form, as in *this is a strange phenomena*, but it is best to stick to the traditional singular and plural distinction. For similar examples, see NOUNS, SINGULAR AND PLURAL.

P

phosphorus, phosphorous

The correct spelling for the noun denoting the chemical element is **phosphorus**, while the correct spelling for the adjective meaning 'relating to or containing phosphorus' is **phosphorous**. Over 90 per cent of the examples of **phosphorous** in the Oxford English Corpus should have been spelled **phosphorus**. Note that some uses which sound adjectival, such as *a phosphorus bomb* and *the deadline for reducing phosphorus levels*, in fact use the noun as a modifier and are therefore spelled **-rus**. True adjectives are found in expressions such as *phosphorous acid*.

pianist

People on both sides of the Atlantic commonly find that
'America and England are two countries separated by a common
language', as George Bernard Shaw put it. That his witticism has
more than a grain of truth is graphically illustrated by a word
as seemingly straightforward as **pianist**. In Britain you put the
stress very firmly on the letter **i**: /**pee**-uh-nist/. Stateside, you
stress it in the same way as you would *piano*, with the stress
very firmly on the letter **a**: /pee-**a**-nist/.

plead

In a law court a person can **plead guilty** or **plead not guilty**. The
phrase **plead innocent** is not a technical legal term, though
it is commonly found in general use.

plethora

A **plethora** is not simply an abundance of something, but
rather an overabundance, as in: *the bill had to struggle
through a plethora of committees and subcommittees.*
In sentences such as *a plethora of play spaces and equipment*,
the looser meaning of 'abundance' is often not considered
good style.

pore, pour

Pour and **pore** are often confused. If you want to describe
'studying or reading something intensely' with the phrase to
pore over, the correct spelling is as shown, not **pour**.

practice, practise

It is easy to get confused about when to write **practice** and when
practise. Which spelling you should choose depends on whether
you're using the word as a noun or a verb, and whether you're
following British usage or not. In British English spell the word
with a **c** when using it as a noun, as in *practice makes perfect*.
When using one of its verbal forms you should spell it with an
s, as in *practising Christians*. In the US the word is always
spelled with a **c**.

pre-

The prefix **pre-** is often joined to the word it qualifies without a hyphen, e.g. *prearrange*, *predetermine*, *preoccupy*. But when the word begins with **e-** or **i-**, or if it looks like another word, it is usual to insert a hyphen, e.g. *pre-eminent*, *pre-ignition*, *pre-position* (to distinguish it from *preposition*).

preferable, preferably

Both **preferable** and **preferably** are traditionally pronounced with the stress on the first syllable, in British and American English: /**pref**-ruh-buhl/, /**pref**-ruh-bli/.

preposition

A preposition is a word such as *after*, *in*, *to*, or *with*, which usually comes before a noun or pronoun and establishes the way it relates to what has gone before (*the man **on** the platform*, *they came **after** dinner*, and *what did you do it **for**?*).

The superstition that a preposition should always precede the word it governs and should not end a sentence, as it does in the last example given above, seems to have developed from an observation by the 17th-century poet John Dryden. It is not based on a real appreciation of the structure of English, which regularly separates words that are grammatically related.

There are cases when it is either impossible or sounds stilted to organize the sentence in a way that avoids a preposition at the end, as demonstrated by Churchill's famous *This is the sort of English up with which I will not put*. By the same token, the pithy phrase *I want to meet the people worth talking to* becomes convoluted when reorganized as *I want to meet the people with whom it is worthwhile to talk*.

The following are cases where it is generally impossible to reorganize the sentence.

▶

p

First, in relative clauses and questions featuring phrasal verbs (verbs with linked adverbs or prepositions): *what did Marion think she was up to?*; *they must be convinced of the commitment they are taking on*; *budget cuts themselves are not damaging: the damage depends on where the cuts are coming from*.

Second, in passive constructions: *the dress had not even been paid for*; *we were well looked after*.

Last, in short sentences including an infinitive with *to*: *there are a couple of things I want to talk to you about*.

In conclusion, in more formal writing you might consider not leaving a preposition dangling at the end of the sentence when you are absolutely sure that putting it elsewhere will not result in the sentence becoming stilted or unnatural. Generally, however, finishing a sentence with a preposition is a natural part of the structure of English; those who object to it are perpetuating an antiquated shibboleth.

presently

Presently has two meanings. The older, meaning 'now', dates from the 15th century and is the dominant meaning in American English, as in *he is presently chair of the committee*. The second meaning is 'in a while, soon', and used to be the chief meaning in British English, as in *he will see you presently*. Nowadays the first meaning is just as common in British English as the second, and just as correct, despite the objections of some traditionalists.

principal, principle

The words **principal** and **principle** sound the same but mean different things. **Principle** is normally used as a noun meaning 'a fundamental truth or basis underlying a system of thought or belief', as in *this is one of the basic principles of democracy*. **Principal** is normally an adjective meaning 'main or most important', as in *one of the country's principal cities*. **Principal** can also be a noun when used to refer to the most important or senior person in an organization: *the deputy principal, a principal with the Royal Ballet*.

program, programme

The standard spelling of the noun and verb in British English is **programme**, except when referring to computer programs: *TV programme*; *programme of study*; *he programmes the film festival every year*; but *computer program, can you program in Perl?* In American English and most other varieties **program** is used for the noun and verb in all contexts. When used as a verb, the forms are **programming**, **programmes** or **programs**, according to context, and **programmed**. In the US the spellings with a single **m**, **programing** and **programed** are accepted, though not very common.

pronouns

A pronoun is a word such as *I, we, they, me, you, them*, etc., and other forms such as the possessive *hers, theirs*, and so forth and the reflexive *myself, themselves*, etc. They are used to refer to and take the place of a noun or noun phrase that has already been mentioned or is known, especially in order to avoid repetition, as in the sentence *when June saw her husband again, she wanted to hit him*.

When a pronoun refers back to a person or thing previously named, it is important that the gap is not so large that the reader or hearer might have difficulty relating the two, and that ambiguity is avoided when more than one person might be referred to. Here is an example (where the ambiguity is deliberate) from a play by Tom Stoppard:

SEPTIMUS: Geometry, Hobbes assures us in the *Leviathan*, is the only science God has been pleased to bestow on mankind.

LADY CROOM: And what does he mean by it?
SEPTIMUS: Mr Hobbes or God?

pronunciation

People often say the second syllable of **pronunciation** as -ouns-
(pruh-**nown**-see-**a**-shuhn), and misspell it with an -**ou**-,
pron**ou**nciation. Both of these may have logic on their side, since
the verb is **pronounce**. But here, as so often, actual usage
contradicts logic, and in standard English only **pronunciation** is
acceptable.

prophecy, prophesy

The words **prophesy** and **prophecy** are often confused.
Prophesy is the spelling that should be used for the verb
(he was prophesying a bumper harvest), whereas **prophecy** is
the correct spelling for the noun (a bleak prophecy of war
and ruin).

prosciutto

You pronounce this Italian word /pruh-**shoo**-toh/. The correct
way to spell it is with the letter **i** before the **u**, not the other way
round, as often seen on menus. It may help to recollect the right
order if you remember that in fascist, another Italian word, the
same combination of letters -**sci**- is also pronounced as a **sh**
sound.

prospective

Prospective is an adjective describing a likely future event or
situation, as in prospective students, and prospective changes in the
law. For its use in phrases where **perspective** is the appropriate
word, see PERSPECTIVE.

prove

For complex historical reasons **prove** developed two past
participles: **proved** and **proven**. Until recently, in British English
proved was generally used for the past participle, and **proven**
survived only in dialect, particularly in the Scottish legal phrase

not proven (usually pronounced /**proh**-v'n/), and adjectivally: *he has a proven track record* (generally pronounced /**proo**-v'n/). In the US, **proven** is much more common as the standard past participle than in Britain (*she has proven to be an outstanding manager*), but its use has been increasing recently in Britain; although this is perfectly correct, some traditionalists baulk at it.

purposely, purposefully

These are often confused, but in principle they mean somewhat different things. If you do something **purposely**, you do it on purpose, deliberately: *this administration purposely misled the American people*. If someone is **purposeful**, they are resolute and determined by nature. So, if they do something **purposefully**, they do it with great resolve and determination: *he got up and strode purposefully towards the trees*. To check if you are using the right word, try replacing it with *on purpose*. If you can replace it, as in the first example, then **purposely** is the right word to use.

queer

The word **queer** was first used to mean 'homosexual' in the 1920s. It was originally, and usually still is, a deliberately offensive and aggressive term when used by heterosexual people. In recent years, however, some gay people have taken the word and deliberately used it in place of *gay* or *homosexual*, in an attempt to deprive it of its negative power by using it positively. This use of **queer** is now well established and widely used among politically minded gay people (especially as an adjective or a noun modifier, as in *queer rights*) and at present it exists alongside the other, deliberately offensive use.

race

In recent years using the word **race** has become problematic because of the associations of the word with the racist ideologies and theories that grew out of the work of 19th-century anthropologists and physiologists. Although still used in general contexts, it is now often replaced by other words which are less emotionally charged, such as *people(s)* or *community*, as in

p

q

r

community relations, and **racial** is often replaced by *ethnic*, as in *ethnic minority*.

rack

The relationship between the forms **rack** and **wrack** is complicated. The most common noun meaning of **rack**, 'a framework for holding and storing things', is always spelled **rack**, never **wrack**. The figurative meanings of the verb, deriving from the type of torture in which someone is stretched on a rack, can, however, be spelled either **rack** or **wrack**: *racked with guilt* or *wracked with guilt*; *rack your brains* or *wrack your brains*. In addition, the phrase **rack and ruin** can also be spelled **wrack and ruin**. In the contexts mentioned here as having the variant **wrack**, **rack** is always the commoner spelling.

random

The long-established meaning of **random** that everybody knows is 'done or happening without method or conscious decision': *here are some random thoughts*. The newer meaning, 'peculiar, strange, or unpredictable', can strike people above a certain age as novel and alien. As a result, it is still informal in tone. First appearing in the 1970s, it is now well established among people below a certain age, especially in the US: *you are so incredibly random!* In these two examples, **random** functions as an adjective. People also use it as a noun, to mean someone who is somewhere by chance, or who is not part of a particular group: *randoms are a fundamental ingredient at any good party*.

raring to do

This colourful, informal phrase means 'eager and enthusiastic to do something': *she was raring to get back to her work*. It is an American gift to our language. Some people say and write **rearing to do** something, which many people would consider wrong. But those who use **rearing** are in fact right to make the connection with the image of a rearing horse: **raring** is an American dialect form of **rearing**.

re

Some people claim that, strictly speaking, **re** should only be used in headings and references, as in *Re: Ainsworth versus Chambers*, but not as a normal word meaning 'about', as in *I saw the deputy head re the incident*. However, the evidence suggests that **re** is now widely used in the second way in official and semi-official contexts, and is now generally accepted. It is hard to see any compelling logical argument against using it as an ordinary English word in this way; it can, though, sound pretentious when used in everyday speech or writing, and *about* would probably serve better.

re-

In modern English, the tendency is for words formed with prefixes such as **re-** to be unhyphenated: **restore, remain, reacquaint.** One general exception to this is when the word to which **re-** attaches begins with **e**: in this case a hyphen is often inserted for clarity: **re-examine, re-enter, re-enact.** A hyphen is sometimes also used where the word formed with the prefix would be identical to an already existing word: **re-cover** (meaning 'cover again', as in *we decided to* re-cover *the dining-room chairs*) not **recover** (meaning 'get better in health'). Other prefixes such as **pre-** behave very similarly.

rearing to do

For the use of **rearing to do** to mean **raring to do**, see RARING TO DO.

r

reason

1 Some people object to statements like *the reason why I decided not to phone* on the grounds that what follows *the reason* should express a statement, using **that**, not imply a question with a **why**: *the reason that I decided not to phone* (or, more informally, *the reason I decided not to phone*).

2 Some people also object to the phrase *the reason ... is because*, as in *the reason I didn't phone is because my mother has been ill.* They object on the grounds that either *because* or *the reason* is

unnecessary. It is supposedly better to use the word **that** instead (*the reason I didn't phone is that...*) or to rephrase altogether (*I didn't phone because...*).

Nevertheless, both the above usages are well established and, though more elegant phrasing can no doubt be found, they are generally accepted in standard English.

Red Indian

The term **Red Indian**, first recorded in the early 19th century, has largely fallen out of use, associated as it is with a historical period and the corresponding stereotypes of cowboys and Indians in the Wild West. If used today, the term may cause offence: the normal terms are now **American Indian** and **Native American** or, if appropriate, the name of the specific people (Cherokee, Iroquois, and so on).

reference

To **reference** something has a precise technical meaning in the field of bibliography, and a more general one. The technical meaning is 'to provide a book or article with citations for the sources of information mentioned', as in: *each chapter is referenced, citing literature up to 1990*. From this has developed a broader meaning of 'to mention or refer to': *one British Computer Society paper is referenced on page 35 of the White Paper*. Using the word in this somewhat broader way to mean that something is mentioned, often with a precise indication of where it is mentioned, is perfectly legitimate. But using it as a supposedly stylish replacement for the simpler **refer** or **mention**, as in *the media referenced our association in almost 40 articles*, may well irritate people alert to the nuances of language.

referendum

For information on which plural form to use, see LATIN PLURALS.

refute

The core meaning of **refute** is 'prove (a statement or theory) to be wrong', as in *attempts to refute Einstein's theory*. From the

1960s on, a more general meaning has developed from the core one, meaning simply 'deny', as in *I absolutely refute the charges made against me*. Traditionalists object to this second use but it is now widely accepted in standard English. However, it is wise to avoid it in writing for a more conservative audience.

regalia

The word **regalia** comes from Latin and is, technically speaking, the plural of the adjective *regalis,* meaning 'royal'. However, in the way the word is used in English today it behaves as a collective noun, similar to words like *staff* or *government*. This means that it can be used with either a singular or plural verb (*the regalia of Russian tsardom **is** now displayed in the Kremlin* or *the regalia of Russian tsardom **are** now displayed in the Kremlin*), but it has no other singular form. For more information, see NOUNS, SINGULAR AND PLURAL.

regard

See WITH REGARD TO.

register office

The form **register office** is the official term, but **registry office** is the form most often used in informal and non-official use.

regretfully, regrettably

The adjectives **regretful** and **regrettable** are distinct in meaning: **regretful** means 'feeling regret', as in *she shook her head with a regretful smile*, while **regrettable** means 'causing regret', as in *the loss of jobs is regrettable*. The adverbs **regretfully** and **regrettably** have not, however, preserved the same distinction. **Regretfully** is used as an adverb of manner to mean 'in a regretful manner' (*he sighed regretfully*), but is also used to mean 'it is regrettable that' (*regretfully, mounting costs forced the branch to close*). In this second use it stands in for **regrettably**. This use is now well established and is included in some modern dictionaries without comment.

reign, rein

The correct spelling of the idiomatic phrase is **a free rein**, not **a free reign**; see FREE REIN.

relative clauses

1 A **relative clause** is one that is connected to the main clause of the sentence by a word such as *who*, *whom*, *which*, *that*, and *whose*. The underlined part of the following sentence is a relative clause: *the items, <u>which are believed to be family heirlooms</u>, included a grandfather clock worth around £3,000.*
There are two types of relative clause:
defining (or **restrictive**) **relative clauses** and
non-defining (or **non-restrictive**) **relative clauses**.

- Defining relative clauses provide information which is essential to specify the noun or noun group to which they refer.
- Non-defining relative clauses give information which is additional and could be left out without affecting the meaning of the sentence.

Take the two sentences: *the books which were on the table are John's* and *the books, which were on the table, are John's.* In the first sentence the relative clause introduced by *which* uniquely identifies a specific group of books (the ones on the table) and states that they, and only they, are John's. In the second sentence the clause merely offers the additional information that John's books happen to be on the table; the fact that they are on the table does not distinguish them uniquely from other books which are not John's.

2 As you will see in the example above, defining clauses are not separated from the rest of the sentence, but non-defining clauses must be separated by commas. Ignoring this distinction can lead to unintentionally ▶

ambiguous or even comic effects. For example, the mistakenly defining relative clause in *if you are in need of assistance, please ask any member of staff who will be pleased to help* implies contrast with another set of staff who will not be pleased to help. A comma is needed before *who*.

3 Whether a relative clause is defining or non-defining also determines the choice between *that* and *which* when referring to things. If the clause is defining, either *that* or *which* can be used, e.g. *the coat that/which he had on yesterday was new* (we are identifying the coat by saying it is the one he had on yesterday, as opposed to any others he may have). However, in non-defining clauses, only *which* can be used: *that coat, which he had on yesterday, was made of pure alpaca and cost a bomb* (this is a coat we already know about and have referred to, and, by the way, he had it on yesterday). In the following example *that* should have been replaced by *which*: *the new edition of his book, that was first published in 2001, has proved even more successful than the first edition.*

relatively

The use of **relatively**, as in *it was relatively successful*, has been criticized on the grounds that there is no explicit comparison being made and that another word, such as *quite* or *rather*, would therefore be more appropriate. But even if no explicit comparison is being made **relatively** is often used in this way and is acceptable in standard English.

research

In British English, **research** is traditionally pronounced /ri-**serch**/, with the stress on the second syllable. In US English, the stress is reversed and comes on the first syllable: /**ree**-serch/. The US pronunciation is becoming more common in British

English and, although many people dislike it, it is now generally accepted as a standard variant of British English.

restaurateur

The word **restaurateur**, meaning a 'restaurant owner', comes directly from the French. The common misspelling *restauranteur*, copying the spelling of **restaurant** with an **n**, is found in nearly 10 per cent of uses of this word in the Oxford English Corpus.

restrictive relative clauses

See RELATIVE CLAUSES.

reverend

As a title, **Reverend** is used for members of the clergy; the traditionally correct way to refer to them is *the Reverend James Smith*, *the Reverend J. Smith*, or just *Mr Smith*, but not *Reverend Smith* or simply *Reverend*. On an envelope, for instance, especially where *Reverend* is abbreviated, *the* can be omitted: *Rev. J. Smith* or *Revd J. Smith*. Other words are prefixed in titles of more senior clergy: bishops are *Right Reverend*, archbishops are *Most Reverend*, and deans are *Very Reverend*, and these are treated similarly: *the Most Reverend Andrew Jones*; *Rt Rev. C. Brown*.

robust

Some words are, arguably, overused, and thus quickly become rather clichéd. **Robust** is one of them. In its meaning of 'uncompromising and forceful', it is a facile choice when someone is cornered and has to defend themselves, as in these two examples: *ministers were last night preparing a robust defence of Government economic performance; a rather more robust rebuttal of the allegations against her*. Synonyms which can deliver you from the tyranny of cliché include **assertive, forceful, forthright, rigorous,** and **vigorous**.

round

Round and **around** are interchangeable in some contexts, but not all. In many contexts in British English you can use either, as in *she put her arm round him*; *she put her arm around him*. There is, however, a general preference for **round** to be used for definite, specific movement (*she turned round; a bus came round the corner*), while **around** tends to be used in contexts which are less definite (*she wandered around for ages; costing around £3,000*) or for abstract uses (*a rumour circulating around the cocktail bars*).

In US English, the situation is different. The normal form in most contexts is **around**; **round** is generally regarded as informal or non-standard and is only standard in certain fixed expressions, as in *year-round* and *they went round and round in circles*.

rubbish

Rubbish used to be exclusively a noun, but in British English is now quite often used as a sort of adjective: *people might say I was a rubbish manager; she's rubbish at maths*. This use is still rather informal, and is best avoided in more formal writing.

's

There are a few special instances in which it is acceptable to use an apostrophe to indicate plurals, as with letters and symbols where the letter **s** added without punctuation could look odd or be undecipherable: *dot your i's and cross your t's; he rated a string of 9.9's from the jury*. However, in the formation of plurals of regular nouns it is incorrect to use an apostrophe, e.g. *six pens, not six pen's; oranges—6 for £1, not orange's—6 for £1*.

Sami

Sami is the term by which the **Lapps** themselves prefer to be known. Its use is becoming increasingly common, although **Lapp** is still the main term in general use.

sat

For the use of **sat** in sentences like *we were sat there for hours*, see SIT, STAND.

scarcely

Scarcely, like **barely**, should normally be followed by *when*, not *than*, to introduce a subsequent clause: *they had scarcely pulled to a halt when Rale flung the door open.*

scone

There are two possible pronunciations of the word **scone**: /skon/, rhyming with **gone**, and /skohn/, rhyming with **tone**. In US English /skohn/ is more common. In British English, the two pronunciations traditionally have different regional and class associations: /skon/ is standard in Scots, but in England tends to be associated with the north, and the northern working class, while /skohn/ is associated with the south and the middle class. In modern British English, however, the first pronunciation is increasingly common.

Scottish, Scot, Scots, Scotch

The terms **Scottish**, **Scot**, **Scots**, and **Scotch** are all variants of the same word. They have had different histories, however, and in modern English they have developed different uses and connotations. The normal everyday word used to mean 'of or relating to Scotland or its people' is **Scottish**, as in *Scottish people*; *Scottish hills*; *Scottish Gaelic*; or *she's English, not Scottish*. The normal, neutral word for 'a person from Scotland' is **Scot**, along with **Scotsman**, **Scotswoman**, and the plural form **the Scots** (or, less commonly, **the Scottish**). The word **Scotch**, meaning either 'of or relating to Scotland' or 'a person/the people from Scotland', was widely used in the past by Scottish writers such as Robert Burns and Sir Walter Scott, but it has become less common nowadays. It is detested by Scots (as being an 'English' invention) and is now uncommon in modern English, though occasionally used by unsuspecting American tourists. It only survives in certain fixed phrases, as for example *Scotch broth*, *Scotch egg*, *Scotch mist*, and *Scotch whisky*. **Scots** is used similarly to **Scottish**, as an adjective meaning 'of or relating to Scotland'. However, it tends to be used in a narrower meaning to refer specifically to the language spoken and used in Scotland, as in *a Scots accent* or *the Scots word for 'night'*.

S

seasonal

The words **seasonal** and **seasonable** are sometimes confused.
Seasonal means 'relating to a particular season' (*seasonal fresh fruit*) or 'fluctuating or restricted according to the season' (*there are companies whose markets are seasonal*). **Seasonable** is a rather rare word which means 'usual for or appropriate to a particular season': *in December the magazine carried cartoons and songs, including a seasonable Christmas carol.*

sensual, sensuous

The words **sensual** and **sensuous** are frequently used interchangeably to mean 'gratifying the senses', especially in a sexual sense. Strictly speaking, this goes against a traditional distinction, by which **sensuous** is a more neutral term, meaning 'relating to the senses rather than the intellect', as in *swimming is a beautiful, sensuous experience.* **Sensual** relates to gratification of the senses, especially sexually, as in *a sensual massage.* In fact the word **sensuous** is thought to have been invented by Milton (1641) in a deliberate attempt to avoid the sexual overtones of **sensual**. In practice, the connotations are such that it is difficult to use **sensuous** in the non-sexual meaning. While traditionalists struggle to maintain a distinction, the evidence from the Oxford English Corpus and elsewhere suggests that the 'neutral' use of **sensuous** is rare in modern English. If a neutral meaning is intended it is advisable to find alternative wording.

sex

On the difference in use between the words **sex** and **gender**, see
GENDER.

S

sexist language

It is very important to make sure that you do not unwittingly offend people by what might be considered sexist uses of language. Roughly since the 1970s, certain previously

▶

established uses of language have come to be regarded as discriminating against women, either because they are based on male terminology, e.g. *businessman*, or because women appear to be given a status that is linguistically and socially subsidiary, e.g. *actress*. Specific aspects of this are dealt with at the entries for **-ess**, **gender-neutral language**, **man**, and **-person**.

Different groups and individuals have different sensitivities to these issues, but there are some general guidelines that can be followed.

1 Where there is a choice between a word which specifies gender and a word which does not you should use the one which does not, unless the gender is relevant to the context. So, *chair* or *chairperson* is the gender-neutral word for the person running a meeting or a committee, as is *spokesperson* for someone who makes statements on behalf of a group or organization, and *head teacher* for someone in charge of a school. On the other hand, to say *she's a shrewd businessperson* rather than *she's a shrewd businesswoman* might sound somewhat forced. For more information see MAN.

2 In some cases the term which previously applied exclusively to males is used to refer to males and females, since the female form has negative connotations which the male does not. Accordingly, *actor*, *author*, *editor*, and *poet* are used irrespective of gender, e.g. *she is not only radiantly beautiful but a great actor*. For more information see -ESS.

3 When you are referring to groups of people in general, using words such as *each*, *everybody*, *anyone*, or nouns such as *individual*, *person*, *applicant*, *speaker*, and so forth, you should avoid using *he* or *his* to refer to them. Instead you can generally use *they* and *their*, and this use is perfectly acceptable nowadays, as in *each speaker will have their expenses reimbursed within one month of submitting*   ▶

a claim. The alternatives to *they*, *their*, etc. are the rather cumbersome *he or she*, *his or hers*, etc. Invented forms such as *s/he* have not become established in general use. For more information see GENDER-NEUTRAL LANGUAGE.

4 When referring to the whole of humanity, phrases such as *the human race*, *humankind*, should be used instead of **mankind**. For more information, see MAN.

shall

There is considerable confusion about when to use **shall** and when **will**. The traditional rule in standard British English is that **shall** is used with *I* and *we* (first-person pronouns) to form the future tense, while **will** is used with *you*, *he*, *she*, *it*, *they* (second and third persons), e.g. *I shall be late*; *she will not be there*. To express a strong determination to do something the traditional rule is that **will** is used with the first person, and **shall** with the second and third persons, e.g. *I **will** not tolerate this*; *you **shall** go to the ball*. In practice, however, **shall** and **will** are today used more or less interchangeably in statements (though not in questions). Because both **shall** and **will** are usually contracted in speaking (*we'll*, *she'll*, etc.), there is often no need to make a choice between **shall** and **will**. This has no doubt helped weaken the distinction. The interchangeable use of **shall** and **will** is an acceptable part of standard modern British and US English.

she

1 For a discussion of whether to say *I am older than she* or *I am older than her*, see PERSONAL PRONOUN and THAN.

2 The use of the pronoun **he** to refer to a person of unspecified sex, once quite acceptable, has become problematic in recent years and is now usually regarded as old-fashioned or sexist. One of the responses to this has been to use **she** in the way that **he** has been used, to refer to people in general, irrespective of gender, as in *only include your child if you know she won't distract you*. In some types of writing, for example

S

books on childcare or child psychology, use of **she** has become quite common. In most contexts, however, it is likely to be distracting in the same way that **he** now is, and alternatives such as *he or she* or *they* are preferable. See also GENDER-NEUTRAL LANGUAGE.

sheer

The two verbs **sheer** and **shear** have a similar origin but do not have identical meanings. **Sheer**, the less common verb, means 'to swerve or change course quickly', as in *the boat sheers off the bank*. **Shear**, on the other hand, usually means 'to cut the wool off (a sheep)' and can also mean 'to break off (usually as a result of structural strain)', as in *the pins broke and the wing part sheared off*.

sherbet

The tendency to insert an **r** into the second syllable of **sherbet** is common; this misspelling happens in around 10 per cent of the uses of **sherbet** in the Oxford English Corpus.

should

1 As with *shall* and *will*, there is confusion about when to use **should** and **would**. The traditional rule is that **should** is used with first person pronouns (*I* and *we*), as in *I said I should be late*, and **would** is used with second and third persons (*you, he, she, it, they*), as in *you didn't say you would be late*. In practice, **would** is normally used instead of **should** in reported speech and conditional clauses: *I said I would be late*; *if we had known we would have invited her*. In spoken and informal contexts the issue rarely arises, since the distinction is obscured by the use of the contracted forms *I'd, we'd*, etc. In modern English, uses of **should** are dominated by the meanings relating to obligation (for which **would** cannot be substituted), as in *you should go out more often*, and for related emphatic uses, as in *you should have seen her face!*

2 For the use of **should of** instead of **should have**, see HAVE.

S

sight

On the confusion of **sight** and **site**, see SITE.

similar

The standard construction for **similar** is with **to**, as in *I've had problems similar to yours*. However, in British English, the construction **similar as** is sometimes used instead, as in *I've had similar problems as yourself*. This is not accepted as correct in standard English.

simplistic

Simplistic is first recorded in its modern meaning as recently as the 19th century. It differs from **simple** in implying a simplicity that is excessive or misleading rather than direct and useful: *'If you don't like what's on TV, just turn it off' is a simplistic remedy*.

sink

Historically, the past tense of **sink** has been both **sank** and **sunk** (*the boat sank; the boat sunk*), and the past participle has been both **sunk** and **sunken** (*the boat had already sunk; the boat had already sunken*). In modern standard English, however, the correct past is **sank** and the past participle is always **sunk**.

sit

Using **sat** (the past participle of **sit**) instead of **sitting** in such statements as *we were sat there for hours* is considered non-standard and dialectal by some people. It should be avoided in formal writing, but is acceptable and widely used when speaking in British (though not in US) English. See also STAND.

site

Confusion can arise between the words **site** and **sight**. As a noun, **site** means 'a place where something is constructed or has occurred' (*the site of the battle; the concrete is mixed on site*), while **sight** chiefly means 'the faculty or power of seeing' (*he lost his sight as a baby*).

S

skulduggery

This rather colourful-sounding word, deriving from the Scottish word **skulduddery**, ultimately has nothing to do with skulls, and was originally spelled with only one l. However, through a process of FOLK ETYMOLOGY, the spelling most commonly used these days is with **-ll-**, though strictly speaking this is incorrect.

slow

The word **slow** is normally used as an adjective (*a slow learner*; *the journey was slow*). It is also used as an adverb in certain specific contexts, including compounds such as *slow-acting* and *slow-moving* and in the expression *go slow*. Other adverbial use is informal and usually regarded as non-standard, as for example in *he drives too slow* and *go as slow as you can*. In such contexts standard English uses **slowly** instead. The use of **slow** and **slowly** in this respect contrasts with the use of *fast*, which is completely standard in use as both an adjective and an adverb; there is no word 'fastly'.

smell

The past tense and past participle of **smell** are both either **smelled** or **smelt**, and both forms are equally correct. **Smelt** is slightly preferred in British English, and **smelled** in American.

sneak

The traditional standard past form of **sneak** is **sneaked** (*she sneaked round the corner*). An alternative past form, **snuck** (*she snuck past me*), arose in the US in the 19th century. Until very recently **snuck** was confined to US dialect use and was regarded as non-standard. However, in the last few decades its use has spread in the US, where it is now regarded as a standard alternative to **sneaked** in all but the most formal contexts. In the Oxford English Corpus, there are now three times more US citations for **snuck** than there are for **sneaked**, and there is evidence of **snuck** sneaking into British English in a big way too.

soon

In standard English, the phrase **no sooner** is followed by **than**, as in *we had no sooner arrived than we had to leave*. This is because **sooner** is a comparative, and comparatives are followed by **than** (*earlier than*; *better than*, and so on). It is incorrect to follow **no sooner** with **when** instead of **than**, as in *we had no sooner arrived when we had to leave*.

sort

The construction **these sort of**, as in *I don't want to answer these sort of questions*, is technically ungrammatical. This is because *these* is plural and needs to agree with a plural noun (in this case **sorts** rather than **sort**). The construction is undoubtedly common and has been used for hundreds of years, but is best avoided in formal writing. See also KIND.

spastic

The word **spastic** has been used in medical contexts since the 18th century. In the 1970s and 1980s it became a term of abuse, used mainly by schoolchildren and directed towards any person regarded as incompetent or physically uncoordinated. Nowadays, the use of the word, whether as a noun or as an adjective, is likely to cause offence, and it is preferable, in the medical sense, to use phrasing such as *a person with cerebral palsy* instead.

specially

On the differences between **specially** and **especially**, see ESPECIALLY.

S

speed

Which is the correct past of **speed**? **Speeded** or **sped**? When the meaning is 'to go fast', the past tense and past participle are **sped**: *the car sped past*; *by that time she had sped down the road*. But if the meaning is 'to break a speed limit'; or if the verb is followed by **up**, **speeded** is the appropriate form in British English. Typical examples are: *he often speeded to get there in time*; *the reform process needs to be speeded up*. In American English **sped** is often used also in the second type of context, but sounds markedly odd to British ears.

spell

The form for the past tense and past participle is **spelt** or **spelled**. **Spelt** is more usual in British English, especially in the primary meaning 'to write or name the letters of a word'; **spelled** is more common in American English and in the phrasal verb **spell out**, meaning 'explain in detail'.

spill

The forms for the past tense and past participle are either **spilled** or **spilt**, and are equally correct. However, **spilled** is used much more often for both forms. There is no evidence of American and British usage being different.

spinster

The development of the word **spinster** is a good example of the way in which a word acquires unfavourable connotations to such an extent that it can no longer be used in a neutral way. From the 17th century the word was put after names as the official legal description of an unmarried woman: *Elizabeth Harris of London, Spinster*. This type of use survives today in some legal and religious contexts, as in the often humorously used *spinster of this parish*. In modern everyday English, however, **spinster** cannot be used to mean simply 'unmarried woman'; it is now always a derogatory term, conjuring up a stereotype of an older woman who is unmarried, childless, prissy, and repressed.

split infinitive

You have to really watch him; *to boldly go where no man has gone before*. It is still widely held that it is wrong to split infinitives—separate the infinitive marker **to** from the verb, as in the above examples. The dislike of split infinitives is long-standing but is not well founded, being based on an analogy with Latin. In Latin, infinitives consist of only one word (e.g. *crescere* 'to grow'; *amare* 'to love'), which makes them impossible to split: therefore, so the argument goes, they should not be split in

English either. But English is not the same as Latin. In particular, the placing of an adverb in English is extremely important in giving the appropriate emphasis: *you really have to watch him* and *to go boldly where no man has gone before*, examples where the infinitive is not split, either convey a different emphasis or sound awkward. Nowadays, some traditionalists may continue to consider the split infinitive an error in English. However, in standard English the principle of allowing split infinitives is broadly accepted as both normal and useful.

spoil

The forms for the past tense and past participle are either **spoiled** or **spoilt**, and are equally correct. However, there is a difference between American and British usage in that the spelling **spoilt** is rarely used in the US for either the past tense or the past participle, but in Britain it is as common as **spoiled** for the past participle, e.g. *we've been spoilt in recent years*.

spring

In British English the standard past tense is **sprang** (*she* sprang *forward*), while in US English the past can be either **sprang** or **sprung** (*I* sprung *out of bed*).

squaw

Until relatively recently, the word **squaw** was used neutrally in anthropological and other contexts to mean 'an American Indian woman or wife'. With changes in the political climate in the second half of the 20th century, however, the derogatory attitudes of the past towards American Indian women have meant that in modern North American English the word cannot be used in any context without being offensive. In British English the word has not acquired offensive connotations to the same extent, but it is nevertheless uncommon here too and now regarded as old-fashioned.

stand

Using **stood** (the past participle of **stand**) instead of **standing** in such statements as *my husband was stood on the other side of* the fence is considered non-standard and dialectal by some people. It should be avoided in formal writing, but is acceptable and widely used when speaking. See also sɪт.

stationary

The words **stationary** and **stationery** are often confused. **Stationary** is an adjective which means 'not moving or not intended to be moved', as in *a car collided with a stationary vehicle*, whereas **stationery** is a noun which means 'writing and other office materials', as in *I wrote to my father on the hotel stationery*. Around five per cent of the uses of **stationary** in the Oxford English Corpus are incorrect.

stood

For the use of **stood** in sentences like *we were stood there for hours*, see STAND.

stratum

In Latin, the word **stratum** is singular and its plural form is **strata**. In English, this distinction is maintained. It is therefore incorrect to use **strata** as a singular or to create the form *stratas* as the plural: *a series of overlying strata* not *a series of overlying stratas*, and a *new stratum was uncovered* not *a new strata was uncovered*. For further examples, see NOUNS, SINGULAR AND PLURAL.

subscribe

For the mistaken use of **ascribe** to to mean **subscribe to**, see ASCRIBE.

S

subjunctive

1 The **subjunctive** is a form of the verb expressing a wish or hypothesis in contrast to fact. It usually denotes what is imagined, wished, demanded, or proposed, as in the following examples: *I wish I were ten years younger; if I were you; the report recommends that he face* ▶

the tribunal; it is important that they be aware of the provisions of the Act.

2 The subjunctive is a legacy of Old English. It was common until about 1600, then went into decline, being retained in certain structures, such as following *if* or *as if,* and in certain fossilized phrases such as *as it were, be that as it may, come what may, far be it from me, God save the Queen, heaven forbid, perish the thought, so be it,* etc.

3 In modern English the subjunctive can be distinguished from the ordinary (indicative) form of the verb only in the third person singular present tense, which omits the final **s** (*God save the Queen*), and in the verb 'to be' (*I wish I were* and *it is important that they be aware*). It is regarded in many contexts as optional, and using it tends to convey a more formal tone.

4 The subjunctive has become very common, following American usage, in 'that' clauses after verbs such as *demand, insist, pray, recommend, suggest,* and *wish*: *fundamentalist Islam decrees that men and women be strictly segregated; she insisted Jane sit there; it was suggested he wait till the next morning.* For more conservative British writers this use still has a distinctly transatlantic feel; in all cases it can be replaced by a construction with *should,* e.g. *it was suggested that he should wait till the next morning.* See also LEST.

5 Another area where usage seems to be changing is in phrases such as *as if I were you, if it were up to me,* etc. People often say *if I was you* and *if it was up to me,* but the subjunctive is preferable in writing.

substitute

Traditionally, the verb **substitute** is followed by **for** and means 'to put (someone or something) in place of another', as in *she substituted the fake vase for the real one.* From the late 17th century on, **substitute** has also been used with **with** or **by** to mean 'replace (something) with something else', as in *she substituted the real vase with the fake one*. This can be confusing, since the two sentences shown above mean the same thing, yet the object of the verb and the object of the preposition have swapped over. Despite the potential confusion, the second, newer use is well established, especially in some scientific contexts, and though still disapproved of by traditionalists is now generally regarded as part of normal standard English.

suffice it to say

The traditional form of this phrase includes the word **it**: *suffice it to say he was not pleased*. However, the winds of change are buffeting this little word clean away, so that nowadays it is just as common to hear and see **suffice to say**. Nearly half of the examples in the Oxford English Corpus are in that form. The way the original phrase has been whittled down is an interesting example of how people can change English forever by being economical with words; see also AS FAR AS.

sulphur

In general use the standard British spelling is **sulphur** and the standard US spelling is **sulfur**. In chemistry, however, the **-f-** spelling is now the standard form in all related words in the field in both British and US contexts.

superior

When you compare two things, you normally link them with the word **than**: *my brother is older than me*. But **superior** is an exception to this rule. You use the word **to** instead: *restaurant industry managers consider US beef to be superior to Canadian and Australian beef*. A second difference between superior and other adjectives is that you cannot put the word **more** in front of it. So, it is correct to say *A is far superior to B*, and wrong to say *A is far more superior to B*.

supersede

The standard spelling is **supersede** rather than *supercede*. The word is derived from the Latin verb *supersedere* but has been influenced by the presence of other words in English spelled with a **c**, such as *intercede* and *accede*. The **c** spelling is recorded as early as the 16th century but is still generally regarded as incorrect and should be avoided in any kind of formal writing.

swim

In standard English, the past tense of **swim** is **swam** (*she swam to the shore*) and the past participle is **swum** (*she had never swum there before*). In the 17th and 18th centuries **swam** and **swum** were used interchangeably for the past participle, but this is not acceptable in standard modern English.

syllabus

Both **syllabuses** and **syllabi** are correct as plurals of **syllabus**, though in speech the first will sound more natural, the second slightly academic. For more guidance on words with more than one plural, see LATIN PLURALS.

sympathy

On the difference between **sympathy** and **empathy**, see EMPATHY.

tableau

Tableau comes from French, and is singular in meaning. The plural in English and French is **tableaux**. It is therefore incorrect to use **tableaux** in sentences such as *his pictures are a tableaux of military life behind the front line*. For further examples of this kind of mistake, see NOUNS, SINGULAR AND PLURAL.

s
t

text

At the moment there seems to be no agreement on which is the 'correct' form for the verb **text** in the past tense: **text** or **texted**. **Text**, as in *I text you but you didn't reply* is often heard, but **texted** is also used, and is found in writing. If to **text** is a regular verb, like *love*, then **texted** is the correct past tense and participle. However, people may be treating it as an irregular verb, like *put*, with the same past form as the present, perhaps influenced by the fact that **text** sounds like a past participle, as though it were 'texed'. It will be interesting to see which form wins out in the long run.

than

Traditionalists hold that personal pronouns following **than** should be in the subjective rather than the objective case: *he is smaller than she* rather than *he is smaller than her*. This argument is based on analysing **than** as a conjunction, with the personal pronoun ('she') standing in for a full clause: *he is smaller than she is*. However, many would argue that **than** in this context is not a conjunction but a preposition, grammatically similar to words like *with*, *between*, and *for*. If it is a preposition, the personal pronoun is objective: *he is smaller than her* is standard, in just the same way as, for example, *I work with her* is standard (not *I work with she*). Whatever the grammatical analysis, the evidence confirms that sentences like *he is smaller than she* are uncommon in modern English and only ever found in formal contexts. In speech they would certainly sound affected or pompous. Uses involving the objective personal pronoun, on the other hand, are almost universal. For more explanation, see PERSONAL PRONOUN and BETWEEN.

thankfully

Thankfully has been used for centuries to mean 'in a thankful manner', as in *she accepted the offer thankfully*. Since the 1960s it has also been used to mean 'fortunately', as in *thankfully, we didn't have to wait*. Although this use has not attracted the same amount of attention as **hopefully**, it has been criticized for the same reasons. It is, however, far commoner now than the traditional use, accounting for more than 80 per cent of uses of **thankfully** in the Oxford English Corpus. For further explanation, see HOPEFULLY.

that

1 The word **that** can be omitted in standard English where it introduces a subordinate clause, as in *she said (that) she was satisfied*. It can also be dropped in a defining relative clause where the subject of the subordinate clause is not the same as the subject of the main clause, as in *the book (that) I've just written* ('the book' and 'I' are two different subjects). Where the subject of the subordinate clause and the main clause are the same, use of the word **that** is obligatory, as in *the woman that owns the place* ('the woman' is the subject of both clauses).

2 It is sometimes argued that, in defining relative clauses, **that** should be used for non-human references, while **who** should be used for human references: *a house that overlooks the park* but *the woman who lives next door*. In practice, although it is true to say that **who** is restricted to human references, the function of **that** is flexible. It has been used for human and non-human references since at least the 11th century. In standard English it is interchangeable with **who** in this context.

3 People are often unsure whether there is any difference between the use of **that** and **which** in sentences such as *any book that gets children reading is worth having* and *any book which gets children reading is worth having*. The general rule is that in defining relative clauses, where the relative clause serves to define or restrict the reference to the particular thing or person described, **which** can replace **that**, as in the example just given. However, in non-defining relative clauses, where the relative clause serves only to give additional information, **that** cannot be used: *this book, which is set in the last century, is very popular with teenagers* but not *this book, that is set in the last century, is very popular with teenagers*. In US English it is usually recommended that **which** should be used only for non-defining relative clauses.

t

thee

The word **thee** is still used in some traditional dialects (e.g. in northern England) and among certain religious groups, but in standard English it is restricted to archaic contexts. For more details see THOU.

their

1 Do not confuse **their** and **there**. **Their** means 'belonging to them', while **there** means principally 'in/to that place', as in *almost 3,000 people made their living there*.

2 On the use of **their** to mean 'his or her', see THEY.

theirs

1 There is no need for an apostrophe in **theirs**.

2 On the use of **theirs** to mean 'his or hers', see THEY.

them

On the use of **them** in the singular to mean 'him or her', see THEY.

themself

1 The standard reflexive form corresponding to *they* and *them* is **themselves**, as in *they can do it themselves*. The singular form **themself**, first recorded in the 14th century, has re-emerged in recent years corresponding to the singular gender-neutral use of *they*, as in *this is the first step in helping someone to help* themself. The form is not widely accepted in standard English, however. Compare OURSELF.

2 On the use of **themselves** to mean 'himself or herself', see THEY.

thence

Thence and **from thence** are both used to mean 'from a place or source previously mentioned', as in *they intended to cycle on into France and thence home via Belgium; this is not a commodity which can be transported from thence*. Some traditionalists maintain that 'from' in **from thence** is unnecessary, since the word already contains the idea of 'from', so that effectively you are saying 'from from there.'

thesaurus

Thesaurus is pronounced /thi-**saw**-ruhs/, emphasizing the second syllable. Both **thesauruses** and **thesauri** are correct as plurals, though in speech the first will sound more natural, the second somewhat academic. For more guidance on words with alternative plural forms, see LATIN PLURALS.

they

The word **they** has been used since at least the 16th century as a singular pronoun to refer to a person of unspecified sex (and its counterparts **them**, **their**, **theirs**, and **themselves** have been used similarly). In the late 20th century, as the traditional use of **he** to refer to a person of either sex came under scrutiny on the grounds of sexism, this use of **they** became more common. It is now generally accepted in contexts where it follows an indefinite pronoun such as *anyone*, *no one*, or *someone* or a noun used to refer generally to males and females, such as *person*, *student*, *applicant*, *employee*, etc., as in **anyone** can join if **they** are a resident, **each** to **their** own, **any student** using these facilities **is** responsible for their belongings. The use of **they** after singular nouns is now common, though less widely accepted, especially in formal contexts. Sentences such as *ask **a friend** if **they** could help* are still criticized by some for being ungrammatical. Nevertheless, in view of the growing acceptance of **they** and its obvious practical advantages, this use after a noun is now an established pattern in English. Where you wish to avoid it, you can often do so by rewriting the whole sentence in the plural: **any student** using these facilities **is** responsible for their belongings can become **any students** using these facilities **are** responsible for their belongings.

thou

In modern English, the personal pronoun **you** (together with the possessives **your** and **yours**) covers a number of uses: it is both singular and plural, both objective and subjective, and both formal and familiar. This has not always been the case. In Old English and Middle English some of these different

t

functions of **you** were supplied by different words. Thus, **thou** was at one time the singular subjective case (*thou art a beast*), while **thee** was the singular objective case (*he cares not for thee*). In addition, **thy** was equivalent to the modern *your*, and **thine** was equivalent to the modern *yours*: *in the sweat of thy brow shalt thou eat bread*; *for thine is the kingdom, the power, and the glory*. The forms **you** and **ye**, on the other hand, used always to mean more than one person. By the 19th century they had become universal in standard English for both singular and plural, polite and familiar. In present-day use, **thou**, **thee**, **thy**, and **thine** survive in some traditional dialects but otherwise are found only in archaic contexts.

though

Though and **although** are virtually interchangeable, the only difference being that **though** tends to be less formal than **although**.

thusly

First coined in the 19th century as a humorous form of **thus**, **thusly** is now quite commonly used in the meaning of 'in this way'. Many people consider it superfluous, and it should probably be avoided in writing. Compare IRREGARDLESS.

till

In most contexts, **till** and **until** have the same meaning and are interchangeable. The main difference is that **till** is generally considered to be the more informal of the two and occurs less frequently than **until** in writing. **Until** also tends to be the natural choice at the beginning of a sentence: until *very recently, there was still a chance of rescuing the situation*. Interestingly, although it is commonly assumed that **till** is an abbreviated form of **until** (the spellings *'till* and *'til* reflect this), **till** is in fact the earlier form. **Until** appears to have been formed by the addition of Old Norse *und* 'as far as' at least several hundred years after **till** was first used.

t

time

People are sometimes unsure about where to put the apostrophe in phrases such as *in a week's time*, or *in two years' time*. To help you decide if the apostrophe comes before or after the letter **s**, first try rephrasing the previous examples using the word **of**: *in the time of a week, in the time of two years*. Then look carefully at the final letter of the relevant word as it now appears. The correct place to put the apostrophe is immediately after that letter. Apply this method to the phrase you are unsure about, and you will not go wrong.

titivate

The verbs **titillate** and **titivate** sound alike but do not have the same meaning, and to use the wrong one could be unfortunate. **Titillate** is the commoner word and means 'to stimulate or excite', as in *the press are paid to titillate the public*. **Titivate**, on the other hand, means 'to adorn or smarten up', as in *she titivated her hair*.

toothcomb

If you have ever wondered what a **toothcomb** is, and why on earth anybody would want to comb their teeth, wonder no more. There is no such thing. The forms **toothcomb** and **fine toothcomb** come from a misreading of the noun **fine-tooth comb**, meaning a comb with very finely spaced teeth. In modern standard English the versions **finetooth comb** and **fine toothcomb** are largely acceptable, if implausible.

tortuous, torturous

Tortuous and **torturous** have different literal meanings. **Tortuous** means 'full of twists and turns'. **Torturous** is derived from **torture**, and means 'involving or causing torture'. A *tortuous route* is one that is twisting and winding, and a *torturous death* is one that is extremely painful. In their figurative meanings both words can mean 'difficult or complex', and it is in this sense that they overlap. A *tortuous judgement* is one that has many complicating features, and a *torturous judgement* is one that is painfully difficult to make. **Tortuous** is used more often to express this meaning of 'difficult or complex', and is the better and more accurate choice. The overlap in meaning also occasionally leads to **tortuous** being used incorrectly for **torturous**, as in *my family, for whom this has been a tortuous ordeal, have been a tower of strength*.

transpire

The standard general meaning of **transpire** is 'to come to be known' as in *it transpired that Mark had been baptized a Catholic*. From this a looser sense has developed, meaning 'to happen or occur': *I'm going to find out exactly what transpired*. This looser sense is first recorded in US English in the late 18th century, and was listed in US dictionaries from the 19th century onwards. It is often criticized for being jargon, or for being unnecessarily long when *occur* and *happen* would do perfectly well. The newer meaning is very common, however, and generally accepted in most contexts, except by purists.

treason

Formerly, there were two types of crime to which the term **treason** was applied: **petty treason**, the crime of murdering one's master, and **high treason**, the crime of betraying one's country. The crime of petty treason was abolished in 1828 and in modern use high treason is now often simply called **treason**.

tribe

In historical contexts, the word **tribe** is broadly accepted (*the area was inhabited by Slavic tribes*). However, in contemporary contexts, used to refer to a community living within a traditional society today, the word is problematic. It is strongly associated with past attitudes of white colonialists towards so-called primitive or uncivilized peoples living in remote, undeveloped places. For this reason, it is generally preferable to use alternative terms such as *community*, *nation*, or *people*.

-trix

The suffix -**trix** has been used since the 15th century to form feminine agent nouns corresponding to masculine forms ending in -**tor**. Although a wide variety of forms have been coined, few of them have ever had wide currency. In modern use the suffix is found chiefly in legal terms such as *executrix*, *administratrix*, and *testatrix* but also in the word *dominatrix*.

try and

Some people consider it is incorrect to use **try and** plus an infinitive in sentences such as *we should try and help them*, and suggest that *we should try to help them* is the only correct form. In practice there is little discernible difference in meaning, although there is a difference in formality, with **try to** being regarded as more formal than **try and**. The construction **try and** is grammatically odd, however, in that it cannot be used if **try** has the form **tries**, **tried**, or **trying**. So, for example, sentences like *she tried and fix it*, *she tried and fixed it*, and *they are trying and renew their visa* are not acceptable, while their equivalents *she tried to fix it* and *they are trying to renew their visa*, as well as *try and get over it* and *it is vital that they try and come*, undoubtedly are. For this reason **try and** is best regarded as a fixed idiom used only in its infinitive and imperative form.

Two words or one

The spelling of English words is not fixed forever, and changes over time. We no longer spell **pathetic** as *pathetick* with a final **k** as Doctor Johnson did, and we put a letter **b** in **doubt**, even though no one did before the 15th century. Similarly, a number of common words in English started out as two-word phrases which always functioned as single ▶

t

units of meaning and eventually became fused in a single word, such as **forever**, **somebody**, or **everyone**.

As regards writing words in single units or separately, in current English there are two tendencies worth commenting on. On the one hand there is a tendency to join together fixed expressions which have for a long time been written separately, e.g. **thankyou** for **thank you** and **straightaway** for **straight away**. This trend continues the well-established process which fused **for** and **ever** into **forever**, and **some** and **body** into **somebody**, and it is probably more likely if there is a direct analogy with an existing word: **anymore** is analogous to **anyone** and **anybody**.

On the other hand, an opposite process can also be observed with a very limited group of words: some people write as individual words terms such as **nonetheless** which are standardly written as a single word.

Of the two trends, the first appears to be much the stronger. For instance, in the Oxford English Corpus, the phrase **some time** now appears as **sometime** in 32 per cent of all cases in American English and 19 per cent of all cases in British English: *we really want to do a live record sometime*.

The move towards writing fixed expressions as one word is stronger in American than in British English. For instance, in American English **someday** has now become more or less standard, and **anymore** and **underway** look set to follow. Although the same trend is apparent in British English, it lags behind. The one exception is **thankyou**, which, relative to **thank you**, is more common in British than American English.

Fused forms almost always emerge first in informal English, used in contexts such as chatrooms and weblogs, and are slower to spread to more formal, edited text such as newspapers and magazines. In formal British English it is therefore probably still best to avoid most of them.

The shift towards writing single words as their component parts is far less strong: in the Oxford English Corpus ▶

nonetheless is written as **none the less** in 6 per cent of cases. We will have to wait and see whether it becomes more prevalent in the future, but for the time being writing such words this way will generally be considered mistaken in formal written English. See also ALBEIT, AWHILE, EVERYDAY, EVERYONE, HOWEVER, WHATEVER, WHENEVER, WHEREVER, WORTHWHILE.

un-

The prefixes **un-** and **non-** both mean 'not', but there is often a distinction in emphasis. **Un-** tends to be stronger and less neutral than **non-**: consider the differences between *unacademic* and *non-academic*, as in *his language was refreshingly unacademic* (i.e. not obscure and full of technical argon); *a non-academic life suits him* (i.e. a life in which he does not have to study or teach).

uncharted, unchartered

People sometimes wrongly use **unchartered** instead of **uncharted** in phrases such as *the uncharted waters of the Indian Ocean* or *uncharted territory*. To avoid this mistake it is helpful to remember that the image suggested is that of going into unexplored—literally or figuratively—places that have not been mapped. A **chart** is a kind of map used by navigators, hence the image of **uncharted**.

unexceptionable, unexceptional

There is a clear distinction in meaning between **exceptionable** ('open to objection') and **exceptional** ('out of the ordinary; very good'). However, this distinction has become blurred in the negative forms **unexceptionable** and **unexceptional**. Strictly speaking, **unexceptionable** means 'not open to objection', as in *this view is unexceptionable in itself*, while **unexceptional** means 'not out of the ordinary; usual', as in *the hotel was adequate but unexceptional*. But, although the distinction may be clear in these two examples, the meaning of **unexceptionable** is often indeterminate between 'not open to objection' and 'ordinary', as in *the food was bland*

u

and unexceptionable or *the candidates were pretty unexceptionable*.

uninterested

On the difference between **uninterested** and **disinterested**, see DISINTERESTED.

unique

There is a set of adjectives, including *unique*, *complete*, *equal*, *infinite*, and *perfect*, whose core meanings are absolute. Therefore, according to a traditional argument, they cannot be modified by adverbs such as *really*, *quite*, *almost*, or *very*. For example, since the core meaning of **unique** (from Latin 'one') is 'being only one of its kind', it is logically impossible, the argument goes, to modify it with an adverb: it either is 'unique' or it is not, and there are no in-between stages. In practice, however, these adjectives are so commonly modified by *quite*, *almost*, etc. that such uses go unnoticed by most people and must by now be considered standard English.

United Kingdom

See BRITAIN.

unlike

The use of **unlike** as a conjunction, as in *she was behaving unlike she'd ever behaved before*, is not considered standard English. It can be avoided by using **as** or **in a way that** with a negative instead: *she was behaving* as *she'd never behaved before*; *we do it in a way that isn't pushy or overtly political*.

unsociable, unsocial

There is some overlap in the use of the adjectives **unsociable**, **unsocial**, and **antisocial**, but they also have distinct core meanings. Generally speaking, **unsociable** means 'not enjoying the company of others', as in *Terry was grumpy and unsociable*. It can also mean 'not conducive to friendly social relations', as in *surfing the Net is an unsociable habit*. **Antisocial** means 'contrary to the laws and customs of a society', as in *aggressive and antisocial behaviour*. **Unsocial** is usually only used to describe hours 'falling outside the normal working day', as in *employees were expected to work unsocial hours*. It is therefore incorrect to use it in phrases such as *violence and unsocial behaviour*.

unthaw

Logically, the verb **unthaw** should mean 'freeze', but in North America it means exactly the same as **thaw** (as in *the warm weather helped unthaw the rail lines*); because of the risk of confusion it is not part of standard usage. **Unthawed** as an adjective always means 'still frozen', but it is best avoided because many contexts may be ambiguous.

until

On the differences between **until** and **till**, see TILL.

untouchable

In meanings relating to the traditional Hindu caste system, the term **untouchable** and the social restrictions accompanying it were declared illegal in the constitution of India in 1949 and of Pakistan in 1953. The official term for 'untouchables' today is **the Scheduled Castes**.

upmost

Upmost is a somewhat rare adjective and a variant of **uppermost**. It refers to the position of something, as in *the upmost layer*. Through a process of FOLK ETYMOLOGY it is sometimes incorrectly used instead of **utmost**: e.g. *with the upmost care*, instead of *with the utmost care*; *to do your upmost*, instead of *to do your utmost*.

upon

The preposition **upon** has the same core meaning as the preposition **on**. However, in modern English **upon** tends to be restricted to more formal contexts or to established phrases and idioms, such as *once upon a time* and *row upon row of empty seats*.

us

People are often unsure whether it is correct to say *they are richer **than us***, or *they are richer **than we*** (or ***than we are***). For a discussion of this topic see PERSONAL PRONOUN AND THAN.

use

1 The construction **used to**, as in *we used to replace the picture tubes in our television sets when they failed*, is standard English, but difficulties arise with the formation of negatives and questions. Traditionally, they are formed without the auxiliary verb *do*, as in *it **used not to** be like that* and ***used** she **to** come here?* In modern English this question form is now regarded as very formal or old-fashioned, and the construction with *do* is broadly accepted as standard, as in ***did** they **use to** come here?* Negative constructions with *do*, on the other hand (as in *it **didn't use to** be like that*), though common, are informal and are not generally accepted.

2 There is sometimes confusion over whether to use the form **used to** or **use to**, which has arisen largely because the pronunciation is the same in both cases: /**yoos** too/. Except in negatives and questions, the correct form is **used to**: *we used to go to the cinema all the time*, not *we use to go to the cinema all the time*. However, in negatives and questions using the auxiliary verb *do*, the correct form is **use to**, because the form of the verb required is the infinitive: *I didn't use to like mushrooms*, not *I didn't used to like mushrooms*.

utmost

For the occasional confusion between **upmost** and **utmost**, see UPMOST.

various

In standard English the word **various** is normally used as an adjective, e.g. *dresses of* various *colours*. It is sometimes also used as a pronoun followed by *of*, as in *various of her friends had called*. Although this use is similar to that of words such as *several* and *many* (e.g. *several of her friends had called*), it is sometimes regarded as incorrect.

venal, venial

Venal and **venial** are sometimes confused. **Venal** means 'bribable, corrupt', as in *venal consulate officials have reportedly swindled untold thousands*, whereas **venial** is used to refer to a sin or offence that is excusable or pardonable, as opposed to a *mortal* sin: *a venial sin, a venial mistake*.

verbal

Some people claim that the true meaning of the adjective **verbal** is 'of or concerned with words', whether spoken or written (as in *verbal abuse*), and that it should not be used to mean 'spoken rather than written' (as in *a verbal agreement*). For this meaning it is said that the adjective **oral** should be used instead. In practice, however, **verbal** is well established in this meaning and in certain idiomatic phrases (such as *a verbal agreement*) cannot be simply replaced by **oral**.

verbs formed from nouns

English is remarkably free-and-easy in the way it can use the same word in many different grammatical functions. A very common word like *down* can be used as an adverb, preposition, adjective, verb, or noun, as in *she looked down*; *I walked down the stairs*; *he's been so down lately*; *he downed his drink*; *she had a real down on Angela*; conjunctions can become nouns, as in *too many ifs and buts*; proper nouns can be used as adjectives, as in *a very Hollywood view of life*, and so forth. Yet despite this grammatical freedom there is one particular process of forming new words which often offends purists and traditionalists: forming verbs from nouns. The name by which this process is known, **verbing**, first recorded as long ago as 1757, is, appropriately, an example of this selfsame process, since it derives from a noun. For whatever reason, many people object to the creation of new words in this way. There is a story from a while ▶

V

back that an American wished to contact an Oxford don, to which the reply was: 'I am delighted that you have arrived in Oxford. The verb "to contact" has not.' Yet respectable and well-thought-of verbs have for several centuries been formed from nouns (and occasionally adjectives) by these methods:

- by using exactly the same word (e.g. *to question*, *to knife*, *to quiz*, *to service*)
- by adding a suffix such as *-ize* (*to prioritize*, *to randomize*)
- by shortening the noun (*to edit*, *to diagnose*, *to televise*)
Nobody objects to *pepper* as in *his conversation was peppered with risqué anecdotes*, or to *floor* as in *his question floored me*.

It might be some people's aversion to new words in general that puts them off these formations; or they might be put off by the fact that many of them come from the mistrusted worlds of business and politics, and so have a feeling of jargon. Whatever the reason, there is no doubt that **verbing** is a very productive process and will continue to add new words to English. Below are a few more examples of recent and not so recent words, together with their first date, if known, in that meaning.

to access	to gain access to	1962
to author	to write	1940
chipmunking	keying frenetically on a mobile phone while in the middle of another activity, such as a meeting	
to contact	to get in touch with	1929
to enthuse	to fill with enthusiasm	1827
to interface	to interact	1967
to offshore	to move a business operation abroad	1987
to podcast	to put audio files on the Internet for downloading	

V

waive, waiver, wave, waver

Waive is sometimes confused with **wave**. **Waive** means 'not to insist on', as in *he will waive all rights to the money* or *her fees would be waived*, whereas the much more common word **wave** means 'to move to and fro'. A **waiver** is the act of **waiving** a right or claim (or a document recording that) whereas **to waver** means mainly 'to falter' as in *her voice wavered; he never wavered in his resolve*.

was, were

On whether it is more correct to say *if I was a rich man* or *if I were a rich man*, etc., see the article on the SUBJUNCTIVE.

well

In many varieties of English, people below a certain age now quite commonly use **well** to emphasize any adjective: *she is well thick; Jack said he was well chuffed; this is a well cool bar; a technology now well familiar*. Using **well** like this is still markedly informal even in speech, and should be avoided in any kind of serious writing. It is, nevertheless, a logical extension of some old-established ways of using **well** for emphasis.

well-

1 The adverb **well** is often used in combination with past participles to form adjectival compounds: **well** *adjusted*, **well** *intentioned*, **well** *known*, and so on. As far as hyphenation is concerned, the general stylistic principle is that if the adjectival compound comes before the noun (i.e. when used attributively), it should be hyphenated (*a* **well**-*intentioned remark*) but that if it stands alone after the verb (i.e. when used predicatively), it should not be hyphenated (*her remarks were* **well** *intentioned*).

2 In combinations with **best**-, such as **best**-*built*, **best**-*dressed*, **best**-*intentioned*, **best**-*looking*, the hyphen is used irrespective of the position of the word, e.g. *the* **best**-*looking man I know, she's the* **best**-*looking of the whole clan*. See also HYPHENATION.

W

were, was

On whether it is more correct to say *if I was a rich man* or *if I were a rich man*, etc., see SUBJUNCTIVE.

whatever

In its emphatic use (e.g. *whatever was she thinking of?*) **whatever** can also written as two words (*what ever was she thinking of?*). In its other meanings, however, it must be written as one word, e.g. *do whatever you like*; *they received no help whatever*.

whence (also from whence)

Strictly speaking, **whence** means 'from what place', as in *whence did you come?* Accordingly, some people maintain that 'from' in **from thence** as in *from whence did you come?* is unnecessary, since the word already contains the idea of 'from', so that effectively you are saying 'from from where'. The use with *from* is very common, though, and has been used by reputable writers since the 14th century. It is now broadly accepted in standard English.

whenever

In its emphatic use (e.g. *whenever shall we arrive?*) the one-word form **whenever** may also be written as two words (*when ever shall we arrive?*). In its other meanings, however, it must be written as one word: *you can ask for help whenever you need it*; *I'll do it at the weekend or whenever*.

wherever

In its emphatic use (e.g. *wherever can he have got to?*) the one-word form **wherever** may also be written as two words (*where ever can he have got to?*). In its other meanings, however, it must be written as one word: *meet me wherever you like*; *it should be available wherever you shop*; *use wholegrain cereals wherever possible*.

whether

On the difference between **whether** and **if**, see IF.

which

On the differences between **which** and **that** in relative clauses, see THAT.

whichever

Whichever should always be written as one word, e.g. *you're safe with whichever option you choose*. However, do not confuse it with constructions in which the separate words *which* and *ever* quite legitimately come together, e.g. t*his reminds me of the 5-year development plans, none of **which ever** worked*.

while

On the distinction between **worth while** and **worthwhile**, see WORTHWHILE. For **a while** versus **awhile,** see AWHILE.

white

The word **white** has been used to refer to the skin colour of Europeans or people of European extraction since the early 17th century. Unlike other labels for skin colour such as *red* or *yellow*, **white** has not been generally used in a derogatory way. In modern contexts there is a growing tendency to prefer terms which relate to geographical origin rather than skin colour: hence the current preference in the US for African American rather than *black* and European rather than *white*.

who, whom

1 There is a continuing debate in English usage about when to use **who** and when to use **whom**. According to formal grammar, **who** forms the subjective case and so should be used in subject position in a sentence, as in *who decided this?* The form **whom**, on the other hand, forms the objective case and so should be used in object position in a sentence, as in *whom do you think we should support?* (where it is the object of *support*); and after a ▶

W

preposition: *to whom do you wish to speak?* Although some people still use **who** and **whom** according to the rules of formal grammar as stated here, there are many more who rarely use **whom** at all; it has retreated steadily and is now largely restricted to formal contexts. So formal has it become, indeed, that the American humorist Calvin Triller observed, 'As far as I'm concerned, "whom" is a word that was invented to make everyone sound like a butler'.

2 The normal practice in modern English is to use **who** instead of **whom**: *who do you think we should support?*; *who do you wish to speak to?* In the second example, the preposition *to* is moved to the end of the sentence. Such uses are today broadly accepted in standard English, and in both the previous examples using **whom** could have sounded starchy and off-putting.

3 Many people use **whom** so rarely that when they do venture into these further reaches of grammar they use it inappropriately. The most common mistake made with **whom** is to use it to refer to the subject of the sentence: e.g. *a leader who has been linked to Al Qaeda and whom US officials have said is behind other attacks*. What has happened here is that **whom** has been used in the mistaken belief that it is the object of the verb *have said*, whereas it is the subject of the phrase *is behind other attacks*. It is very common for this mistake to be made after verbs such as *say*, *claim*, *suspect*, *think*, etc.

4 A second mistake, based on the correct notion that **whom** is the appropriate form after a preposition, is to use it when it is part of a complete clause introduced by a preposition, as in: *the camera is trained almost exclusively on one of the participants, regardless of whom is talking*. **Who** should be used here, as it is the subject of *is talking*.

5 On the use of **who** and **that** in relative clauses, see RELATIVE CLAUSES and THAT.

w

whoever

In the emphatic use (*whoever does he think he is?*) **whoever** can also be written as two words. In its other meanings, however, it must be written as one word: *whoever wins should be guaranteed an Olympic place*; *come out, whoever you are.*

whom

On the use of **who** and **whom**, see WHO.

who's

A common written mistake is to confuse **who's** with **whose**. The form **who's** represents a contraction of **who is** or **who has**, while **whose** is a possessive pronoun or determiner used in questions, as in *whose is this?* or *whose turn is it?*

why

On the phrase **the reason why**, see REASON.

will

On the differences in use between **will** and **shall**, see SHALL.

-wise

In modern English the suffix **-wise** is attached to nouns to form a sentence adverb meaning 'concerning or with respect to', as in *confidence-wise, tax-wise, price-wise, time-wise, news-wise,* and *culture-wise.* The suffix is very productive and widely used in modern English but many of the words so formed are considered inelegant or not good English style. If you want to avoid using -**wise**, the solution is often to omit the word entirely, or to recast the sentence. For instance, *we were late time-wise, but so was everyone else* is just as good without *time-wise*, while *until things get better business-wise* can be reworded as *until business gets better.*

W

wish

People say both *I wish I were rich* and *I wish I was rich*, but the second form is often viewed as incorrect. On this question, see SUBJUNCTIVE.

with regard to

The correct form of this phrase, meaning broadly 'about', is to use **regard** without a final **s**: *suspicion with regard to British intentions*. However, possibly because of the influence of the phrase *to give one's regards to someone*, people often say and write **with regards to**. It is best to avoid doing this in formal or academic writing, since many people are likely to consider it a mistake.

worthwhile

When the adjective **worthwhile** is used before the noun (i.e. attributively) it is always written as one word: *a worthwhile cause*. However, when it stands alone and comes *after* the verb (i.e. when used predicatively) it may be written as either one or two words: *we didn't think it was worthwhile* or *we didn't think it was worth while*.

would

1 On the differences in use between **would** and **should**, see SHOULD.

2 For a discussion of the use of **would of** instead of **would have**, see HAVE.

wrack

On the complicated relationship between **wrack** and **rack**, see RACK.

wreak

The past participle of **wreak** is **wreaked**, as in *boll weevils wreaked havoc on the US cotton industry*. An alternative expression is **wrought havoc**, as in *over-fishing has wrought havoc in some areas*. **Wrought** is an archaic past tense of **work** and is not, as is sometimes assumed, a past tense of **wreak**. There is therefore no justification for the view, sometimes expressed, that **wreaked** is an incorrect form.

ye

The history of the use of **ye** is complex. In the earliest period of English it was used only as the plural subjective form. In the

13th century it came to be used in the singular, equivalent to
thou. In the 15th century, when **you** had become the dominant
subjective form, **ye** came to be used as an objective singular
and plural (equivalent to **thee** and **you**). Various uses survive in
modern dialects.

your

Note the difference between the possessive **your** (as in *what is
your name?*) and the contraction **you're**, meaning 'you are'
(as in *you're looking well*). Note also that neither **your** nor **yours**
should be written with an apostrophe.

yourself

There are two ways of using **yourself** to which nobody will
object, and one which some people will criticize. The innocuous
uses are:

1 to refer to the person you are speaking to: *did you hurt yourself?
help yourself to some cake, Tim.*

2 to emphasize the word **you**: *you are going to have to do it yourself;
did you do it yourself?*

Staff who deal with the public, in businesses such as restaurants,
call centres, and the like, quite often use **yourself** in a rather
different way, as a substitute for **you**: *is this soup for yourself?
is the appliance for yourself, sir?* Using **yourself** in this way should
be avoided in any kind of formal writing, and is considered
wrong by some people even in speech. Arguably, however, it
fulfils a useful function in the situations mentioned. **Yourself**
sounds more formal and less direct than **you**, and is thus
intended to be more polite.

y